# HEARTS IN HARMONY

*By*
*William H. Elder*

ISBN-13: 978-1-57258-612-3 (Paperback)
Library of Congress Control Number: 2009942456

# TABLE OF CONTENTS

# PREFACE

"Above the distractions of the earth He [God] sits enthroned; all things are open to His divine survey; and from His great and calm eternity He orders that which His providence sees best" (Ellen G. White, *The Ministry of Healing*, p. 417).

The three men of our trilogy, *Hearts in Harmony*, were, without question, products of providence. The time, place, and sequence of their births brought them together at a very important transitional period in the history of God's people.

Samuel, the senior member of the trio, was a child of miracle birth, and before he had reached his teen years, he became the judge, chief priest, and anointed prophet of the nation of Israel.

His impeccable manner of life won him favor with God and the people, but his sons were not prepared spiritually to succeed him, and thus the rule of the judges ended with Samuel. But Samuel's ministry was not over. God chose Samuel to anoint the first two kings of Israel, Saul and David, and to mentor Jonathan, the first prince of the nation. Thus he became the first note in the harmony of the trio of hearts.

Many students do not consider Jonathan a major player in Bible chronology, but close study reveals otherwise. While he never reached the eminence of Samuel or David, he played a vital role in the transition from the role of the judges to the rule of the kings. Then, at the expense of his own succession to the kingship, he became an intercessor between his father, King Saul, and his dear friend, David, the newly anointed king of Israel. Certainly he didn't realize the prophetic implications in his unselfish role as the mediator between his father and David.

In Jacob's vision of his sons' futures, he prophesied that Judah's posterity would wield the scepter (rule as king) until Shiloh (Christ) would come. Saul was a Benjamite, and thus according to the prophecy, his heirs could not have fulfilled this prophecy. David was from the tribe of Judah and would qualify. Thus Jonathan's unselfish ministry and unblemished life gave him his place as the second note in the *Hearts in Harmony*.

David was the beneficiary of the mentorship of the venerable Samuel, and the royal gifts and protection of his dear friend Jonathan. In the providence of God, David was born to be a king. His manner of life was not as pure and unblemished as Samuel's and Jonathan's, but his deep love for God and his contrite repentance for his sins confirmed his love relationship with the One who loves to forgive and restore.

He became the signet king of Israel and all of the succeeding kings of Israel were known as the sons of David. The Messiah (Jesus Christ) was called the "Son of David." Thus David was assured his place as the third note in the trio, *Hearts in Harmony*.

# INTRODUCTION

## SAMUEL'S HEART

Samuel was dedicated to the Lord's service even before his conception, and at the age of four, he was physically given to Priest Eli to work in the temple.

He was invested with the offices of priest, prophet, and judge at the tender age of twelve, and as one writer observed, "Placing one hand in the hand of Christ, and with the other taking the helm of the nation, he holds it with such wisdom and firmness as to preserve Israel from destruction" (*SDA Bible Commentary*, vol. 2, p. 1011).

He was truly a man after God's own heart and was spoken of by God Himself in Jeremiah 15:1 as an equal to Moses, an intercessor for His people.

In his old age, Samuel was disappointed with his sons in whom he had invested confidence and responsibility, but he didn't chide them.

He was deeply hurt when the people asked for a king, but the hurt was not entirely for himself but mainly for the King of Kings who the people rejected after centuries of leading them, fighting their battles, and healing their backsliding.

Samuel was privileged to anoint and mentor the first two kings of Israel. Then, after challenging a final gathering of the people at Mizpah as to the fairness and integrity of his judgments during his long tenure among them, he stepped into the twilight. He spent the last days of his life among his beloved teachers and students in the schools of the prophets.

Surely when the saints of earth are honored and Samuel receives his crown of glory, he will wave it in honor before the throne and gladly acknowledge that the faithful lessons of his mother, through the merits of Christ, have crowned him with immortal glory.

# SAMUEL'S HEART

## CHAPTER 1

"Well, what kind of thank offering is Mrs. Barren going to present to Jehovah this year?" Peninnah laughed shrilly as she jeered at Hannah. "I'm carrying another baby for our beloved Elkanah, but you haven't given him even one child in ten years. You are hopeless. If I were you, I would give up and allow him to divorce you."

Hannah cringed at the sarcasm in the voice of her tormentor, but she knew that Peninnah was right, even though her intentions were evil. It was a public shame to be a barren wife in Israel. In fact, some spiritual leaders believed that there were serious spiritual problems in the lives of women who could not bear children, and the wives with fruitful wombs were in full agreement with these religious leaders.

For several years now, Hannah had endured the harassment of Elkanah's second wife. She had suffered without retaliation on her part, but her heart was bleeding from the grievous gibes. She was a very pious woman, and her prayers ascended daily to the ears of the Lord, but her womb remained closed.

Most of her tears were shed in the privacy of her closet, but often her heart became so full of hurt that she knelt, crying and pleading to the Lord, wherever the occasion found her. Several times, Elkanah had observed the agony of his favorite wife and had said nothing, but today her pain tore his heart. He waited until her tear ducts were empty then took her in his arms.

"Hannah," he spoke with feeling. "Why do you weep? Why do you not eat, and why is your heart grieved? Am I not better to you than ten sons?"

She nodded against his chest. "Yes dear, you are very good to me. I have no complaint. But Elkanah, in our ten years of marriage, I have not once conceived. Thus I am unprofitable to you, so you have my permission to divorce me and marry someone else."

Elkanah patted his wife's shoulder. "Hannah, I love you. I don't want to marry someone else even though you haven't given me an heir. We must be patient, and perhaps someday soon Jehovah will answer our prayers and open your womb. Now I must go up to the temple and assist in offering the evening sacrifice, but before I go I want you to promise me that you will dry your tears and eat the meal that has been provided for you."

"Yes, I will eat," she promised, but her heart was still heavy.

As she was eating, Peninnah came into the room and immediately began to torment her rival. "I noticed that you got my husband's attention again by your whining. Let me tell you Mrs. Barren; one of these days he's going to get tired of all your tears and you won't have anyone to listen to your whimpering then. Like I said, you should offer to let him divorce you and either replace you or let him spend full time with me. I can give him all the children he would ever want."

Hannah didn't tell her that she had suggested to Elkanah that he divorce her. She knew that Peninnah would greet the news with another slur.

Hannah finished her meal in silence and then walked to the entrance of the tabernacle. It was getting dark now, and the evening sacrifices were finished. The tabernacle appeared to be empty, so she knelt just inside the front door and again poured out her heart to Jehovah.

In her agony a new thought came to her as if sent from heaven. She framed the thought immediately in silent prayer. "O Lord of hosts, if you will indeed look on the affliction of your maidservant and remember me, and not forget your maidservant, but will give your maidservant a male child, then I will give him to the Lord all the days of his life, and no razor shall come upon his head."

Hannah had become so intense in the presentation of her petition that she hadn't seen Priest Eli who was sitting quietly on a seat by the doorpost of the tabernacle, but the spiritual leader was observing Hannah with deep interest. He noticed that she had come from the hall where many travelers were still eating and drinking, and he wondered if perhaps she had imbibed too much of the strong wine that was being passed around freely. Possibly she felt guilty about her over indulgence and had come to what she assumed was the empty temple to pray for forgiveness.

Eli watched the woman closely as her lips moved but her voice was not heard. She needed reproof, so he spoke to her loudly enough so that she would hear but no one else would be alerted.

"How long will you be drunk? Put your wine away from you."

Hannah was hurt and ashamed that the high priest would think she was a common drunk. She was quick to rebut his accusation.

"No, my lord, I am a woman of sorrowful spirit. I have drunk neither wine nor intoxicating drink, but have poured out my soul before the Lord. Do not consider your maidservant a wicked woman, for out of the abundance of my complaint and grief I have spoken until now."

Eli was contrite. He had misjudged this mother in Israel who had a special burden on her heart, and he had probably hurt her deeply. He remembered the many times he had come to the temple while the city was sleeping to agonize before the Lord for his wayward sons. Some nocturnal people, or early risers, could easily have misunderstood his actions as he poured out his soul to God.

His voice was gentle as he spoke again to Hannah. "Go in peace, and may the God of Israel grant you your petition which you have asked of Him."

Even as the high priest was speaking, the burden lifted from Hannah's heart. And it felt as if her prayer had already been answered. She bowed before the man of God in thanksgiving and hurried away from the temple. Her heart was singing and her countenance was no longer sad.

The next morning every member of Elkanah's family arose early and worshipped together, ate their morning meal, and then prepared for the return trip to Ramah. As each person worked in preparation for the departure, Peninnah was her same old obnoxious self. She bossed everyone around and, of course, insulted Hannah at every opportunity.

In contrast, Hannah was sweet to everyone as usual, and her spirit appeared completely in opposition to what it had been only yesterday, and Peninnah wondered what had happened to her hated rival. Had Hannah slept in Elkanah's arms last night and been reassured by him that her desire for a son would be fulfilled soon? The second wife grimaced with pain at the thought, but perhaps it was so.

In her frustration, Peninnah intensified her efforts to upset the radiant Hannah, but her evil efforts sparked no negative effects in her rival. Hannah kept sweet and kept smiling.

As soon as the family arrived back at Ramah, Hannah requested a meeting with Elkanah. He was very pleased to grant the petition of his favorite wife. When she came into the room, he greeted her with a hug and a kiss and invited her to be seated across from him. His eyes were full of questions, but he waited for her to speak. He knew that she was a woman of few words.

Hannah bowed in a show of respect and then seated herself. "My lord, on our last night at Shiloh, I was privileged to speak to Priest Eli, and he gave me encouragement that I would like to share with you."

He nodded. "By all means, tell me what his message was," the eager Elkanah offered.

"After the evening sacrifices were finished, I went to the temple to pray. I thought that I would be alone. I didn't see Eli, who was sitting on a seat by the doorposts, but he saw me and noticed that I had just come from the hall where many were eating and drinking. When he saw my lips moving in wordless prayer for the Lord to open my womb, he assumed that I had been drinking excessively and was praying for forgiveness. He decided to chide me. Naturally, I was hurt deeply that he would think me to be a fallen woman.

"So I explained to him the burden of my prayers. He was immediately contrite and sympathetic to my problem. Then he gave me the assurance that the Lord had heard my prayer and would answer soon according to His mercy and grace. I accepted his assurance as a promise from Jehovah, and the burden immediately lifted from my heart. So Elkanah, I believe that now I am ready to bear you a man child." Her face was beaming as she finished, and Elkanah was ecstatic.

"My dear Hannah," he exclaimed. "God is good, and I agree with you that He is now ready to open your womb and give me an heir according to your prayer. This very night we will do our part to fulfill your petition." So Elkanah lay with his wife Hannah, and the Lord opened her womb and she conceived.

Everything seemed to go wrong on the day that Hannah knew for certain that she was with child. The loom on which she was weaving some woolen cloth broke down because of her nervous fingers. She broke one of Peninnah's favorite pottery dishes and then tore the sleeve of Peninnah's oldest son's shirt as she was washing.

Peninnah was livid. "Can't you do anything right?" she stormed. "You are worse than my children, always daydreaming instead of keeping your mind on your business. What a story I've got to tell Elkanah when he comes in from the field tonight."

Peninnah chose to forget that only last week she had broken two bowls and had to make a trip to the marketplace to replace them.

Hannah was pained by her clumsiness, but she was not intimidated by Peninnah's ire. During the years, she had become immune to the venom of her tormentor. Besides, Hannah reasoned, God had now given her a reason for joy and happiness that would dissolve any rancor or bitterness toward poor, unhappy Peninnah.

Hannah kept the secret of her pregnancy to herself for several more weeks, lest she find that she had misread the signs. Finally, all doubts were wiped away, and she resolved that she must share the news with Elkanah today.

She went to meet her husband as he came in from the field. Her face was radiant, and Elkanah knew that she had good news for him. "My lord, Elkanah," she exclaimed. "Rejoice with me for I am with child."

For a moment, he was immobile; then he grabbed her in his big strong arms and lifted her off of her feet. While she was still in his arms, he offered a prayer of thanksgiving to Jehovah for answering their petition so quickly.

Hannah was unsure if she should share the news of her pregnancy with Peninnah, but she finally decided that it was her duty to share the news with all of the family members. She was quite sure that her jealous rival would greet the news with some form of insult, and she was correct in her expectation.

"Peninnah, I have found that I am with child, and since you are one of the closest members of my family, I wanted you to know."

Peninnah didn't receive the announcement with a pleasant face and joyful embrace. She slowly took the cooking pot from the stone fireplace, set the pot aside, and turned to face Hannah. There was open contempt in her eyes.

"Humph," she snorted. "I don't see any evidence of your pregnancy. Besides, you are so frail that you might not be able to carry a baby to full maturity. If I were you, I wouldn't pick any names until it is out of the womb. And," she added with a toss of her head, "if you are with child, as you believe, it might be a girl instead of the man child you want to give Elkanah."

Hannah nodded. "You are correct, Peninnah. Even though Elkanah and I asked particularly for a son, Jehovah might choose to give us a daughter. If that is what God gives me, I will love her with all my heart and rear her in the fear of the Lord, the same as with a male heir."

Peninnah turned away in frustration. No matter how hard and how often she tried, she couldn't raise the ire of Hannah.

Hannah's pregnancy was by no means an idle time. Her nimble fingers were sewing and knitting garments for the expected child, while her joyful mind created songs of thanksgiving and prayers to the Lord. Neither did she shirk her responsibilities in the home, although Peninnah constantly accused her of daydreaming and idleness.

Elkanah was a loving and tender spouse to his favorite wife during this difficult time. His devotion to Hannah irritated Peninnah and increased her harassment, but Elkanah's kind attention to Hannah's every need tended to mitigate the persecution of her rival.

"Elkanah, I am in need of the midwife, for my labor pains have begun," Hannah announced.

Elkanah immediately hastened to the village to bring the midwife. She was the woman who had certified Hannah's pregnancy.

Peninnah had been trained in midwifery and was quite proficient with the practice. In fact, she had delivered two of her own babies without the assistance of an attendant midwife. But neither Hannah nor Elkanah felt that they could trust her with Hannah's delivery, although Hannah wished fervently that she could.

The midwife came quickly, and the birth was soon consummated. The aide laid a wrinkled, red faced, but perfectly formed, baby boy in the arms of a weary, but joyful mother. Hannah looked into the face of her first-born son and exclaimed, "I will name him Samuel, for my prayers were 'heard of God.' Truly he is a miracle child."

As was expected, Peninnah and her brood were critical of the new baby and especially of Hannah's mode of training.

"He is ugly," the older son offered, which probably reflected his mother's attitude.

"You are spoiling him badly," Peninnah stated with a toss of her head. "If you are going to give him to Eli at the temple, he will grow up lazy, just like his own two sons, and he will be an idle lout his entire life."

Fortunately, there was a bright spot in Peninnah's family. The older daughter, Livi, reflected more of the kind and caring traits of her father, than the crude and evil personality of her mother. She was a happy child and was always civil and responsive to Hannah. She immediately fell in love with her half brother, Samuel, and even though she was only four years old, she would play with him and care for him faithfully. She was often the target of Peninnah's chiding.

Hannah bore the sarcasm and criticism of Peninnah patiently and increased her prayer to Jehovah for wisdom and resolution in her training of this gift from God.

"Elkanah, will it be all right with you if I do not go with you to Shiloh for the yearly sacrifice until our son is weaned? I believe that the Lord would rather for me to stay at home and continue his training until he is weaned. Then, of course, we must give him to the temple service in fulfillment of our vow, and he will minister before the Lord forever."

Elkanah pondered his wife's suggestion for a few moments before he spoke. "Yes, Hannah, I agree with you that you should stay here at home until the baby is weaned. I will offer a special thank offering to the Lord for this special gift from heaven. Then, as you say, when he is weaned, we must take him to the temple and leave him there to minister before the Lord. I know that it will pain our hearts greatly to be separated from him while he is still a child, but, at the same time, it will be a joy for us to fulfill our vow."

Hannah stayed at Ramathaim Zophim each year with the child, Samuel, while the rest of Elkanah's family went to Shiloh to sacrifice before the Lord. But the time came for the child to be weaned, and Hannah could no longer delay the fulfillment of her vow to the Lord.

# SAMUEL'S HEART

## CHAPTER 2

"Look mother, I can eat bread and lentils just like Shamar." Samuel demonstrated his new accomplishment to Hannah with limited success. "I don't need your milk anymore." Then his tender little heart smote him. "You don't mind, do you mother?"

Hannah smiled sweetly on her exuberant little son, but her heart was churning. "No son, it's all right with me if you don't need to nurse anymore. I'm so glad that you can eat at the table with the family. Now we will be able to go to Shiloh when your father goes for the yearly sacrifice."

The lad clapped his hands in glee. "Great! Father, did you hear what Mother said? We will go to the temple with you and . . . ." Suddenly he remembered, and his little chin trembled. "But I won't be coming home with you. I'll stay there with Eli, Hophni, and Phinehas." As he spoke the last sentence, he suddenly felt homesick, and he hadn't gone anywhere as yet.

"You probably won't be there very long," Shamar reminded him with a smirk. "You eat so sloppy that Eli will probably kick you out, and you'll come home crying."

"That's enough," Elkanah rebuked his oldest son. "If I remember, you were worse than sloppy in your eating habits when you were Samuel's age." Elkanah saw Peninnah glaring at him from across the table, but he ignored her.

"Yes, Samuel, you will stay with Eli and work for the Lord at the temple. Your mother dedicated you to the Lord for service in the tabernacle even before you were conceived, and I concurred with her pledge. You will have a great privilege of serving the Lord at such a young age."

Samuel's tear ducts had been threatening to overflow at the thought of leaving home, but his father's words encouraged him, and his eyes sparkled again with anticipation of his place at the temple.

"Humph," Peninnah snorted. "He's too young to be of any help in the temple. He'll be underfoot up there all the time, so if you ask me, I look for Eli to send him home with the family."

She continued. "If he's old enough to work at the temple, he should be doing his share out on the farm. Shamar is doing most of the work now."

"Oh, I like to work out in the field, Aunt Peninnah. I helped Shamar gather some stones for the stone fence yesterday. Didn't I Shamar?"

"Yeah, but you mostly got in my way," Shamar grunted, taking the cue from his mother.

"I think it will be wonderful to have my brother serving in the temple," Peninnah's older daughter, Livi, broke in. "Samuel is always kind and courteous, which is more than I can say for Hophni and Phinehas. They are very rude. I noticed that they take women into a side room at the temple and stay with them for a long time while people are lined up waiting to offer their sacrifices. I don't trust them, but I would trust Samuel. "

Livi smiled at her younger half brother. Livi was Samuel's only true friend in Peninnah's family. She would take his side when her brothers would tease and insult him.

"Thank you, Livi," the grateful brother whispered. "I hope that I will always make you proud of me."

"I'm sure you will," Livi responded with admiration for her younger brother.

The flax harvest had been good for the family of Elkanah, and already Hannah had processed the flax stems and spun many sheets of beautiful linen cloth. Some of these sheets she would sell for a good price in the marketplace, but one of the finest sheets she set aside for her son, Samuel. She had also woven many sheets of woolen cloth, and one of the finest of these she chose for a robe for her little son. She believed that only the best should be worn before the Lord.

"Come, Samuel," she called. "I must measure you for your ephod and robe." The boy came quickly.

While Hannah was measuring her little son for his garments to be worn at the temple, Peninnah entered the room. She watched Hannah work for a few moments with a scornful look on her face. Then she observed haughtily, "Aren't you taking a lot for granted with this miracle baby? Eli might not let such a puny little thing stay at the temple, and what you're making wouldn't fit too well out on the farm. I would surely want to make sure that he's going to stay at the temple before I did all that work."

Hannah smiled. "I feel quite certain that Eli will accept him. Samuel was born for the temple service, and I have dedicated him to that office. The Lord has impressed me that I have made the right decision to give him to the temple."

"Humph," Peninnah retorted. "You're a strange person, and you have some crazy plans for what you call this miracle child of yours."

"Father, why are you planning to take three bulls to Shiloh this year? Don't you usually take only one for the family?" Samuel was full of questions.

Elkanah patted his favorite son tenderly on the shoulder, and his eyes were misty. "Samuel, this will be your first year to go with us to the annual sacrifice, and these three bulls are for your special dedication as well as for the family. One bull will be a burnt offering that will consecrate you to the Lord forever, and the other two bulls are for our sin and peace offering. We will also take an epah of flour and a skin of wine for your consecration."

Elkanah hesitated for a moment; then he grasped the hand of his little son and led him to a seat. "Samuel, I'm quite sure that your mother has told you about some of the dangers you will face at Shiloh and also of some of the duties you will be expected to perform at the temple."

The boy nodded but was mute.

"I also need to talk to you about conditions there at Shiloh. Eli is old and is getting slow. His sons, Hophni and Phinehas, have charge of almost all of the sacrifices that are offered at the temple; they are not good men. Some of our wiser and more outspoken men have called them 'sons of Belial,' not to their faces, of course, but in many public gatherings. These sons of Eli cheat many of the worshipers and also have immoral relations with many of the women who come to the temple to worship. They claim that they are holy men and therefore can have their way in every situation without question.

"You must stay close to Eli and shun these evil men. They will, no doubt, resent your childhood and will expect you to do their bidding without question, but as I have said, stay close to Eli and ignore the wishes of these men. The Lord will deal with them in His time. Now, you must remember that you are also a Levite, and therefore have as much right to minister at the sanctuary as Hophni and Phinehas. Whatever Eli asks you to do, do it as unto the Lord. Never neglect your daily prayers or the reading of the holy scrolls."

The trip from Ramathaim Zophim to the city of Shiloh was usually a very pleasant time for Elkanah's family. Other families from the area and from along the route of travel joined with them in the trek to the holy city.

On this particular trip, the main topic of conversation between both the adults and children was the anticipated dedication of Samuel to the service of the temple. The children were awed by the thought and would touch Samuel timidly as if they regarded him more than human flesh.

The adults were divided in their support for a child aide to the priest. Some agreed with Peninnah that Samuel was too young to leave his family and much too young to assist in the temple services. Many of these families were special friends of Peninnah and, of course, were openly critical of Hannah for giving her son away at such an early age. But many others, with tears in their voices, commended Hannah for her unselfish gift and, in the same breath, voiced the wish that a son of theirs would be eligible for such a sacred work.

Hannah was not deterred by the criticism nor overly elated by the approval. She smiled and nodded and continued on her difficult journey.

Since every family in the caravan was bringing live cattle for sacrifice at Shiloh, the pace of travel was very slow. But the distance from Ramathaim Zophim to Shiloh was not far, so in the late evening of the first day, the spire of the temple was seen in the distance. As little Samuel saw the temple for the first time, his heart began to beat rapidly at the thought that this would be his home. Then his thoughts began to cycle, and fear of the unknown caused his brow to furrow. His heart began to churn. Hannah saw the troubled look on the face of her little son, and she put her arm around him as they made their way into the city.

The hour was late by the time Elkanah's family was settled. But Hannah was still determined to go for prayer to the very spot in the temple where, a few years before, she had been given the assurance from Eli that Jehovah would open her womb and give her a child. This visit was so different from the last one. Her heart was no longer heavy with an unfulfilled desire. Instead, she was now singing the praises of the God who had answered her prayer.

She spent so much time there in the darkness of the temple alcove that Elkanah came looking for her. He didn't chide her or interrupt her prayer. He knelt with her for a time with his arm around her as their hearts united in praise and thanksgiving to God who had given them such a precious son.

Sleep didn't come easily to Hannah that night. She had no regrets about her decision to dedicate Samuel to the sanctuary service, since he had been born with that purpose in mind. But the thought of permanent separation from her miracle four-year-old son was daunting to her. He was so young and vulnerable and had been such a joy to her in the last few years. He was always so obedient and attentive to her desires. Also, he was somewhat of a buffer zone to her, since his attitude toward the taunting of Peninnah and her sons was always so pleasant and positive that sometimes they even appeared ashamed of their own rude remarks. Yes, Samuel would be missed in the Elkanah home.

Samuel slept soundly even though of late he had experienced several bad dreams because of the thoughts of parting from his parents and the unknown he would be facing at the temple. But he had now accepted the idea as Jehovah's plan for his life, and he believed that it would be a joy to serve God under Eli the priest.

Everyone was up early in Elkanah's camp, and the chores and the breaking of the fast were soon over. It was now time for the morning sacrifice and the dedication of Samuel to the service of the temple.

Father Elkanah selected the finest of the three bulls, and leading the beast, the family proceeded to the temple area. Elkanah expected to see Hophni and Phinehas monitoring the morning sacrifices, but instead, Eli was in his place. Elkanah thought that perhaps Hophni and Phinehas had imbibed too much of the sour wine during the previous evening service and were sleeping off a hangover. According to rumors, this had happened quite often of late.

Hannah was glad to see that Eli was presiding. It seemed providential for it would make her presentation of Samuel so much easier. She touched her husband's arm. "May I speak to the priest before you offer the sacrifice?"

"By all means, you must have the privilege," Elkanah responded.

Hannah faced the aged man of God with a smile on her face and a song in her heart. "My lord," she said. "You probably don't remember your maidservant, but five years ago at this time I was praying to the Lord in the temple entrance with a heavy heart. I was a barren woman at that time and was praying that the Lord would look with mercy on my barrenness and would give me a son that I could dedicate to the temple service. You were sitting by the doorpost of the tabernacle as I was praying and you misjudged me. You thought that I was drunk from the sour wine that was passed around at the eating house. When you found that I was not drunk, but rather was pressing my burden before the Lord, you assured me that Jehovah had heard my prayer and would certainly give me the son for which I was asking.

"The Lord did answer my prayer and granted the petition I asked of Him. He opened my womb and gave me a son that his father and I are presenting this morning for dedication to the service of the Lord in His temple for all the days of his life."

When she spoke these words, the Spirit of the Lord rested upon Hannah, and she lifted her hands toward heaven and prayed a beautiful prayer, a song of praise and prophecy. As she prayed, the Spirit gave her insight into God's future plan for His people through the life and atonement of the Messiah. She saw in vision the final triumph of God's people, and her inspired ear heard the songs of the redeemed as they will stand on the sea of glass with a new song on their lips.

She was given a greater understanding of the character of the God who answered her prayer, and she made an indirect appeal to her rival, Peninnah, to put aside arrogance and give herself to the Lord. Possibly Peninnah, who was standing by and listening to the prayer, would have a change of heart and become a sweet companion to Hannah in their home.

As Hannah finished her prayer, she presented Samuel to Eli for dedication. Eli could hardly believe his ears. In his many years in the priesthood, he had never received such a request as this one. He looked at the small child standing before him wide-eyed and expectant, and then his eyes rested on the parents. They were so earnest and were giving to the Lord their very best.

The aged priest recovered slowly from his initial shock, reached out, and put his hands on Samuel's head. His thoughts were cycling. *He is so small to be separated from his parents,* he reasoned. *Possibly he will get so homesick for his mother that he will be of little use to the temple service.* He reminded himself that he was much too old to care for a weeping child. Perhaps the mother would secretly welcome his refusal of the child, since she would then be released from her vow to give the child for his entire lifetime to the service of the temple. But even as his negative thoughts surfaced, the Spirit of the Lord impressed his heart that this child before him was a providential gift from the Lord. The parents were really only the willing givers.

Eli thought of his own sons who had become so evil and self-determined. He felt he had lost almost complete control over the priesthood. Possibly this little boy could help him in his declining years to restore a sense of dignity and justice in his ministry to the people.

Eli was a very heavy man and was slow in both his physical movements and mental thoughts. The mother and father were waiting for his response.

As his thoughts cleared, Eli gently patted the top of the head of the little four-year-old boy who was standing patiently at attention. Then, he turned to the mother. "My dear lady, the Spirit of the Lord has brought to my memory just now the experience of your special prayer session here at the temple several years ago. I thought at first that you had been drinking too much sour wine, and I chided you unfairly. Then I found, by your own testimony, that you were greatly troubled in spirit because you were barren. So by inspiration, I assured you that the Lord would certainly answer your prayer, and today this little boy is the proof of that answer."

Eli turned his attention again to the child, Samuel. He placed his trembling hand again on the boy's head and lifted his own face to heaven. His voice was firm as he framed a homily of welcome and a prayer of dedication.

"I welcome this child to the service of the Lord's temple with some misgivings. He is so young and will certainly become homesick and yearn for you, his father and mother. I am also sure that you will long many times to have him with you that you might clasp him to your bosom. But since the Spirit of the Lord has impressed me that this child was born for service in the Lord's temple, we must not frustrate the wishes of the Lord. So, with the laying on of hands and with prayer, we will dedicate Samuel to the purpose for which the Lord has called him."

Eli reached down and grasped Samuel under his chin and looked into the wide, clear eyes of the son of Hannah. He saw fear in the young eyes, but with his wisdom of many years in the priesthood, he also saw determination on Samuel's face. The boy was looking into Eli's eyes without wavering.

"My son," Eli spoke kindly. "Do you wish to leave your father and mother and stay with me and my sons here at the temple?"

"Yes, my lord," Samuel answered quickly. "Mother and father have given me to the Lord."

"Very well," Eli responded. "We will now have your prayer of dedication."

He indicated that Elkanah, Hannah, and Samuel should kneel, but because of his ponderous size, he remained seated. Hannah grasped the precious form of her little son to her breast, while Eli and Elkanah put their hands on Samuel's head.

The priest intoned a beautiful prayer of dedication for Samuel, petitioning the Lord to bless the parents for their wonderful gift. He prayed that Samuel would become a great man of God and would always be inclined to hear and follow the leading of the Lord. (No doubt, as he prayed, he was thinking of his own wayward sons.)

He closed with the statement, "Anoint this child now with your Spirit and give him power with God and with men. Thank you, Lord, for hearing and answering this prayer. Amen."

Elkanah and Hannah added their "Amen's" to that of the priest, and even the voice of little Samuel was heard.

The aging priest arose from his seat with difficulty, grasped the hand of little Samuel, and turned toward the rear of the tabernacle. It was a silent farewell to his father and mother.

Samuel looked back at his parents as he was led away, and for a few moments, his young heart felt a pang of loneliness, but the thought that he would be serving the God of his father and mother calmed his heart. He resolved to be brave and obedient.

Eli took Samuel in through the back door of the tabernacle and showed him the many rooms where he, his sons, and other keepers of the temple lived. Samuel was hoping that his bed would be in Eli's room, but it was not to be. He would be in the room next door to Eli. There was a bed on the floor and very sparse furnishings. The boy did notice a table next to his bed with what he believed to be a holy scroll on top of it. Several candles were spaced around the room to provide him light for the evening and early morning hours.

Eli then gave him his assignments, which were quite comfortable for a four year old. He was to care for his room every day and put out the towels, knives, and basins for the daily sacrifices. Most of the morning hours would be spent in a class with Eli and another elderly priest, Ahimaaz, who were to be his instructors. He would also be assigned two or three intercessory prayers a day.

Sleep didn't come easily to the little priest from Ramah that first night. He lay on his bed in the dark and thought about his father and mother and his home of yesterday. For a moment, a tiny tinge of homesickness touched him, but he was comforted by the thought that only a short time ago his mother and father had prayed for him, and even now he was in their thoughts. Next, his favorite sister, Livi, came to mind. She was always so loyal to him, and she was also thinking of him at the moment. His thoughts settled on Aunt Peninnah. He loved this crabby lady even though she was often mean to him and his mother.

His mother, Hannah, had often assured him that underneath her cross exterior Peninnah had a good heart and one day would change. She encouraged Samuel to pray for her daily, even though it was quite evident that Peninnah did not reciprocate the act. The lad, on his bed at Shiloh, couldn't have known that today Aunt Peninnah had suffered that change of heart for which he and his mother had faithfully prayed.

As Peninnah watched and listened to the dedication of the tender little boy of four to the priesthood, the sweet and fervent prayer offered by her rival was used by the Spirit of God to break the critical heart of Peninnah. She had immediately gone back to the room to weep and pray, and there is where Hannah found her.

Hannah was alarmed. She took Peninnah in her arms and tried to soothe her. "Peninnah, what is wrong? Are you ill or hurt? Have I said something that has hurt you? If I have, please forgive me."

Peninnah shook her head. "No, Hannah, I am the one who has done the hurt. I have been so jealous of you and mean to you that I cannot stand myself any longer. But you have never said a nasty word back to me, and I have wished, many times, you would. Also, I have been so unkind to that sweet little boy of yours that you dedicated to the service of the tabernacle today.

"As I watched you so unselfishly giving up your only child for life and heard your wonderful prayer of submission and prophecy, my heart was broken. Hannah, will you please forgive me for all of the evil things I have said to you. I want to be friends from now on, instead of rivals. Now I know that you are Elkanah's favorite wife. He told me so when he married me. I know that he also loves my children and me, and I want to be worthy of his love. Hannah, I am sure that I won't be perfect in my attitude toward you, but please pray that the Lord will help me to improve every day."

She paused and her eyes misted again. "I only wish that I could see little Samuel and ask for his forgiveness, but that won't be possible right now, so I will write him a letter of apology."

Peninnah finished and lifted her tear-stained face to Hannah. Hannah hugged her again, and they were in each other's arms when Elkanah entered.

Elkanah was wide-eyed. "What is happening?" he wanted to know. "Have you two had a spat and are making up?"

Peninnah disengaged herself from Hannah's arms and faced her husband. "No, Elkanah, we have not had a disagreement." She again became teary eyed. She dried her eyes and continued. "Elkanah, I have confessed to Hannah how unkind I have been to her and little Samuel for so long now, and I have asked for her forgiveness. She has never said an unkind word to me in return, so the blame is all mine."

She changed her direction. "Elkanah, I know that I have also hurt you and the children by my evil tongue, so I ask for your forgiveness and understanding."

Elkanah took Peninnah into his arms and dried her tears away. "Yes, dear, I gladly forgive you. I am so happy for your change of heart."

There was great joy and sweet unity in the Elkanah family from that day on.

Samuel had fallen into a light sleep when Hophni and Phinehas entered the back of the tabernacle. They were loud and were laughing foolishly. Samuel had observed a few drunks in the city of Ramah, and the brothers were acting and sounding just like these rogues on the street. A shudder of revulsion passed through his small frame as he thought of these evil men ministering to the needs of God's people. He knew that sooner or later he would be meeting the two and, at the moment, he hoped that it would be later.

Samuel arose early the next morning, had his worship, cleaned his room, and then put out the towels, knives, and basins for the morning sacrifices. As he worked, he felt a sense of gratefulness for the small privilege of serving his Lord in His temple.

The morning sacrifices would not begin for some time, so he lingered at the entrance of the temple and greeted the people as they came for prayer

Many of the people were surprised to see a child at the temple, so they stopped and questioned him. "What is your name, my son? Where are you from? What are you doing at the temple?"

The first two questions were easy to answer without apology. "My name is Samuel, and I am a priest in training," he would answer quickly. "My mother and father dedicated me to the temple service even before my birth."

Most of the people would ponder Samuel's last answer for a few moments then pass on with a shake of the head. It was very evident that these people could not grasp the idea of any loving mother or father giving up such a sweet little boy.

When Eli came out to offer the morning sacrifices, Samuel made sure he was available to run any errands that might be needed. Eli seemed to appreciate the help of the little boy and gave him assignments that probably should have been handled by an adult resident priest. Neither Hophni nor Phinehas showed up for the morning services. They were, no doubt, sleeping off the effects of the sour wine of which they had imbibed much too freely the day before.

It was after the morning session with Eli and Ahimaaz that Samuel met the brothers. He was returning to his room from the toilet as one of the brothers was on his way to use the facility. The priest's eyes were bleary from his hangover, but when he saw Samuel, his eyes widened and he became alive.

"Ha, little boy what are you doing here in the tabernacle? Don't you know that this is off limits to children?" His voice was loud and shrill.

Samuel faced him. "I live here," he responded firmly.

"You live here? Since when and why?"

"Since yesterday. My mother and father brought me here, and your father dedicated me to the temple service for the rest of my life."

The priest couldn't believe what he had just heard. He shook his head to clear his muddled thoughts. The noise in the hall had aroused the other brother, and he came out to see what the commotion was all about.

"Look here, Phinehas. This little urchin is telling me that his father and mother left him here yesterday and father dedicated him to the temple service. So he lives here now."

The brother identified as Phinehas laughed coarsely. "So father has started dedicating babies for the temple service? What in the world will he think up next? When this word gets around the country, the people will laugh father out of his job. Of course, he doesn't get much done anymore, so perhaps, if we can get up earlier in the morning," he nudged his brother meaningfully, "we should also take over the morning services."

"I agree with you," Hophni responded quickly.

At this moment, Eli opened the door to his room and stepped out into the hall. The brothers turned on him with venom. "What's the meaning of this, Father?" Phinehas wanted to know. "This little boy tells us that you dedicated him yesterday to the temple service. Surely you were just patronizing the boy's parents for the day, and you will send him home; won't you?"

Eli answered slowly but firmly. "My sons, I had the same thoughts at first that you are having. I planned to refuse the offer of the parents and send the boy home with them. But as I pondered, the Spirit of the Lord impressed me deeply to accept the gift of the father and mother and dedicate him immediately for the temple service. I could not frustrate the will of the Lord, so the boy will stay." Eli patted Samuel's head as he made the last statement.

"Well," Phinehas growled. "I'm certainly going to let the people know that Hophni and I had no part in this silly arrangement. You will have to bear all the blame,

Father, and I am quite sure there will be a ground swell of criticism when the news gets around."

"I will take all the blame," Eli agreed. "But I rather think that before long most of the people will be rejoicing with me."

Hophni and Phinehas walked away, muttering to themselves. To their credit, the brothers came home early that evening, and Samuel noticed they didn't exhibit any symptoms of drunkenness. However, Samuel noticed that they still took women into the side rooms of the temple and spent much time with them while people waited impatiently to offer their sacrifices.

Samuel was in his room the night Eli faced his sons as they came in from their work. The walls of the rooms were thin, so Samuel could hear every word of the exchange between Hophni, Phinehas, and Eli. Even as a young boy, Samuel could feel the pain in the voice of Eli.

"My sons," he addressed them. "I am not hearing good reports of your ministry to our people. Some of the people are telling me that you send your servants with a three-pronged flesh hook and take all of the meat that the hook will bring up. They complain that they hardly have enough meat left for a good sacrifice. Then, if they don't give you the giant's share, you threaten to take it by force. You even take the meat before they have a chance to burn the fat. Some of the people are getting so discouraged that they are threatening to stop bringing sacrifices. But the worst of your sins is your fornication with women who come to the temple. Some of those women have complained to me that you forced them, and they have wept in my presence. Furthermore, the husbands of others are stirred up by your relations with their wives and are threatening to rebel."

"Now, Hophni and Phinehas, you are sinning against the Lord grievously, and I cannot intercede for you. You will have to bear your own guilt. Also, as you might know, you are discouraging the people and causing them to sin."

Phinehas broke in. "Father, you have said yourself that we are holy men. We pray for the people and intercede for them, so we have a right to expect a large part of their sacrifices and the favors of the women we choose. We believe that our requests of them are for their best interest."

Eli couldn't believe what he was hearing. He knew that he had been lax in the training of his sons, but he had warned them since early childhood of the sins of fornication and stealing. How had they gone so wrong?

It was difficult for Samuel to give into sleep that night. The sad appeal of Eli to his sons and Phinehas' self-righteous reply kept resonating in his mind. Before sleep claimed him, he promised God again that, in His divine strength, he would be strong and obedient in his walk before the Lord.

Samuel was becoming more and more a blessing to the ministry of Eli. As he grew in wisdom and stature, he was also growing in the love and respect of the people to whom he was ministering.

He looked forward each year to the visit of his family from Ramah. When he had reached his fifth birthday, his mother brought a baby brother to visit him as he ministered before the Lord. Also, a changed and radiant Peninnah brought him a robe that she had made with her own hands.

# SAMUEL'S HEART

## CHAPTER 3

The man of God came to Eli unannounced, uninvited, and unnamed. Perhaps he was an angel. He came with a message from God, and he delivered the charge with firmness and without preamble. The morning sacrifices were over, and Samuel was in his training class with teacher Eli when the messenger came, and since he was not dismissed, he heard the entire text of heaven's condemnation of Eli's priesthood.

Even at the tender age of five, Samuel had grasped the fact that God was not pleased with the ministry of Eli's sons, but Samuel hadn't assessed any blame to Eli for the deportment of his sons. They were grown men and responsible for their own actions. However, according to the man of God, heaven was assigning a large part of the prevailing corruption to Eli because of his lax manner in dealing with his sons.

The messenger reminded Eli of the Lord's choice of the tribe of Levi to offer the spiritual sacrifices of the people before him even from the day of their release from Egypt.

"However," the man of God continued. "You have corrupted His holy ministry by honoring your sons above the honor accorded to Him. Therefore, what could have been a forever ministry by your house will be cut off with shame. Your sons, Hophni and Phinehas, will both die in one day and all other descendants of your house will be cut off."

The man of God ended his message with the assurance that God would fill the void created by the loss of Eli's household with a faithful priest who would obey the Lord in all his ways. The man of God left as abruptly as he came. The aged priest arose painfully, dismissed Samuel with a wave of his hand, and went to his room. He was a beaten man.

Samuel thought that Eli would call his sons in, and after acquainting them with the message of the man of God, dismiss them from the temple ministry. At least this would delay the judgment of the Lord, but Eli did nothing. Possibly they would have laughed at his statement of dismissal and gone on with their evil ministry. Samuel wondered if Eli had even shared the message of the man of God with his sons.

Five years had passed since Samuel had begun his ministry at Shiloh. He had never been back to Ramah during those five years, but his family visited him at least once a year and would bring him gifts and their love. He was now a familiar and welcome figure at the temple, and no longer did the people pass by the holy place and shake their heads in disbelief at the sight of a child ministering to their spiritual needs. He was growing daily in stature and wisdom and in the esteem of the people.

Hophni and Phinehas continued their evil ministry in the temple, and it seemed to Samuel that they were becoming even bolder in their cheating of the people with the sacrifices and the fornication with the women. For a time, they ceased their illicit relationships with women when one woman accused Hophni of forcing her to have relations with him. Hophni adamantly denied the charge, and when the woman could not get a public hearing, she took her own life.

Because of their behavior, there was a public outcry against the two brothers, so much so, that they feared for their lives. They suspended their daily ministry in the temple for several weeks, and when they did return, they seemed very chastened. They humbly asked the people to choose the parts of the animal sacrifices they desired to give to the priests, and they did not take any of the women worshipers in the side rooms of the temple. They were pleasant to the people and civil to their father and Samuel. When they were seen in the marketplace, their wives were usually with them.

However, the change in the lives of the two brothers was only temporary. It is a law of human nature that the change in outward deportment must be the result of an inward transformation or the character manifestation will not last. Soon, the two corrupt priests were again indulging their lusts and selfish desires in their ministry to the people. In fact, they went beyond the boundaries of their former conduct.

It was when Samuel reached his tenth birthday that the Lord put His seal upon the boy priest's ministry. To this point in his life, the lad did not know the Lord God as his personal Friend and Savior. Through the practice and consistent teaching of his mother, he had early developed a sweet and kind spirit and a love for his mother's God, but he still needed the change of heart that every follower of God must experience.

Because of the moral failure of Eli's house, the word of the Lord was precious in those days. There was no open vision. The law of God was well nigh forgotten, and every man did what was right in his own eyes. But the Lord was preparing to make drastic changes in the spiritual leadership of Israel, and He would make sure that adequate warning was given to the people and also to the present priesthood.

It had been five years since the man of God had warned Eli of troubles to come because of the sins of Hophni and Phinehas and of his own neglect to curb their sinful excesses. During this extended period, no positive changes had been made in the lives of the two brothers. Thus, for the sake of His people, Israel, God could not wait much longer to end the flawed ministry of the house of Eli.

Samuel was now wearing the linen ephod and was accepted by the people as a divinely called priest in Israel. His daily schedule at the temple enlarged with the passing months and years.

After a long day of service, Samuel had gone to his bed. He lay awake for a time, pondering the experiences of the day before giving into a light sleep. He awoke to the sound of a voice speaking to him in the night.

"Samuel!"

Since he didn't yet recognize the voice of God, he assumed that Eli had called him. He immediately arose from his bed and ran to Eli. "Here I am for you called me," he said.

Eli was puzzled. "No, Samuel, I did not call you. Go back to your room and lie down again."

The Lord called again. "Samuel."

Again Samuel ran to Eli thinking that he was the one who had called him. Eli again assured him that he had not called, so Samuel went back to bed.

When God called the third time, Eli knew that it was the Lord who was calling Samuel. So he said, "Samuel, go and lie down in your place, and if the voice calls again, say, 'Speak, Lord, for your servant is listening.'"

And the Lord called Samuel again, and He said, "Samuel, I have seen that, even as a child, you have walked before me in purity of heart and integrity, thus I will trust you with a message of my coming plans for the house of Eli. I will bring to pass disaster against the house of Eli, which will make the ears of all Israel tingle. When I begin, I will not cease until I bring to an end his priesthood because of the sins of his sons, which he has not restrained. Thus, I have sworn that the iniquity of the house of Eli will not be purged with sacrifice or offering, but rather with the death of everyone in his succession. The Lord has spoken."

Samuel was deeply troubled. Eli had become like a father to him during his few years at the temple, and he had learned to love the aged priest very much. Eli's two sons hadn't fared so well in his evaluation process, but because of his training at his mother's knee, Samuel pitied the evil men rather than hating them. He completely understood why God planned to end the evil ministry of the two rebels. However, according to the message he had just received, Eli was just as responsible for his son's deportment as were the sons themselves, thus all alike would die.

Samuel lay down on his bed again, but sleep fled from him. He pondered the implications of the message he had just received. Not only was it a statement of God's plans for Israel, it was also a seal of his call to the ministry. The God of the universe had descended to share with him, a ten-year-old boy, the future of the priesthood of Israel.

Suddenly he felt much older than his ten years. In a span of only an hour, he had passed from a helper in the temple to a prophet of God and a divinely recognized priest. His childhood was gone. He slipped to his knees beside his bed and poured out his young heart in a prayer of renewed dedication to God.

Samuel rose early the next morning, opened the doors of the house of God, and completed his chores before the morning sacrifices. He saw Eli at a distance and tried to avoid him, but Eli remembered.

"Samuel," he called. "I know that the Lord spoke to you last night, and you must tell me everything that He said to you. Don't withhold anything, for the Lord will be disappointed with you if you keep back any part of the message." So Samuel told him everything that the Lord had revealed to him that night.

Eli realized that as the boy priest and prophet related to him the divine message Samuel was really not the one who was speaking. The Spirit of God was speaking through the boy. Samuel was only the mouthpiece.

Thus, the experience left the lad breathless and without strength.

For sometime after Samuel had finished, Eli sat unmoving and with head bowed. Samuel dared not interrupt his thoughts. Finally, Eli slowly rose, patted Samuel on the arm, and said sadly, "It is truly from the Lord, so let Him do what seems good to Him." He turned toward the entrance of the temple.

Samuel repressed the desire to run after the chastened priest to console him and then chide him for his inaction. He wanted desperately to question Eli about why he refrained from disciplining his sons, since the Lord had twice warned him that the evil lives of his sons and his own reluctance to correct them was the reason for the Lord's decision to bring an end to Eli's priesthood.

Samuel busied himself for the balance of the morning with temple chores, and at the noon hour, he took his meal in the temple kitchen. As he walked back to his room for the midday rest, he passed Hophni and Phinehas coming from their rooms. The lad noticed quickly that the brothers were angry. They blocked his path and glared at him for several moments as if they would like to physically attack him.

Hophni spoke up. "Father tells us that you have been seeking a grievance against us from the Lord, and only this morning, you told father a strange tale about how God is planning to kill the three of us soon."

He choked on the last sentence, and Phinehas took over. "I suppose you think that God would make you the high priest if we were gone." Both of the brothers laughed shrilly.

"What do you have to say for yourself, you boy prophet of doom?"

Samuel faced them without fear and looked them both in the eyes. Pity welled up in his heart for these two rebels. "Hophni and Phinehas, I hope that your father didn't relate to you that I have sought a grievance against you from the Lord, for that is not true. However, it is true that God gave me a message of warning against you two and your father because of your evil deeds and your father's unwillingness to restrain you. I wasn't aware that your father would share this message with you, but I am very glad he did.

"Perhaps you could defer this calamity the Lord has promised to bring against you if you would resign your functions as priests and by prayer and intercession ask God to change your lives."

For a moment, Samuel was amazed at the words he, a ten-year-old boy, had spoken to these grown men. But then he realized that the words were not really his. God had used him as a mouthpiece.

As Samuel finished, the two angry rebels acted as though they would physically hurt him, but there were several people standing nearby listening to the exchange. So the two gritted their teeth, clenched their fists, and walked away in anger.

Samuel watched them go with pity in his heart; then he went to visit with Eli. He was anxious to visit with the high priest, for he hadn't realized until his confrontation with Hophni and Phinehas how much the divine message given to him last night must have affected the venerable priest and judge. God had bypassed the senior priest and given His message to a priest apprentice, a ten-year-old boy. This must have been very humiliating to an aged and experienced judge and priest such as Eli.

Also, the tenor of the message directed against Eli and his sons was dire and irrevocable in content. It appeared that Eli and his sons had turned the final corner in their sin against the Lord, and there was no remedy. Certainly Eli would have good reason to be depressed.

Samuel found Eli in his room, and the boy was invited into his presence. The two sat in silence for a few moments; then Samuel spoke. "Master Eli, I met Hophni and Phinehas a few moments ago, and they accused me of seeking a grievance against them from the Lord. I felt badly about their charge, since it is not true, and I was hoping that you did not concur with them in their belief." He paused and waited for Eli to answer.

Eli was quick to rebut. "Samuel, my sons have no good reason to believe such an untruth, and as for me, I hadn't given that possibility one thought."

"Thank you, Master Eli. They also told me that you had reported to them that I had received a revelation from the Lord last night to the effect that the three of you would soon die by the Lord's hand. They were quite loud in their accusation and several people were standing nearby, listening to the exchange. I fear that because of those people, this news will travel far in a few days. Did you warn your sons to be careful in discussing this revelation from the Lord with the lay people, or had you planned for the people to hear it?" Samuel paused and looked expectantly to Eli for an answer.

Eli stirred in his chair and a shadow passed over his face, but his answer was firm. "Yes, Samuel, I want the people to know about your God-given revelation. In fact, I have already made plans to send this news by couriers tomorrow to the utmost boundaries of Israel. This news not only affects me and my sons, but every family in Israel. You see, if the Lord follows through on His threat, there will be an immediate change in the leadership of Israel. Perhaps the people will be so alarmed by such a possibility that there will be a great revival of godliness in Israel."

"But," Samuel remonstrated, "news of this kind could also serve to weaken your influence with the people."

Eli shook his head. "I am afraid, my son, that my influence, and certainly the influence of both Hophni and Phinehas, is at its lowest level since I was installed as high priest. So perhaps this message to the people could, at least, give us their sympathy."

Samuel was shocked. "But Master Eli, you have been a faithful high priest and judge in Israel for many years, so you need honor and esteem, not sympathy."

Eli looked at the earnest young lad before him for several moments, and an impossible passion filled his heart. *O Lord, I wish this boy were my son.*

He answered Samuel's statement as if he were absent from the body. "My son, I am sure that I have been much more than lax in the discipline of my two sons. You see, I was quite old when they were born, and their mother died when they were very small. Because of my heavy workload as both judge and high priest, I allowed a nurse to rear them for me. She was more doting and careless in their training than I was, so they have grown up selfish and evil."

Samuel marveled that the Lord was giving him the ability to visit with Eli as if he himself were an adult. He pressed his advantage.

"Master Eli, would you consider dismissing your sons from the temple ministry? Perhaps if you would do this, the Lord might see fit to defer the punishment he is planning to visit on you and your sons?" He wondered if the high priest would chide him for daring to suggest such a change, but Eli answered without apparent bitterness.

"I have thought of that measure many times, and I actually told them once several years ago that I was replacing them. They took the matter as a joke, and I didn't have the heart to follow through. Now it is too late. They would defy any order I would give, and they have enough of their kind in the city that would support them." Eli bowed his head in resignation.

Then he brightened again. "Samuel, my son, you have been the bright spot in my life and ministry for six years now, and I have greatly appreciated your obedience to my orders and to the Lord's commands. Your purity of life has been an example to my sons and to all Israel, but at the same time, you have been a thorn in the sides of my sons. You have made them feel very guilty, and I'm sure that they have acted out their guilty feelings many times by being rude to you."

The old priest paused for a moment; then he continued. "Many times I have wished that you were truly my son in the flesh."

With these parting words, Eli dismissed Samuel, and the young prophet retired to his room.

True to his promise, Eli sent out couriers the next day with the message of Samuel's revelation. Every family in Israel was to be summoned to the town hall of their particular city for the public reading.

In the city of Ramathaim Zophim, Elkanah's family heard the courier's announcement, and the hearts of Elkanah, Hannah, and even Peninnah and her children were stirred by the news that God had called Samuel to be a prophet. He had been given a message for the priesthood and for all Israel.

The announcement of Samuel's revelation from God made his name a household word in all of Israel. People who had lost faith in the priesthood of Eli and his sons began to bring their civil cases before Samuel. At first, the young prophet refused to hear their cases in deference to Eli, but the high priest urged him to listen to the people, so he began making court decisions.

Because of his consistent prayer life and spiritual approach to all of the people's problems, Samuel made fair and just decisions, and his fame spread.

Soon other cities were making requests for his service as a judge, and the ire of Hophni and Phinehas became violent toward him. On several occasions, the intervention of nearby laymen saved the boy from serious bodily harm.

Eli was always helpful and supportive of him, and Samuel could readily see that there was no jealousy on the part of the aged high priest, but rather fatherly pride.

He assisted Samuel in working out an itinerary that included Ramah, the city of his birth. In his visits to the cities, he found the land of Israel in spiritual shambles. His young heart was pained, and he began to exhort the people to turn to the Lord before His wrath would be poured out. Heathen idols had been set up in many of the temples dedicated to the Lord God of Israel, and at his bidding, many of these idols were destroyed, and the people began to worship the Lord again.

Samuel knew that because of the continuing corrupt example of Hophni and Phinehas the reformation begun in the cities would only be temporary. The dire consequences of the brother's sins and Eli's neglect would only be requited by the death of the family, according to Samuel's prophecy.

Samuel also found that the enemies of Israel were becoming bolder in their contacts because of Israel's sins. They were threatening the safety of Israel by moving their outposts closer to the boundaries of Israel. Their raiding parties were constantly making forays into the outlying farms and small towns. To Samuel, the situation looked dismal.

Samuel apprised Eli of the critical situation, but the high priest only shrugged his shoulders. He made no move to notify the army commander. The Israelite army at that time was actually under the direction of the high priest, but because of Eli's lack of interest in its function, Captain Azel was the recognized leader.

Samuel went to the captain with his concern. Azel welcomed the priest into his headquarters but listened rather listlessly to Samuel's report.

"I am fully aware of the situation," he answered with a shrug, "but I take my orders from the high priest, and . . . ," he smiled insolently, "he hasn't been around to give any orders for several years now."

A few weeks later, Samuel heard that a large Philistine army had gathered at Aphek and was threatening to invade Israel. Captain Azel marshaled an Israelite force of approximately 50,000 men at Ebenezer, and the two armies soon joined in battle.

Israel met the enemy with great expectations. They were presuming that God was on their side and thus the pagans would soon turn tail and flee before them, but their hopes were quickly dashed. The Philistines fought fiercely, and soon it was the Israelites that were in flight.

Their initial optimism was replaced with stark fear. Men were falling by the score, and four thousand men were left dead on the battlefield. The army was in disarray.

Because of the late hour, the Philistines didn't follow up their advantage, but it was quite evident that they would regroup for a second offensive the next day.

As the disheartened fighting men of Israel trooped back to camp, the elders of Israel summoned Captain Azel to their headquarters. They felt that unusual tactics would need to be employed in the offensive tomorrow or the enemy would soon overrun the land.

"Why did the Lord defeat us today before the Philistines?" they asked Captain Azel and one another. "We will need to meet them again tomorrow, and we must have better plans," they concurred.

They soon came up with a new strategy for meeting the enemy, and there was complete unanimity, but they didn't present their plan to the Lord for approval. Neither did they ask the new prophet of Israel to bless the plan with prayer.

# CHAPTER 4

Two years had now passed since God's announcement through Samuel that Eli's priesthood would come to an end by his violent death and that of his sons. For a time, the divine decree had tempered the evil actions of Hophni and Phinehas, but the passing of time had emboldened them in their sins against heaven. Later, God predicted this very human tendency: "Because the sentence against an evil work is not executed speedily, therefore the heart of the sons of men is fully set in them to do evil" (Ecclesiastes 8:11, NKJV).

It was early in the morning, and seldom were Hophni and Phinehas astir at this hour. Samuel had risen early as usual, and after his devotions and the morning meal of gruel, bread, and goat's milk, he had dressed for the morning services.

Most of the time, the twelve-year-old priest took care of all the morning sacrificial services so that Eli could sleep late and conserve his strength. Hophni and Phinehas were not morning people, and, as a usual practice, they were often sleeping off the effects of their drunkenness from the night before.

Samuel had noticed unusual activity in the hall in front of his room as he dressed for the day. The footsteps sounded like those of Hophni and Phinehas, but since he had seldom known them to be astir at this time of the morning, he concluded that other temple aides were responsible for the noise. However, as Samuel came from his room, he was surprised to see Phinehas going out the back door. He knew that Hophni must have preceded his brother for the two were inseparable.

The mind of the young priest was puzzled. What could be so important to the two men that it would serve to rouse them from their beds at such an early hour? He remembered that last night, as he was reading in his room, a group of men, who had introduced themselves as the leading elders of Ebenezer, had met Hophni and Phinehas in the hallway in front of his room.

The men had told the brothers, in a very excited manner, of a battle between Israel and the Philistines that had been fought that very morning near the city of Ebenezer. Israel had suffered a very humiliating defeat and 4,000 men had died in the battle. Samuel had heard several of the elders weep aloud as they recounted the painful loss.

The spokesperson continued. "We are certain that the pagans are planning to follow up their advantage and attack us again tomorrow. We must be sure that our army will not suffer another defeat, because, if that were to happen, the Philistines would overrun our country. We have a plan to discuss with you, to strengthen our army and save our nation."

At that point, the brothers invited the Ebenezer delegation into Hophni's room, and Samuel did not hear the plan the group was proposing. Samuel was quite sure that the early morning activities of Hophni and Phinehas had to do with the proposal of the leaders from Ebenezer.

The young priest finished getting ready for his day before going to the temple to prepare for the morning sacrifices. As he entered the front of the temple, he noticed that the door to the room where the Ark of the Covenant was stored was open and there were sounds of activity within, so he immediately went to investigate. He found Hophni and Phinehas within, obviously preparing the Ark for removal.

Samuel stood just inside the door for a few moments with mouth agape, wondering just what the brothers had in mind for the Ark. Until this moment, Samuel had never seen the sacred chest. He had a key to the room where it was stored, but his sense of the holiness of God would not allow him to open the room and gaze on the Ark. Also, he knew that the high priest was the only one who was supposed to touch it or even look on it. Each year during the eight years that Samuel had been at the temple, Eli had used the Ark in the service of the Day of Atonement, but Samuel had not been asked to assist him.

It was a belief in Israel that, for many centuries, the presence of the Lord had been manifested in the sacred vessel, and here the two carnal priests were treating the Ark as though it were a part of the morning service. The brothers glanced at Samuel as he stood in the door but made no move to recognize his presence.

Righteous anger boiled up in the young priest's throat, and he found his voice. "What are you planning to do with the Ark of God?" he demanded in a voice that was bigger than he was.

Phinehas stopped working for a moment and with a smirk on his face looked at this brother. "Did you hear a noise somewhere?" he asked insolently. "Or am I just hearing things?"

Hophni laughed coarsely. "Yes, you heard the voice of the new prophet of doom asking us what we are planning to do with the Ark. Evidently it's too dark in here for his heavenly vision to see what we're doing." Both brothers laughed heartily at Hophni's sarcasm.

Hophni straightened up. "Little man, we have no obligation to explain to you what we are doing, but just so you won't die of curiosity, I will tell you what our plans are. We are preparing the Ark to travel to Ebenezer. There was a battle yesterday between our national army and the Philistines. Our army was soundly defeated, and 4,000 men died on the field. The men of Ebenezer have reason to believe that the Philistines will attack our army again today, and we must take unusual steps to prevent another defeat. So we are taking the Ark to the battle today so that the Lord will fight for us against our enemies. Now are you satisfied?" Hophni stopped speaking and resumed his work on the Ark.

Samuel was aghast. "No, I'm not satisfied!" he said with heat. "You can't use the Ark like that! Only the high priest is supposed to touch this sacred chest. It would be pure arrogance against the Lord for you to use this holy vessel as you are planning. Surely, if your father knew about your intentions, he would stop your plans immediately."

Both men stopped working and looked at Samuel with hate in their eyes. Phinehas answered. "Our father does know about our plans for the Ark, and although he has the same old woman ideas about the Ark that you do, he has no intention of stopping us. Now little prophet, get out of our sight and let us finish getting this vessel ready for travel." The brothers then ignored Samuel and bent to their task.

Samuel had one last parting comment. "By handling the Ark with carnal hands, you obviously do not believe that it is sacred. So then, what good will it do you in your battle against the pagans?"

The brothers ignored the question and kept at their work.

Samuel deferred his morning chores for a time in order to visit with Eli. He reasoned that surely the high priest had not thought of the serious consequences that could result from taking the Ark into the battle area. If the sacred chest were damaged or taken by the enemy, the entire nation of Israel would stand guilty, and the people would possibly rise up and dispossess him of his holy office immediately. The situation seemed very critical to the young priest and prophet, and he was convinced that Eli should see that the plan was aborted immediately.

Eli was awake, and he listened patiently to Samuel's appeal. Then, with a helpless shake of his hoary head, he answered. "Samuel, my son, I know that you are right and what my sons are doing is wrong. I am against their evil plan with all my heart. But they ignored my counsel and would certainly defy any order that I would give for them to stop. So I will leave the matter in the Lord's hands, and you must do the same." The aged priest spread his hands in frustration and turned away with his aide toward the temple.

Samuel knew that to speak further with Eli would not be profitable, so he left the high priest's presence with a heavy heart and took charge of the morning services. He finished the morning sacrificial service and then watched helplessly as the brothers brought the Ark out the front of the temple and placed it on a cart drawn by two oxen. The sacred chest was draped with a black cloth, but the shape was unmistakable. The brothers headed with their sacred cargo toward Ebenezer. The young priest and prophet wondered for a moment if he would ever see the sacred vessel again. It was a prophetic thought.

Samuel stood for sometime looking after the disappearing Ark. Then he saw Eli coming from his place led by his faithful aide, Libni. Eli was almost completely blind now. He could no longer lead out in the services of the temple, but often he would assist Samuel by handing him instruments and offering prayers.

Lately, he had assumed the position of the head elder of the city by sitting at the gate of the city. He would welcome visitors to the city and meet with couriers from other cities with messages for Shiloh.

The aged high priest couldn't have known that today the prophecies of the man of God and Samuel would meet their fulfillment. The judgments of God had been deferred for seven years, but today the axe would fall and a new chief priest would be installed in Israel.

Samuel was ready to begin the evening services when a messenger came from the battlefield. He had passed Eli at the city gate without notice and had come directly to the temple and to Samuel. The man was wild of eye, and his clothes were torn, but he had the looks of a warrior. Samuel invited him in and questioned him. "Who are you? Where are you from, and who do you represent?"

"I am a Benjamite, and I come from the battle of Ebenezer." He paused for a few moments as though he were trying to remember the details of the message he was bringing. He shuddered; then resumed. "The pagan Philistines attacked us again today as they did yesterday. Our army suffered a very humiliating defeat in the battle yesterday, and 4,000 of our troops died in the battle. So our army commanders and the elders of the city of Ebenezer got together to determine what went wrong and what we should do to prevent a defeat today. They came to Shiloh last night to ask your priests to bring the Ark of the Covenant to the battlefield so that the Lord would fight for us against our enemies. Your priests brought the Ark to the battle today with the hope that the pagans would be defeated."

At this point, Samuel felt like shaking the man soundly and demanding that he get to the point. But the messenger was methodical.

"When the Ark came into our camp, the entire army was excited. We thought surely the presence of God was among us now and thus our enemies would be afraid to attack us. Every man in our army shouted loudly. We put the two priests and the Ark right in the middle of our army so that we could protect the holy men and the sacred Ark.

"When our men shouted, the Philistines found that we had the Ark of God with us, and they were afraid. Several of our men heard the pagans shout, 'We are all dead men because the Ark of their God is fighting for them.'

"But something terrible happened." The man shuddered as he remembered, and a spasm of pain creased his face. "Our men seemed confused from the very start of the battle, and the Philistines seemed very determined. They fought like mad men, and it almost seemed as if the Lord was fighting for our enemies rather than for Israel. Men were falling all around me even worse than yesterday.

"It soon became evident that we were losing the battle, so we fled before the Philistines. In our fear, we forgot about the priests and the Ark. Suddenly we remembered, and quite a few of us went back to get the priests and retrieve the Ark. But we found that the two priests were dead and the pagans had taken the Ark to the rear of their army. There was no way that we could rescue it."

The man bowed his head in agony, and it was difficult for him to continue. Finally, he found his voice again. "Several of our army leaders have estimated that we lost at least 30,000 men, more than half of our entire army."

Suddenly the messenger looked at Samuel as if he were seeing him for the first time. There before him was a lad of twelve years. "You aren't the high priest, are you?" He was puzzled.

Samuel smiled. "No, I am not the high priest; however, I am acting in his place at this time. The high priest is at the city gate, so you must have passed by him as you entered the city. I will take you to him now, and you must tell him what you have just related to me."

They found Eli sitting on a bench without a back, nodding in the warm sunshine. As Samuel and the Benjamite approached him, the high priest turned toward their footsteps.

"Master Eli, we have a messenger here who has just come from the battlefield. He wishes to speak with you."

Eli's face lighted up, and he answered quickly. "Yes, by all means give me your report."

Samuel watched the facial expression of Eli carefully as the warrior gave his report. The change in his visage was slow, but when the Benjamite told him of the death of his two sons and the loss of the Ark, a spasm of pain, like that of a woman giving birth, convulsed his face. He fainted, and his ponderous form fell off the seat backward. Samuel leaped forward to catch him, but it was too late. He struck the ground heavily, and the jolt broke his neck. He died immediately. He had judged Israel for forty years, and he was ninety-eight years old. Samuel's prophecy of three years earlier was almost totally fulfilled in a single day.

Samuel walked with the messenger back to the temple, and there he dispatched several temple aides to bring Eli's body back to the temple. Samuel took the Benjamite to the temple kitchen and requested the temple maids to prepare a meal for him and a room for the night. He then went to visit with the wives of Hophni and Phinehas. He found the wife of Phinehas in the early pains of childbirth. Her mental torment at the news of the death of her husband and father-in-law and the loss of the Ark was so great that she died during childbirth. Upon delivering a living child and with her dying breath, she named him Ichabod—"the glory of the Lord has departed from Israel."

As the twelve-year-old priest and judge finished his work for the day, he suddenly felt lonely. Eli, his mentor of eight years, was gone, and the two irritating and profane brothers were lying dead on the battlefield. They would not be back. There was no one to counsel him or chide him. In the space of one day, he had become the only legitimate priest and judge in Shiloh. Thus, all of the activities of the temple and the civil cases would be under his direction from this moment forward.

The words of the man of God spoken seven years earlier resonated in his ears as though they had been spoken but yesterday: "Then I will raise up for myself a faithful priest who will do according to what is in my heart and in my mind . . ." There was more, but right now the balance seemed of no import. He had no idea that on the day when the man of God spoke these words, the prophet was talking about him. But it had to be. He thought of the priest Ahimaaz who had been of great help to him in his early years at the temple, but Ahimaaz was no longer ambulatory and was confined to his home.

Samuel dropped to his knees in the temple room and poured out his heart in renewed dedication to his God. He shared with God his insufficiency and his great need, and he begged earnestly for divine wisdom to guide him in all the decisions he would make in future days. He stayed on his knees for a long period of time, and the Lord met with him. The meeting wasn't in the form of a dream or a vision; neither did the Lord call him by name as he had that night two years ago. The communication was by impressions that were so strong and well defined that Samuel knew they were from the Lord. He listened carefully. The impressions came slowly and were etched in his mind. They didn't appear to come in sequence but rather in degrees of importance.

The first impression advised him to warn the people to vacate Shiloh immediately. The Philistines would soon follow up their advantage by settling in the cities close to their boundaries, and of course, they would put in bondage every Israelite that remained in those cities. Shiloh would certainly be one of the choice cities for Philistine occupation.

He must send out couriers early the next morning announcing to all Israel the news of Israel's defeat at Ebenezer. The riders would also carry a report of the death of Eli, his sons, and daughter-in-law; the loss of the Ark of the Covenant; and the threat of an immediate Philistine invasion of Shiloh, thus necessitating the removal of the temple services and judicial center from Shiloh to Ramah.

He must schedule an immediate burial service for Eli and the daughter-in-law and would find out from the army captain if there were any plans to recover the bodies of Hophni and Phinehas from the battlefield. The two rebels didn't deserve any special consideration, but since they were recognized as legitimate priests by many in Israel, they should have proper burials.

He sent a temple servant to the army commander asking about his intention for recovery of the bodies of the priests. The servant came back quickly with the news that since many Philistine soldiers were still astir on the battlefield, any plans for recovery of specific bodies would be futile.

The sudden and modest burial of Eli troubled Samuel. This aged priest had given his entire life to the service of his people, and now he was going to his final rest without proper recognition from the many people who loved him, but it had to be.

Samuel was warned that he must make haste to close out all activities at Shiloh lest the Philistines find him there. He must not overstay. He did take time, however, to decide what temple furniture he must take with him to Ramah. He also determined what primary roles he would assume in the city of his birth.

He had never been officially invested with the office of high priest. Eli had mentioned to him several times that he planned to dedicate him to the office of high priest on his fifteenth birthday in order to bypass his corrupt sons, but now that would never happen. It was probably the best, since now that the Ark was gone there was no immediate need for a high priest.

Samuel was a priest and also a judge, and he knew that there would be a need for his services in Ramah. Ramah would function as the center for the sacrificial services and the judicial system for all of Israel. He was also a prophet but that office was subject to God's time and call.

The move of the temple equipment and its services from Shiloh to Ramah was very painful for Samuel. The transition of the offices of chief priest and judge from Eli to him would have been difficult even if he could have stayed on at Shiloh where he was well known and accepted by the people. But in Ramah he could expect little honor, since he would always be remembered as the miracle child of Elkanah and Hannah.

He remembered, however, that the few times he had sat as a child judge at Ramah many people had brought their grievances to him and had accepted his decision as from the Lord.

He was also comforted by the thought that the move from Shiloh to Ramah was not a plan of his own devising but was dictated by the Lord Himself. He had confidence that the God who had dedicated him to the temple service as a child would not err in placing him where he was needed most.

It was a homecoming for the twelve-year-old judge and priest, since he had been back to the city of his birth only the few times while serving as a judge. Of course, he had seen his family and Aunt Peninnah's family each year as they came for the yearly sacrifices at Shiloh.

His heart was always warmed by the thought that the two families he dearly loved were united in spirit since the day of his dedication at Shiloh. Hannah and Peninnah were no longer rivals but were now close sisters, members of the same family.

Two days after Samuel arrived in Ramah, a messenger brought the news that the Philistines had taken over Ebenezer, Shiloh, and the surrounding cities, and the shattered Israel army had offered no resistance. At the announcement, Samuel remembered the army.

He wondered. Since the disastrous defeat at Ebenezer was there still an organized group that would constitute an army? Was Captain Azel still in charge, or had he fallen at Ebenezer? If any part of the army still existed, who was feeding the soldiers and paying them for their services? He must find the answer to these questions immediately.

He knew that Eli had served as the nominal head of the army, thus as Eli's successor, it would now be his responsibility. So he must call for the captain and find out what needed to be done to restore the military defenses of Israel.

A courier soon found Captain Azel, and he came to Ramah at Samuel's request. Samuel recognized him as the same man with whom he had talked about the Philistine threat before the battle at Aphek, but he was a chastened man. There was none of the insolence with which he had answered Samuel at that time. Samuel seated him and then studied the man for a few moments before he spoke. Azel fidgeted uncomfortably before the gaze of the twelve year old.

"Captain Azel, I appreciated your answering my summons. I need to ask you a few questions."

"Yes, my lord," the captain answered civilly.

"How many men are left in your army?"

"We numbered them yesterday. There are 20,049, but quite a number were wounded and are in immediate need of a physician."

Samuel nodded. "I will send a physician back with you to care for these men. We must not lose them."

"How are you feeding them?"

"We are living off the land, my lord. Our supplies from the temple were cut off when the Philistines moved into Shiloh. But many of the faithful in Israel have been bringing us food. I do fear, however, that before long many of our men will desert unless we can restore their pay and provide regular food lines for them."

"Where is your army camped at this time?"

"We are staying in the country near Bethel."

"Very well. If you can forage for a few more weeks near Bethel, I will make plans to have your troops moved to Ramah, and hopefully we can provide them with their pay and a regular plan for feeding them."

Azel arose and bowed. "Thank you, my lord, for your assurance. The men will be very grateful for your interest and effort."

Samuel dismissed the captain, and at the same time, he invited a physician from the city to go to Bethel with the captain to care for the troops. He then went to visit with his father.

"Father, I am now working out of temporary headquarters, but since I will not be able to return to Shiloh, I will need a tabernacle here where I can carry on my work as priest and judge. When the Philistines settle down, I will resume my itinerary, but Ramah will be my base."

Elkanah looked long at his son who, at twelve years old, was a priest, a judge, and a prophet. What a blessing he had been to his family and to all of Israel.

He made a quick decision. "Son, God has blessed me with much earthly goods, so I will make a thank offering to Him. I will build a tabernacle for your work as a priest and judge and will dedicate it to God's honor. If you will draw the plans, I will set men to work on it immediately."

Samuel hugged his father with feeling. "Thank you, Father. I knew that you would have the answer. I will draw the plans for you this very evening."

"There is one more item that I need to discuss with you."

Elkanah nodded and waited.

"Since Eli was the nominal head of the army, as his successor that responsibility is now mine. Thus I must make provision for the pay and the rations of the troops. I visited with Captain Azel today and found that the 20,049 survivors of the battle of Aphek are camping in the country near Bethel and are literally living off the land. Quite a number are badly wounded so I invited a physician from the city to return to Bethel with the captain and care for the wounded.

"We will soon need to move the troops to Ramah and provide them with pay and food. In the past, Eli furnished their pay and food from the temple offerings, but that will not work here. I have made plans to send out a tax notice to all of Israel so that the army will be paid and fed. However, they will also need housing in the city. Since you are a member of the city council, will you see that plans are made to house them and feed them? We will certainly need a standing army to take care of Philistine raids and possible feuds among our own people."

Elkanah nodded. "Our next meeting is tomorrow night, and I am sure that the members will look with favor on the idea of housing the army here in Ramah."

"Thank you very much, Father, for easing my mind on this weighty matter."

Elkanah smiled. "You are welcome, son. Please remember that every member of your blood family stands ready to help in any way we can. We do not want to interfere with your work, so we will simply stand by."

The Philistines appeared content to settle in the peripheral towns of Israel and made no move to annex other cities. However, they roamed the country at will and were bold in their show of control.

Samuel chafed under the pagan's occupation, but his earnest prayers brought no dreams, visions, or impressions regarding any possible liberation. He knew that he must be patient. God would declare the time for the yoke to be broken.

As Elkanah had promised, a beautiful new tabernacle was soon ready for sacrificial and judicial services, and Samuel was in business. His workday soon became long, but never tedious. He always enjoyed giving to his people the blessings and counsel God gave to him.

The years passed swiftly. Samuel knew that the Ark of God had been returned by the Philistines and had settled in Kirjath Jearim in the house of Abinadab on the hill.

Abinadab consecrated his son Eleazer to keep the Ark, and it stayed there for twenty years. The Lord didn't give Samuel any vision, dream, or impression to retrieve the Ark, so he patiently let it reside at Kirjath Jearim.

During the twenty years the ark was in Kirjath Jearim, Samuel kept his twice yearly visits to Bethel, Gilgal, and Mizpah, but he always returned to Ramah, for his home and the center of his sacrificial and judicial work were there.

His mother, father, and Aunt Peninnah died during this period, and the family mourned for them. Samuel grew close to his brothers and sisters, but his closest relative was Livi, Peninnah's oldest daughter. One day she came to him with a suggestion that changed his life.

# CHAPTER 5

Samuel's older half sister Livi hovered over her favorite brother like an old mother hen caring for her lone chick. He was her happy responsibility. She had been married for several years already to a prosperous merchant in Ramah and was blessed with three lovely children, but she still doted on Samuel. Often she would bring him meals as he worked in his study and would sit and visit with him as he ate.

Today she had a special reason for her visit. She had good news for him. Her manner was different than usual, so Samuel put aside his quill and faced her.

"Samuel," she breathed, her eyes wide with excitement, "I have a new friend that you must meet, so please don't disappoint me. She is beautiful, smart, and of marriageable age, and since you need a wife, I am anxious for you to get acquainted with her."

A shadow passed over her face momentarily as she spoke. "There is one little problem. She already has a suitor, but I am confident that, with your charm and art of conversation, you can overcome such a handicap quite easily." Her eyes were pleading. "You will set aside your work long enough to meet her and possibly court her, won't you?"

Samuel smiled and hugged her. "Livi, I am certain that the grace of God and much practice has made me quite fluent in my visits with the people and my public discourses, but I am not sure that I would be a good wooer. I would probably be tongue tied around such a beautiful lady as you have described."

She slapped his hands playfully. "Nonsense! You have a gift of putting people at ease, and I am sure that before

long she would be sitting at your feet and looking at you with adoring eyes as I have done many times."
She hesitated. "Brother, I'm sure that with your humility you don't realize how handsome and charming you really are. If you were not my half brother and younger by several years, I would have pursued you and pestered you until you would have married me. Of course, that was before I met Zeruiah," she added with a smile and twinkle in her eyes.

"You will let me introduce you to her, won't you?" she asked with a plea in her voice.

Samuel laughed. "Livi, I wouldn't think for one moment of disappointing my favorite sister. So tell me more about this angel in the flesh. What is her name, and who are her parents, and, oh yes, who is the fellow that is squiring her now?"

She relaxed as she answered. "Her name is Belah, and her parents are Shepi and Zoran. Her father is a banker in the city, so it is possible that you have met him."

Samuel nodded. "Yes, I have met the banker, Shepi. He appears to be a very nice fellow."

"Oh yes," she agreed. "The family has a spotless reputation in the city, and the suitor of Belah is Uzal. He is the son of the tanner, Anah. Uzal works for his father, and from what I hear, he is a very hard worker. He does have one apparent and obnoxious weakness, however. He has been taxed for public drunkenness several times. Each time his father quickly paid his tax so there has never been any prison sentence. News like this travels around town quite quickly, you know."

Samuel looked at his appointment schedule as he spoke. "How and when did you plan for me to meet Belah? Knowing you as I do, I am sure that you have already formed a flawless plan with fanfare and bells."

She laughed musically. "Well, I didn't want to lose the advantage if you would agree, so I have planned for an evening of fun, games, and refreshments at my home tomorrow night, an hour after sunset. The guests were picked carefully. There will be Belah, of course, and several married couples that are friends of Zeruiah and me. You and Belah will be the only unmarried guests." She paused with a look of uncertainty on her face. "Samuel, do you think that my intentions will seem too obvious?"

He laughed heartily. "Well, it would certainly have all of the earmarks of a setup. Have you discussed this with Belah? She might resent me from the very start if she thinks that I am trying to come between her and her present boyfriend."

Livi's face brightened. "Oh yes, I have discussed this matter with her. She knows of my interest in having you meet her, and she is all for it. You see, I don't think she has any deep emotional ties to Uzal even though they have kept company for more than a year. So, my loving brother, she will be there tomorrow night with all of her beauty and charm and will be awaiting your presence."

He patted his sister's arm. "Good, I will look forward to the occasion." He hesitated for a moment. "By the way, as you remember, I was supposed to be gone this week and next, but the meetings were postponed. Did you presume that I would be here?"

Her eyes flickered guiltily. "I have to confess," she said timidly. "I came by to see you last week, but you were out for an hour or so. Your schedule was open on your desk, and I noticed the postponement, so I took advantage of the news to plan this assemblage. That wasn't nice of me to pry like that, was it?"

Samuel waved his hand. "Livi, my schedule is hardly ever a secret, and it would never be so to you, so you didn't commit any type of sin. You can pry into my agenda any time you feel a need."

She arose then, hugged him, and kissed him on the cheek. "Thanks so much, brother. I was afraid that I had overstepped."

"Never!" Samuel assured her.

Samuel was greeted by a radiant Livi as he arrived at her home for the assemblage. She gave him an embrace, a kiss on the cheek, and ushered him into the living room where several couples were already seated. He recognized three of the men as merchants in the city even before introductions were made. Then Livi introduced him to the gorgeous Belah. The introduction took his breath for a moment. Livi hadn't overrated her beauty and poise at all. She was elegant. Both acknowledged the introduction without apparent embarrassment, and then, at Livi's suggestion, they sat down together to visit and get better acquainted.

Belah was interested in his work. "I have heard so much about you from so many in the city," she said with awe in her voice. "And I have seen you at a distance several times, but because you are so busy and such a public figure, I never dreamed that I would ever have the privilege of meeting you personally. But," she said with a brilliant smile, "it happened."

She continued. "Livi tells me that you have a circuit that you follow twice a year in your ministry and that you minister to many people during this tour." She paused and waited for his response.

"Yes," he admitted. "I have a regular circuit that I follow quite religiously. The people in these cities expect me, and I don't like to disappoint them. Along with my writing, this keeps me busy. That's probably why I haven't met you before. But now that I've met you in the flesh, I would certainly like to get better acquainted."

She blushed slightly, and her chin came up. "I would like that," she affirmed.

"Tell me about yourself and your family," he pressed. "Livi has told me that your father is Shepi, one of the local bankers. I have met him. Livi also told me that your mother's name is Zoran, but she wasn't sure if you had brothers and sisters."

"Yes, you have heard right. Father is a banker and mother's name is Zoran. I do have two older brothers, Tolan and Jarih. They are both married and have moved to Gibeah. They are also into banking. I have no sisters."

Samuel waxed boldly. "Lady Belah, if you would have been blessed with sisters, I am very sure that they would not have reached the plateau of your beauty."

Now, he pressed. "Could I have the privilege of visiting you in your home and getting better acquainted with you?"

A look of uncertainty clouded her pretty face. "Lord Samuel, since you have asked to visit me at home, which I am quite sure means you would like to court me, I will share something with you that must be kept in confidence." She shuddered as she spoke.

He nodded but didn't speak.

"The man who has kept company with me for more than a year, whose name is Uzal, is very jealous." Again, she shuddered. "He has threatened to kill anyone whom I would allow to court me, and I am certain that he means every word. I have turned several prospective suitors away without explanation because of the danger that he would pose for them, but because I esteem you so highly and also because of my friendship with Livi, I felt a need to share this onus of mine with you. I have determined never to marry Uzal, but since I would not want to endanger others, I have contented myself with the thought of remaining a virgin for the rest of my life." She looked to Samuel for understanding.

He was silent for a few moments; then he faced her. "Lady Belah, I greatly admire your concern for those who would desire to court you, and of course, that would include me, since that is my intention. But it wouldn't be fair for you to allow this man to hold you hostage for the rest of your life with his insane jealousy. You would have so much to offer a marriage of love with your beauty and sweetness. Someone must challenge this evil fellow. Now, since I am a man of God, I do not indulge in fighting. However, even God fights for those He loves and who love Him in return, so I must face this man and attempt to reason with him. If he will not listen to reason, I will need to resort to other methods. I have practiced jousting with the soldiers and have become quite proficient at the art. I am also better than average at hand-to-hand combat without weapons, so with your permission, I will meet this man as soon as possible, and we will see where the Lord will lead from there."

She had been listening wide-eyed.

Samuel continued. "I would want you to understand that I expect no personal commitment on your part. Since you hardly know me, you do not know, at this point, whether you would want to pursue a serious friendship with me. Also, perhaps you are in love with one of the men you had to turn away. However, as I mentioned before, I would like to visit you and get better acquainted."

She nodded and whispered, "I would like very much to have you visit me."

He grasped her hand, and she didn't resist. "Do I have permission to visit with this man, Uzal?"

"Yes, yes, you may," she agreed quickly. "But please be very careful, for he is a very strong and violent man."

"That I will do," he assured her. "Now, perhaps I should not monopolize your time further, for you will want to visit with others here at Livi's assemblage." He squeezed her hand and she responded.

The balance of the evening at Livi's assemblage was rather painful for Samuel. Although he visited and bantered with the guests, his mind was on the call he must make the next morning at the home of Anah, the tanner, and his son Uzal. As the guests were leaving, he also prepared to leave. He could plainly see the look in Livi's eyes pleading for him to stay by, but he ignored her silent request. He felt a need to hurry home and spend much time in prayer in preparation for his confrontation with Uzal tomorrow. He placed the burden of his heart before the Lord, asking for wisdom and tact in dealing with this man who had made this evil threat.

He wasted no time the next morning. As soon as he was sure that most business establishments in the city were open, he ventured forth.

Anah's tanning center was next door to their very palatial home, and the sign on the front door welcomed visitors. So Samuel entered and stood just inside the front door for several minutes. Several of the workers in the shop looked his way momentarily then continued to work at their tables. He was simply ignored.

Finally the man whom Samuel had picked as Uzal left his work and came over to where the prophet was standing. "What may I do for you?" he asked with a smile.

Samuel looked him over for a few moments until Uzal's smile began to fade. Samuel noticed that he was a big man, well-built, and his face was kindly with smile wrinkles around his mouth. It wasn't the stern visage that Samuel had expected.

The priest extended his hand. "I am Samuel," he said simply.

The man grasped Samuel's hand, and then his face lighted up with apparent recognition. The smile returned larger than ever. "You are the priest and prophet, Samuel?" he asked somewhat incredulously.

"Yes, I am," admitted Samuel somewhat taken aback by the man's attitude.

Uzal dropped Samuel's hand and called to his father. The elder merchant responded quickly. "Father," Uzal said excitedly, "this is the priest and prophet, Samuel, the man who healed our little Benjamin last year."

Uzal grabbed Samuel's hand again. "We have been wanting to meet you and thank you for what you did for our family." The father, Anah, grabbed Samuel's other hand in his exuberance.

Uzal was speaking again. "Do you remember the little boy who was dying of blood poisoning? His mother, my sister, was bringing him back from the doctor because the doctor had given him up to die. My sister had stopped along the way to weep for her dying child; then you came along and saw her crying. You took them both in your arms and prayed for the little boy, and he was healed." By this time both of the men were weeping, and even some of the workers were brushing misty eyes.

The memory of the incident came to Samuel immediately, "Yes, I remember the little boy. He is your sister's child?"

"Yes," Uzal nodded. "And you should see him now. He is active, and all of the credit goes to you."

"No," Samuel corrected him. "God is the one who healed the lad. But He did see fit to use me for the occasion."

The father, Anah, had left them for the moment and gone to the interior of the shop. He returned with a beautiful fur that he extended to Samuel. "As Uzal said, we have wanted to meet you since the day little Benjamin was healed. We wanted to give you a token of our thanks. Now this gift is not intended as a payment of any kind. It is just our way of saying how much we appreciated you noticing Aronah and Benjamin and taking them in your arms and praying over them. We will never forget." Both men were again teary-eyed.

Samuel looked at the lovely fur for a long moment. He had made a habit of refusing all personal gifts, because he knew that men were often corrupted and bribed by gifts. He did accept the gifts of the people in public meetings because that was the source of his income along with the temple offerings. But he reasoned that he could not afford to offend these grateful people. He must accept this gift.

He held up the fur. "Thank you from the bottom of my heart," he said with another handshake from the men.

Now Uzal spoke up. "My lord, Samuel, you must have had a purpose of your own to visit us. Please tell us what you had in mind?"

Samuel's heart began to race and his lips were dry, but he was composed. He faced Uzal and their eyes met. "Yes, I did have a purpose for my call," he admitted. "And possibly you won't approve of the reason," he added with a smile. "I would like the privilege of courting Belah, the daughter of Shepi and Zoran, and I wanted your permission."

The smile faded from Uzal's face, and for a moment, a flash of pain took its place, but he answered very kindly. "I am deeply in love with Belah and have threatened to kill anyone who would attempt to court her. I haven't changed my mind as far as others are concerned, but I could not forbid you the privilege. You have my permission. You are a man of God and were so kind to visit me and ask my permission." He smiled now. "I won't give you my blessing since I love her so much and want her for my wife. But I will not interfere with your courtship of her in any way." He sighed as he finished.

Samuel grasped his hand. "Thank you very much, and may the best man win."

Uzal's face brightened. "That's right. May the best man win. I have a bit of the advantage since I've known her much longer," he said smugly and patted Samuel on the arm.

Samuel headed for Livi's home as soon as he left Uzal. He was afraid that he had hurt his sister's feelings last night when he had ignored her silent plea to stay. Also, he wanted to acquaint Livi with the gist of his visit with Belah last night and the visit with Uzal and Anah this morning.

Livi hugged and kissed him at the door and then led him into the living room. She seated him across from her, and he could see the big questions in her eyes.

"Livi," he said apologetically. "I hope you were not hurt by my refusal to stay by last night, but I had a very important reason to leave when I did. I will explain my actions now."

"I had a wonderful visit with Belah last night, thanks to you, and we became acquainted very quickly. Sister dear, you did not overrate her one bit. She is very beautiful, sweet, and smart and a very interesting conversationalist. We became so relaxed in our conversation that I asked her about her present suitor, Uzal. She talked about him freely and even shared with me about a very deadly threat he had made against anyone who would attempt to court her. He is actually holding her hostage for she admitted that she had turned several would be suitors away without explanation because of her fear for their lives.

"When I asked her if I could visit her and get better acquainted, which of course, she knew meant that I was asking to court her, she told me about Uzal's threat. She said that it was because of her great esteem for me, and her friendship with you, that she felt the need to share. I asked her permission to confront Uzal and reason with him. She gave her permission somewhat reluctantly because of her fear of what he might do to me.

"Livi, I am certain that the Lord's hand is in this matter. For when I faced Uzal at his father's tanning business, he immediately recognized me as the priest who had taken the little boy who was dying of blood poisoning and prayed over him and the Lord healed him. He was overwhelmed. The little boy was his sister's child and a favorite of the family.

"Both Uzal and his father, Anah, were happy to meet me and to express their heartfelt thanks for that miracle. The father, Anah, gave me this beautiful fur as a token of their appreciation." Samuel opened the package and showed his sister the gift from Anah and Uzal.

"Now," he said with a smile and a pat on Livi's arm, "I am giving this beautiful gift to my favorite sister." He placed the fur in Livi's lap.

Livi looked at the fur for a few moments, and when she lifted her head, her eyes were misty. "Samuel, it is so sweet of you to give me this gift, but perhaps later you would like to give this to Belah during your courtship."

Samuel shook his head. "No, Livi. This doesn't belong to Belah. It belongs to you. It is a brother's token of appreciation to a sister who is so loving and caring. Livi, you have been such a blessing to me. I love you very much." She hugged him and tears were in her eyes.

"Now, I must tell you about Uzal's reaction when I asked his permission to court Belah."

Livi leaned forward expectantly.

"The thought pained him at first, and he reminded me of the threat he had made against those who would attempt to court her. He admitted that she was the love of his life, but he was so grateful for my help to his little nephew and that I had come to ask his permission that he gave his consent quite freely. So I have his permission without any rancor or bloodshed."

Livi grasped his hands. "Samuel, that is wonderful. You are a rare person in the art of handling people. Now, I'm sure that you are bursting at the seams to tell Belah, and I'm also sure that she is eagerly awaiting your visit and report. Are you planning to visit her this afternoon?"

"Yes, I had planned to visit her this afternoon if she is available."

Livi leaned toward him. "Let me send Othan to her home with a note from you requesting a visit with her this afternoon. He can wait and bring back her answer."

"Yes, I would like that," Samuel agreed.

Othan was soon on his way to Belah's home with the note, and within the hour the servant came back with her answer. She would be awaiting Samuel's visit.

Samuel ate a light dinner with Livi, and in the early afternoon, he was ready for the visit with Belah.

Belah met Samuel at the door with a welcome smile on her face, but there were question marks in her eyes. She led him to a seat in the living room and seated herself in an opposite chair.

Samuel opened the conversation. "I am sure that you are interested in the outcome of my visit with Uzal, so I will tell you about the visit first and then perhaps we can chat about other matters that are of interest to both of us."

She nodded. "Yes, please tell me about your visit."

"Well, as you might have expected, I went into Anah's tanning shop anticipating a battle, but there was not one harsh word spoken during the entire time of my visit."

A quizzical look replaced the questioning look on her beautiful face.

"You see, when I am not studying or writing or holding court circuit, I am often visiting in the homes of the people and praying with them. So during the latter part of last year, I was coming home one day from a visit on the far side of the city. On the road, I met a young woman with a young boy in her arms, and she was weeping loudly. Instinctively, I stopped and asked the lady what her trouble was. She showed me the leg of her little son that was almost to drop off because of gangrene. She had been to see the doctor, but he had given her no hope. She had waited too long. The little boy was in a coma and would have died soon.

"I took them in my arms and petitioned the Lord for healing for the lad, and the Lord answered my prayer immediately. The little boy jumped down from her arms and began to run and play. The mother was so grateful that I thought, for a moment, she would try to worship me. This woman was the daughter of Anah, the tanner, and sister of Uzal.

"Both Anah and Uzal recognized me and were very liberal in their thanks for my part in the healing. I reminded them that the healing was from God and that I was only His instrument.

"Uzal then asked me what the purpose of my visit was. So I told him that I had come to get his permission to court you. He then told me about his threat to kill anyone who would dare to court you, but since I had done their family such a great favor and also had been so kind to ask his permission, he gave me full freedom to court you. He promised that he would not interfere in any way with our relationship. So now, Lady Belah, there are no restrictions. May I court you? I warn you that I am very serious in my courting."

She drew in her breath, relaxed against the back of her chair, and laughed. "My lord, Samuel," she said with deep feeling. "What a man of the people you truly are? Certainly you may pay court to me without any restrictions, and I am glad to hear that you are serious about our relationship, for I too am serious." He grasped her hand, and they looked into each other's eyes.

"Now, would you be so kind as to tell my mother what you have just shared with me? She has been so concerned about my relationship with Uzal and the threat he has made. We haven't told father about this threat because he would have immediately faced both Anah and Uzal, and he is not as tactful as you are."

Samuel laughed. "I can certainly relate to your father, for I had fire in my eyes when I first faced Uzal, but the Lord settled the matter without bloodshed.

"Now, as to telling your mother about the results of my visit, that would be good. Also, I would like very much to meet your mother."

Belah brought her mother, Zoran, into the room, and Samuel found her to be very lovely and sweet. She welcomed the account of his visit with Anah and Uzal.

"I'm so glad that you visited with Uzal," she agreed. "I have been very concerned for Belah because of his attitude."

Samuel took advantage of the moment. "Lady Zoran, I have asked your daughter for the privilege of courting her, and she has made me very happy by saying 'yes.' Could I be so bold as to ask you for the privilege of courting her?"

Zoran's face brightened. "I certainly concur with my daughter. You are welcome in our home at all times. I fully trust my daughter in your presence. I am quite sure that my husband would give the same answer if you were to ask him."

"That I plan to do," Samuel answered quickly. "And thank you, Lady Zoran, for your confidence."

He rose to go and Zoran added. "I hope that the relationship between my daughter and you grows stronger each day."

When Samuel left the home of Belah and Zoran, he headed immediately to the bank to receive her father's permission. He wanted to make the circle complete. The banker was in his office, and Samuel was ushered in. Both men acknowledged that they had met before, so Samuel was somewhat relaxed for his tender mission.

Shepi wasted no time, for he was all business. He leaned forward and fixed Samuel with piercing eyes.

"Since you are a prophet, a priest, and a judge, how am I supposed to address you?"

Samuel laughed. "You aren't the first to ask that question. It appears to pose quite a problem, but since I have no desire to put myself above the people, whatever fits the common man is all right with me. I like for people to call me Samuel."

The banker relaxed. "Very well, I'll call you Samuel. Now Samuel, how may I help you?"

Samuel cleared his throat. "Last night at the home of my older sister, I met your lovely daughter. I was greatly impressed with her poise and personality, and I would like very much to court her. Both your wife and daughter have given their consent, and I have come to ask your consent."

He paused a moment and waited for Shepi's reply. The banker laughed, "I suppose that since you have already received permission from the majority of my family, and especially from my daughter, my sanction would hardly be needed. But before I give you my answer, I would like to ask you a few questions, if I may."

"By all means," Samuel agreed.

"Belah already has a suitor by the name of Uzal, the son Anah. What are your plans for handling this impediment?"

Samuel answered quickly. "I met with Uzal this morning and received his permission to court your daughter."

Shepi's eyes were wide. "Do you mean that you asked a man who has courted Belah for more than a year to let you oppose him for her affection?"

"That's correct," Samuel agreed. "You might want to ask your daughter about the details."

The banker shook his head. "You must be quite a unique person to get such a strange concession from a man like Uzal."

"Now another question—and perhaps I am prying—are your intentions serious enough that you would consider asking for Belah's hand in marriage?"

"That is my intention," Samuel answered quickly.

Shepi hesitated; then plunged ahead. "Since you are a judge, as well as a priest and a prophet, I hear that you have a court circuit that takes you away from Ramah for weeks at a time. How would you handle a wife on those terms and especially children, if they are involved?"

Samuel laughed. "Lord Shepi, you should have been a lawyer. You ask some very probing questions. In answer to your question, I could pare my court travel down some, and I could also take a wife along. I have very pleasant and adequate housing for these trips and the food is excellent. I also could train someone to help me on my circuit. A child in the family would pose a problem, but I can assure you that I would plan my work to the child's advantage. Have I given you adequate answers or would you expect more?"

Shepi smiled. "You have done very well with your answers, and I am satisfied. You have my full permission to court my daughter." He hesitated. "I personally would like very much for you to win the affection of Belah. However, Uzal is a very determined man, and you will certainly need to work hard to beat him out."

Samuel nodded. "I also am a very determined man, and your lovely daughter, Belah, is certainly worth the effort."

Samuel left Shepi's office with a troubled heart. He chided himself for his concern since his visit with the banker had been very successful. But the question Shepi had asked about the possible conflict with his work and a family had stirred his memory. He had thought many times of how the magnitude of his work could seriously interfere with plans for a wife and a successful, peaceful domestic life. But since he had no specific person in mind when these thoughts had arisen to trouble him, he had easily put them aside as a future consideration.

Now Belah was in the picture, larger than life, and thus a decision was mandatory and immediate. Would it be fair to Belah to subject her to the rigors of travel to Bethel, Gilgal, and Mizpah twice a year? She had lived a tender life and would possibly be appalled by the thought of travel and lodging in these strange places. He would need to know her feelings before he would ask her to marry him. He must be frank and fair with her.

The priest, prophet, and judge, who had been the source of counsel to thousands of God's people from his early childhood, felt a great need to petition the Lord for wisdom before he made any further calls. God had been his ever present mentor from the first day that personal accountability had become his pleasure, and divine wisdom was needed so much at this moment of his life.

As he knelt and poured out his heart in prayer, the thought came to him forcefully that he was the only door of hope for Belah's hostage relationship with Uzal. She had confided to Samuel the night of Livi's assemblage that she had determined never to marry Uzal but rather to remain a maiden for the rest of her life. But now he, Samuel, had come into her life, and she had indicated to him in many ways that she would gladly reverse her decision at his suggestion. He determined while on his knees that he would not disappoint her.

For several minutes he considered the magnitude of his work as a circuit judge and priest in relationship to Belah's welfare, and suddenly another forceful thought came to him from the Lord. It was as plain as the message the Lord had given him in his childhood to relay to Eli.

"Samuel," the voice said. "I gave you as an assignment sometime ago to establish a training center for dedicated young men who will assist you in your work, and you have not as yet moved to obey me." The divine chiding was sweet and firm.

Samuel responded with a repentant heart. "Lord, I will carry out this commission immediately, and at the same time, I will consecrate your people, Israel, at Mizpah. Please give me much wisdom for this assignment."

He determined while on his knees that he would visit Belah early the next morning and ask for her hand in marriage. Then he would send out couriers to the farthest boundaries of Israel, hopefully with the news of his impending marriage, and also to call the people together at Mizpah for a national dedication. During this meeting he would choose the young men for the training center. The next few days and weeks would be a very busy time for Samuel, the judge, priest, and prophet.

Samuel sent a servant to the home of Belah requesting an appointment, and she was waiting for him. The look on her face was expectant. She seated him, and he grasped her hand and faced her. "Lady Belah, you will remember I warned you that my courtship of you would be serious." He dropped to one knee. "Lady Belah, will you marry me?"

His abruptness took her breath for a moment, but she recovered quickly. "Lord Samuel, I would consider it a great privilege to become your wife."

He smiled and kissed her hand. "Thank you for that answer. Now you must know that my life is a very busy one. Besides the court that I hold here in Ramah, the intercessory sacrifices I make for the people, and the book I am writing, twice a year I have a court circuit at Bethel, Gilgal, and Mizpah. However, I have received an order from the Lord to set up a training center here in Ramah to prepare young men to assist me in my work. Of course, I will still have a very busy life. Would this be troubling to you?" He paused and waited for her response.

Her face was very composed as she spoke. "Lord Samuel, it would be a pleasure and challenge for me to join with you in your work. Perhaps I can hold up your hands as Aaron and Joshua did for Moses."

He laughed. "What a beautiful answer. You have certainly eased my troubled heart. I have confidence that we will be very happy together."

They set the date for the wedding and then received the permission and blessing of both her father and mother.

# SAMUEL'S HEART

## CHAPTER 6

Samuel awoke from a troubled sleep with a heavy heart. As he lay for a few minutes on his bed, he reflected on the reason for his pain. The thought came to him that, at this moment, he should be the happiest man in all Israel. His work was greatly inspiring, and he would soon be married to the most wonderful woman in the land. These thoughts were pleasing, but they did not fully assuage the distress that held his heart hostage.

For twenty years he had judged Israel from his home in Ramah. Besides twice a year visits to Bethel, Gilgal, and Mizpah where he held judicial sessions, he also traveled the length and breadth of the land and spoke to the people. His message was always the same: "Repent of your evil ways, put away your strange gods, and turn to the Lord with all your heart."

His own heart was greatly troubled. In many of the cities that he visited, the people seemed content to allow the Philistines to wield authority over them. Enemy soldiers were very visible in the land, and pagan priests carried on their profane exercises without interference. Pagan altars were in the groves and high places and some of the altars were even besmirched with live human sacrifices to the heathen gods.

Many of the elders of the cities shared Samuel's concern and had joined with him in prayer for a spiritual revival among the people and for physical liberation from the oppression of the pagans. However, God was delaying an answer as they pressed their petitions.

Samuel knew that there would never be a time when military force would rid the nation of the presence of the pagans. In the first place, the diminutive Israelite army was merely tolerated by the Philistines as a caretaker body. Also, most of the troops had lost their desire to be free from enemy occupation. They were satisfied.

Thus, God alone could suffice to break the yoke of bondage, and there were now evident signs in the land that God was preparing to bare His holy arm in defense of His people. Stirrings of spiritual revival were becoming more and more evident, and Samuel was greatly encouraged. He renewed his appeals in the cities.

"If you will return to the Lord with all your hearts, put away the foreign gods from among you, prepare your hearts to seek the Lord, and serve the Lord only, He will deliver you from the hands of the Philistines." The people believed and responded. They put away Baal and Ashtaroth and served the Lord only, and the Lord was pleased with them.

Samuel was now ready to call a meeting of all Israel at Mizpah, where he would make a statement to the people before the Lord. Then they would pray together for the Lord to deliver His people.

There was another item Samuel must take care of while the people were together at Mizpah. It was a pleasant task for him. At the instigation of his half-sister, Livi, he had met and fallen in love with Belah, daughter of Shepi and Zoran of Ramah. He had conducted a very bold and successful courtship and had persuaded her to become his wife. He would announce to the people at Mizpah his upcoming marriage to Belah.

It was a solemn meeting at Mizpah. The people came from every corner of Israel, but they came with divided hearts. Some came doubting that God would work a miracle to deliver them from such inflexible enemies as the Philistines, while others came expecting the Lord to do great things for them.

As Samuel looked over the vast host of Israel, he was gratified to see in the very front his brothers and sisters and Belah and her parents. As he looked closer, he saw his former rival, Uzal, his father, Anah, and their families. As he met the gaze of the tanner's son, Uzal smiled a greeting. Evidently there were no hard feelings. Samuel lifted his hand, and the people quieted immediately. They gave him their full attention.

"Fellow Israelites," the judge and priest addressed his countrymen. "God has been waiting on us for several years to have this meeting. He has longed to have us unite in revival and reformation, and your presence here today is a testimony to your personal desire for a revival in the land. The Lord has never wanted us to serve the heathen nor bow down to their gods. He wants us to serve and worship Him only. Is it your desire today to confess your sins and to pray for revival in the land and liberation from our enemies?"

The people shouted in unison. "Yes, yes, that is our desire!"

"Very well, then. We will fast for the rest of this day, and tomorrow I will pray and offer a sacrifice for you, and then we will look to the Lord for our salvation."

Again, the people shouted with one voice. "We will wait on the Lord, and He will save us from our enemies."

The people fasted and prayed for cleansing from sin, and the Lord drew near. As they prayed, the Philistine army moved toward them with the plan to attack. The lords of the Philistines heard that thousands of Israelites were gathered at Mizpah. Naturally, they thought that the people were planning to revolt and wanted to nip this thing in the bud.

As the people saw the pagan soldiers advancing toward them, many of the Israelites feared for their lives and began to rail on Samuel for bringing them to this place, but many others took courage in the face of the enemy.

"Surely the Lord will save us out of the hands of these heathens. Didn't He promise that if we would confess our sins and turn to Him with all our hearts that He would deliver us? We believe that God will keep His promise."

As Samuel saw the pagan army drawing closer—as yet, God had not made any move to deliver His people—the heart of Israel's judge and priest was tested with fire. He sacrificed a little lamb and then knelt by the altar and poured out his heart to God. He felt the presence of people around him and noticed that Belah was on one side and Livi was on the other. His brothers and sisters had also drawn close, and Shepi and Zoran were there.

Then again he saw Uzal. "We believe with you, Master Samuel, that God will deliver us," the son of Anah said.

A giant thunderclap suddenly shook the heavens and the earth and was followed by a rumbling and roaring in the heavens as if an enormous giant was struggling to break his chains. Bolts of lightning kept pace with the roar of the thunder. The jagged shafts flashed from the sky to hilltops and then danced like miniature dervishes along the tops of the hills and trees. The skies, that only a few moments earlier had been cloudless, were now dark and threatening. An eerie chill was in the air, and the wind began to move the trees in a grotesque fashion.

The Philistine army was moving to attack the Israelites, but the violent celestial display confused them and filled their hearts with fear. Suddenly they remembered the judgments of the God of the Hebrews at Ashdod, Gath, and Ekron when they had uncovered the Ark of God. Conviction fastened on every heart that God was angry with them and would surely open the heavens and pour out a scourge upon them all.

They spoke to one another. "We are all dead men, for the God of Israel is fighting against us. Let us flee from this place." They were soon in total disorder as they fled before the Israelites.

The Israelites followed up their advantage and pursued the fleeing host. Bodies of the Philistines littered the road from Mizpah to below Beth Car. It was a crushing defeat for the heathen nation and a great victory for God's people. It was the same area where twenty years before the battle results were reversed. At that time the Israelites had been put to flight, the Ark of God was captured, and Hophni and Phinehas slain.

As the people returned from pursuing the Philistines, Samuel again called them together at Mizpah. He had other items to discuss with them.

The people were flushed with the victory over the Philistines, and Samuel knew that it would be natural for many to take credit to themselves for the triumph. Inspired, he led them in a song of praise to God as the Israelites sang when the pursuing Egyptian army was drowned in the Red Sea.

"I will sing to the Lord, for He has triumphed gloriously. The Lord is my strength and song, and He has become our salvation. He is our God and we will praise Him; our Father's God and we will exalt Him. The Lord is a Man of war; the Lord is His name. He has become glorious in power; He thundered from the heavens and dashed the enemy in pieces."

The hills around Mizpah resonated with the voices of the people as they joined in the song of triumph. Then Samuel led the thousands in a prayer of renewed dedication. But there was still another part of the celebration of victory. Samuel took a stone and set it up on the road from Mizpah to Shen, and he called it Ebenezer—stone of help.

"Thus far the Lord has helped us," Samuel said, "and He will continue to help us as we continue to worship and serve Him." Samuel held up his hand again and the clamor hushed. "This is a day for rejoicing," he shouted.

The people responded, "Thanks be to the Lord, for He is good."

"The Lord has driven the enemy from our land," Samuel continued, "and He has restored to many of you your homes that were taken by force. So, remember when you return to your homes, go with a prayer of thanks in your hearts."

And again the people shouted, "Amen, the Lord is good."

"Now, I have two more special announcements to share with you." The people were quiet. "Some time ago God instructed me in a dream to set up a center of training in Ramah for our young men. These young men will be trained in many areas of manual labor, and all will be trained in the study and use of the word of the Lord. Perhaps some of these students will be able to assist me in my work as a judge.

"I am hoping that several of our learned elders will be willing to spend time in the training of these young men. I have been remiss in carrying out the wishes of the Lord in this matter, but I will tarry no longer.

"To you young men who would desire to be a part of this training program, I invite you to meet with me tomorrow at the tabernacle in Ramah. I will be personally contacting the elders who will assist in instructing you."

Samuel hesitated and looked at Belah and her parents who were standing before him. "As you may know, I began my ministry in the temple at Shiloh at age four. I am now thirty-two years old and have served you as judge, priest, and prophet almost my entire life. To this time, I have walked alone among you, but that is soon to change. You will remember that God said of our father Adam, 'It is not good for man to be alone.' So He made our mother Eve to be his wife—his helpmate. God has also seen that it is not good for me to be alone, so He has persuaded Belah, daughter of Shepi and Zoran of Ramah, to be my wife—my helpmate."

At this news the people clapped and again responded with "Amen."

"The wedding will be in Ramah, and you are all invited. We will live among you at Ramah, where I will continue to minister to your needs. I will also keep my circuit to Bethel, Gilgal, and Mizpah.

"Now that the Philistines are no longer among us I would like the Ark to return to this area, but since we do not have a temple in which to house it, we will leave it at Kirjath Jearim where Eleazer, the priest, is caring for it."

Samuel dismissed the people, but they were loath to leave the area. They knew that God had been at work in their behalf, and they could still feel His presence among them. They felt secure.

Finally they left by groups to return to their homes with a new determination to serve the Lord with all their hearts.

Belah and Livi assured Samuel that they would take care of all plans for the wedding so that he could devote his time to organizing the training center, so he made his way to the tabernacle.

He felt a bit guilty because of his delay in starting the school after God had so plainly instructed him as to its importance. He wondered if perhaps God would withhold His blessings as a rebuke, but his fears were quickly put to rest as young men came from every part of the kingdom, eager to learn more about God and His plan. Leading elders from several cities also came to offer their services as instructors.

Samuel was elated. The number of prospective students had exceeded his fondest hopes, and the response for instructors was more than adequate. He would even have to winnow out some of the teachers, and a few of the students would need to wait for the next term.

Immediate housing would have to be in tents, and the instructors and students would need to build their own living quarters.

Samuel sat in assemblage with the instructors and worked out a course of study. Thus, in only a few days time, the school of the prophets was ready for business. Samuel made plans to dedicate the school at the time of his wedding to Belah

Because Samuel was a national figure in Israel, his wedding was a national occasion. People came from all over the kingdom to pay honor to a man they loved very much.

Belah was a beautiful bride, and Samuel was a very handsome bridegroom. Livi watched the two with thankfulness in her heart. She felt so good that she had played a part in joining these two lives together.

While the two were being congratulated, a little boy broke from the line, ran up to Samuel, and hugged his legs. The priest had no idea who the little fellow was until he saw the mother hovering near, smiling at the antics of her little son. He immediately recognized her as Aronah, Anah's daughter and Uzal's sister. This was the child that had been healed of gangrene only a year before.

Samuel halted the guests, reached down, and picked the little boy up in his arms. The man and the boy hugged each other for a few moments while the crowd watched and Uzal, Anah, and the child's mother wept.

Samuel held up his hand. "Friends, let me tell you about this little boy I am holding. About a year ago, I was returning to my home from the city when I met this little boy, Benjamin, and his mother on the road." He paused and motioned for the mother, and she timidly came.

"This mother, Aronah, was weeping and holding her child who was dying from gangrene in his leg. She had been to the doctor, and he had pronounced her child incurable. I took the child in my arms and prayed for him, and the Lord saw fit to heal little Benjamin immediately. You can see that he doesn't have a scar on his leg. Benjamin is the grandson of Anah, the tanner, and the nephew of Uzal." He pointed the two men out in the crowd.

As Samuel finished speaking, there was a chorus of "Amens" from the crowd, and many wiped tears from their eyes. The little boy hugged Samuel tightly again and went to his mother. It had been a tender moment.

Life with Belah was very sweet and rewarding, but the demands from the people didn't give him enough time with his new bride. The question Shepi asked him before he consented to Samuel's courting his daughter haunted him. How could he handle this heavy program and still care for a wife? Belah was also deluged with invitations from the women of the city to assist them in various projects. The two often wished for anonymity so that they could spend more time with each other, but they never complained nor disappointed the people.

Samuel was glad when the birth of their firstborn, Joel, forced Belah to refuse all requests for a time. Soon they secured a nurse for the baby, and again Belah was gone from home much of the day.

Soon two more children—a boy, Abijah, and a daughter, Hagan—graced their home. These two children curtailed Belah's activities for a time, but soon the mother was too busy again.

Samuel was frustrated. The children's nurse and Shepi and Zoran were spending more time with their three children than either of the parents.

A crisis was developing in the family of Samuel and Belah. Both parents were hurting because of the neglect they were subjecting their precious little family to but neither had the answer for their dilemma. The man who had successfully counseled many of the families of Israel had no counsel for himself.

# CHAPTER 7

"Father, will you borrow some of my money?" Joel asked, his eyes beaming with anticipation.

Samuel was interested in his older son's sudden desire to share his treasure. "Well, son, do you have a lot of money to loan?"

"Yes, I do. I have a lot more money than Abijah." He held up several coins in his grubby little hands. "See."

"My, you do have a lot of money. Where did you get so much wealth?"

The little boy assumed a very businesslike manner. "I ran errands for Grandfather Shepi, and he paid me all of this money." He leaned toward his father and lowered his voice as if he were sharing a deep secret. "Then grandfather showed me how to make a lot more money from these coins."

Samuel lowered his voice almost to a whisper to match the mysterious attitude of his little son. "And what did Grandfather Shepi tell you to do in order to make a lot more money?"

Joel looked around to make sure no one was listening. "He said for me to loan this money to people and charge them a big amount of . . . ," he hesitated, and his brow furrowed as he tried to remember the big word his grandfather had used.

Samuel helped him. "Charge them a large amount of usury?"

Joel relaxed, and a smile creased on his face. "That's it Father, 'usuree'."

"I've already loaned Abid and Rami money, and when they pay me next week, I'll have twice as much money as I have now." He sat back with a very satisfied look on his face. "Grandfather said that if I saved my money and loaned it only to dep . . .," again he struggled.

"Dependable people," Samuel supplied.

"Yes, dependable people." He looked at his father with a look of admiration on his face. "Father, you sure do know a lot about loaning money."

Samuel's heart swelled a bit at the statement of confidence from his older son.

"Shaul and Ethan wanted to borrow some of my money, but they aren't dep . . . ." He looked at his father again for help.

"Dependable people."

"Yes, so I wouldn't loan them any," he spoke the statement in the air of a banker who has had the final word.

"But you would loan me some of your money?"

"Yes, I would Father. You are the most dependable person I know."

"Thank you, son." Samuel rumpled the hair of his precious little boy, but his heart was hurting, and he felt a deep sense of guilt. He was neglecting these precious little ones that God had given to Belah and him, and at the moment he had no idea how to correct the situation.

His workload had multiplied during the passing years, and Belah was much too busy with community affairs. They had such little time together as a family anymore. They had chosen an excellent nurse and mentor for the boys, and she was doing a good job in teaching them the fundamentals of education and social interaction. The lads were always well mannered and courteous, but they were not spiritually inclined. They were always obedient and respectful to their parents and were attentive and quiet during the family worship periods and the Sabbath services, but their interest in Jehovah and their spiritual history was minimal. Money and business were already the driving forces in their young lives.

This present experience with Joel was a case in point. Samuel was certain that Shepi and Zoran were wielding a greater influence over the youngsters than either Belah or himself. His heart twisted in pain at the thought. Shepi was teaching the boys the tricks of making money, and Joel was a ready pupil. He had much more of an appetite for figures than did Abijah.

But what Shepi had taught Joel about undue usury was evil. It was poor training for a growing mind. God had warned the Israelites while they were on their way from Egypt to Canaan against charging too much usury, and the law was still in force spiritually. However, there wasn't any law in the books of the land against undue usury, so it was legal to charge as much as a person would pay. But Joel must learn that God did not approve of such an oppressive practice.

Joel was sitting quietly, waiting for his father's response. Samuel was cautious and didn't want to undermine the boy's trust in his grandfather, nor did he want to estrange his father-in-law, but he must speak up.

"Son, your Grandfather Shepi is a very rich man, and he has a lot of influence in this city. Your Grandfather Elkanah was also a rich man. God desires for His people to prosper, so there is nothing wrong with being rich. Abraham and Jacob were rich and many others of our forefathers.

"Since you are good at making money, perhaps someday you will be richer even than your grandfathers, but you must be sure that every shekel you make is honest."

The boy nodded but was mute.

"As you know, we have laws. Some of our laws were made by men and some given by God. One of the laws that God gave to our forefathers had to do with usury."

Joel's eyes widened. "Does God charge usury?"

"No, son, God doesn't charge usury. But he knew that our people would charge usury when they loaned money, so He gave us a law to cover the practice."

The boy relaxed, but his eyes were still wide with wonder.

"God commanded us not to charge usury to the poor people among us; however, we could charge the stranger usury. When our people settled in Canaan, they needed to borrow money. The lender could charge a fair price for his money. Grandfather Shepi and your uncles, Tolan and Jarih, would have to close their banks if they didn't charge usury to those who borrow from them. But the rate of usury should always be fair. God wouldn't like for us to double our money within a week. Do you understand?"

Joel nodded. "Father, I wouldn't charge you nearly as much as I charged Abid and Rami. Would that be all right with God?"

Samuel hesitated. He hadn't expected this kind of rebuttal.

"Well, son, I wonder if you have charged Abid and Rami too much usury. Perhaps you should give them back at least half of the total when they pay you."

The boy shook his head vigorously. "Oh no, Father, you don't understand. Abid and Rami's parents are rich. They give the boys a lot of spending money each week." He frowned and shook his head again. "But they spend their money foolishly, and by the middle of the week, they need more money. Then they ask me to loan them some of my money."

"You see, Father, Abijah and I don't spend our money foolishly like they do, so I have money to loan. And Father, you are a poor man and can't give Abijah and sister, Hagan, and myself a lot of money to spend each week, so we have to earn our own money." He stopped and lowered his voice again. "I have more money in a purse in my bedroom, and so does Abijah, but not as much as I do. And Father, Abijah and I both share with Hagan." He stopped and looked at Samuel with questions in his eyes.

Samuel's eyes misted over at his son's speech. He looked at the precious youngster for a long moment and then put his hand on the boy's shoulders. "Son, I am so glad to hear that you and Abijah share your money with your sister and also that you don't spend your money foolishly like Abid and Rami.

"It seems that your mother and I have given you the wrong impression about our finances. We are not poor people. We don't have as much money as your grandparents, but God had given us more than we really need.

"I suppose that because my childhood was spent at the temple I have never had a thought about providing you children with spending money, and I doubt if your mother has thought about it."

Joel broke in. "That's all right, Father. We don't need money from you and Mother. We do lots of chores for Grandfather Shepi and Grandmother Zoran, and other people often ask us to do chores for them. We don't charge them, but they usually pay us something."

He paused for a moment. "But Father, since you and Mother have money, you don't need a loan from me, do you?"

"No, son, I don't need a loan, but since you were so thoughtful to offer me a loan, I am going to give you a 'pim.' I will also give your brother and sister a 'pim,' but you shouldn't consider this gift as the beginning of a weekly or monthly spending money. Do you understand?"

Joel's face brightened. "Thank you, Father, very much."

Samuel was reminded that he had not, as yet, resolved the issue of the exorbitant usury fee. "Son, I hope that you will pray about the matter of your usury fee, and perhaps the Lord will impress you to lower your rate to not more than half of the loan itself. Would you do that?"

"Yes, Father, I will do that."

"Joel, do you remember the times your mother and I have read the Scriptures to you, Abijah, and Hagan about payment of tithe to the Lord on all of our earnings?"

There was a puzzled look on the youngster's face. "Yes, I remember Father, but I thought that payment of tithe was only for grown-up people. Do you mean that God also expects children to pay tithe?"

Samuel suddenly suffered a pain in his heart and guilt washed over him. *What am I doing*? he thought. *I am busy every day of the week ministering to God's people—counseling them, dedicating their babies, burying their dead, settling their differences, offering sacrifices for their sins—but, at the same time, I am neglecting my own blood family*.

He offered a silent prayer for forgiveness and wisdom and then turned to his little son again. "No, son, the payment of the tithe is also the privilege of children and is the basis of God's spiritual and material blessings."

Joel nodded. "Father, if you will help me to figure the tithe that I should pay, I will be glad to pay, and I'm sure that Hagan and Abijah will also be glad to pay their tithe."

Samuel rose and hugged his son to his breast. "Thank you, son, for giving me the time for such a special visit with you."

Samuel was very pensive that evening, and Belah wondered what was bothering the judge of Israel. He never brought the burdens of his work home with him, and his mood was quickly noticed by his wife. She studied him for several moments. He was almost forty years old now and was a very handsome man, but the pressures of his work were leaving their marks on his features. There were silver threads among his dark hair and lines were forming permanently on his forehead.

She clasped his hand, kissed him tenderly, and then invited him to share with her. "Tell me, dear, what it is that is troubling you today? Would you share with me?"

He hugged her and they sat down opposite each other. It had been too long since they had taken time from the busyness of their lives to talk to each other heart-to-heart. He sat with head bowed for a moment while she waited patiently.

"Belah, I had a good visit with Joel today, and it made me aware of a grave sin I have committed. I have sadly neglected the training of our children. I have relied too much on Zonau, their nurse, and your father and mother. The revelation filled me with a deep sense of guilt. Joel opened the conversation by asking me if I would borrow some money from him."

The parents smiled together at the unconventional question from their child banker. "I asked him if he had a lot of money, and he assured me that he did. He showed me several coins and then informed me that he had more coins in a purse in his bedroom. He said that Abijah also had a stash there. Furthermore, he said that he and Abijah shared some of their money with their sister."

There was an incredulous look on Belah's face.

"I asked him where he got so much money, and he informed me that he and Abijah ran errands for Shepi and Zoran and other people, and these folks gave them money. That part of the conversation made me feel good. In fact, I was proud that the boys were showing such good business sense so early in their lives. But then he shared information with me that made me feel guilty.

"He said that he had already loaned two of his friends money at one hundred percent usury. Thus, when they pay him next week, he will have twice as much money.

He said that your father had given him the idea of charging so much usury."

There was a stricken look on Belah's face, and she covered her face with her hands for a few moments.

Samuel continued. "Now, the reason he offered to loan me money is because he thinks that we are poor. We don't give the three of our children money to spend like the other parents did. He didn't say this to condemn us, but rather, he spoke out of sympathy for us."

Belah smiled. "Our little boy has a big heart."

"Yes, he does," agreed Samuel.

"I was at a loss for words for a time. I explained to him the evil that could result from charging too much usury. I also assured him that we were not poor people, but because of our background, we had not thought of giving the children regular weekly spending money. Then we talked for a few moments about tithing his increase. He was very willing to tithe, and after our visit, he skipped off to make more money. I came home with my heart full of guilt."

The two looked at each other for several moments without speaking. Then Belah broke the silence. "Samuel, please, let me share your guilt. I have been much too busy with national and community projects and have put too much of the children's training on the shoulders of Zonau. I have noticed that she rarely disciplines any of the three. She loves them so much, and they love her in return. She has confided to me that it would break her heart to punish one of them.

"Of course, my parents spoil them beyond reason. The children are much more loving and respectful to Mother and Father than any of my brother's children are. Mother has told me that many times. Also, Father has told me that he has already made plans to leave his banking enterprise to Joel and Abijah. However, I am quite sure that my brothers have plans for their sons when father passes." Her face twisted in pain. "It could be a nasty problem." She looked at Samuel and spread her hands helplessly.

"I have never laid the rod on either of the three, and I don't remember ever seeing you chastise them." She paused and groped for more words to express her frustration.

Samuel patted her hand. "Belah, dear, you have assumed too much of the blame. My portion is much greater than yours.

"As I was visiting with Joel this morning, the Spirit of the Lord smote me. I was reminded that I have been so busy judging and counseling our people that I have denied time to my own flesh and blood." He choked up for a few moments and then continued. "I prayed earnestly for the Lord to help me arrange my work so that I can spend more time with you and the children." He shook his head as if to clear the obstruction.

"I don't know how it will happen, since the people are so demanding, and I have allowed them to completely control my time. But I will trust the Lord to answer my prayer for the good of our family."

She put her hand on his arm. "Samuel, you belong to the people, so don't disappoint them. I will make some major adjustments in my time with the people so that I can spend more time with the children." She spread her hands again in frustration. "I know that I am not a good disciplinarian, since I could not bring myself to punish one of them, but I will make an effort to be there for them."

Samuel noticed that as the years passed Joel and Abijah spent more and more time at the bank with Shepi. They had shown an unusual aptitude for finances, and Shepi was a good teacher. It was obvious that he was training them as his successors to his bank and the time for his retirement was imminent.

Shepi knew that it was time for him to make a change. Twice now he had lost his directions on his way home from work, and Zoran and Belah finally found him wandering in an unfamiliar neighborhood. His banking business was suffering because of his forgetfulness. He was certain now that he must turn his banking business over to his grandsons.

For some time now, he had mentored Joel and Abijah in the mechanics of his business, and he had found them to be apt learners. He was quite sure that soon they would surpass his sons in the matter of finance.

At this same time, Samuel was attempting to get the boys interested in the sacred art of judicial determination. He had allowed them to sit in judgment on several minor cases, and he was pleased with their decisions. He was hoping that they would follow in his footsteps and become judges in the land, rather than follow Grandfather Shepi in the banking business.

The boys were old enough now to make their own decisions, and they opted for banking. Money had become almost an obsession to them in their young lives. Because of the home training and the love and respect for their father, spiritual values were a consideration to them, but they were secondary to the material. They joined their grandfather at the bank, and Samuel continued his work with a heavy heart.

Since his sons were no longer available to assist him in his work, Samuel looked to the schools of the prophets for a helper. There were several of the young men that were spiritual and showed some promise of good judgment, but as yet, the Lord had not impressed him to choose any of them.

Shepi was dead. The retired banker had died quietly in his sleep, and the community was in mourning for him. The banker had oftentimes been hardheaded and highhanded in his dealings with the people in matters of finances, but he was still beloved by most.

Belah's brothers and their families and Belah and her family met together to share their pain. And while they were still in mourning for Shepi, Zoran also died. The two had been very close in life, and now they were united in death.

Samuel spoke words of comfort and consolation to the families, and the words were a balm to his own heart. He had learned to love these two people like his own father and mother. And they had returned his love with approving his marriage to their daughter and other fond favors through the years.

There was no indication on the part of the brothers, Tolan and Jarih, when they left to return to Gibeah that they would soon be back for a visit to Ramah. But here they were when Samuel returned from a visit to Mizpah. Their faces were stern.

Tolan, the older of the two, was the spokesman. "We are here to protest your decision to let your sons work in our father's bank when he was aged and doting. As you should know, we and our sons have the first right to our parent's inheritance, so we are demanding that your sons vacate our father's office immediately so that our sons can have their rightful property."

For a few moments, Samuel stared them down; then he spoke deliberately. "You men are well aware that I had nothing to do with the installation of my sons in your father's banking office. That was your father's idea. I preferred to have them work with me, but even though your father was aged and doting, he was more persuasive than I was, so my sons chose banking over the judicial occupation.

"Now, I am wondering why you didn't face your father on this issue. My sons have been in the office for more than a year, but you didn't mention the matter until now."

For a few moments, the brothers were mute; then Jarih found his tongue. "Well, we knew that your boys had sweetened up our father in his old age, and we didn't want to cause the folks any trouble by stirring things up, so we decided to wait it out."

Samuel was unimpressed. "I see. Now, from what my sons tell me, the business is doing extremely well under their management. As a compromise, why don't you let one of your sons work with one of my sons for a month or so while my other son works at your bank in Gilgal. That way there wouldn't be any drastic change in administration at the bank. Perhaps the boys would be in favor of a working relationship like that."

The brothers shook their heads in unison. "No, no, we're not in favor of a relationship like that," Tolan countered. "We want our father's business, because it is our right."

Samuel sat back. "My sons are of age now, and I cannot demand that they do anything. In this matter, I would not demand for them to give up the business even if I could do so. They didn't ask for the business; your father asked them to take it. Why he didn't ask one of your sons, I wouldn't know. My sons helped your father in the bank so often during the years, and he told me many times how much of a blessing they were to him. They have worked very hard since they have taken over from your father, and the Lord has blessed them."

The brothers weren't giving up easily, since the stakes for them were high. "If your sons don't give up the business willingly, we will take this issue to court," Tolan threatened.

"In that case, I'm quite sure you would lose, since I am the supreme jurist of the nation," Samuel informed them.

For the moment, the brothers had forgotten that for many years their brother-in-law had been interpreting and enforcing the laws of the land through the national court system. They were mute.

Samuel continued. "I have been speaking for my sons, and I shouldn't have presumed to do so. They are of age so they must speak for themselves. Your sons are also of age and should be here in your place pleading their case. So, either you two should speak with Joel and Abijah or we should let our five peers sit down and discuss this matter without interference from the three of us." He looked at the brothers for confirmation.

Tolan was adamantly opposed. "Your sons have the advantage, since they are already installed in the office."

"Perhaps you are right," Samuel agreed. "So let me talk with my sons and the other members of my family about your contention, and if you will come back within a week, either the boys or I will have a final answer for you."

The brothers grudgingly agreed to Samuel's proposal, since they had no other option.

After an evening meal that night at Samuel's and Belah's home, Joel, Hagan, and Abijah and their mates sat down around the table with their parents to discuss the challenge brought by Belah's brothers.

Samuel opened the discussion. "I felt quite sure," he admitted, "that since you boys have been running the bank without Shepi's help for more than a year now that the brothers were content with your takeover and would not launch a protest. It seems now, however, that they were simply waiting for Shepi's passing.

"Because of the attitude they demonstrated today, I have reason to believe that every member of their six separate families will keep up this protest until it becomes a nationwide issue. That could be very embarrassing to our families and especially to me. They threatened to take the issue to court, but their ardor was cooled somewhat when I reminded them that I was the supreme jurist in all of Israel.

"I believe that eventually the families will take the issue to the people. If they do, I will be forced to arbitrate or will need to pick an impartial person to decide the dispute since my immediate family is involved.

"However, if I do excuse myself, your case will be weaker and theirs stronger because the laws tend to give much more consideration to the sons of the family. Jurists feel that the daughters should get their inheritance through marriage."

He paused, and for a few moments, there was silence around the circle. Joel broke the silence.

"Father, I am sorry that our uncles have involved you in this issue. You are such a busy man. Since Grandfather Shepi installed Abijah and me in the bank more than a year before his death and neither Mother or you had anything to say in the transaction, I feel that this dispute should only involve the cousins.

"Abijah and I have worked very hard in the bank since we took it over from grandfather. It had always been a thriving institution because Grandfather Shepi was a very wise businessman, but it has grown considerably in assets since we have assumed the management, so we would certainly feel cheated if we were forced to hand everything to our cousins. They haven't worked one day in this bank. I can't understand why they would desire the bank, since I understand that grandfather left them a liberal portion of his wealth."

Samuel nodded. "Yes, Shepi and Zoran left a generous share to each of the brother's children, and you boys were given the bank."

"I thought so," Joel agreed. "So if it would be all right with Abijah, perhaps we can sit down with our cousins and work out a sensible division of the assets of the bank. We would ask them if it would be all right for you to sit as the arbitrator, Father, but if they object, you could appoint an impartial judge. Do you think that the cousins would agree to meet with us? After all, every one of us is now an adult, and we should settle our own disputes."

"You have proposed a very sensible plan, Joel, and it should work. However, I suggested a similar plan to the brothers this morning, and they rejected it immediately. I am fairly certain that whatever assembly of this nature that will take place between our families, the fathers will speak for the sons.

"Regardless, why don't you boys contact your cousins and suggest a meeting with an impartial arbitrator present. I am not suggesting that the arbitrator give you a final verdict on the matter, but rather, this person will make sure that the assembly is conducted properly. He could also suggest a further course of action if the five of you cannot agree."

The family nodded in unison. "That is good counsel, Father," Abijah conceded.

The next day a mounted courier took a message from Joel and Abijah to the cousins at Gibeah, requesting an assembly for the five of them at the bank in Ramah two days hence. The courier returned empty-handed.

The following day a courier arrived at Ramah with a message for Joel and Abijah, informing them that any assembly between the families would have to include the fathers, since it was their inheritance that had been appropriated.

The boys brought the message from the cousins to Samuel that evening. "Father, give us counsel," they begged. "We need to get this issue settled, so should we agree to a joint meeting with the fathers and the sons?"

Samuel took the terse message, spread it out before the Lord, and prayed about it in the presence of his sons. When he arose, the way was clear to him.

"Sons, the Lord has indicated that the only solution to this dispute is for every member of the three families of Shepi and Zoran to meet together with an impartial arbitrator in charge. In that case, everyone would have to agree beforehand to accept the verdict without recourse." He paused for a few moments.

"It is painful for me to say this, but as I have already mentioned, the judgment could possibly go against the two of you because you are the sister's children. Are you willing to abide by the verdict that might take the bank away from you?"

The sons were in pain. "Father, do you think that if we reject the idea of meeting with the fathers and ignore any further communication from them that they will finally tire of the game and leave us alone?" Abijah asked hopefully.

Samuel shook his head. "No, that will not happen. They have seen that the bank is prospering, and thus, they will keep up the fight until they hope that it will be theirs. So, prolonging a decision on the business will simply increase the bitterness."

The sons made a very difficult decision. They would meet with the uncles and cousins with an impartial arbitrator and would accept the verdict of the judge.

Samuel admired the willingness of his sons to sit in arbitration with the uncles and their families. It was a generous concession on their part, since they could have held the bank and dared the uncles and their sons to dispossess them.

Communications were exchanged between the families, and an impartial arbitrator was certified. The judge was from Mizpah, and he set the date and the rules of the assembly between the two families.

It was a tense time for the families as they met at the bank in Ramah. But Samuel, with his wisdom and charm, helped to mitigate some of the tension.

Since the two sons of Shepi and Zoran were several years older than Belah, they had never been close to their sister, but they had bonded closely with each other. They had accused their parents many times of partiality to their sister, so they had no natural feelings for Belah or her family. Thus they were in this meeting to get what should have been theirs if it were not for the advantage their sister had with their parents.

By previous agreement with Joel and Abijah, Samuel and Belah did not take part in the proceedings. It was very difficult for them to hear lies from the lips of the brothers and sons and not intercede on behalf of their sons, but they held their peace.

The judge disappointed Samuel, since he gave his opinion without open prayer. It seemed so secular to the spiritual priest and judge.

The verdict was what the family had feared. The sons of the brothers were given the bank, and the assets were divided between the five sons with Joel and Abijah receiving major shares.

Samuel feared for the attitude of his sons. He was quite sure they would be bitter, because they had done so well in the bank. Samuel had heard a few clients complain that they had been cheated, but others praised the boys. Now they had no future. They were shorn of a living, but Samuel had a plan.

# CHAPTER 8

The facial expression of the elders was very grim, and their physical movements stiff but deliberate as they met with Samuel at the tabernacle in Ramah. Samuel's thought's cycled as he wondered about the apparent gravity of their mission. Since the Lord had not forewarned him that such a delegation would be visiting him, he was mentally unprepared to face such a large group, but he must meet with them.

As he seated the group and welcomed them to Ramah, the thought struck him that his sons were in deeper trouble than he had at first imagined. They were possibly the focus of the evident anger of the group. Several times during his judicial circuits, he had received disturbing news about the unethical actions of his sons.

Many people were accusing them of taking bribes and thus rendering unfair decisions in a number of major cases. There were also rumors that they were operating an illegal lending institution and were charging undue usury rates to those who were borrowers.

Samuel was pained in his heart. He remembered that he had suffered some major misgivings when he appointed them as judges several years ago. But he had desperately needed their help, and they had needed the employment. He had hoped with all his heart and prayed earnestly that they would judge the people fairly and live exemplary lives.

He realized now that he had expected too much from them. The training they had received from their grandfather, Shepi, in the area of finance was a greater factor in their lives than the spiritual training received from their father.

Samuel had considered several times the counsel he had given to Eli regarding the high priest's erring sons, Hophni and Phinehas. "Master Eli, if you would dismiss your sons from the priesthood perhaps the Lord would see fit to suspend the evil He has prophesied against your house." He was only a child priest then but he had spoken to Eli as a father.

Now the onus was on him. No, the Lord had not sent a prophet to warn him of a curse on his house as He had Eli, but the Lord had spoken to him through several groups of elders who had brought complaints against his sons. And to compound his sense of guilt, he had merely mentioned these public indictments to his sons.

At first he had excused his inaction with the thought that his son's conduct was not really evil in nature, but he knew better. He would have immediately dismissed others in Israel who would have presumed to practice the same behavior.

He shook his head to clear his thoughts. The delegation was waiting for him. He led them in prayer and then sat back and waited for them to present their case. After a few moments of hesitation, the spokesman arose, painfully awkward in manner. As Samuel watched, he reflected that perhaps the group had drawn straws to determine the spokesman and this man had drawn the short straw. It was evident he hated his assignment.

Finally, the man assumed a minimum of poise and began his speech. "Esteemed Judge," he addressed Samuel. "We want you to know that we love and respect you very much."

Every member of the group nodded in agreement and said, "Yes, yes," in unison.

"You have been a fair judge and faithful priest among us from your childhood," the man continued. "You have ministered to our fathers and to us and our children." He paused and swallowed hard. "But you are an old man now and you will not be able to serve us much longer.

Your sons have ministered among us for several years, but they are not like you. Sometimes they take bribes and thus are not fair in their decisions, so we have decided . . . ," he looked helplessly at Samuel. "We have decided that we need a king to rule over us. One who will lead us and fight our battles like the nations around us."

Samuel couldn't believe his ears. The man was still speaking, but Samuel was not listening—the people were requesting a king to assume a large part of his ministry, which hurt him deeply, but the reason they were giving for wanting a king was even more painful to him. They wanted to be like the nations around them. He shuddered as he considered this unholy request.

Their desire to be like the nations around them had led them into deep troubles so many times in the past. But they refused to learn the lessons God was attempting to teach them for so many years now. They were a called out people. They were supposed to be different from the people around them, not like them. They were intended, by God Himself, to be a peculiar people.

As he mused, visions of past experiences of God's people passed before him. He saw the defeat of the Israelites at Ebenezer, the death of Hophni and Phinehas, and the loss of the Ark of God. As a child he was greatly traumatized by this tragedy, but he remembered that God had predicted this experience through him. However, He hadn't realized that the spiritual problems of Israel reached far beyond the evil lives of Hophni and Phinehas until that incident.

He remembered that after the death of Eli and the forced move from Shiloh to Ramah, he saw, with more mature eyesight, the depth of the apostasy of Israel. In his travels he beheld the people worshipping pagan idols in the groves and on the high places. He remembered his agonizing efforts to correct the evils of the people and the encouragement of seeing the first signs of repentance and renewal that grew into a great revival at Mizpah. He heard again the thunders at Mizpah and saw the Lord bare His holy arm in defense of His people.

Twenty years earlier the Philistines had been victorious over Israel at Ebenezer because of Israel's apostasy. Then he saw the result of repentance and turning to the Lord—the great victory of Israel over the Philistines.

The scene swept through the years since Mizpah. He was again seeing the sure signs of apostasy in the land. In many places he saw pagan altars in the groves and high places. He noticed that the Philistines were slowly infiltrating the outlying areas of Israel, and the people were accepting them and associating with them. His heart was sick unto death.

The drone of the spokesman brought his mind back to the present. He remembered that the people were asking for a king. Soon the spokesmen ended his appeal and sat down. All eyes were now focused on Samuel.

Samuel stood up and looked intently into the eyes of every member of the commission. They moved uneasily in their seats. His thoughts were churning, but his voice was calm.

"Brethren, I have heard your request and will certainly consider it immediately. As you surely are aware, of course, I will need to place this matter before the Lord." The men nodded in agreement.

"He has been our King of kings for many centuries now," Samuel continued. "He has fought our battles, and when we have depended on Him, He has never failed us. No other people have such a great King as we have!" The men stirred uneasily in their chairs. " So if you are to have a king from among our people, God will have the final choice." The men nodded again in unison.

"I am calling an official meeting one week from today at Ramah. At that time, I will tell you about the decision of the Lord regarding a king for you. Will that be all right with you?

There was a shout. "Yes, Master Samuel, that will be all right with us."

"Very well then. Thank you one and all for coming."

He finished and left the room. He must share the burden and the pain of his heart with his Friend, the King of kings and Lord of lords.

He went to his favorite room in the tabernacle, where he had met with the Lord many times before, and fell on his knees before the Lord. For many minutes He was mute as he knelt there. Then he felt the presence of the Lord draw near as he waited. The Lord didn't speak to him audibly at first as He had many times in the past, but it seemed to Samuel that the presence enfolded him in tender arms and the divine hand was gently massaging the aching muscles of his heart.

Samuel spoke, "Lord, I have served Your people with a faithful heart since only a child. I have judged them fairly and have made atonement for their sins. I have delivered Your messages to them without fabricating or improvising and have held them up before You in prayer. Now they have rejected my ministry for them and are asking for a king so that they can be like the pagan nations.

"Lord, I do not believe that it will be good to give them a king. They will no longer depend on You but rather look to the king and will forget You." Samuel felt divine fingers on his lips, and he ceased his speaking.

"Samuel." The Lord spoke at last. "I know you are hurting. But you must heed the voice of the people, for they haven't rejected you, but they have rejected Me. They no longer want Me to rule over them.

"From the day I brought them out of Egypt even to this present day, they have been a disobedient people. They have repeatedly forsaken Me and served other gods, just like they are doing now.

"I have rebuked them many times and chastised them by giving them into the hands of their enemies. When they have turned back to Me in repentance and true sorrow for their sins, I have delivered them from their enemies and restored them to their land again, but they backslide again and again.

"Samuel, you must heed their voice and give them a king. But you must forewarn them of the behavior of a king who will rule over them when you meet with them next week. You must not spare any of the details. And my Spirit will give a lash to your words.

"Here are the rules of conduct that they must expect from the king. I will bring them to your memory as you meet with the people. I will be with you in your search for a king, and I will impress you as to his identity. I will also be with you as you transfer the power of rulership from yourself to the king.

"But, Samuel, your work is not finished. I will need you to mentor the new king, and there will possibly be times when you will need to discipline him for Me. Also, you will need to continue your work as the chief priest and as the director of the training school for the young men of the nation."

Samuel felt the immediate presence of the Lord leave him then, but the aura of divine presence was still with him as it had been during his entire lifetime. He remained on his knees for some time, loath to leave that holy place. Then he arose and went home to Belah.

As Belah greeted her husband, she noticed a particular appearance about him that reminded her of the description of Moses as he came down from Mount Sinai. Moses face had been shining and radiant. So also was Samuel's face, and she knew that he had been in session with the Lord. She had seen the signs several times before, but why, she wondered, was his countenance so troubled? She knew that he would soon share with her, so she waited. They sat down together, and he took her hand, but for several moments, the words wouldn't come.

"Belah," he finally said with effort. "An assemblage visited with me this morning that claimed to represent the voice of the people, and they asked me to appoint a king to rule over them."

He stopped and put his head in his hands. Belah knew that he was in agony of spirit, but she was silent. She caressed his back as he fought for self-control. Finally, he straightened up and continued. "I assured them that I would call a national meeting next week and would relay the Lord's answer to them at that time. Then I dismissed them and went into my prayer room to put the request before the Lord.

"I had an extended session with the Lord, and I was surprised at His answer regarding the people's request for a king. He chided me a bit at first.

"He said, Samuel, they are not rejecting you but rather are rejecting Me. Then He said plainly, 'You must honor their request and give them a king.'"

Samuel shook his head. "Belah, I will admit that at first I thought they were rejecting me, and I reacted much too humanly. I felt self-pity for a few moments, but as I thought further, my heart is more troubled thinking that they have rejected God than if they would have rejected me."

He spread his hands helplessly. "Belah, I almost feel that my ministry to these people has been a failure."

He looked at his wife, and she consoled him. "No dear, your ministry hasn't been a failure. Look at all of the promising young men you have inducted into the training school at Ramah and at Kirjath Jearim. Also, there are so many dedicated teachers in the two schools. You have done a great work among these people."

He felt better listening to Belah, and she continued. "Look at the many centuries God has ministered to these people with the hope that they would love and serve Him. But most of the people through these centuries have disobeyed Him and hurt Him, and now they have added to their sins by asking for a human king instead of being content with the King of kings. And . . . ," she paused, her eyes filled with wonder. "God is willing to step aside, in a sense, and let them put a king in His place."

She turned to Samuel. "Dear, we serve such a wonderful God, don't we?"

Samuel nodded. "Yes, Belah, He is wonderful."

Samuel remembered something else about the meeting. "Belah, the spokesman for the group said that the reason they were requesting a king was because I was growing old and our sons were not like me—they are taking bribes and are cheating some of the people."

A spasm of pain flashed across Belah's face, but she was mute.

Samuel continued. "I had heard the same criticism twice before from the elders of Beersheba, so I confronted the boys with the accusations. They admitted rendering judgments in favor of two families who had given them substantial gifts. They claimed, however, that at the time they thought the judgments were fair. They said that one of the families who had lost the case was related to an influential elder of the city and that elder was the one making the complaint. They denied that they had cheated anyone but admitted that they had made several loans and had charged undue usury." He shook his head. "It appears as though the boys are trying to mix judging and banking, and it isn't working. The boys love us very much, and it would crush them if they knew that their unorthodox activities had forced me out of office prematurely, so I have decided not to tell them about the criticism from the delegation that met with me this morning."

He looked to Belah for confirmation, but he could see that she was not in agreement.

"No, Samuel. You must tell them the truth. I am sure that the truth will hurt them deeply, but at the same time, it could be of help to them. We have shielded them too much, and we must not continue."
He saw her logic. "I am sure that you are right, Belah. I understand that both Joel and Abijah are in the city tonight visiting their in-laws, so perhaps we should invite them over and tell them about the request from the elders."

She nodded. "I will send Rauh with a message to them right away."

There was a bit of tension in the room as parents and sons met. Both Joel and Abijah remembered the last meeting with their father. He had met them at Beersheba and had faced them with the accusation of the elders. They wondered now, *Have more complaints of our misdeeds found there way to our father's ears*? They feared the worst.

After prayer Samuel began his difficult monologue. "Joel and Abijah, a delegation of elders from several cities, including Beersheba, met with me this morning and presented a very unusual request from their people." He hesitated, remembering the pain, for a few moments and then plunged ahead.

"They asked me to appoint a king to rule over them like the nations around them." The sons drew in their breath sharply, and their eyes widened in similar shock and pain, but they didn't interrupt.

"They gave two reasons for their request. I am now an old man and will not be able to judge them much longer, and you two are not qualified to be judges. They said that you both had been charged with bribery and cheating at Beersheba." The pain in his heart was slowing his speech now, and he recognized that he had even slurred some of his words.

Joel recognized that Samuel had finished, so he spoke up. "Father, I am so sorry for the trouble we have caused you, and I am sure that Abijah shares my pain. Now, it appears that partly because of our activities you will have to give up your work as the national jurist. We know that you love your work and the people love you, so this will be very difficult for you.

"It is true that we have done some stupid things at Beersheba. We took gifts from two families while we were deciding their case in the court. We were certain that they were in the right and would have won the case regardless, but it gave the losers reason for accusing us of taking bribes. Then, as we admitted to you, we did charge undue usury on some loans."

He spread his hands helplessly. "I certainly am not blaming Grandfather Shepi, but he did endow us with an unreasonable affection for money. And," he added, "it isn't compatible with the work we were commissioned to do.

"Abijah and I have talked about going back into banking at Gilgal. So perhaps now is the time for us to make a change."

He stopped, and a look of uncertainty spread over his face. "But, Father, I am sure that you have already placed this request before the Lord. What was His answer?"

"Yes, Joel, as soon as the assemblage left, I went to my prayer room in the temple and placed the people's request before the Lord." He paused and closed his eyes as he relived the precious experience.

"God came very near to me as I prayed, and He comforted my heart. He said, 'Samuel, you must heed the voice of the people. They have not rejected you, but rather, they have rejected Me. Ever since I brought them out of Egypt to this present time, they have rejected Me time after time. Nevertheless, you must heed their request and give them a king.'"

Samuel paused and looked longingly at his sons, Joel and Abijah, "I crave for you the same experiences I have had as the Lord has met with me. He has been such a true Friend and has given me the wisdom to judge the people these many years. God promised me that He would assist me in my search for a king and would identify the king to me."

The people gathered by the thousands at Ramah to hear the Lord's answer to their petition for a king. It was the largest assemblage Samuel had seen in his long tenure as judge and priest. He faced them at the appointed time, and the vast crowd became quiet.

"You have requested a king, and as I promised, I have placed your petition before the Lord. He was disappointed by your request. But He reminded me that from the day He brought our forefathers out of Egypt to this present time your fathers and now you, who are gathered here today, have forsaken Him and have served the gods of the nations around us. He reminded me that He has always been your King and has fought your battles and has loved you with an everlasting love. He said that it was not for your best good to have a human king; nevertheless, He will honor your request and choose a king for you."

He paused, expecting the people to make a response, but they were mute.

"He charged me to forewarn you of the behavior of the king who will rule over you. The king will take your sons and induct them into his army. They will drive his chariots and be his horsemen. Some will even run before the chariots. He will appoint captains over his thousands and over his fifties, and they will fight his battles.

"He will appoint some of you to make his weapons of war and equipment for his chariots. He will take some of your lands for his own and will press some of you into service to plow his ground and reap his harvests. He will plant vineyards and olive groves and will give some of these lands to his servants.

"He will even take your daughters to be perfumers, cooks, and bakers. He will take a tithe of your grain and vintage and even of your income as merchants, and he will give it to his servants and officers.

"He will take the finest of your young men, your menservants, and maidservants, and of your donkeys and oxen and put them to work in his fields.

"He will take a tenth of your sheep and your cattle, and you will not have any recourse.

"You will chafe under his reign, and you will cry out to the Lord for relief, but He will not hear you in that day, for you have rejected Him."

Samuel paused and looked over the sea of faces before him.

"Now, I have forewarned you about the behavior of the king as the Lord asked me to do. I have held nothing back. Do you still wish for the Lord to choose a king to rule over you?"

There was silence for a few moments in the assemblage before the voices rang out. "Yes, we want a king to rule over us like the nations around us. We want a king that will judge us and fight our battles."

"Very well, I will now place this before the Lord here in your presence."

Samuel knelt before the people and prayed to the Lord. The Lord answered immediately. "Heed their voice and give them a king."

Samuel relayed the Lord's answer to the people. He then dismissed the people and turned toward his prayer room in the tabernacle.

Belah joined him. "May I meet with you and our Lord in the prayer room?" she asked uncertainly.

He grasped her hand. "I would love to have you with me when I meet with the King of kings," he said as he squeezed her hand.

They knelt together on the floor of the prayer room, and their arms went around each other as Samuel poured out his heart in prayer. The Lord came very near. Belah felt His presence but didn't hear His voice as He spoke to Samuel.

"Samuel, I have already chosen the man who will be the king of My people, Israel. You will meet him within three days time. His name is Saul, son of Kish, of the tribe of Benjamin. He lives at Gibeah. My angels hid three of the donkeys of Kish, and Saul will soon be searching for them. The donkeys will be found quickly, but Saul will not be the one to find them. He and his servant will continue their search until they arrive at Ramah. That is when you will meet him, for he will come to you with a plea to tell him where he can find his father's donkeys. You will assure him that the donkeys have already been found, and he is to be a special guest at a sacrificial feast you have prepared for the people. I will give you further instructions the day before you meet him regarding this man whom I have chosen to be king."

The voice ceased, and Samuel knew that the audience was ended. He had been unconscious of any movement around him while the Lord was speaking to him, but now he felt the arm of Belah still encircling his waist. His arm was also around her, and he squeezed her gently. She responded in kind.

As in the past times, the immediate presence of the Lord had left the room but the sacred sensation still remained. Samuel and Belah arose from their knees and left the prayer room. They spoke not a word until they were out of the room for fear of disturbing the bond that connected them with the Eternal.

Belah looked into his eyes, and gratitude was in her voice. "Samuel, thank you so much for allowing me the privilege of sharing this precious time of divine association with you. This has been the most spiritual moment of my entire life."

For the moment he was mute, and she sensed that he was still overwhelmed by the voice of God. He shook his head and looked at Belah as if he were seeing her for the first time.

"Belah, God told me that the man He has chosen as king will meet me at the time of the sacrificial feast two days from today. The man has been seeking several of his father's lost donkeys, and he will come to me to see if I can use my powers as a seer to find the lost donkeys. God said that He would give me further instructions before the man arrives."

She squeezed his arm, and her eyes were wide with wonder. "Samuel, that is awesome. I was sure that the Lord was speaking with you, but all I heard was a sound like thunder."

"I was so glad that you were able to share this experience with me. I cherish these special moments with my Lord"

"I will be inviting the elders from Zuph and Benjamin to meet with me for a sacrificial meal day after tomorrow. According to the word of the Lord, that is the time I am to meet the man who will be king. I will invite you to join us at the feast in Zuph."

Her face became serious. "Samuel, are you sure that the elders will accept the presence of a woman at such a sacred feast? Will they accept me because I am your wife?"

Samuel's face broke into a smile. "I don't have much to fear from the elders anymore. And besides, I am the one who is hosting the feast."

She relaxed. "It will be such a privilege to be with you when you meet the newly appointed king."

Samuel made arrangements for the sacrificial feast at Zuph. About thirty men in all were invited, but none of the thirty suspected the real reason for the celebration.

As Samuel and Belah were preparing to go to Zuph, the Lord met with Samuel again and gave him instructions regarding the man who was to be anointed king of Israel.

"Samuel, as I have mentioned, the man whom I have chosen is of the tribe of Benjamin. His name is Saul, the son of Kish, and he is the finest in the land. You will notice that he is head and shoulders taller than anyone else in Israel, which will be pleasing to the people. Many of the people have heard stories about the giant sons of 'Anak' who were kings of the tribes who opposed our people as they were coming out of Egypt. They want a king who is like these pagan kings, and this man, Saul, is the largest man in Israel.

"As soon as you see this man, My Spirit will tell you, 'This is the man.' You will tell him that you have been expecting him and that he and his servant will be special guests at a sacrificial feast you have prepared. He will be surprised that you know him and are treating him so royally, for I have not given him any indication that he has been chosen as the king of Israel. At this time in his life, he is a very humble man and would certainly be overwhelmed at the thought of being a king, so you must be very careful in your dealings with him. Anoint him secretly, and then tell him of specific incidents that will happen to him on his way back to his home.

"He will meet two men by Rachel's tomb in Benjamin near Zelah. He will not know them, but these men will know him and will tell him that his father's donkeys, which were lost, have been found, and now his family is worried about his welfare. After he leaves these men, he will come to the famous terebinth tree of Tabor. There he will meet three men on their way to Bethel to sacrifice to the Lord. One of these men will be carrying three goat kids, another three loaves of bread, and the third will have a skin of wine. These men will greet him and for no apparent reason will give him two loaves of bread.

"After that, he will come to the hill of God where a Philistine garrison is located. There he will meet a group of prophets coming down from the high places with a stringed instrument, a tambourine, a flute, and a harp, and these men will be prophesying as they are traveling. Saul will join them, and the Spirit of God will come upon him, and he will also prophecy and become a changed man.

"Tell him that God has arranged for him to see all of these signs so that he will know that he has been chosen by the Lord for a special work. These signs will also assure him that the Lord will be with him. He is to go to Gilgal, where you will meet with him within seven days and will show him what he is to do."

All of these things happened to Saul just as Samuel had predicted, and Saul wondered what all of these things meant.

He had heard that the elders of Israel had requested a king, and Samuel had promised that the Lord would fulfill their request, but Saul had no idea that the Lord would choose him for such an office. He thought, *Isn't the tribe of Benjamin the smallest in Israel? And my family is the most insignificant of this small tribe.*

Saul went back to his home and found that during the time he had been seeking for his father's donkeys a son, Jonathan, was born to him by his wife, Ahinoam. He rejoiced with his family over the birth of his son, but he didn't tell his wife or his father about His anointing by Samuel at Zuph. It was still a mystery to him.

Samuel was also puzzled. He had anointed Saul to be king according to the directions of the Lord. Then he had relayed to Saul, by inspiration from God, the providential experiences that he would meet on his way back to Gibeah.

Samuel thought that surely the Benjamite would understand that God had chosen him to be king over Israel. But Saul had gone back to Gibeah and was again working on his father's farm as if nothing of importance had happened.

Samuel wondered what God would do next to let Saul know that he should take his place as king over Israel. He sought the Lord in prayer for divine direction, and the Lord came to him.

"Samuel, I am pleased with Saul thus far. He understands that I have spoken to him through you, but he doesn't want to be presumptuous. He is still working for his father, but he is waiting for further directions from you.

"I want you to call all Israel together at Mizpah, and there I will choose Saul to be king in the sight of all the people. Perhaps then he will sense his responsibility to take his place at the head of Israel."

Samuel sent out couriers to the ends of the nation with an appeal for the people to meet at Mizpah, where the Lord would choose by lot the king of Israel. The people came by the thousands to Mizpah.

Samuel addressed them. "The Lord gave me this message. The Lord brought your forefathers out of Egypt and delivered them from the hands of the Egyptians and the evils that threatened them along the way. He brought them safely to this place where we live today and has cared for your fathers and you these many years. But you have now rejected the Lord your God who has delivered you from your adversaries, and you have requested a human king, a peer of your own to rule over you. God could have denied your request, but because of His great love for you, He is granting your petition for a king. Now, all of you come near, and you will see the Lord choose your king by lot."

When the lots were cast, the tribe of Benjamin was chosen. Then the family of Matri was chosen, and finally, Saul, the son of Kish, was chosen. But when they sought for him, they couldn't find him. Then Samuel bowed before the Lord and asked the Lord to reveal to Him where Saul could be found, and the Lord answered. "He was overwhelmed by the thought of being chosen king and has hidden among the equipment."

Several of the young men ran to find Saul, and they brought him out to stand before the people.

Samuel said to all the people. "Behold the man that God has chosen to be your king. He is head and shoulders taller than any other man in Israel, and there is no one like him."

Then the people shouted with one voice, "Long live the king."

Samuel was again inspired to relate to the people the behavior of royalty. As he looked out over the sea of faces, he was struck with the superficial thinking of the people. Their lives were so free now compared to the heavy taxes and conscription that a king would impose. But their minds were made up; they wanted a king, and they would have a king.

Samuel wrote down in a book the predicted behavior of a king and ordered that it be put in the library of the capital city, Gibeah of Benjamin. It would serve both as a reference book for the people and also as a testimony against them. Samuel dismissed the people, and Saul went back to his home in Gibeah. This time some valiant men went with him and became the royal guards. Samuel went back to his home in Ramah.

Samuel was not satisfied with the results of the meeting at Mizpah. Saul had been publicly proclaimed king of Israel, but he had not yet been coronated, and Samuel wondered if the shy Benjamite would know how to assume his place as king of Israel. Since Israel had never had a human king, there were no records, and the Lord had not given specific instructions regarding the location of the royal headquarters, the recruiting and funding of a standing army, and the formation of a council to assist the king.

Rumors had come from Gibeah that Saul had again assumed work on his father's farm and the royal guards were simply cooling their heels. Samuel wondered what the Lord would do next to put the new king to work as head of Israel.

The answer to Samuel's reflections came quickly. Nahash, king of the Ammonites, desired to enlarge his dominion, and he knew that Israel was vulnerable at this time. So he came up with his army and encamped against Jabesh Gilead. The people of Jabesh Gilead were peace-loving people, so they immediately proposed to serve Nahash if he would make a covenant with them.

But the evil king refused to be satisfied with mere subordination on the part of the Jabeshites. He demanded that every male in the city have their right eye put out so that reproach would be brought on all Israel. The Jabeshites made a counter proposal. "Give us seven days to find someone in Israel who will save us. If at the end of seven days no tribe comes forward to save us, we will put ourselves in your hands."

Nahash had heard that many years ago the inhabitants of Jabesh Gilead had been an odor in the nostrils of the other tribes of Israel because they had refused to go to war against the tribe of Benjamin. So the Ammonite king readily agreed to the proposal.

The people of Jabesh Gilead sent messengers to every city in Israel informing them of the intentions of the Ammonites, and they pleaded for help from their brethren. And there was great lamentation throughout the land of Israel.

The sad news came to Saul's attention as he came in from the field, and he was greatly touched in his heart by the plight of the people of Jabesh Gilead. The Spirit of

God came upon the newly appointed king, and he made a very radical decision. He took the yoke of oxen with which he had been working in the field, killed them, hewed their bodies into many pieces, and sent these pieces of flesh by courier to every village and city in Israel. A message was attached to the grisly parts stating that any able bodied man in Israel who did not join with him in fighting the Ammonites would have their own oxen mutilated as these beasts were.

The response of the people exceeded the expectations of the new king. Three hundred and thirty thousand men from Israel and Judah joined Saul at Bezek to fight against the Ammonites. Saul proved his merits as a skillful military leader by defeating the Ammonites so soundly that no two men were left together. Samuel was greatly encouraged by the brilliant military strategy of the new king and the good response of the people to his leadership.

"Surely now," the aged prophet reasoned, "Saul will assume his rightful place as king of Israel." But as Samuel waited before the Lord, he was reminded that there was one more step in the installation of the new king. There must be a coronation ceremony, and Samuel must publicly transfer the leadership from himself to Saul.

Samuel called the people together once again, this time at Gilgal. He made sacrifices of peace offerings there, and the people hailed the new king. Then, with Saul by his side, Samuel made his final speech to the people as their leader and judge.

"Look, I have heeded your voice and have appointed a king over you this day."

And the people shouted, "Long live the king."

"I have served you as a judge, priest, and prophet from my childhood to this day. I am now an old man and must give the scepter to a younger man of God's choosing." As he spoke, Samuel handed a wand to Saul, representing the transfer of leadership from himself to the new king.

And again the people shouted, "Long live the king."

"Now, I must hear from your lips a response of my leadership among you these many years.

"Whose ox or whose donkey have I taken, or whom have I defrauded? Whom have I oppressed, or from whose hand have I received any bribe to blind my eyes? Tell me and I will restore it to you."

The people responded with one voice, "You have not defrauded us or oppressed us, nor have you taken anything from any man's hand."

Then Samuel once again reviewed before them the way the Lord, the King of kings, had led their forefathers from Egypt to this land He had promised them. The prophet reminded them that their fathers had rebelled against the leadership of the Lord, and God had sold them into slavery. Then when they had repented and turned to Him again, He had rescued them from the hand of the enemy with men like Jerubbaal, Gideon, Jepthah, and Samuel.

"But you have rejected the King of kings and have chosen to have a human king rule over you as the nations around you. If you fear the Lord and serve Him and obey His voice, both you and the king that you have chosen will live in peace before Him. But if you do not obey the voice of the Lord, the hand of the Lord will be against you as He was against your fathers. And He will send the thunder and rain on you so that you will see how great is your wickedness in His sight."

As Samuel spoke these words, he bowed his head in prayer, and the Lord sent a mighty burst of thunder and rain upon the people. Then the people feared greatly for their lives and begged Samuel to pray for them that the Lord might not kill them for their sin of asking for a king.

And Samuel said, "Do not fear. You have done this wickedness, but God has forgiven you. Do not turn aside now from following Him."

Then Samuel took a crown that he had made especially for the new king of Israel, and he placed it on Saul's head in the sight of all the people. And again the people shouted, "Long live the king."

## SAMUEL'S HEART

# CHAPTER 9

In an unusual gesture for the aged priest, he embraced the new king of Israel warmly, but Saul returned the tender clasp rather woodenly. It was quite evident to Samuel that Saul was not an emotional man. Perhaps that personality trait would work to the king's favor in the long run, Samuel reasoned, since it could make him more impartial in his judgments.

As the two embraced, the scene was a moving one to the assembled Israelites. The hoary head of the aged priest, who had served them for many years, was tried and tested by the years of service, but the dark locks of the younger king appeared to demonstrate one untested as yet by time and circumstances.

As the two leaders finished their farewells, Samuel dismissed the people and went back to his home in Ramah. Saul finally took over the duties of ruling Israel from his home in Gibeah.

Samuel returned from the coronation of Saul at Gilgal with high hopes for a successful reign for the new king. Saul had shown such a deep sense of humility at the time he was chosen king by lot at Mizpah. Then, his brilliant military leadership in the battle against the Ammonites had won the hearts of all Israel. Thus the spirit was strong in the land, and the people were praising the new king.

*Perhaps,* Samuel reflected, *the selection of a king to rule over Israel might work better than I had thought at first.*

He was immediately reminded by the Spirit of God that the results would be dependent on the continued spiritual deportment of both king and people. The true

King of kings and Lord of lords would still be in charge, and the obedience of the king and people to His commandments would determine whether there would be blessings or curses in their future.

Samuel had been considering the future of his ministry as a judge in this new political order. He realized that there could be times when this office could infringe on the authority of the king, so he felt a deep need for the Lord to give him open guidance in this area, but the Lord was silent.

The Lord had told him that he would be expected to mentor the new king. Of course, counsel would only be given by request from the king, and Samuel had a feeling that such requests from Saul would be very rare.

Samuel did hear that Saul had appointed a council of elders to assist him in his governmental affairs, but later, word came to the priest that the council had met only once during the first year of Saul's reign.

Samuel continued his priestly ministry to the people, and after a time when no direct divine counsel was given him, he decided that he must keep his judicial office in Ramah open and continue his itinerary to Bethel, Gilgal, and Mizpah. It was apparent that Saul had no interest in judicial matters.

Mentoring the new king was certainly not time-consuming to Samuel. He was invited by Saul only once in five years to visit him at the palace in Gibeah. The occasion was the dedication service for the beautiful and functional palace for the royal family and the administrative center for the nation. During this visit Saul did not ask for any counsel from the aged and experienced priest and judge. The king appeared to have all the answers.

Samuel met the queen during his visit to Gibeah and the king's two children, Jonathan and Merab. He was deeply impressed with the grace and piety of Ahinoam, but he noticed an aura of sadness about her, and he wondered.

A few days after his return from Gibeah, he spoke of his impression of the queen to Belah. "Belah dear, I was very much impressed with her and the behavior of her two children. She certainly fits into the royal mode, but she doesn't seem happy. In fact, she appears to be sad."

A look of pain flashed over Belah's face. "Samuel, I'm very sorry. I should have shared this news with you immediately, but I was afraid that it would diminish your confidence in the king, and I know how much you want him to succeed."

"Last week when Joel's wife, Nona, visited me, she brought a bundle of news from Gilgal. According to her report, King Saul is no longer living with his family at Gibeah. He has moved with most of his army to Gilgal and is living in tents. Evidently the move had nothing to do with the defense of Israel but rather is the area where several secondary wives or concubines are living. Nona said that at least one of the women has a child by the king. According to rumor, he visits his family in Gibeah when he desires to spend the night with his wife, so perhaps the queen has good reason for her appearance of sadness."

Belah hesitated for a few moments before continuing. "Samuel, isn't there direct counsel from the Lord in the writings of Moses that kings should not take multiple wives?" She looked to Samuel for confirmation.

"Yes, Belah, there is. The Lord anticipated that someday Israel would ask for a king. He was not to multiply wives or horses or be greedy and get much silver and gold. Also, the king was admonished to write a copy of these requirements and God's commandments and study them daily so that his leadership would always be just and fair."

The two were silent for several moments; then Belah spoke. "Samuel, are you sure that Saul knows about these restrictions?"

Samuel felt a twinge of guilt. "I am quite sure that he doesn't, and I am to blame. I wanted to sit down with him after his coronation and have a heart-to-heart chat with him, but . . . ," Samuel spread his hands helplessly. "He was in a hurry to leave, and besides, he is not the type of man who invites one-on-one conversation. I hoped that later he would call me and ask for counsel, but that has never happened. He has chosen to go his own way."

Samuel sighed. "I feel guilty now because I didn't insist on giving him an orientation."

Belah patted her troubled husband on the knee. "Dear, you must not feel guilty. Almost everyone in Israel knows that God had never sanctioned multiple wives. There are some that have rebelled against God's plan and have taken more than one wife, but there is strife in most of these families. I know that your father had two wives, but later, he was sorry for his choice. He excused his actions with the thought that your mother would be permanently barren and thus would not be able to give him an heir." Belah stopped speaking abruptly again and looked intently at Samuel.

"Are you planning to visit with Saul and explain God's counsel to him?"

Samuel thought on the question for a few moments. "I haven't received any impression from the Lord to give the king a late indoctrination, but He did ask me to mentor the king. Saul has never given me that opportunity, and since he has been supreme commander of the nation now for several years, he might consider any counsel from me as interference. However, to satisfy my own heart, I will pass on to him this counsel from God."

Belah nodded. "Hopefully he will accept it as from the Lord and will benefit from it."

Samuel sent a letter to Saul at Gilgal, requesting a meeting with him, and soon the king replied with favor. Saul met the aged priest graciously and ushered him to a seat in an arbor near his tent. It was quite an inelegant setting for a meeting between the king and the chief priest, but Saul appeared comfortable with his crude outpost.

Samuel was not given to small talk, so after a few pleasantries, he came to the main reason for his visit.

"King Saul," Samuel addressed the ruler, "I had hoped we could spend time together at the beginning of your kingship to get better acquainted and so that I could acquaint you with some very important counsel that God gave through Moses to a king of Israel. You see, God anticipated that a time would come when Israel would ask for a king, so He gave some very definite directions for the king."

Samuel took a sheet of papyrus from his bag. "I have written these requirements down for you and will leave the list with you. Here are the mandates. The king shall not be greedy and collect much silver and gold. Neither is he to multiply unto himself horses or wives. He is to write these injunctions along with the other commandments down and read them daily so that his reign will always be just and fair."

Samuel lowered the sheet and looked at the king. Saul's face had darkened and the veins in his neck were distended, but Samuel ignored these signs of anger.

"Rumors have come to my ears that you have taken several wives, and I was greatly concerned that I had been remiss in not sharing the information with you much earlier in your reign." He stopped and waited for the king's response.

Saul swallowed hard as he fought for self-control. Finally, he spoke. "Master Samuel, I was certainly not aware of these restrictions that the Lord had placed on the king centuries ago. I wish that you would have called these to my attention years ago, but you should not shoulder all of the blame. I planned several times to call on you asking for counsel, but I made the mistake of waiting for you to call on me, so I will share your guilt.

"It is true that I have taken two concubines from this area, and one has given me a son. At this point I am not sure how I could end these relationships. However, I am planning to move back to Gibeah with my army, and perhaps that will take care of some of the rumors." He spoke the last sentence rather sharply and bitterly.

The king arose from his seat to indicate that the visit was over. "Thank you very much for your visit and counsel. I have always been a great admirer of yours."

Samuel went back to Ramah and to Belah with a heavy heart. The thought haunted him that his visit with Saul was much too late, and therefore, his counsel was ineffective.

Saul had given him a mild rebuke for not acquainting him with God's counsel to the king much earlier, and Samuel felt that the mild criticism was fully justified. He should not have waited for Saul to come to him. He should have gone to the king. God had told him to mentor the king and that meant that he should have been the aggressive one.

He did not entertain the idea, for one moment, that Saul would put away his concubines. He was quite sure, however, that he would move back to Gibeah, which would make his relationships with the women more discreet. Also, it would give the impression that he was a more faithful family man.

Belah was dead. Samuel had lost his dearest earthly friend. But in this time of deepest grief, the aged priest never faltered in his trust and devotion to his Lord. He stood like a tree in a great storm.

Belah had been ill for many months, and the ministry of the physicians had been ineffective on her behalf, but she bore her suffering silently and with grace, and even in death, her face reflected the inner peace that had sustained her for so many years.

Mother Belah, as she was known by many in Israel, would be sorely missed. Her counsel and encouragement had lifted the hearts of thousands. The king and his royal family attended the burial services and offered their consolation to Samuel and his family.

Belah was buried in the family tombs at Ramah. After the services Samuel observed the time of mourning and turned again to his priestly and judicial ministry.

Samuel was surprised to see the young Prince Jonathan among his visitors, and he wondered about his mission. He had met Jonathan only twice before and these brief meetings had impressed him with the humility and devotion of the prince. He was a serious young man.

Samuel seated the prince, and for a few minutes they chatted amicably together. "Prince Jonathan, rumors have come to me that you have recently joined the royal army as a foot soldier. I'm sure your father is pleased with your decision."

Samuel was quite certain that a bit of pain showed for a moment on the face of the prince, but he answered easily. "Yes, it was a very difficult decision for me. While my choice pleased my father, it disappointed my mother and my Grandfather Kish. They were hoping that I would choose to manage the vast estates of my grandfather."

He hesitated for a moment, and then continued. "I really preferred the pastoral over the military, but after much prayer I decided to join the army. That brings me to the purpose of my visit."

The prince put his head in his hands for a few moments then straightened up and looked to Samuel for understanding.

"Perhaps what I will share with you is a betrayal of my father's trust and a violation of army regulations, but since you are the spiritual leader of our nation, you need to be aware of the unlawful acts of our army leaders. I am speaking about my father and Captain Abner, who is my uncle."

"From my earliest childhood, Mother taught me that God is to be first in everything. He is to be first in our hearts and in our homes. He is to have the first of our flocks and of our grain. And when He gives us victory in battle, He must have the first and the best of the spoil. My father and Captain Abner ignore this divine right. When the battle is over, they immediately divide up the spoil between themselves and the troops, and often there is none left for the Lord, or perhaps what is left is inferior.

"I spoke to my father about this neglect several years ago, and he chided me for my impertinence. When I spoke to Captain Abner about this sin, he laughed at me."

The prince spread his hands in frustration. "I have prayed often about this matter, but the Lord hasn't given me any answers. Then, I felt impressed to share my burden with you with the hope that because of your many years of experience you might give me counsel. You see, Master Samuel, I am fearful that God will withhold His blessings from our nation because of the sins of our leaders."

Samuel looked tenderly at the troubled young prince, and his heart went out to him. He thought, *What a treasure the nation has in this young man. Certainly Israel should prosper when he succeeds his father as king.*

Samuel leaned forward. "Jonathan, your mother was right. God is supposed to be first in everything done under the sun, and what your father and Captain Abner are doing is not pleasing to Jehovah. However, I have found that the king does not accept counsel graciously. He is a very proud and determined man, and since he is the king he can make his own rules to a point. So I am fairly certain that he will not change his practice.

"Nevertheless, I must speak to your father about this trespass, and I will also visit with Captain Abner. I have never met Captain Abner before, so it will be our first conversation. Perhaps these men will prove my prediction wrong and will honor the Lord again with the first fruits. I will not mention your name in my visitation."

Jonathan smiled and arose to leave. "Thank you, Master Samuel, for hearing me out. And thank you for not mentioning my name. My father would, without fail, dismiss me from the army and might even charge me as a traitor if he knew that I had shared his misconduct with you."

He straightened his shoulders. "However, I was prepared to suffer the consequences if you felt a need to mention me as your source."

Samuel's heart swelled with pride at the courage of the prince. He shook his hand warmly.

The day after Jonathan's visit, Samuel sent a message by courier to the king requesting a meeting with him. A return message, written by the king's scribe, informed Samuel that the king was currently involved in several national problems and, therefore, could not make room in his schedule at this time. He would notify Samuel when his schedule was clear.

Samuel waited patiently, but the king's invitation was long delayed. Samuel felt a bit guilty that he hadn't been able to fulfill his promise to Jonathan, but he also knew that he could not press the king. He was sure that an uninvited visit to Saul would doom any possibility of success for his appeal.

He sent a message to Jonathan explaining the reason for his delay in visiting the king, and he received an immediate reply of understanding from the young prince.

One day a courier trumpeted the news in Ramah that a dedication service was planned for Prince Jonathan as captain of one thousand men of the royal army. The courier added that Jonathan and his men would remain at Gibeah, and Saul and Abner and the other two thousand men of the royal army would move back to Gilgal. Samuel made plans to attend the ceremony at Gibeah.

The army was already performing for the crowd when Samuel arrived, and the people were cheering lustily. The aged priest tried his best to be inconspicuous, but he was too prominent a public figure to remain unnoticed. Soon, a servant of the king sought him out and invited him to sit with the royal family.

Samuel hadn't visited the royal family for many years, and he was surprised to see how the family had increased. Besides Jonathan, there were two younger sons and two daughters. They were all very courteous and well behaved, which spoke highly of their mother's training.

Samuel noticed particularly how enthusiastic the boys were about the antics of the troops. He divined that these two would not have the pain that their older brother, Jonathan, experienced in choosing the military over the pastoral as a career. They would be ready as soon as their age would allow them to take up arms for their country.

The king was very congenial as he visited with Samuel, although he seemed a bit defensive. "I am very sorry that I have not yet scheduled the visit that you requested, but . . ." he spread his hands expressively, "there has been such a rash of national problems and enemy incursions lately that I have spent most of my time in the field." He looked to Samuel for understanding.

Samuel nodded. "Yes, I have heard that the Philistines have been quite bold of late, and there are rumors that they are considering a major war with Israel in the near future. Have you made preparation for meeting such a challenge?"

Saul's face darkened, and he answered rather sharply. "As I mentioned to you, our army has been harassing their garrisons and driving them back from our borders. Now, I am beginning a new strategy. I am leaving Jonathan here in Gibeah with one thousand troops, and Captain Abner and I will move to Gilgal with the remaining two thousand. We will be able to cover more territory and demonstrate greater strength. Perhaps the enemy will change their mind about waging war with us."

"Yes, hopefully, that will be the case." Samuel agreed.

Samuel watched with interest as Prince Jonathan demonstrated his skill on the field. It was evident that he had been a good student, since he carried out his part in the public displays flawlessly and with flair. He was a dashing figure on the field, and Samuel was quite sure that the hearts of many of the maidens present beat a bit faster as they watched him.

The king personally took charge of the installation service, and since it was father and son, the service was a special delight to the crowd, and Jonathan took his place at the head of an army of one thousand men.

Samuel had been asked by the king to have the prayer of dedication, and then he was privileged to congratulate the young army captain. Jonathan cast aside his rigid military bearing when Samuel came by, and he clasped the aged priest to his breast. It was obvious that he loved and respected this eminent sage of Israel.

Over the next few months, Samuel heard good reports from Jonathan's army camp. The prince had carried out successful raids against the Philistine outposts and had corrected the evil practice of Captain Abner and the king regarding the spoil that was taken in these incursions. Now, the large share was dedicated to the Lord before the men were treated. Samuel was pleased. No reports came out of the camp at Gilgal, and Samuel wondered if the King and Abner were expecting Jonathan to keep the enemy at bay.

Then one morning a courier brought an urgent message from the king, requesting a visit from Samuel within seven days. The reason given for the request was that a large Philistine army was on the move to Michmash with the intention of attacking Israel. Samuel was asked to bring divine instructions with him as to how to deal with such a large enemy force.

Samuel remembered his conversation with Saul at the time of Jonathan's installation as army captain. He had specifically asked the king if he was making preparation to deal with a large Philistine army that was rumored to be preparing to march to Michmash. Saul had showed anger as if he considered the question impertinent. Then he replied that he believed the raids Jonathan and Abner would wage against the enemy outposts would discourage the pagans from planning an all out war. Evidently Saul now realized that he had underestimated the pagans.

Samuel immediately made plans to visit the King at Gilgal within seven days. He petitioned the Lord earnestly for the next five days for word to take to the king, but the Lord was silent. Then the night before he was to leave for Gilgal, the Lord came to him.

"Samuel," the voice said. "You will be greatly disappointed when you meet with Saul tomorrow at Gilgal. You will find a disobedient man. Instead of asking you or Ahijah to seek my counsel in regard to the Philistines, he will have grown impatient and willfully offered an unlawful sacrifice himself. I cannot allow this sin in the supreme leader of my people.

"Therefore, Samuel, you will deliver a message to him from Me that I have rejected him as king. He will not have a successor. Tell him that I have chosen someone else to take his place—a man after my own heart. I will reveal that person in due time."

Samuel was crushed. "But Lord," he protested, "couldn't You give him another chance? He has done many things that have helped our people."

"Samuel," the Lord said again, "Saul has disappointed Me in many ways, some that you are not aware of. So you must trust Me when I determine that he is not the right man to rule Israel."

Samuel was repentant, and he fell on his face before the Lord. "Yes, Lord, I do trust You. I know that You are always right, but Lord, what about the young prince, Jonathan? He is such a wonderful person and would make a good king."

The Lord answered. "Samuel, you have spoken well. Jonathan has pleased My heart, but he will not be king, and he will accept the rejection with grace. Samuel, I know that it will be difficult for you to deliver My message to Saul and Jonathan tomorrow. The young man will also be present, but I will give you special grace and strength for the occasion."

Samuel felt the immediate presence of the Lord leave the area, unlike other times when the aura remained.

The next day Samuel met Saul at Gilgal and delivered the message from God to the guilty king. He saw the evidences of the king's guilt, the crude altar and the fresh ashes of the sacrifice, and he was convinced of the Lord's proper judgment. He also saw the large host of Philistines across the gorge and the discouraged group of Israelite soldiers. He wondered momentarily what plan the Lord had in mind for dealing with these pagans.

*Surely*, he reasoned, *God will not allow these heathens to take control of the country of Israel as they did at the death of Eli.*

However, God had not revealed to Samuel His plans for stopping the Philistines. One thing Samuel did know is that God had not forgotten His people.

Samuel saw Jonathan standing straight and tall in front of his troops. He wanted so much to reach out to the prince, but he refrained.

His work was over, so he returned to Gibeah.

The next day a messenger came from the battlefield at Michmash with the announcement that the Lord had used Prince Jonathan and his armor bearer to destroy the Philistine army. The herald said, with a flourish, that the pagans had been chased all the way to Ajalon and many thousands had been slain. There was great rejoicing in the city of Ramah. Samuel was so glad for Jonathan that he wanted to call him to Ramah immediately to congratulate him, but the Lord restrained him.

"Samuel," He said. "I know how much you love Jonathan, and you must realize that I also love him, but I have a special work for him to do, and he must be severely tested in the preparation. He is a son of his mother and thus is spiritually inclined. He is also a humble man, which is very essential for the part I have for him, but he is young and needs more trial by fire. I will make sure that he is not hurt in the process."

Samuel sank back on his bed, satisfied with the Lord's statement.

The victory at Michmash, although not attributable to Saul, appeared to renew the king. He began to attack his enemies on all sides with vigor. He fought against Moab, the Ammonites, the kings of Zobab, and Edom, and of course, against the Philistines. Everywhere he turned he was successful in war, and his enemies were troubled. He searched for good men in Israel and built up a much larger army than he had at Michmash.

One night the Lord appeared to Samuel with a message that surprised the aged priest, but it also pleased him. God was again noticing Saul.

"Samuel," the Lord said. "The Amalekites have filled up their cup of iniquity. They fought against My chosen people when they were on their way to this land, and they have been a thorn in the side of Israel since that day, so I have committed them to complete destruction. I am sending you to Saul with a message that he is to wage war immediately against these enemies. He is not to save anyone, man, woman, or child. Neither is he to take any spoil from them. He must destroy all of their animals and their goods, including their wealth. There are to be no exceptions."

Samuel met Saul at Gibeah. His heart was light, and his hopes were high for the king and Jonathan. This was a pleasant task.

The king greeted him with reservation, but when he heard the assignment from the Lord, he relaxed. "Blessed are you from the Lord," he cried. "I will carry out the Lord's wishes with dispatch."

Jonathan was with his father when Samuel visited, and he was extremely pleased with the divine mandate. Saul sent messengers throughout Israel asking for volunteers to join him in this war against Amalek. Two hundred and ten thousand men from Israel and Judah joined him at Telaim.

Saul demonstrated his brilliant military skill against the Amalekites, and when the battle was over, not a man, woman, or child remained alive except for King Agag. Also, the best of the stock and goods were kept for the benefit of the army. Jonathan protested against this blatant disobedience against the Lord's command, but his appeal was ignored.

Samuel was preparing to retire for the night when the Lord came to him.

"Samuel," the Lord called. "I greatly regret that I have set up Saul as king over Israel. I gave him another chance as you requested, and he has disobeyed Me even worse that before. He is a willful man, and I cannot trust him to carry out My will. You must visit him tomorrow without fail and give him My final message."

Samuel fell on his knees before the Lord and cried out in prayer the entire night. Then he arose, dried his eyes, and, without further rest, went to find Saul. He soon found that the guilty king had gone to Carmel where he set up a monument to himself to commemorate his victory over the Amalekites. Then he had bypassed Ramah and gone on to Gilgal with his unholy property.

Samuel met him at Gilgal. The king came out to meet Samuel with a smile and a greeting. "Blessed are you of the Lord! I have performed the commandment of the Lord." Samuel was amazed that the king was so callous that he could utter such blasphemy.

The priest spoke slowly and deliberately. "If you have performed the Lord's commandment, what then is the meaning of the bleating of the sheep and the lowing of the oxen that I hear?"

Saul spread his hands. "The people insisted that we save the best of the oxen and of the sheep to sacrifice to the Lord, but . . ." he added lamely, "the rest of the stock we have destroyed completely as the Lord directed."

Samuel was silent for a few moments; then he spoke tersely. "Be quiet now, and I will tell you what the Lord said to me last night."

The king remained quiet with bowed head.

"The Lord said, 'When Saul was little in his own eyes, I took him and made him ruler over all of the tribes of Israel and anointed him king.' Now the Lord sent you on a mission to destroy all of the Amalekites. You were not to spare man, woman, or child, and you were not to take one item of plunder. You were to destroy everything!

"Now tell me, why didn't you obey the command of the Lord? Why did you think it was right to reserve a portion of the spoil?"

Samuel paused and looked to Saul for an answer.

"I have obeyed the voice of the Lord," Saul explained. "I utterly destroyed the Amalekites. I saved King Agag for a short time as a trophy, but I will do away with him soon. It was the people that took a part of the loot that should have been destroyed."

Samuel looked at the king intently for a few moments. "Listen to the Lord's decision," he commanded. "I do not accept burnt offerings and sacrifice in place of obedience. To obey is always better than sacrifice. Rebellion against Me is as the sin of witchcraft and stubbornness is as iniquity and idolatry. Because you have rejected the word of the Lord, He also has rejected you from being king."

When Samuel finished, Saul fell to his knees before the priest." I have sinned," he finally admitted. "I have transgressed the commandment of the Lord because I feared the people. Now please forgive me and return with me that I may worship the Lord."

Samuel's face was set. "I will not return with you," he stated firmly. "You rejected the Lord, and He has rejected you as king."

Samuel turned to go, but Saul caught the edge of his robe and it tore in his hand.

"Just as you have now torn my robe, God has torn the kingdom from you and given it to a man who is better than you," Samuel said. "I will return and worship with you, but this is the last."

Samuel remembered Agag. "Bring Agag to me," he ordered.

Samuel hacked the evil king to pieces before the Lord. Then he worshipped with Saul and returned to Ramah.

Samuel mourned for Saul and especially for Jonathan until the night God came to him again.

"Samuel, how long are you going to mourn for Saul, seeing that I have rejected him as king over Israel?" God chided him. "Rise and take off your robe of mourning, for I have a special task for you to do."

Samuel spoke. "Yes, Lord, I will cease my mourning for Saul if that is your will, for I do not want to offend You."

"You haven't offended Me," the Lord said. "I too have mourned for Saul, but I can no longer trust him."

Samuel dared to answer Him. "Lord, could you give him one more chance for the sake of his devoted son Jonathan. If Saul is rejected while he is still on the throne it would mean that the son would not succeed him. As I have said to You before, Jonathan is such a wonderful young man and would make a good king.

"Now, I know that you have told me that you have a work for him to do other than being king, so I will bow to your decision, but I wanted You to know what was on my heart."

"Samuel, you must trust Me. I have great confidence in Jonathan. He is truly a model of piety and loyalty, but I must repeat: I have a special work for him to do, but it is not as king. I have chosen someone else to be Saul's successor.

"Tomorrow morning you must fill your horn with oil and go to Bethlehem to the home of Jesse. You must anoint one of his sons to be king over Israel, and I will point out to you the one I have chosen."

Samuel sat up in his bed. He was trembling, and his heart was beating wildly. "But Lord," he protested, "if I anoint someone else to be king, Saul will surely hear about it and will kill me. Since I have told him twice now that You have chosen someone else to take his place on the throne, he will surely monitor my travels. Probably he will have spies observing my contacts with those who might replace him. So, Lord, You will surely be sending me to my death by this assignment."

Samuel could feel a hand touching his shoulder, and the voice was tender. "Trust Me, Samuel. I care for you very much and would certainly not send you to your death deliberately. But I do need you to go for Me.

"I have a plan. Take a heifer with you to Bethlehem and invite the city elders and Jesse and his family to attend a sacrifice to the Lord. Then you must listen carefully for My voice, and I will name for you the one who is to be anointed."

The next day Samuel journeyed to Bethlehem, and he invited the elders of the town and the family of Jesse to attend a sacrifice to the Lord. It had been many years since Samuel had visited Bethlehem, and at first the elders of the city trembled with fear that he would call them to account for some public sin, but when he invited them to a sacrifice, they relaxed.

Some thought it strange that Samuel asked Jesse to bring his sons before him, but Jesse was pleased to obey. The sons were all handsome and hardy, and Samuel thought that any of them would make a good king, but God cautioned him as the sons passed by. "Don't look on the outward appearance, Samuel, for I have rejected each of these seven. Man looks on the outward appearance but I look on the heart."

Samuel was troubled. The Lord had rejected them all, and Jesse had made no move to bring any other sons to the priest's attention. But God spoke to Samuel. "There is another son. Ask Jesse to bring him to you."

Samuel's face brightened. "Jesse, do you have other sons besides these?"

"Yes," the Bethlehemite answered. "There is the youngest. He is tending the sheep."

"Please send for him immediately," Samuel directed.

When the young man, David, was brought before him, Samuel knew immediately that this was the chosen of the Lord. He was handsome and clear-eyed, and he had an aura of spiritual power about him.

"Arise and anoint him," the Lord ordered. "He is the one I have chosen to be the next king of Israel."

Samuel was getting feeble. He could no longer make his judicial trips to Bethel, Gilgal, and Mizpah, and his work at Ramah was greatly reduced.

His aged heart was saddened by the news of Saul's dementia and cheered by the report of the bonding of Jonathan and David.

Later, when Saul harassed David from place to place, Samuel realized what God had in mind for Jonathan. He became the intermediator between his father and David. He had the loyalty of both, and David was spared several times by the intervention of the prince.

Samuel's work was done, and he died at Ramah. The king declared a time of mourning for the saint of Israel, and the people mourned. Many were constrained to say, "Would to God we had not rejected him in favor of a king."

He was buried beside his beloved wife, Belah, at Ramah.

A Christian writer of yesteryear commented on the life of Samuel. "A life consecrated as was Samuel's is of great value in God's sight."

# JONATHAN'S HEART

## INTRODUCTION

I have a treasured book in my library that features a brief biography of twenty-six Bible characters. The list is very diverse. It includes Ezekiel, Noah, Moses, and Job, among others, and even the renegades Balaam and Judas.

On the first page of a very concise introduction, the author makes the statement, "In the Old Testament I chose Jonathan as the ideal." But in the total list of the twenty-six characters, he never again mentions the name of Jonathan.

That seems to be the manner in which most religious writers view Jonathan. He is a model of love, faith, humility, and loyalty, and yet, he is not worthy of a full biographical sketch.

Even the Apostle Paul omits the name of Jonathan in his list of Hebrew worthies of faith. He does mention the harlot Rahab, the weak-spined Samson, the skeptic Gideon, and the foolish Jephthah, and they are worthy of mention, but Jonathan stands out above them all.

Paul does, however, allude to Jonathan in a generic fashion: he "became valiant in battle, turned to flight the armies of the aliens." (NKVJ, Heb. 11:34)

That's precisely what Jonathan did at Michmash. He ignored the overwhelming advantage of the enemy in terms of physical numbers and with the ringing assurance—"for nothing restrains the Lord from saving by many or by few"—resonating there in the valley, he and his armor bearer routed the great host of the pagans and won a signal victory for the Lord of hosts and for Israel.

He refused to rebel against the Lord in behalf of his legitimate succession to the kingship of Israel. Instead, he gladly gave the tokens of his position as prince and his love and loyalty to his friend David. Yet, he never abandoned his father. He was early bereaved of the love of his life, Zereth, and also his own life. However, he died in the assurance of eternal life spiritually.

**JONATHAN'S HEART**

# CHAPTER 1

Saul tiptoed around in the darkness hoping not to awaken his sleeping wife, Ahinoam. He knew exactly where every piece of furniture was located in the medium-sized room, but he still managed to stub a toe and bruise a knee in the search for his clothes and the provisions for his trip.

As he closed the door silently behind him, his heart twisted in pain. He imagined the disappointment of his dear wife when she awakened and found his bed empty. She would weep quietly for a time; then she would accept his decision and forgive him. That was her nature. She would never chide him when he returned.

*But,* he reasoned, *this time I really should have made a different decision.*

He had promised her repeatedly that he would be with her for the birth of their first child, and he was reneging on his promise. The reason for his absence was simply to find two of his father's donkeys that had strayed away.

This wasn't the first time Saul had chosen to break a promise to his wife in favor of pleasing his father. In fact, the times of denying Ahinoam's claims had multiplied in the past few months. There were two noxious reasons for his sin.

Saul worked for his father, Kish, who was a very wealthy farmer with vast properties, many herds of cattle, sheep, and donkeys, and a large number of servants. Saul was a very diligent worker, but he was inept in the handling of finances. Thus, through the years, he had incurred a massive indebtedness to his father, and now his father owned him as an adult. So Saul had to choose his father's wishes over those of his wife.

The second reason was even more odious. Saul was not monogamous. Over the objections of his wife, he had taken several concubines soon after his marriage to Ahinoam, and several times he had preferred these libertine women rather than his primary wife.

The night after Saul left to find his father's donkeys, Ahinoam's labor pains began. As the hours passed, the pains increased in intensity, so she sent her maid to call the midwife. The practitioner came quickly.

The midwife was a veteran, so she was very methodical. At the time she had no idea that she was delivering the future prince of Israel. But had she been privy to this fact, it probably would have made little difference in her procedure and attitude. She had assisted in the birthing of scores of Israelite babies, and to her mind, they were all the same, miniature globs of messy, squalling human flesh. There was no beauty or appeal in the entire lot of them.

Her actions were automatic. She pulled the baby from the vaginal canal, cut the umbilical cord, cleaned his clogged air ducts, and slapped the little fellow on his bottom until he began to protest. Then she washed his body with a wet cloth rubbed in aromatic oils, wrapped him in a blanket, and placed him in the arms of his new mother.

At that moment a drastic change occurred in the perspective of this new life. The little body that had been nameless and unimportant to the midwife became an object of value and beauty in the eyes of Ahinoam. She hugged the little body, looked into the red, wrinkled face of her newborn son, and exclaimed, "I will call him Jonathan for Jehovah has given him to me."

Jonathan was scarcely a week old when Samuel secretly anointed his father, Saul, as king over Israel at Ramah. Then a few days later, Samuel called all Israel together at Mizpah and introduced Saul to the people as their new king.

As Saul became the first king of the nation, baby Jonathan became the first prince and successor to the throne. It is possible that Saul was the only man in all Israel who would have satisfied the people as their king. They had heard the stories handed down from their fathers about the kings of the pagan people that opposed the Israelites on their way from Egypt to Canaan—kings such as Og, king of Bashan and Sihon, king of the Amorites. These men were giant sons of Anak.

The people also desired a physical giant to lead them in their military conquests, and Saul was the largest man in all of Israel. When Samuel introduced Saul to the people at Mizpah, he stressed the fact of Saul's size. As the anointed king stood among them, Samuel said, "Do you see him whom the Lord has chosen? There is no one like him among all the people."

As the people looked at the new king standing head and shoulders above them, they shouted, "Long live the king."

Saul was anointed king by Samuel at Ramah and proclaimed king to the people at Mizpah, but it wasn't until after his masterful victory over the Ammonites at Bezek that he was officially installed King at Gilgal. Once again, the people cried out, "Long live the king."

The new king disassociated himself from his father's farm, and as a thank offering for his son's elevation to the kingship of Israel, Kish forgave all of Saul's indebtedness. It lifted a heavy load from the shoulders of the new king.

As soon as Saul arrived back at Gibeah of Benjamin, he gave orders for a palace to be built at Gibeah for the royal family. At the present time, only the king, Queen Ahinoam, and Prince Jonathan comprised the royal family. Later, there were two daughters, Merab and Michal, and two more sons, Abinadab and Malchishua.

The palace, or castle as some referred to it, was more functional than ornate, which pleased the people. The walls were six to eight feet thick, which gave good protection from enemy siege, and there were large iron gates. The largest room was the throne room where Saul held court and entertained with state dinners. There were comfortable quarters for the royal family and many rooms for guests. It was interesting that soon after the palace was finished, Saul moved with his army to Gilgal and lived in a tent.

Growing up royalty is a very difficult experience for anyone, and Jonathan was not an exception. Although he was, by nature, modest and unassuming, the attention and adoration of the servants, court attendants, and palace guards at times resulted in the display of poor manners and attitude. But his mother, Ahinoam, was patient and consistent with her son's spiritual training, and Jonathan was a good listener and student.

"Come, Jonathan, it's time for your story," she would call him as he worked at his morning chores or played with his friends at midday. There was also a story and prayer at bedtime. His mother followed a curriculum of spiritual education that Jehovah had delivered to Israel during the Exodus from Egypt. Moses, the great leader and prophet, had recorded the rules of time and content for the Israelite parents to follow.

"You shall love the Lord your God with all your heart, and all your soul, and with all your might. And these words that I command you today shall be in your heart; you shall teach them diligently to your children and shall talk of them when you sit in your home, when you walk by the way, when you lie down, and when you rise up. You shall bind them as a sign on your hands, and they shall be as frontlets between your eyes. You shall write them on the door posts of your house and on your gates." Ahinoam had written this divine instruction on a slate, and little Jonathan memorized it.

Jonathan loved the stories his mother told him about the miracles God performed for their relatives when they were traveling from Egypt to Canaan. His favorite was the crossing of the Red Sea without a boat or ship. Ahinoam would act out this miracle, and he would clap his hands and shout with glee.

Later, Jonathan would dramatize the miracle for the benefit of his playmates. He had a vivid imagination and a knack for performing, so the children would gather around him expectantly.

"Our distant relatives had been slaves in Egypt for hundreds of years," he began, and the children drew in their breath. "But one day God said, 'Moses, take my people out of Egypt and lead them to the land of Canaan.' That's where we are now. So they all started out. There were so many of them and most were walking. Some mothers had babies and children like us. "They soon came to the big Red Sea, and they couldn't get across to the other side. It was wide and deep, and they didn't have any boats or ships. Then they looked back and saw a big Egyptian army coming to get them and take them back to Egypt." The children gasped and their eyes widened.

"But the Egyptians couldn't see our people because God had brought a big cloud clear down from the sky to the ground between the Egyptians and our people." The children cheered and clapped.

Now, Jonathan assumed a perplexed look. "But how were they going to get across that big sea?"

The children shook their heads and Jonathan waxed dramatic. He knelt and placed his hands together. "Moses prayed to the Lord, and the Lord sent a strong wind to blow on the sea, and soon the water in front of the people divided and made a road through the middle of the sea. There were big walls of water on both sides, and the bottom wasn't muddy. The people cheered and thanked the Lord. Then everybody started across the sea. There were a lot of rocks on the bottom, but no one stubbed their toes." Some of the children looked down at their bandaged toes.

"The children and older people would touch the walls of water, and they didn't get their hands wet." Jonathan would act as though he were touching a wall of water and then would show his dry hands to the wide-eyed children.

"When the people all reached the other side of the sea, they looked back and saw the Egyptians coming into the sea, and all the people wondered how God would deliver them from the Egyptians. But do you know what happened?" The children shook their heads in wonderment.

"Well, God waited until all of the Egyptians and their horses and chariots were in the middle of the sea, and then the wheels started coming off of their chariots and their horses became lame. The Egyptians became afraid. They tried to go back the way they came, but God turned the water loose, and all of the Egyptians were drowned. Not one of them got back to Egypt." Tears coursed down the cheeks of several of the children for their hearts were tender. Jonathan's eyes were also misty.

Jonathan loved to visit his paternal grandparents, Kish and Noona, at Zelah. His grandfather was a wealthy landowner with thousands of sheep, goats, cattle, and donkeys roaming the fields and plains. Dozens of servants cared for the large flocks, while many others tilled the fields of grain and vegetables.

Jonathan knew that his father had been born on this farm and had worked for his father, Kish, until he became king. In fact, Saul had been away from home looking for two of Kish's lost donkeys when Jonathan was born.

As Jonathan roamed his grandfather's properties, he would dream of the day when he would have his own holdings with large flocks and herds and many servants. His childish mind envisioned even greater vistas than those of his grandfather; in fact, his empire would be the largest in all of Israel.

Several times his dreams suffered some downsizing due to experiences with the herd of goats. There was a very mean male goat in one of the herds that the shepherds had named Satan. He was certainly well named because of his disposition, and he was the undisputed leader of the herd. The servants always guarded the prince carefully when they were in the area where Satan was grazing. But one day Jonathan got out of the cart to pet one of the baby kids, and the male goat took advantage of Jonathan's posture. The goat came running and butted the lad squarely in the buttocks, and Jonathan tumbled head over heels. The outlaw didn't follow up on his success or the prince could have suffered serious hurt. The herders rescued Jonathan and drove the goat away.

A few days later, Jonathan asked for the privilege of milking one of the older nanny goats that the herders claimed was the tamest goat in the entire herd. Jonathan started out eagerly on his new task, but he quickly ran into trouble. He didn't understand the proper procedure for drawing the milk from the udder, and the goat became irritated over his ineptness. She began to move about in her stall and managed to step on one of his toes. Then to add insult to injury she stepped in the partially filled pail of milk. Jonathan was so ashamed with his failure that he slapped the nanny on her rump, and she retaliated by kicking him. His vision of a large goat flock for his storybook farm was dimming rapidly.

The event that dealt a blow to his childish plan for thousands of goats was a death of a young kid that the herders had been doctoring for several weeks, and Jonathan had joined them during his visits. In only a few days, he became so emotionally attached to the frail little creature that he cried unashamedly when it died. He demanded that the little body be buried with honors.

The prince decided that he would leave the raising of goats to others, and he would add a few more sheep to his flocks to compensate for the absence of goats. He reasoned that he had always liked sheep better than goats anyway. His mother was mainly responsible for his preference. In her stories she had recited that a lamb was a symbol of the Redeemer who would come sometime in the future to save the world. She also reminded the prince that Moses had become the most humble man on earth mainly because of the patience he had developed when caring for his flocks of sheep.

One day Jonathan went to his grandfather, Kish, with a request. "Grandfather, may I work for you so that I can buy one of your lambs? I want to be a humble man like Moses."

Kish stifled a laugh. His grandson was deeply in earnest, and he didn't want to make fun of his childish sincerity. "Jonathan, I will give you a lamb if you will promise to care for it faithfully. You will find that sometimes you would like to be at play, but you will have to feed the lamb. You will need to clean up after it and clean its fleece. Also you must remember that Moses cared for his flocks for forty years, so he cared for many little lambs and their mothers. Are you sure that you want a lamb to care for?"

"Yes, Grandfather, I do want a lamb. I will promise to be faithful in caring for it. But I don't want you to give me a lamb as a gift; I want to work for it. I'm strong now so I can work hard." Jonathan flexed his muscles to prove how strong he was.

"All right," Kish conceded. "I can see that you are strong for your age, so I will tell my supervisor, Ahmed, to give you some work to do. He will tell you when you have earned enough to pay for a lamb. You may have your choice from the flocks. Does that sound fair to you?"

"Oh yes, I like that. When can I start?"

So Jonathan bought a little lamb and brought it home. He cared for it faithfully and tenderly even when his friends were at play.

As Jonathan grew older, his dreams of great farms and herds began to be replaced by visions of a place in the king's army. It wasn't the thoughts of heroism and great exploits that directed his interest toward a career in his father's army, for his tender heart revolted at the thought of taking life.

An experience he had suffered when he was only ten years old made him very sensitive to the value of every form of life. And for a time after this experience, the thought of army life became repulsive.

He was playing with a group of boys who loved to hunt birds and small game. They had crude homemade weapons such as bows and arrows and slings with which they were quite proficient, and they usually came home with small animals and birds. Jonathan had become quite skillful in the use of the sling, but his usual targets were tree limbs and fence posts.

Today, however, he reluctantly entered into the spirit of the hunt. He took aim at a bird that had just lighted in a bush, and his aim was true. The bird fell dead. When he reached the place to claim his prize, however, he found that he had killed a mother bird that was in the act of feeding her nestlings. He reached down and picked up the little body, but his heart was sick. He immediately excused himself and left for home, but it seemed that the hungry cheep of the little orphaned birds followed him all the way. He took a shovel from a shed and buried the mother bird along with his bow and arrows and sling.

Ahinoam could sense that there was something very heavy on the heart of her little son. "Jonathan, come and sit on my knee and tell me what it is that is troubling you."

Jonathan's eyes were very teary as he told of his sin. "Mother, I did something terrible today. I killed a little mother bird as she was feeding her nestlings. I am so sorry. Do you think God will forgive me?" He turned his misty eyes to his mother.

Ahinoam patted her penitent son on his head, "Yes, son, God will forgive you, but He is also sad for the untimely death of this little mother bird. We must think about those little baby birds that have been orphaned. You should take a basket, line it with cloth, then take those little birds from their nest, and bring them to the house. You will feed and water them by hand until they can fly. Are you willing to do that?"

The prince nodded eagerly. "Oh yes, Mother, I will be glad to feed those orphaned little birds, and perhaps they will become pets." He hesitated. "Mother, I buried the little mother bird along with my bow and arrows and sling. I promised God that I wouldn't kill anymore of his little creatures."

Tears welled up in the eyes of Ahinoam as she hugged her precious son to her breast. "God will be glad for your promise, Jonathan, and He will smile and nod His head as you feed those little birds."

The experience with the mother bird and her nestlings took some of the edge off of Jonathan's desire to become a member of the king's army. But as he continued to visit his father at court and mingle with the troops as they jousted and came in from battles, he felt a need, even as a child, to help correct some of the wrongs that he could see.

One of the evils he had noticed was the practice of the king regarding the spoils of war. His mother had impressed on his mind that all credit for victories in battle should be given to the Lord and the greater part of the plunder should also be dedicated to Him. But Jonathan noticed that his father and Captain Abner chose to keep the primary part of the spoils for their own use and also allowed the troops to take liberal portions. Very little was left as an offering for the Lord.

The prince pondered over this habit on the part of the king, and later he spoke out against it. "Father, is it true that the Lord gives you success in your battles against the enemies of our people?"

The king thought on this question from his firstborn for a few moments before answering.

"Well, son," he responded. "The Lord does favor us in battle since we are His chosen people, but He expects us to be well prepared and very aggressive in the war against our enemies. What did you have in mind, Jonathan?"

The prince hesitated for a moment; then spoke what was on his heart. "Since the Lord favors us and gives us special wisdom in battle, shouldn't He be the one to receive the first part of the spoils of war rather than the troops and yourself?"

The king's face reddened and the muscles around his mouth began to twitch. "Who gave you that idea?" he snapped with venom in his voice.

"Mother did," Jonathan admitted frankly. "She reminds me often that God should always be first in our gifts, but I noticed that you gave Him only what was left."

"You are an impertinent lad," the king observed heatedly. "And your mother is a nosy old woman. Don't ever mention this subject to me again. Do you understand?"

"Yes, Father," Jonathan said meekly. "I am sorry to make you angry."

Jonathan had reached a very important milestone in his young life. He had just celebrated his twentieth birthday, and it was now time for him to decide on his life's occupation. His heart was torn as he pondered the choices.

He had never lost the desire to be a landowner and merchant like his grandfather, Kish. His interest had sometimes waned because of the experiences he had suffered, but the dream had not disappeared. The fields and flocks still excited him and the thought of riches and power always made his heart beat faster. He knew that his mother prayed and hoped for him to choose the pastoral life, and he always liked to please her, but the king's army had a stronger claim on the loyalties of his heart.

He was the prince of Israel and the successor to his father, the king. Thus the protection of his people, Israel, from the pagans that surrounded them weighed heavily on his heart. For some time now, the press of national business had occupied the majority of the king's time, and thus, the army had been inactive. Abner should have led the troops in raids against the Philistine garrisons, but he was not an aggressive man, and he dallied with the rest of the army. As a result, the Philistines had become more aggressive against the border towns of Israel. They plundered the herds and flocks and even killed some of the herders. It was evident that offensive measures must be planned against them or they would soon take over the border towns.

There were also the evils in the army that needed correction. The king and Abner both were party to these malignant offenses rather than opposing them, so Jonathan chose a career in the army against the wishes of his own heart. Jonathan dreaded the visit with his mother to tell her of his choice. He knew that she would weep for a time before accepting his decision as the best for his life. He was right in his assumption. She wept for only a minute then faced her firstborn son.

"Jonathan," she said through her tears, "I felt that you would choose to serve in the army rather than deciding on a pastoral career, but my heart is quite at peace because I know that your decision was not based on a desire to make war. You have such a tender heart, my son, and army life will be very difficult for you at times. The army is a killer implement. You will leave widows and orphans in your wake and some young men like yourself will be crippled for life. You might be a casualty of war, and that would break my heart.

"Now Jonathan, you are a born leader of men, and one day you will be promoted to be a captain of your own regiment. Then you will be personally responsible for spiritual leadership of your men. You must lean heavily on the Lord, consult Him for every major decision that you will need to make. Do not neglect your daily devotions with Him. The Spirit of the Lord in your heart will give you compassion to those who will be innocent victims of your battles. And son, I pray that one day soon you will choose a godly wife from among our people who will share your love for Jehovah and His law."

Ahinoam arose then and clasped Jonathan to her breast. Then she prayed for him through her tears. She was a small lady, and the prince was a large man, but she held her firstborn as she had when he sat on her knee.

It was initiation time for the new recruit. "Foot soldier Jonathan, step forward two paces," Captain Abner ordered. Jonathan broke rank from the army lineup and quickly stepped forward two paces. The captain looked the new recruit over slowly and deliberately from head to toe as though he was seeing the prince for the first time.

Actually, Abner and Jonathan were related. Abner's father, Ner, and Saul's father, Kish, were brothers, so the prince was a nephew to Abner. Abner had known Jonathan since his birth.

"Foot soldier Jonathan," Abner repeated. Jonathan knew the captain enjoyed rolling the phrase, "foot soldier Jonathan," over his tongue. It fed the ego of the veteran army man, since he was now superior to the prince of Israel and could order him around at will. Jonathan brought his thoughts quickly under control because Abner was still speaking.

"I must remind you that since you are now a foot soldier in the king's army your relationship to royalty will not count in this company. You will be treated as all of the other soldiers are treated. You will sleep in tents with your army mates, eat at their table, march with them, and fight side by side with them in battle. Your times of leave from your duties will be of the same duration and subject to the same rules as apply to all of the men. You will be expected to stand for inspection morning and evening, and you must be on time every time. Any infraction of the rules will result in either time in the guardhouse or lashes at the stake. The type of punishment and the degree will be determined by a panel of your peers that have been chosen by army administration. Serious infractions will become a part of your army record."

The captain paused for a few moments as though he was trying to think up another regulation to put on the new recruit. Then he said officiously, "Foot soldier Jonathan, do you have any questions?"

Jonathan looked his uncle in the eye and said clearly, "No, I do not."

"Very well, you may return to your former position."

Jonathan stepped back in line and bowed slightly. He was now officially in the army. He was glad for the decision he had made.

The prediction made by Jonathan's mother that Jonathan would one day be the captain of an army regiment was fulfilled two years after his enlistment as a foot soldier in the king's army.

It was the moment and the position that Jonathan had been expecting for some time now, but he wondered if he was really ready for such a big task. During his two years of service, he had seen so many evils in the ranks that the King and Abner had tolerated and even encouraged. Now he would be inheriting these practices, and he felt momentarily overwhelmed. His only hope was that God would give him wisdom and strength to meet the challenge.

Jonathan's installation was a royal pageant. The troops were dressed in their best and, of course, were on their best behavior. Many of the citizens from the city and surrounding areas were present. Jonathan's mother, brothers, and sisters were there, and a special citizen of Gibeah of Benjamin whom Jonathan would meet and fall in love with later, was on a front row. She thought the prince looked very handsome and dashing.

As the commission was delivered, Jonathan stood straight and tall before his father, the king. His gaze never wavered. He had learned his army discipline well and had been a model soldier now for two years.

"Foot soldier Jonathan," the king intoned officiously. "I am now presenting you with a commission as a captain in the king's army, and I am assigning you one thousand of our finest troops to be stationed here at Gibeah of Benjamin. You will be totally responsible for the conduct and upkeep of these men. But if for any reason the armies will be combined for a time, you and your men will answer to me. Is that clear?"

"Yes, my lord," Jonathan responded.

"You have proven yourself to be a good soldier. I have noticed, as has Captain Abner, that you are always at the forefront of the troops when in battle but you are never rash. So I am quite certain that the men assigned to you will be pleased to have you as their commander." As the king spoke these words, there was an approving murmur among the army men.

Saul continued. "Captain Jonathan, as the king I speak for our great nation, welcome to your new responsibility in the king's army. You may respond."

"Thank you, my lord," Jonathan stated. "I am greatly humbled by the honor and responsibility you have bestowed upon me. I realize that only by the blessings of our Lord will I be able to fulfill this most important assignment. I will do my best." The prince bowed before the king and the onlookers and returned to his place with the troops.

The two years the prince had spent in the king's army made him painfully aware of the multiple problems he was inheriting from the flawed leadership of his father and Abner.

Abner had been commander of the king's army for several years, but he was not a religious man and was accustomed to leading the troops into battle without divine direction. Jonathan determined that his regiment would have the blessing of the Lord in every incursion. Also, the men assigned to Jonathan would expect a share of the spoils of battle immediately. The king had trained them that way. Jonathan decided that he would meet these challenges to his leadership in due course.

There was a priest of the Lord at Shiloh, Ahijah, the son of Ahitub, Ichabod's brother, the son of Phinehas, the son of Eli, and he was wearing the Ephod. Jonathan had visited with Ahijah on several occasions and found him to always be willing to make inquiry of the Lord for the people of God. Jonathan determined that he would ask the priest to inquire of the Lord before every incursion as to whether this raid would be for the glory of the Lord. The prince was confident that by means of the Urim and Thummim the Lord would answer every request and he would be careful to obey His decisions. If the Lord said no, Jonathan would call off the mission. Most likely, some of the soldiers would question his behavior as an overly pious practice because of their former associations with Abner, but some would welcome this spiritual approach.

It was at the end of the first successful battle of Jonathan's command when a few of the radicals tested his leadership. When the time came to gather up the booty of sheep and oxen and personal belongings, about a score of these men came to Jonathan, and their spokesman stepped forward.

"Captain Jonathan," he spoke in a respectful tone, "we have voted that the spoils be handed over to us so that we can divide them among the men. Of course, you can have your share first. This is the way the king divided the stock and the goods. We believe that this is a fair plan since we fought the enemy for these things."

Jonathan listened respectfully while silently praying to the Lord for wisdom. He nodded to the man as the group stepped back in line. "Thank you for sharing your convictions with me. As some of you are already aware, I do not see eye to eye with the king on this matter. The Lord is the One who has given us this victory; therefore, His share must come first. The best of the stock will be given to the priest to be used for thank offerings. The rest of the stock, along with the personal property, will be put in a general fund, and every man in the regiment will get his share.

"The questionable practice of taking the Lord's share for our own has led to the wrong idea as to why we are at war with our pagan enemies. We are not warring with these heathen neighbors in order to enrich ourselves with their personal properties but rather to drive them out of this territory that Jehovah promised to our fathers many years ago. If they would have obeyed Him and been faithful to Him, He would have driven these people out of this land long before our time, but they failed Him and now these heathen peoples are all around us and continually threatening us. Only with the strength of the Lord can we hope to have success in the war against these enemies, so we must honor Him as our leader in every incursion that we make."

The men in question were surly and pouty for a time but made no other outward show of insubordination at that time. Jonathan was quite sure, however, that this was not the last that he would hear from them.

Jonathan's assessment proved correct. At the very next incursion on a Philistine garrison, while the Prince was tending to other duties, the men who had challenged Jonathan before took some stock and personal property to a hidden location. Evidently, they were certain that their clandestine operation would remain hidden from the captain, but Jonathan's aide gave him the news.

Jonathan made no mention of this breach of an official order as the troops finished their assignment at the battle site and marched back to camp. But as soon as everyone was in place, he called the entire regiment to attention. As he looked over the lineup, he asked the men whom he knew to be the offenders, to step forward two paces. For a few moments, he said nothing, and the men became uneasy.

"Is it true that you," and Jonathan called each man by name, "took part of the spoils in defiance of the order that I gave at our last raid?"

For a few moments, none of the men responded. Then with set jaw, each man confessed. "Yes, I am guilty."

"I'm sorry," the prince said firmly. "I had hoped that all of you men would cooperate, but perhaps I expected too much. Each of you will have to be punished for this infraction. We cannot abide insubordination in our camp. I will offer two choices for your penalty, and you will choose individually. Either you will suffer twenty lashes at the whipping post or you will spend one week of supervised labor. If you choose this latter course, you will spend every night of that week in the guardhouse. An extra ten lashes or an extra week will be added to the punishment if you fail to immediately reveal where you have hidden the booty, and you must have it back in camp by nightfall. Our scribe will record your names and the punishment you choose. The penal officer will administer your punishment and will officially record when your sentence has ended. Since this is your first offense, this indiscretion will not show on your service record."

Most of the men chose the lash, and to the credit of each, they never challenged the order of the commander again. Jonathan's unquestioned fairness with his troops, combined with his undeviating demands for obedience to official orders, made him a favorite with the soldiers. The men also knew that he would never ask the lowest ranking among them to take care of any situation that he himself would be reluctant to do.

Several well-planned raids that Jonathan's regiment waged against the Philistine outposts were disappointing. The prince had hoped to capture some crafted swords and spears to replace the homemade weapons his troops were forced to use. But only two swords and two spears were taken in several raids. The soldiers manning these garrisons had fled at the first sound of trouble, and their weapons went with them.

There was one commodity, however, that was captured that made the men rejoice. Horses were in abundance around these outposts, and soon more than half of Jonathan's army was mounted. They had only a few saddles and bridles and most of the horses were unbroken, but the men had great fun breaking the horses to ride and fashioning rope bridles for them. Several of the men suffered bruises and one broke a finger, but soon the entire herd of horses was carrying a soldier without complaint. The men became adept at riding bareback. Now half of the regiment was able to reach farther into enemy territory than ever before.

Jonathan noticed that the defense of several of the enemy garrisons was weaker than ever before, and he wondered why. His troops completely sacked several outposts and captured much spoil with hardly any resistance. The few defenders fled before the Israelites and left everything but their implements of war.

On the last incursion before Michmash, one of the defender's servants was captured. Jonathan thought to turn him loose but his attitude was so surly and haughty that the prince decided to put him in the guardhouse for a few days.

"Ha," the man spat as he was being led into the prison, "you should turn me loose now, for in a few days none of you will be around to turn the key."

Jonathan stopped him. "What do you have in mind?" he asked.

The prisoner assumed a posture of contempt. "Right now thousands of our soldiers are on their way to Michmash. They will soon crush your armies and take over your country. Then they will turn me loose."

Jonathan was concerned about the prisoner's statement, but he put it out of mind for the moment. He wasn't surprised, however, at what happened next.

# JONATHAN'S HEART

## CHAPTER 2

The courier's horse was dark with sweat, and there were red streaks across the flanks where the rider's spurs had gouged the flesh. It was evident that the messenger had not spared his mount.

The sight of the abused animal raised the hackles of Jonathan, who always cared tenderly for his horses. He thought about giving the man a lecture, but his thoughts were interrupted by a loud shout from the messenger.

"A message from the king for Captain Jonathan," the man cried out before his mount came to a full stop. Jonathan was standing just outside his tent, and he raised his hand. The rider raced over and handed him an official cylinder sealed with the king's seal.

Jonathan unrolled the dispatch quickly and read the cryptic note that had been written by the king's scribe, Pena.

"Captain Jonathan, you are commanded to bring your entire body of troops to Gilgal immediately. The enemy is assembling a large body of troops here to the east of Beth Aven and is threatening to attack at any moment. Do not stop to camp on the way."

There was an official stroke where the king's signature should have been, but since he could neither read nor write, he leaned heavily on his faithful scribe to convey his wishes correctly.

The shout of the courier had aroused most of the men, so Jonathan was able to quickly alert the camp to prepare for travel. Hastily, he wrote a message in reply to his father's order, assuring him that his regiment would arrive in Gilgal posthaste. He gave the dispatch to the courier along with the counsel to spare his horse on the return trip.

Jonathan was concerned about leaving his headquarters in Gibeah of Benjamin so totally vulnerable to attacks by the pagans, especially since his mother, brothers, and sisters were here at the palace at the present time. He reasoned further, however, that possibly the Philistines had reduced every one of their garrisons to caretaker status in order to form the unusually large force that was gathering at Michmash. The thought eased his heart for the moment.

The prince visited briefly with his mother just before his departure. They prayed together as they thought of the dangers that lay ahead.

"Son," Ahinoam admonished him, "be much in prayer and listen carefully for the voice of God. You must also respect and obey the counsel of Samuel, the man of God, for the Lord will surely give him wisdom in this situation."

"I will do that, Mother," he promised as he kissed her good-bye.

It wasn't until Jonathan was well on the road to Michmash that the wisdom of his mother's counsel struck him with full force. She had seen immediately what he had overlooked until now in his rush to get the troops ready for travel. Here he was bringing one thousand troops to join his father's two thousand, while at Beth Aven these few precious souls would face hundreds of thousands of angry pagans in mortal combat. The Philistines would be equipped with professionally crafted swords and spears while the Israelites would fight with crude homemade weapons. As he looked down the lines, he wondered how many would feel so overwhelmed by the odds that they would cut and run.

The reason for the dearth of weapons in Israel was due in part to a flawed decision on the part of the king. After his outstanding victory over the Ammonites at Jabesh Gilead, where he had mustered three hundred and thirty thousand men from Israel and Judah, Saul dismissed all but three thousand of these troops and sent them home with their weapons. The three thousand guards that remained were fully armed, but after years of inactivity, their swords and spears rusted away.

During this period of inertia, the Philistines had infiltrated the land of Israel and carried off all of the blacksmiths. Now the Israelites were ordered to go down to the Philistine outposts to get their plowshares, axes, mattocks, and sickles sharpened, but the Philistines would not allow them to have swords or spears. Jonathan had made frequent incursions against the Philistine garrisons hoping to capture weapons of war, but so far he had garnered mostly stock and provisions and only two swords and spears.

After an all night march, Jonathan's weary legion arrived at Gilgal, across from Michmash. The prince immediately put his army at ease and went to consult with his father. The prince expected the king to have a well-prepared battle plan ready for immediate execution, but he was disappointed. Saul was fretting and in a foul mood and didn't even acknowledge the presence of his son.

After several attempts at conversation without getting a response from the king, Jonathan finally pushed the button that brought a tart answer to his question. "Father, have you consulted the resident priest, Ahijah, regarding the Lord's counsel for dealing with this enemy?"

Saul's eyes were blazing as he turned them on his son. "No, I have not!" he responded through clenched teeth. "And, furthermore, I have no intentions of ever seeking divine advice from that fraud. In fact, I have thought of disrobing him as a priest."

Jonathan was taken aback by his father's venom, but he responded quickly. "I have found Ahijah to be quite accurate in his priestly counsel. Before every incursion our regiment has made into Philistine territory, I have asked

Ahijah to seek the Lord's will for us, and he has always given us true and quick responses."

Saul turned his back on the prince and ignored him. After a few minutes of strained silence between them, Jonathan arose and walked back outside. He thought seriously for a few moments of requesting the counsel of the Lord through Ahijah on his own, but he quickly decided against such a move. With the king in such a surly mood, he would possibly consider such a decision on Jonathan's part insubordination and would probably have him hung on the nearest tree.

The prince took out his glass and scanned the enemy troops camped on the mesa across from the gorge at Michmash. As he looked, his heart sank. It was a much larger group than he had imagined. There were thousands of chariots with their horses and drivers, thousands of cavalry men with their handsome steeds, and the foot soldiers extended far beyond his view. He reasoned for a moment from a human standpoint that the king's cause was a lost one. He shrugged his shoulders helplessly and went to check on his troops. He found his aide in a state of agitation.

"Captain Jonathan," he blurted out, "I am having difficulties with the men. They have noticed that most of the king's troops have already deserted. Some are hiding in the caves, pits, and thickets and others have even gone over to join the enemy. Some of our men want to join with them because they feel that our case is hopeless. I believe that a good talk from you would raise their spirits."

Jonathan's heart went out to this faithful aide who also doubled as his armor bearer. "Nebal, you are right. If you will call the troops to attention, I will speak to them."

Jonathan looked the men over for a few moments as they stood side by side in ranks. He knew every one of these men by name, and he loved each of them, even those who were rascals. Many had families back in Gibeah. He knew that the men were thinking about an impending battle with the immense host of Philistines across the gorge. It would be like fighting a pride of lions with a stick. There could be no future.

He offered a silent prayer before speaking. "Men, I know that you have seen the enemy across the gorge. There are far too many of them for us to fight with swords and spears. We must depend on the God of Israel to fight for us. He has fought our battles many times in the past and has promised help for the present. So we must wait on Him and see what He will do. I understand that many of your peers in the king's army have already deserted. I hope that you will not follow their example. Please stay by and pray, for we have much to lose by playing the coward." He closed with a brief prayer.

Most of the men responded well, and Jonathan was encouraged. The odor of fear was so strong, however, that later a few joined with the king's men in the pits and caves of the adjacent forest.

As Jonathan finished his talk with the troops, the king came out of his tent and looked for several moments at the Philistines at Michmash. Then he looked at the pitiful remnant of his own army and at Jonathan's troops still at attention, and he appeared to make a decision. He called several of his men by name, and they came on the run. Jonathan wondered what his father had in mind.

The king walked over and carefully inspected a site not far from where Jonathan was standing and nodded his head in approval. "Get several men to bring stones to this place," he ordered his aide. "And get others to gather plenty of dry wood."

While the men were responding, he shouted again. "Have two men go to the herds and bring a yearling bull calf. Also, have someone bring the pans, the knives, and the flint."

Jonathan was fairly sure now of what his father's intentions were. He was going to offer a sacrifice to the Lord on his own. Jonathan understood somewhat why his father had chosen this unlawful course—his army and nation were in danger of complete destruction by the hated Philistines, and of course, all of Israel was looking to the king for deliverance. There was no hope of victory in common warfare, so the Lord was their only hope.

It would seem plausible, especially in a crisis, that the rights and functions of the priesthood could be usurped by the supreme commander of Israel, but it didn't work that way. The order and work of the priesthood had been determined by the Lord as Israel was on their way from Egypt to Canaan. The descendants of Aaron of the tribe of Levi had been chosen in perpetuity to minister for the nation in sacrifices and offerings. There were no contingencies built into the plan for crises. Ahijah, the priest, was a Levite, and therefore, he could have offered a proper sacrifice, and he was near at hand.

Samuel, the judge and priest, was scheduled to visit the camp today, and surely he would bring word from the Lord and offer a sacrifice. Samuel was an Ephraimite by birth location, but by genealogy, he was a descendant of Kohath, son of Levi. The prophet had been dedicated to the priesthood from childhood.

As the men were gathering the materials for the sacrifice, Jonathan approached his father. The king ignored him. "Father," he ventured, "I hope that you are not planning to offer a sacrifice to the Lord on your own. That would be presumptuous, and the Lord would not answer."

For a moment it appeared that the king would ignore the intrusion of Jonathan as he continued to watch the men bring the stones. Finally he turned to face the prince with his jaw set.

"Yes, I am going to offer the sacrifice," he said with finality. "Samuel should have been here long before now according to his promise, and I am not sure that he will show up at all. I have found him to be unpredictable in his visits. As you can see, the pagans could decide to attack at any time now, and we have no physical defense against them, so I believe that God would expect me to petition Him for a word." He turned around, and Jonathan knew that the interview was over.

Jonathan watched helplessly as the men formed the altar, stacked the wood, and brought up the bull calf. Then the king commanded the company to gather around as he officiously killed the bull, collected the blood, and lit the fire. He fell on his knees in prayer as the sacrifice burned.

The heart of the prince ached for his father. For some time now, he had seen a gradual decrease in spiritual perception in the life and actions of the king. While the burdens of the kingship should have drawn him closer to the source of all wisdom, he had chosen more and more to rely on his own faulty judgment. His decision to offer the sacrifice was another step in the downward trend in his life.

The fire on the altar had died down. Saul arose from his knees, but there was no answering sign from heaven. Jonathan hadn't expected any divine response from this unlawful sacrifice, for it was like the offering of Cain, which was offered in presumption, rather than faith.

The coals of Saul's sacrifice were still smoldering on the altar when Samuel came into the camp. The king met the priest with a warm greeting, but Samuel's visage was grim. There was no doubt in Jonathan's mind that God had already conveyed to the prophet the fact of Saul's sin.

"What have you done?" he demanded.

Saul spread his hands in frustration. "As you can see, we are facing a grave crisis. The Philistines are gathered across the gorge by the hundreds of thousands." The king pointed across to the camp of the pagans as he spoke. "They are threatening to attack at any time now, and my army is almost gone. Because of such overwhelming odds, the men have deserted by the scores. I waited for you to come and bring word from the Lord, but you tarried, so I felt compelled to offer a burnt offering on my own."

The king paused as though he had finished speaking, and then somewhat lamely, he added a further justification for his actions. "I believe that God expected me, as the king, to seek a word for His people against this great enemy."

Samuel looked at the king for some time before he spoke. Then his voice quivered with emotion.

"You have been foolish. You should have prayed and waited, but instead you stubbornly broke the Lord's commandment. If you would have kept faith, the Lord would have defeated the enemy and would have established your kingdom over Israel forever, but now your rule will end. In your place, the Lord will establish a man after His own heart to be commander over his people. He will replace you soon."

As he finished, Samuel looked around at the soldiers and again looked at the Philistines across the gorge, but he ignored Jonathan who was standing with his regiment. Then the aged priest turned on his heel and left for Gibeah of Benjamin. He had not even mentioned the Philistine threat that now hung like an oversized sword over the head of the king. It was very evident that the prophet's announcement regarding the termination of Saul's kingship had devastated Saul. He stood with slumped shoulders and downcast eyes for some time after Samuel's departure.

Of course, Jonathan was also greatly disturbed by the priest's announcement. Since he was heir to the throne and would be king only by succession, whatever served to affect Saul's political future would also impact his own. There were implications inherent in Samuel's statement that Jonathan couldn't understand at the moment, so he tucked the thought away for future consideration.

Saul moped darkly after the prophet's exit, and no one dared to approach him. Then suddenly he straightened up as if he remembered something and called for the troops to be numbered. This was done quickly, and the remaining number was found to be only six hundred. Jonathan found that fifty of his men had deserted.

The king took his glass and looked for quite some time at the Philistine host across the Michmash gorge. Jonathan watched as his father lowered the glass; his shoulders slumped and the light went out of his eyes. Without a word to anyone, he walked to the outskirts of Gilgal and sat down under a pomegranate tree. He was already a defeated man.

Suddenly the truth dawned on Jonathan, and for a moment his heart paused in its beating. The plans for meeting the daunting enemy across the gorge were his to form and execute. His father had forfeited his leadership for the moment.

Jonathan went inside his tent to meditate and pray. He was positive that traditional warfare would result in an overwhelming victory for the pagans and utter annihilation of the meager armies of Israel. The only hope for Israel was the intervention of Jehovah Himself.

His mother, Ahinoam, had taught him the absolute imperativeness of prayer in all crises, so he bowed there in his tent and prayed earnestly for divine guidance. As he prayed, statements his mother had often repeated came to mind. "With God, one man is an army," and "man's inability is always God's opportunity."

Ahinoam would illustrate these statements with experiences from the Exodus and the time of the judges. The children of Israel, about a million in number, had started out from Egypt by an order from God and were bound for Canaan, the Promised Land. Moses, the great man of God, was leading them. They soon came to the western shore of the Red Sea and to the first great crisis of their journey. There were mountains on one side of them and impassable swamps on the other side, and Pharaoh's handpicked army of six hundred chariots and many horsemen was coming up fast from the rear, determined to take them back to Egypt. The impassable sea was before them. They were in deep trouble. They had no boats, rafts, or ships, and the sea was much too wide and deep for wading or swimming.

The people began to chide Moses and blame God. They cried out, "Lord, here we are. You told us to leave Egypt for a better land, and now we're in this terrible situation." They wrung their hands and cried. "What are we supposed to do?"

Even Moses began to break down and plead to God for direction. It was man's utter inability that enabled God to work a miracle. He made a road through the middle of the Red Sea, and almost one million people crossed without anyone getting their sandals wet or muddy.

As Jonathan meditated on this great miracle, his heart began to sing. God could perform the same size of miracle at Michmash as He did at the Red Sea. Truly his God was a God of miracles.

But there was much more evidence of His power on the Exodus road. As the Israelites went farther into the wilderness, their water supply gave out, and everyone became thirsty unto death. The babies began to whimper because their mothers' milk was drying up. The cattle were lowing because of thirst, and the people were on edge. So again they began to rail on Moses for bringing them into this terrible place. Moses had no appeal but to the Lord of miracles. But God didn't answer Moses for some time. It seemed for awhile as if God had deserted them, but He hadn't.

Soon, in the distance, the people saw palm trees and the cattle smelled water. It was an oasis, and there was water, but it wasn't potable. It was bitter and poisonous, and the people spit it out. So the Lord instructed Moses to cut off a branch from a nearby tree and cast it into the water, and the water became sweet. Moses explained to the people that the branch was symbolic. It represented the promised Redeemer who one day would heal the poisonous water of earth and give eternal living water. It was another mighty miracle of God that changed the composition of that water and made it fit for human consumption.

Jonathan's heart grew stronger in the Lord as he thought on these miracles of the Exodus.

As the people of Israel came near to Mt. Sinai, their food supply gave out. God had miraculously kept their bread from becoming stale, but now their provisions were all used up. What were they to do? Would they have to kill their cattle? Moses prayed to the Lord, and the Lord provided.

The Lord said, "Go out in the morning and your breakfast, lunch, and dinner will be waiting for you."

So the people went out the next morning and the manna was on the ground. For the next forty years, six days a week, every day but Sabbath, the supply of manna was there for them. God was faithful.

As Jonathan thought on these miracles, his cup of faith was being filled to overflowing. The Lord had done so much for His people in times past. Surely He could and would do the same today. Then the prince thought of experiences not many years past. There was Gideon with three hundred men who, by faith, routed the massive army of the Midianites and secured the land of Israel. But Gideon at first was a skeptic. He needed two miracles of the dew on the fleece, a drastic paring of his army of thirty two thousand, and a midnight visit to the Midianite camp before he was ready to obey the word of the Lord.

Later, the warrior Barak, by faith, gained a great victory over the heathen Canaanites. But according to the record, he placed equal dependence on the help of the judge and prophetess Deborah as he did on the Lord.

Last but not least, in the list of great men of faith that came to Jonathan's mind was Jephtah. He showed great courage and faith in his war against the Amorites but poor judgment in his unwise vow that took the life of his only daughter in a pagan type of sacrifice.

Jonathan knew that the unusual achievements of these men were not because of innate ability, but rather the result of Jehovah working through them to accomplish His will. Moses had written by inspiration, "One will chase a thousand and two put ten thousand to flight in the strength of the Lord."

Jonathan was now more convinced that the Lord could use his feeble efforts to utterly defeat the massive army of the Philistines gathered at Michmash. He didn't need the reluctant help of his father or the fearful men of his depleted army. They were like the twenty-two thousand timid recruits of Gideon's band.

Quietly, Jonathan summoned his armor bearer into his tent, and there he shared with the aide the plan of attack that God had put in his mind. Nebal's eyes lighted up with admiration at the boldness, yet simplicity, of the plan, and he immediately agreed to go with the prince. Jonathan loved this young man who was so loyal to him and was also a strong believer in Jehovah.

"Stay by here for a few minutes," Jonathan bade the aide, "while I check on my father, the Israelite sentries, and the general activities of the enemy soldiers on the Michmash rim."

The king was still sitting under the pomegranate tree with his head between his knees. Jonathan could fairly well guess as to the dark thoughts coursing through the mind of the rejected king at this time.

The Israelite sentries were lounging, and there appeared to be very minimal activity in the Philistine camp. Evidently the Spirit of the Lord was holding in check the pagan army for this very moment. Jonathan went back inside his tent and with his armor bearer knelt in prayer before the Lord. The heart of the prince was full to bursting.

"Oh, Lord," he prayed, "I have been reminded again of your miracles of love on behalf of Your people, Israel. You delivered them from their bondage in Egypt and led them every step of the way to this land that You had promised them. You gave them water from the rock to satisfy their thirst and fed them with manna from heaven. You fought their battles for them and won great victories. Despite these many evidences of Your love and care, we are often so thankless and disobedient and thus so unworthy, but You are a God of mercy and forgiveness, and You love to bless Your people.

"Lord, You know that we are facing a great host of the enemy. Our resources are so petty. We are totally dependent on You. You, alone, can deliver us from these enemies and give another great victory to Israel. We are in Your hands. Please use us to Your glory and for the deliverance of Your people, Israel."

Nebal didn't follow in prayer, but he gave a rousing "Amen" as Jonathan finished. The prince could see that his eyes had misted. The two embraced each other and resolutely gathered up their sparse equipment. No one noticed as the pair left. They walked in step to the bottom of the gorge that separated the two armies and assessed the steep walls that they would have to climb. Between the walls through which Jonathan and his armor bearer would climb up to the Philistine camp, there was a sharp rock on one side and a similar one on the other side. The name of the one was Bozez and the name of the other Seneh. These rocks were historical markers. When they reached these rocks, which were out of sight of both armies, they again paused for prayer.

Then Jonathan said to the young man, "Are you ready to go with me to meet the enemy?"

He felt that he must give his aide the same opportunity to withdraw as Gideon did with his thirty two thousand, but the answer of the young soldier was resolute. "Do all that is in your heart. I am with you all the way!"

Jonathan smiled and patted him on the back. "Good. It may be that the Lord will work for us, for nothing restrains the Lord from saving by many or by few."

"Now, here is our plan. We will go out far enough from the base so that the sentries above will see us, and we'll wait for their response. If they say, 'Wait there and we will come to you,' we will stand by and see what the Lord will tell us to do. But if they say, 'Come up to us,' we will go up, for the Lord has delivered them into our hand, and this will be a sign to us."

The eyes of Nebal were shining in expectation. "I am with you all the way."

Jonathan led the way as they walked away from the base of the cliff and were now in full sight of the Philistines sentries at the top of the shaft. The surprised look on the faces of the guards pleased the prince. It was evident that the pagans were not expecting any aggressive actions from the Israelites.

The sentries pointed to the two men below them and then in unison yelled out. "Look, the Hebrews are coming out of the holes where they have been hiding. Come up to us, and we will show you something."

Jonathan knew that the Lord had put these words in the mouths of the enemy, for this was the sign he had asked for. They waved disdainfully at the guards and then went back to the base of the cliff. Jonathan gave his spear to Nebal and kept his trusty sword; then with a prayer in their hearts, they started climbing the steep cliff between the walls of the chasm. They were on their way to fulfill the mission of the Lord. The Lord had impressed Jonathan that they were to spare neither the small nor the great in their slaughter. The Lord would miraculously save those who were not to be destroyed at this time.

Finally, the prince and Nebal reached the top of the crevice and were ready to expose their presence to the sentries. They paused, smiled at each other, and burst out through the opening with a loud yell. The surprised heathen guards must have thought that giant demons were attacking them. The Philistines were totally unprepared. Although they had seen the two Israelites only minutes before and had taunted them to come up and fight, evidently they had no idea that the two foes would accept such a rash challenge. Several of the sentries were relaxing in the sun while others were playing games.

Within a few minutes, Jonathan and Nebal had slain all of the guards, more than twenty, and a few other soldiers in the area. There was no resistance. Then the Lord fought for Israel.

There was a trembling in the camp and among all the people as though an earthquake was assisting the Israelites. The enemy became confused and turned their swords on each other. Men were falling all around the camp. Jonathan knew that the Lord was fighting for them, and his spirits soared.

Soon the noise of the battle reached the ears of King Saul as he dozed under the pomegranate tree, and he suddenly came alive. He looked at the Philistine army on the plateau above him and for several minutes watched the frenzied movements of the enemy troops. He was soon convinced that an alien force of some kind was wreaking havoc in the Philistine camp. The sentries in the Israelite camp had also heard the noise above them and noticed the erratic movements of the enemy soldiers. They had alerted the miniature army.

Saul was now roused to action. "Call the roll," he demanded, "so that we can determine which of us could be doing battle with the enemy at Michmash."

It was quickly discovered that Jonathan and Nebal were missing and thus were surely the cause of the tumult on the mesa.

King Saul was now anxious to be involved in the battle raging on the plain above them, but he was uncertain as to how to proceed. He called for Ahijah the priest to bring the Urim and Thummim, and the nervous priest hastened to comply. But again the impatience of the king spoiled his good intentions.

"Withdraw your hand," he shouted impatiently to the priest.

Then the king turned to the soldiers, "Get ready for battle," he yelled, and the men lined up quickly in battle formation. The troops seemed to smell the fear in the Philistine ranks above them and thus were as impatient as was the king to join in the battle on the plateau. Saul gave the order "forward march" but the men broke rank and raced across the valley, quickly climbed the cliff, and engaged the disoriented enemy troops.

As the cry of the Israelites rang out across the plateau and down to the valley below, the Israelite troops that had taken refuge in the caves and pits hastened to the battle. Also, the soldiers who had defected to the enemy turned against the Philistines, and of course, the barbarians had turned against each other in their confusion.

The Israelite soldiers were soon supplied with crafted weapons and they used them with fervor. The Philistine forces were now in a complete rout. They forgot their fine steeds, tents, and supplies. They desired only to get away from the overwhelming enemy forces that apparently had come out of hiding from somewhere. The Israelites followed hard after the panic-stricken enemy, and thousands were slain on the road to Beth Aven.

King Saul was rejuvenated. He was again in charge as he watched the soldiers fight. But he again made a very foolish decision. He shouted a command to the nearest fighters, and the order was relayed down the line, "Cursed is the man who eats any food until evening, before I have taken vengeance on my enemies."

The position of the king was badly flawed for two reasons. First, by such a command, it became obvious that he was now attempting to take personal credit for the destruction of the Philistine army. Secondly, it was an irrational injustice against the Israelite soldiers. They were pressing hard against the enemy, and they were tiring in the heat of the battle. Had they been allowed to partake of only a few bites of the supplies that were scattered along the way, they would have been strengthened to slay many more of the Philistines.

Jonathan was unaware of the oath his father had imposed on the troops or he too would have complied, since he obeyed his father in every respect except when it was a violation of conscience.

As the chase against the enemy brought Jonathan into a large forest, he came upon a tree with wild honey dripping from a hole in the trunk. The prince was faint from hunger, so he stretched out the rod that was in his hand and gathered some of the sweet stuff. His energy was renewed. As he ate, an Israelite soldier came by and told him of the king's ban on food for the entire day.

Jonathan was saddened by his father's rash order. He knew that the men were obviously tiring, for the chase had been long now and over much uneven terrain. He knew that the bit of honey had greatly renewed his strength and would certainly have been a great blessing to the fighting men. Jonathan was fearful that some type of evil consequence would result from this forced fast.

As the company finished driving the enemy from Michmash to Ajalon, the men were very faint, and Jonathan's fears were realized. The men gave in to their animal nature. There was much spoil that had been taken from the enemy, and the people seized on the plunder. Like a pack of wolves, they slew sheep, oxen and calves on the spot and without benefit of fire began to eat the raw meat, even with the blood. Some of the more conscientious and sensible among the soldiers told the king of the sin of the people in eating the blood. Saul immediately ordered the rest of the men to bring their food supply to a designated place where it was prepared and eaten in proper fashion.

Jonathan watched his father as he strutted about the temporary camp, giving orders and accepting salutes. It was obvious that he was ready and willing to take credit for the Lord's victory at Michmash. As yet he had not acknowledged Jonathan's part in the conquest. The heart of the prince ached for his father.

Suddenly the king stopped his pacing and called out above the noise of the group, "Men, listen! Shall we go down to the camp of the enemy tonight and finish what we started today? We should destroy them completely and not leave a man alive."

The men had followed the king all day without question, and they were eager to complete the destruction of the Philistines. "Do whatever seems good to you. We are with you."

Then the king ordered an altar to be built and asked the priest, Ahijah, to come forward. "Ahijah," he commanded, "ask the Lord if we should go down to the Philistine camp tonight. Will He give the rest of the enemy into the hands of Israel?"

The priest hastened to offer the sacrifice.

Jonathan watched his father's actions with interest and a bit of suspicion. Suddenly he seemed overly conscientious in requesting a word from the Lord. What was his motive?

Ahijah made the request to the Lord as to whether the Israelite army should raid the Philistine camp this night, but the Lord had no answer for the priest or the king.

Jonathan wasn't surprised that the Lord didn't answer his father by the Urim and Thummim, since he had so blatantly ignored this proper course only a few days before. But the prince was taken aback by the reasoning the king used next to cover up his own sin of omission.

"Someone among us has sinned," Saul shouted loudly above the din. The camp became hushed. "The Lord will not answer," he continued, "because there is sin in the camp, and even though it is Jonathan, he shall surely die!"

Suddenly the truth came to Jonathan, and he shuddered with revulsion. Someone had told Saul that Jonathan had eaten the honey in violation to his order, and he was now planning to use this innocent remission to destroy even his own son. Thus he would identify himself in the eyes of his regiment as a ruler who would allow no disobedience, even from his own family.

He made careful and deadly preparations. "You men will be on one side and my son, Jonathan, and I will be on the other," he commanded the soldiers. "Then we will cast lots to see who the wrongdoer is among us."

The prince could see the noose of his father's deception tightening around his neck, but the Lord gave him peace.

When everyone was in place, the King looked proudly up to heaven and spoke these words, "Lord, give us a perfect lot."

When the lot was cast, it pointed to the father and the son. The king appeared surprised, but it was an evident disguise. "Cast the lot again," he ordered. Jonathan was taken.

The king cast accusing eyes at Jonathan and demanded, "Tell me what you have done that has cast this awful spell on Israel?"

Jonathan knew what his father was seeking, so he readily admitted. "I had no knowledge of your prohibition on eating anything until the battle was over, so when I saw the honey dripping from a hole in a tree in the forest, I tasted a little honey from the rod that was in my hand. I immediately gained energy to pursue the enemy, so now I must die."

Jonathan thought surely that his admission would help his father to see the evil rashness of his restriction on the troops, but the king ignored any possible guilt of his own.

Quickly, the king pronounced sentence. "God do so and more also to me, for you shall surely die, Jonathan."

For a few moments, there was silence in the camp. Then there was a stirring. Several of the men from Jonathan's army stepped forward. The prince was surprised to see two of the men whom he had once disciplined quite harshly, step to the front of the group. One of these men was the spokesman.

"If it pleases the king," the speaker said, "we are all opposed to your decision to kill Jonathan. Jonathan must not die. He is the one who accomplished this great salvation in Israel today. Without his faith and courage, we would all have been dead men, including you, O king. So as the Lord lives, not one hair of his head shall fall to the ground, for he has worked with God this day." The men stepped back to their places and waited.

The prince could see the agony in his father's countenance. It was a bitter defeat for him that his royal order was rescinded by the very men who he was supposed to be able to dominate. What was worse, however, was that the men had attributed every facet of today's victory to Jonathan and the Lord. He had not even received honorable mention. The crisis was over, but the king gave in grudgingly. "Very well," he said. "We will drop the matter and march back to Michmash tonight."

When Jonathan arrived back in Gibeah of Benjamin, he immediately went to visit his mother. He knew that she had great concern for his father and himself when they were in battle, and, of course, she prayed earnestly for their safe return. Thus she deeply appreciated a report from Jonathan about the incursion. Usually she heard bits and pieces of news from the soldiers' wives, who were maids in the court, but she knew that Jonathan would give her a true report.

Her eyes were starry as she embraced her first-born warmly and invited him to have a seat. "Son," she breathed, "I have heard news that has made this mother's heart overflow with gratitude. I have been told that you and Nebal engaged the great army of the Philistines because you believed that God would fight for you, and you won a great victory for Israel. Tell me, is it true?"

"Yes, Mother," Jonathan agreed. "It is true. God gave us a great victory, and I am quite certain that the Philistines will be humbled for years to come. But Mother, you deserve much of the human credit for the triumph. You taught me to have faith in God, and you insisted that I memorize the Bible statement, 'One will chase a thousand and two will put ten thousand to flight.' When father became discouraged at Michmash and surrendered his leadership, I realized that God was looking to me to provide leadership against the pagans, so I went to my tent to pray and to review God's miracles of the past. As I prayed and reflected, God impressed me that if I would step out by faith and trust Him, He would give Israel a victory."

Ahinoam's eyes misted over and a lump caught in her throat. "Jonathan, you truly are a wonderful son, and you have a true heart of faith. It is so kind of you to give your mother so much credit."

She leaned forward then, and her face clouded over. "Jonathan, tell me, did your father offer an unlawful sacrifice there at Michmash?"

He hesitated. "Yes, he did, Mother. I felt so sorry for him. His army was deserting by the score. There were only six hundred men left just before the battle. The Philistines were poised to attack at any time, and they could have taken over the entire land of Israel."

"Yes, but he had Ahijah there, and from what I heard, Samuel was scheduled to visit at any time. He surely could have waited for him to bring word from the Lord."

"I pleaded with him to either use Ahijah or wait for Samuel, but he wouldn't listen. His mind was made up."

Ahinoam sat silent for several moments, but she had more on her heart. "Did Samuel come soon after the sacrifice had been offered, and did he chide the king quite harshly? Did he tell him that his kingship was no longer recognized by heaven and someone from another family would sit on the throne of Israel?" A sob shook her breast as she finished.

Jonathan's heart was in pain as he answered. "Yes, Mother, that is all true. I am sure that the news that another king would take his place was the cause of his great discouragement. It took the heart out of him."

Ahinoam looked at her son as if she were searching his soul. "Tell me, son, how did Samuel's announcement make you feel? If your father's rule passes to someone else, your succession will end. Would you be greatly disappointed if you would not succeed your father as king?"

Jonathan thought for a few moments before answering. "Mother, I have had very little time to think about the implications of Samuel's statement. Certainly, I would feel disappointed to give up my dreams of someday being the king of Israel. I have been a prince for all but a few days of my life, and of course, being a prince implies that you are in line to be king. However, if God has picked someone else to be king in my place, I will accept his judgment for He never makes a mistake."

Ahinoam arose from her chair and hugged her son to her breast. Her voice was choked. "Jonathan, I expected that to be your answer. You would make a much better king than your father because of your humility and your submission to the Lord. But as you have said, the Lord knows best, and we must always trust His judgment.

"The Lord doesn't change His mind, but when conditions change His decisions adapt to fit the changed conditions. So, it could be possible that you will still be king. We will wait for His providence."

As Jonathan was reviewing his troops soon after his return from Michmash, a messenger came with a royal order from the king. As the prince unrolled the document written by Pena for King Saul, he wondered what crisis his father could possibly be in now.

"Captain Jonathan," he read. "It has become necessary for my regiment to move back to Gibeah of Benjamin. Since it is wise to have our armies guarding separate areas, you are now ordered to move your troops here to Gilgal. The move is to be made immediately."

Jonathan quickly wrote a response and sent it back with the messenger.

The prince had often wondered why his father had chosen to camp at Michmash when his primary family and royal palace were located at Gibeah. He suspected that the concubines the king had chosen in several of the towns not far from Michmash were the cardinal reasons. His father had children by several of these concubines, but Jonathan had never met any of his half brothers and sisters.

Jonathan moved his army with ease and was soon stationed comfortably at Gilgal.

The victory at Michmash and the move to Gibeah seemed to give King Saul a new lease on life, and for a time, he appeared to put the affront of the troops at Ajalon and the bitter visit with Samuel at Gilgal out of mind. He began to fight the enemies of the Lord on all sides. The timing was overdue for the Moabites, and the Ammorites had become aggressive in their encroachment on the borders of Israel. Jonathan had used his small army of one thousand mainly against the Philistine offensive.

Now the king fought with spirit against these pagans with troops that were fully armed and confident. Saul won signal victories everywhere he turned.

One day as Jonathan was visiting with his father at Gibeah, the prophet Samuel made a surprise visit to the king. Samuel had ignored and avoided the king since the painful parting at Gilgal. But today his visage was pleasant, and his manner rather relaxed. His message to the king from the Lord, however, was brief and to the point. There were no preliminaries.

He read rather officiously. "Thus saith the Lord of Hosts: I will punish what Amalek did to Israel, how he lay in wait for them on the way when they came up from Egypt. Now, go and attack Amalek and utterly destroy all that they have. Do not spare them, but kill man and woman, infant and nursing child, ox and sheep, camel and donkey."

As soon as the prophet finished reading the divine order, he bowed to the king, turned on his heel and left.

Jonathan was pleased with what appeared to be an improved relationship between the aging prophet and his father, as well as a possible second chance offered to the king by the Lord. It was a high moment for the prince.

"Father, my troops will certainly be available to you for this battle if you care to use them," Jonathan offered.

The king responded quickly. "Yes, son, if you will march your men immediately to Telaim, I will send out an official call for volunteers to meet us there. I believe that we will have a good response from all of Israel and Judah."

It was a very impressive army that gathered at Telaim to fight the Amalekites. There were two hundred thousand soldiers from the tribes of Israel along with ten thousand from Judah. All of the volunteers were fully armed from the arsenal of weapons captured at Michmash.

The king, with Jonathan at his side, marched the troops to the city of Amalek and lay in wait in the valley during the darkness of night. Saul sent out spies to reconnoiter the city, and the men found some Kenite families living among the Amalekites. The spies reported back to the king, and Saul immediately sent a message to the leaders of the Kenites.

"I have no quarrel with you," he informed them, "for you showed kindness to the children of Israel when they came up out of Egypt. So now, get out from among the Amalekites, lest I destroy you with them."

The Kenites heeded the king's order and all of them immediately vacated the Amalekite camp.

The king deployed his troops wisely, and the Amalekites were completely routed. In their panic they left their homes and all of their belongings. Saul's men chased them from Havilah all the way to Shur, which is east of Egypt, killing them all along the way. The city was completely destroyed without the loss of even one Israelite soldier.

Jonathan captured King Agag and was about to plunge his spear into the pagan's heart when Saul stopped him. "No, Jonathan, do not kill him. I want to save him for a time as a trophy of war."

"But, Father," the prince protested, "the Lord commanded you to kill every soul, including the women and children. That would surely include the king. You have not yet carried out the order of the Lord if you spare Agag."

Saul glared angrily at his son for a few moments. "Jonathan," he said irritably, "you are not the king. You are only a prince and should not act as a counselor to the king unless you are asked. I am sure that the Lord will not mind if I keep Agag alive for a few days. I will parade him through the streets as a trophy of war, and then I will have him executed."

Jonathan faced his father. "God's order was specific. He said to destroy everyone and, of course, that includes the king. I don't think that God will look with favor on your sparing Agag even for a day, and besides, parading him through the streets is what the heathen kings do. It is their way of bragging about their power over the other nations. Furthermore, Father, please forgive me, but I know that Samuel said for you to destroy all of the cattle, sheep, and donkeys, but you have saved scores of them. Please, Father, don't defy the Lord's command."

Saul turned his back on his son and walked away. Jonathan also walked away sick at heart. He went to his tent to wait for the coming of Samuel.

Samuel came soon, and Saul walked boldly out to meet him. Jonathan held back. The prince could tell by the sad but firm look on Samuel's face that the Lord had already informed him of the king's misdeeds.

Saul appeared not to notice the stern visage of the priest. "Blessed are you of the Lord! I have performed the commandment of the Lord," Saul said.

Jonathan could hardly believe his ears. Surely his father knew that he was lying to the prophet and thus to the Lord.

Samuel was silent for a moment before asking, "Then, what is the meaning of the bleating of the sheep and the lowing of the cattle that I hear?"

"Oh, that," said the king lightly. "The men saved these for a sacrifice to the Lord, but all of the others were destroyed as the Lord commanded."

"Did the Lord ask you to save these animals for sacrifice, or did He ask you to kill them all? Remember, to obey is better than to sacrifice, for rebellion is like the sin of witchcraft, and stubbornness is idolatry.

"Now, because you have rejected the word of the Lord, He has also rejected you as king."

Saul was standing with his head bowed, but now he spoke. "I have sinned against the Lord, because I feared the people. But now, please forgive my sin and return with me to worship."

"I repeat, because you have rejected the word of the Lord, the Lord has rejected you as king over Israel," Samuel said. "The Lord has torn the kingdom of Israel from you today and has given it to a neighbor of yours who is better than you. The Lord will not relent on His decision."

Samuel then worshipped with Saul and put Agag to death. Then he went back to his home in Ramah.

Saul had been able to put the first declaration by Samuel that his kingship was annulled by heaven out of mind, but this second statement by the prophet crushed him. As Samuel left for Ramah, Jonathan saw his father's shoulder's slump, and he was sure that his spirit had died within him.

For some time, the king moped around the camp. Then he turned to Abner, the captain of his army. "Destroy all of the stock and burn their carcasses, then march the army back to Gibeah."

Jonathan waited in his tent until he saw his father mount his horse and follow the army back to his home. Then Jonathan marched his own company back to Gilgal.

# JONATHAN'S HEART

## CHAPTER 3

Jonathan was in love. It was delayed timing for his romantic clock to strike, since he was approaching his thirtieth birthday. To this point in his life, he had not had even a passing relationship with a member of the opposite sex.

Twice before, the king had chosen a possible bride for him from among the daughters of the doctors and lawyers of the city, but Jonathan had rejected them. His answer to his father was, "I do not have time to coddle a wife and still take care of my army and religious duties." But one day his attitude changed in a moment of time, and he felt that now he was ready to coddle a wife.

Since Saul's experience with King Agag of the Amalekites, and Samuel's subsequent reproof, Saul had become morose and bitter. He would sit for hours on his throne with his spear in his hand, and none of his aides dared to approach him. The business of the kingdom was neglected, and the royal agenda was full to overflowing.

The administrators were frantic and were now calling on Jonathan to come to Gibeah and carry on the business of the king. There were court cases for the civilians and disciplinary actions for the soldiers.

Several times as the prince worked in the administration office, he heard sweet music coming from the throne room where his father was ensconced. When Jonathan inquired as to the origin of the music, he was told that a young shepherd lad from Bethlehem had been brought to the palace to play the harp for the king. The shepherd's name was David.

One day Jonathan took a break from his duties at the court to run an errand for his mother. He was to purchase an item at the marketplace. He was rummaging around a bit in one of the shops when he suddenly came face to face with the most beautiful lady he had seen in his entire life. She smiled as their eyes met, and Jonathan's heart skipped a beat. He noticed that an elderly lady was with the girl, and he supposed that she was either a relative or a guardian.

Jonathan instinctively followed them for a few moments, hoping that the girl would drop her handkerchief or lose a slipper so that he could get acquainted with her. The girl did neither and appeared not to notice that the prince was in the area.

It was the girl's consort that provided the opportunity for Jonathan to make the maiden's acquaintance. Suddenly, as Jonathan watched, the elderly lady stumbled on an obstruction on the floor and fell headlong. It was a nasty fall.

The prince leaped forward, bent down, and lifted her small body in his arms. He placed her on a display table that was near. He noticed that her eyes were closed, and he suggested that she was unconscious.

He turned to the girl. "I'm afraid that she might be hurt seriously," he said with compassion. "Should I go for a doctor?"

The girl's eyes were wide with concern, but she was composed. She touched his arm. "Would you be so kind as to carry grandmother to our carriage? It is parked only a few doors away. I will send my driver for the doctor as soon as we arrive home."

Jonathan picked up the slight form and threaded his way through the curious crowd that had gathered. The prince's carriage was positioned close to the girl's coach, and Jonathan motioned for his driver to come.

"Please, go for the doctor," he requested. "The young lady will tell you where to bring him."

Jonathan waited while the girl gave instructions to his driver regarding the name of her grandfather and the location of their home. He recognized the name of the grandfather as an aide to the king. The prince had met the grandfather at the court.

As the maiden turned to him, he offered, "I will ride to your home with you. I am afraid that the jolting of the carriage would be painful for your grandmother."

The girl nodded and smiled her thanks. As they were riding, the girl spoke up. "I'm afraid I've been remiss. I should have introduced grandmother and myself. My name is Zereth and grandmother's name is Mishel. My grandfather, who is a member of the king's court, is Zaccur."

The prince nodded, "Yes, I have met your grandfather at court. I am Prince Jonathan."

Zereth smiled. "I knew who you were," her eyes twinkled. "I have seen you marching your men on the parade ground twice," she hesitated, "and you looked so dashing in your uniform." She blushed as she spoke.

Jonathan laughed. "Thanks for the compliment. May I return the compliment?"

"Certainly, you may," she said warmly.

Jonathan looked at her directly as he spoke. "I have never seen a more beautiful person than you in my entire life."

She blushed even prettier than before, and her chin rose. "Captain Jonathan, that was such a lovely compliment, especially since I know that you have two beautiful sisters whom I have met at court."

The crumpled form in Jonathan's arms stirred and moaned, and the two turned their attention to the elderly woman the rest of the drive to her home.

Jonathan alighted from the carriage with the unconscious woman still in his arms. The girl led him into the house and to the nearest bedroom, and the prince laid the precious bundle of life on the bed.

Then he turned to Zereth. "If I could get your driver to take me to the palace, I would be so grateful. I'm sure that my driver will have the doctor here soon, and you could then direct him to drive back to the compound."

She nodded, showed him to the door, and ordered the driver to take Jonathan home. She grasped his hand, "Thanks so very much for your help to grandmother and me. I'm sure that when grandmother recovers, she and grandfather will both want to thank you personally."

Jonathan waxed bold. "Would it be all right for me to visit your grandmother tomorrow? Furthermore, I would like to get better acquainted with you."

She nodded and smiled. "I am sure that if my grandmother is conscious, she will welcome you, and so will I. Please come."

Jonathan could hardly wait to tell his mother about the beautiful maiden he had met at the marketplace. As he reconstructed in his mind the meeting of Zereth and her grandmother, the thought struck him. He had completely forgotten what his mission was at the town shops in the first place. Here he was coming back to his mother with empty hands.

His borrowed carriage soon met his own coach and driver with the doctor in place. The transfer was quickly made, and he then drove back to the marketplace, purchased the item for his mother, and went back to the palace.

His eyes were starry as he met with his mother, and she knew that he had good news to share with her. "Mother," he said dreamily, "I met a girl this afternoon at the marketplace that I would like to make my wife."

Ahinoam waited, for she knew there would be more.

"I was browsing in the shops for a few minutes when suddenly I came face to face with the most beautiful maiden I have ever seen outside of my own family. She was accompanied by an elderly lady who I later learned was her grandmother. Of course, the only communication we shared was a smile until all of a sudden the grandmother stumbled on an obstruction on the floor and fell headlong. It knocked her unconscious, so I picked her up and at the girl's request carried her to their carriage that was only a short distance away. Since I was concerned that the jolting of the carriage would cause her further pain, I carried her to their home and placed her on the bed. My driver went for the doctor, so I am sure that the little grandmother has received the best of care by now.

"I found out that the maiden's name is Zereth, her grandmother's name is Mishel, and her grandfather, who is an aide to Father, is Zaccur."

Ahinoam nodded. "Yes, I know the grandfather and grandmother and have met the girl. You are certainly right, son. She is very beautiful and Merab and Michal attest to her good character also."

She put her hand on Jonathan's arm. "Now, son, I do not want to dash your hopes, but I have heard from excellent sources that Shema, a son of the leather merchant Jeshua, and Hanan, a son of the banker Bunni, are madly in love with her, and both have expressed publicly that they will marry her soon. I have not heard about her reaction to their claims."

Jonathan was stunned, and for a moment he was speechless. "I'm afraid I have been very naïve. I hadn't given a thought to the possibility that she might have serious suitors. Of course, I should have known that a maiden so beautiful would certainly attract a number of admirers."

He paused for a moment; then forged ahead. "She invited me to visit her grandmother tomorrow and indicated that she would like to get better acquainted with me. I will make the visit and be bold enough to find out if there is any hope for me at that time."

Ahinoam looked at her firstborn with admiration in her eyes. "Jonathan, Zereth could not choose a better mate than you. I have not heard such good reports about the young men who are courting her so perhaps, for her sake and yours, God orchestrated this chance meeting this afternoon in the marketplace. I will be praying for both of you tomorrow as you call on her."

Jonathan hugged his mother. "Thank you, Mother. I have confidence in your prayers, so I will go on this visit with courage."

Jonathan pushed the oversized door knocker at the home of Zereth with some trepidation. A maid answered the door, invited him in, and led him into the living room.

"Lady Zereth is tending to her grandmother right now, but she will be with you in a few moments."

As Jonathan waited he looked around at the rather sparsely furnished room, and he was reminded that the earnings of an aide to the king were quite low—just a bit more than a living wage. He figured then that the maid was probably a relative or someone the grandparents were caring for.

The prince did notice that the room was very neat and clean and was nicely decorated with ornate vases filled with freshly cut flowers. The home was a humble one, with two rooms, a nook, and an open fireplace that served as a kitchen.

He dreamed a bit as he sat. If he would be so fortunate as to claim Zereth for his wife, he would build her a home in Gibeah at least twice the size she was living in now. Of course, when she would join him at Gilgal she would have to share his tent.

His thoughts were interrupted by the appearance of the girl of his dreams. She smiled demurely and held out her hand. "It's so nice of you to come. Grandmother is doing quite well now thanks to you and the good doctor. She is anxious to thank you for carrying her all the way from the marketplace to our home, but she is also embarrassed by her looks and does not speak too well. Would you like to visit with her for a few minutes?"

Jonathan nodded. "I have been anxious about her health and would very much like to see her."

Zereth led him into the bedroom where the grandmother was sitting in bed propped up by pillows. Truly the fall had discolored her face badly, but she was still able to smile.

Jonathan knelt by the bed and took her small hand in his. "I'm so glad that you're on the mend," he said with compassion in his voice.

"Thanks to you," she spoke with difficulty. "It was so thoughtful of you to carry me all the way home from the marketplace. I have recommended you to my granddaughter." She made the last statement with a twinkle in her eyes.

Both Jonathan and Zereth blushed, but Jonathan saved the day. "I'm glad that I was near when you fell, and I was also glad that you were a lightweight."

She laughed. "Thanks again," she breathed and sank back on her pillow exhausted.

Jonathan patted her hand. "You get some rest now and I will come back to visit you again."

The grandmother nodded and smiled.

The girl led him back into the living room and seated herself across from him. "I hope that grandmother didn't embarrass you with her last statement," she stated shyly.

Jonathan was quick to reply. "She surprised me, yes, but I was not embarrassed. Perhaps you were bothered by the implications of her statement?"

Her chin went up. "Not at all. Grandmother is not only very clever, but she is also very wise. She chooses her words well."

They sat quietly for a few moments, and Jonathan broke the silence.

"Lady Zereth, please tell me more about yourself. I find you to be a very interesting person. Besides," he smiled, "as I said yesterday, you are a very beautiful lady."

She laughed. "You are very kind, but I'm afraid that you will not find my history to be an exciting one."

She shuddered, and her eyes misted momentarily, but her voice remained strong. "As you have probably guessed, I am an orphan. I was orphaned at five years of age, but the memory is still quite painful after these fourteen years."

"The killers were bandits from the hills around where we lived. Several families, including my parents, formed a small community for purposes of their work and safety. The men would tend their outlying farms from their homes in the walled city. Someone was always on guard at night, but one morning as the families were breaking the fast, they became vulnerable and the bandits struck. Only five people were spared in the entire community, three of whom were children. I heard the shouts of the bandits before they reached our home, and I crawled under the bed. They looked everywhere but missed my hiding place. An older sister and both of my parents were killed. The bandits set fire to all the homes in the community, so I ran to a small grove of trees near our home. I wandered around in the ruins of the village for two days before my grandparents came and found me."

She was out of breath now and a sob shook her breast, but she smiled bravely and her poise returned. "My grandparents have been as good to me as any parents could have been. Grandmother has taught me social rudiments, and grandfather taught me about God and how to serve him. I feel very fortunate."

She finished and faced him. "That is quite a droll background, don't you think?"

"Not at all," Jonathan replied quickly. "You have kept me on the edge of my seat."

"Now, Prince Jonathan," she said crisply. "I expect a trade. I want to know more about you. I already know that you are captain of an army regiment, son of the King, and have a wonderful mother, two beautiful sisters, and two younger brothers, and are highly respected by all of the people of Israel. But there is a question in my mind about your choice of profession. With your ability you could have become very successful in business. Why did you choose the army? You don't appear to be a man who must fight to prove his manhood. So why don't you resign your army position and take up some other line of work?" Her voice was fairly sharp, but her poise and sweetness of face hadn't changed.

Jonathan took a deep breath before answering. He was a bit perplexed, but he knew the Lord would give him a good answer.

"Lady Zereth, you have certainly given me a challenge. I appreciate your deep feeling against warfare, and I share your feelings. Believe me; I fought the greatest battle of my life with my own heart before I joined my father's army. My wonderful mother impressed on my mind from babyhood the sanctity of human life. Every warrior is some mother's son and is precious to Jehovah.

"However, I remember, and you must also remember, that the Lord ordered our forefathers to drive the heathens out of our land lest the people intermingle and intermarry and thus lose our identity. According to God's promise of several centuries ago, the Lord would have driven the heathens out of our land if our ancestors would have obeyed Him. They disobeyed and lost their advantage. Now we must remove the barbarians through bloody wars."

"You see, the Philistines, the Amorites, the Midianites, and others do not honor boundaries. Lack of aggression on our part is considered as weakness by them. If ignored, they would soon take over our land and enslave us all. I have faith to believe that the Lord will still work for us and with us if we will only believe and obey Him. Of course, it is more difficult now because of the unbelief that we have demonstrated through the years.

"In answer to your question, I could have chosen to be a merchant and live the fat life, but I chose instead to allow God to use me in protecting my mother, sisters, and you and your grandparents through the army. I pray every day that God will use me in His way."

As Jonathan finished, he noticed that Zereth's eyes were shining and a beautiful smile touched the corners of her mouth.

"Lord Jonathan," she breathed, "you truly are an unusual man. You have made the best case for the wars that you must wage as an army commander that I have heard. I also heard about the courage and faith you demonstrated at Michmash. My grandfather vows that we would have been slaves of the Philistines at this very moment if it would not have been for you. He greatly admires you, and I join with him. I am on your side."

Jonathan's hopes lifted. "Lady Zereth, may I ask you a very personal question?"

Her smile gave the answer. "By all means, ask me what you will."

He hesitated; then plunged ahead. "I understand that you have at least two serious suitors in Gibeah. Is that true?"

A look of uncertainty clouded her beautiful face for a moment, and he was afraid that he had overstepped, but she answered without apparent resentment.

"Yes, that is true. Shema, son of Jeshua, and Hanan, son of Bunni, have paid court to me for some time. Why do you ask?"

Jonathan swallowed hard. "Would you have any room for a third suitor?"

There were questions in her eyes as she looked at him. "Lord Jonathan, surely you are not serious about courting an orphan such as myself. You are the prince of Israel and in line for the kingship. My genealogy dates back to Caleb, son of Jephunneh, but since I am a female, the genealogy is worthless. I would think that you would choose a mate from among the daughters of the leading citizens of the city. Remember, my grandfather is almost a slave to your father." She said the last sentence with what might have been a tinge of bitterness.

Jonathan was speechless for a moment; then he reached over and grasped her hand. She did not resist.

"Lady Zereth," he said deliberately and with emotion. "My father has twice chosen daughters from the merchants of the city for prospective brides for me, but I have rejected them both. I am determined to marry for love, and I am certain that I am in love with you."

Jonathan pressed forward. "Are you in love with either of these men, and have you promised yourself to either?"

She hesitated, and then shook her head. "No, I am not in love with either of them, and as yet, I have not promised myself to either, although they have pressed me. I too, would desire to marry for love, but I hardly think that a union between a prince and an orphan would work."

Jonathan was desperate. "Lady Zereth, would you promise to pray about this matter, and I will do the same.

I will visit again within three days, and we will see what the Lord has in mind for us. Would you agree?"

She nodded. "Certainly I will. And I will say at this point, you have stirred my heart as no other man has. Perhaps it is love. We will see in three days."

"Thank you for coming to see Grandmother. She was cheered by your visit.

She looked into his eyes. "I will anticipate your visit in three days."

Jonathan was troubled as he rode back to the palace from his visit with Zereth. He hadn't anticipated the response he had received from the girl with whom he was certain that he was in love. He had prepared himself for outright rejection, but the thought that she would consider herself unworthy to be his wife hadn't entered his mind prior to the visit.

As he thought further, however, he could see her logic. A wedding with a prince would be a royal affair, and she would have nothing to bring to the altar but herself. She had no name, no parental influence, and no experience at court. She would feel completely inadequate as a princess and certainly as a queen.

Ahinoam noticed a puzzled look on Jonathan's face as he came into the room, and she wondered what had taken place between the girl of his dreams and himself. She waited for him to share with her.

"Mother, were you ever overwhelmed with the responsibilities of being the queen of Israel?"

She nodded and waited a moment before she spoke. There was a shadow on her countenance. "Yes, son, I was totally unprepared for the responsibilities of royalty. Remember, your father and I were the first king and queen of Israel. We had no model to follow. Also, I was very young when your father and I married, and only one year later you were born and your father was chosen king.

I am quite sure that I could have handled the position much better had our marriage ties been stronger.

"You see, only a few weeks after our wedding I found that your father had chosen a concubine. So, after the first few weeks of our marriage, your father paid no more attention to me until after you were born. During that first year, he had chosen at least five concubines, so it was very difficult for me. I wasn't certain whether I was truly the first lady of Israel or whether another of the king's mates claimed that title."

She turned anxious eyes to her firstborn. "You can see my quandary, can you not?"

The prince eyed his mother tenderly. He knew her lot with the king had not been an easy one through the years, and the relationship was now deteriorating rapidly, but the situation had not made her bitter. In fact, as she bore his children and endured his criticism, she had become sweeter of nature and more patient of heart. She took care of her duties at court with grace and without complaint.

"Yes, Mother," Jonathan agreed, "I can see your cross."

He arose, hugged his mother, and kissed her on the cheek. As he was seated, Ahinoam spoke again.

"Now, son, I gave too long an answer to your question, for I am certain that you have news to share with me regarding your visit with Zereth."

"Yes, I do have news, but certainly not the kind I expected. I waxed bold and asked her about her relationship with the men, Shema and Hanan. She hesitated before answering, and I was afraid that I might have overstepped, but she admitted frankly that the two men had paid court to her for some time and were pressing her for a decision.

"Then I asked if she had room for another suitor. She seemed very surprised that I had asked such a question.

She said firmly that a union between a prince and an orphan would certainly not work and that I should seek a mate among the elite of the city. I informed her that twice father had chosen a prospective bride for me from the elite of the city, but I had rejected them both. I told her that I wanted to marry for love rather than influence.

"I suspected that she might be in love with one of the men, but she denied it quickly. She said that I had stirred her heart more than any other man she had met, and perhaps it was love. But she still insisted that it would be unwise for us to marry.

"Mother, I was completely frustrated by then, and I sent up a silent prayer for wisdom to know how I should respond. I was inspired to ask her if she would make this a subject of prayer and give me an answer after three days. She assured me that she would gladly pray about it and have an answer for me when I return."

Jonathan looked at his mother and spread out his hands. "So, Mother, I don't have any idea at this time what her answer will be in three days."

Ahinoam smiled and nodded. "I can see why you are so concerned, son, but I believe that you have done all you can, and I have faith to believe that you will have a good answer when you return."

"Thanks, Mother. I certainly hope so."

The next day Ahinoam made a special trip to the home of Mishel and Zereth. She had a good visit with both grandmother and granddaughter and felt very pleased with the success of her venture.

The hours rolled by slowly for Jonathan, but finally the very crucial third day arrived. He was ready for the visit early in the morning, but he painfully waited until close to midday before he turned his steps toward the major moment in his life.

Zereth met him at the door, and to the prince, she seemed especially buoyant and cheerful.

"Would like to see grandmother before we visit?"

"By all means," Jonathan responded. "I am very anxious to see her."

Mishel was seated in a rocking chair in the bedroom, looking much improved. Jonathan knelt and kissed her hand. "I am so glad to see you up and about."

The elderly lady nodded, "The bed was getting so tedious. It's good to be able to walk again."

Her eyes twinkled. "I'm glad for your interest and your visit, but I know that you didn't come particularly to see me. You two go and get to your visit."

Zereth led the prince into the living room, and they sat down across from each other. She seemed tense now and there was a shadow on her face.

"Prince Jonathan," she hesitated, "I want to be very sure of what you have in mind."

He nodded.

"Were you only interested in courting me and getting better acquainted or are your intentions more serious? Are you asking to marry me? I am embarrassed to ask."

He reached over and clasped her hand. "Please, don't be embarrassed. Yes, my purpose is more serious than merely getting acquainted. I am interested in asking you to become my wife."

She relaxed, and the shadow disappeared from her face. There was a smile at the edges of her lips. "Have you asked my grandfather for my hand or are you assuming his consent?"

He laughed. "No, I'm not assuming your grandfather's consent; neither did I want to assume your consent. I wanted to find out first whether you would approve my courting."

"Prince Jonathan, that was an excellent rebuttal. Now, since you mentioned that your father chose prospective brides for you among the elite of the city, perhaps he will not give his approval for you to want and possibly marry a no-name orphan."

He hesitated for a moment. "Lady Zereth, I believe that I can safely share with you some very sensitive facts about my father."

She nodded.

He bowed his head as though in prayer; then he plunged ahead. "My father has not made any decisions for some time now. He sits on his throne with his spear in his hand, and no one dares to approach him. I have been conducting the business of the kingdom for the past several months so you can see that to ask my father, to either court or marry you, would be useless." Jonathan's face twisted in pain, and she squeezed his hand.

"Please forgive me for speaking lightly. I had no idea that the king was incapacitated."

"You couldn't have known," he assured her, "but I thought that surely your grandfather would know."

She shook her head. "Grandfather never discusses palace business."

Her attitude changed. "Now Prince Jonathan, I have thought over and prayed about the matter of our possible relationship, but I must ask, perhaps you have changed your mind?"

The prince cleared his throat. "On the contrary, I am more anxious than ever for the privilege of courting you."

She lifted her chin as she spoke. "If you are as serious about courting me as you say, could we skip courtship? I would entertain a serious question from you if you are ready."

For a moment Jonathan was taken aback by her statement, but he was equal to the occasion. She had opened the door wide, and he must take her at her word. He dropped to his knees. "Lady Zereth, will you marry me?"

She laughed cheerily. "Prince Jonathan, I would consider it a privilege to marry you. Now, I will ease your mind regarding my grandparents. They are in full agreement for me to become your wife, so you need not bother to ask grandfather. And . . . , "she smiled merrily, "since your father is unable to grant his permission, I think you will find that your mother will give her full support."

Jonathan saw the light. "Has my mother been over to visit you?"

Her eyes twinkled, and her chin rose. "I have nothing more to say."

Jonathan had another very painful question to ask. "Zereth, if for some reason I never became the king of Israel would your love for me be just as strong?"

She clutched his arm. "Jonathan, I would be thrilled if you were never to become the king. I have no stars in my eyes to be queen, and I would have you more to myself if you remained simply Captain Jonathan."

They arose from their chairs, and he grasped both of her hands in his. "Zereth," he breathed huskily, "you have just made me the happiest man in all of Israel."

She followed his cue. "Jonathan, I am the happiest maiden in the land." Her eyes twinkled merrily. "Isn't it wonderful that we can be so hilariously happy at the same time and for the same reason?" They laughed together.

Jonathan made an exit from the home in a short time, walking on air. Zereth, the love of his life, would soon be his bride.

As the prince reveled in the success of his new conquest in romance, he suddenly thought of the two men who had been courting Zereth. What a disappointment awaited them, or perhaps the girl had already informed them of her decision to choose him and thus they were now nursing their wounds. He felt sorry for their loss, but he rejoiced in his own victory.

He had a major project to finish before the wedding. He was quite sure that Zereth would live with him in the tent at Gilgal, but it wouldn't be fair to her as the bride of the prince of Israel. He must have a proper house for her to live in.

His thoughts were racing. He would use his privilege as prince to dispatch buyers to Gilgal to build a house that would be ready for them by the time of the wedding. He called the king's aides together and gave assignments for designing, purchasing materials, and constructing the house in Gilgal.

The royal wedding was a national affair. Israelites came from every area of the nation. Every tribe was represented. It was a long tedious journey for them, and since it was only a three day affair, most of the travelers had little rest. Most of the guests brought their families and their tents, and thus the countryside around Gibeah of Benjamin was alive with people, oxen, and horses.

Zereth was a beautiful bride, and Jonathan was dashing. No doubt many of the available maidens of the kingdom gnashed their teeth in disappointment as they saw the handsome prince taking a wife. And, of course, the bachelors in attendance turned green with envy as they beheld the beautiful and graceful Zereth vow her eternal devotions to the prince. Jonathan met the men whom he had bested in the romancing of Zereth. They were both civil, but he could see that they were hurting.

Soon the activities of the wedding were over and the guests began to retire. The tent-city around Gibeah of Benjamin disappeared like snow under a warm spring sun. The royal families were left alone.

Jonathan had made plans to suspend his administrative activities at the royal court immediately after the wedding so that he could move his bride to their new home in Gilgal. He was anxious to get back to his troops. Nebal had done a good job of caring for them in his absence, but he was quite sure that the men were chafing because of their imposed idleness. As he prepared to leave Gibeah of Benjamin, Captain Abner informed him that he must move the king's troops to the Valley of Elah, where the Philistines were massing troops probably with intentions to invade Israel soon.

Jonathan kissed his mother good-bye, and the newlyweds, along with Jonathan's attendants and Zereth's maids, traveled to Gilgal, and Jonathan took his lovely bride into their new home.

The prince found that life with Zereth was one high day after another. She always arose early in the morning to prepare Jonathan for his work with the troops. In the evening she would come running to meet him with arms outstretched. Her embraces were always so warm and her lips so sweet on those of the prince that he was renewed every day.

Jonathan reinstated his weekly raids on the Philistine garrisons with good success. Several of the outposts were completely destroyed by the thrusts of his troops, and the remnants of the enemy forces were forced to flee to their larger stockades.

Life was pleasant and exciting.

# CHAPTER 4

For several weeks now spies sent out from Jonathan's camp reported a heavy Philistine troop buildup at Ephes Dammim in Judah. Jonathan immediately sent these reports to his father and was informed by return couriers that the king's spies had also noted the buildup, and the king was preparing to move his troops to the Valley of Elah to face the enemy army. The spies noticed that the enemy army, as yet, was not as large as the one at Michmash but was still much larger than Saul's two thousand men.

Jonathan waited impatiently for over a month, thinking surely that the king would soon be requisitioning his army, but the order never came. The prince was puzzled at his father's behavior and also that of Captain Abner who had the power to request Jonathan's regiment if he felt it was needed.

Reports came regularly by courier, announcing that neither army had attacked, but that a giant of a man from the Philistine army, Goliath, would come out into no-man's-land every day and challenge anyone from the Israelite army to fight him. The winner would take all.

The prince wondered at the inertia of the Israelites. Why would his father, who was also a giant in size, allow a barbarian to challenge him day after day without answering? Jonathan was tempted to leave his troops with his assistant and go the battle area to challenge the giant, but Zereth cooled the heat of his anxiety with her good counsel.

"No, Jonathan," she said sweetly. "I know how anxious you are to meet the challenge of this giant for our nation's sake, but this is your father's battle until he calls you by official order. He would greatly resent your interference, even though it is very evident that he needs you."

Jonathan laughed. "Zereth, dear, you are a treasure house of wisdom. You have saved me from the lion's jaws on several occasions, so I cherish your advice. I will stay by as you suggest."

She hugged him. "You are so easy to live with."

The next day an excited messenger astride a spent horse rode into the camp and shouted, "Long live the king, and God bless David."

Jonathan knew who the king was whom the courier had lauded, but who was this David he had asked the Lord to bless? The name wasn't entirely unfamiliar to the prince for his mother had mentioned several times that a very gracious shepherd youth from Bethlehem, named David, had spent some time at the royal court playing the harp for Jonathan's depressed father. Ahinoam had testified that the sweet music always calmed the king's nerves and made him much more receptive to her and the court attendants. The prince was quite sure that this was the David of whom the messenger was speaking.

Jonathan invited the courier to dismount and meet with him in the war tent. Zereth was with the prince, so she asked if she could meet with them.

"Certainly, my dear," Jonathan acceded. "You are welcome."

The two sat down facing the messenger and waited for his report. It was an exciting account.

"The king's army was camped in the Valley of Elah, and the Philistine troops gathered across on the opposite side of the valley. Both armies were ready for battle, but before a spear was raised or a sword unsheathed, a giant of a man, who called himself Goliath, came out of the Philistine ranks and began shouting threats and curses at our men.

"Captain Jonathan, this man was more than six cubits in height. Even your father, who is a giant of a man, was no match for his size. Every day he threw a challenge to us. 'Why have you come out to line up for battle? Am I not a Philistine, and you are the servants of Saul? Choose a man from yourselves, and let him come down to me. If he is able to fight with me and kill me, then we will be your servants, but if I prevail against him and kill him, then you shall be our servants and serve us.'

"Then he said something that stirred every one of us. 'I defy the armies of Israel this day; give me a man that we may fight together.' But not a man among us answered him. Every soldier in our entire army was scared, including the king, and we were all ashamed to admit that we were scared.

"After awhile some of our group went to the king and pleaded with him to send for you, Jonathan, for we remembered how you single-handedly routed the entire Philistine army at Michmash, and the army at Michmash was much larger than this company at Ephes Dammim. We were certain that the Lord could use you to conquer these barbarians again. But the king was angry with us. He said that you were busy fighting the enemy in another area, and after all, this was his battle, not yours.

"For forty long days that Philistine giant came out in the valley every day and challenged us, but no one volunteered to fight him. Then one day this young shepherd boy, David, came down from Bethlehem to our camp with food for his brothers and their captain. I remembered later that I had seen this young man at the king's court playing the harp for your father.

"When this shepherd boy heard Goliath come out into the valley and make his daily threats, he wanted to know why none of us had volunteered to go out to fight him. Of course, no one answered him, not even his brothers. In fact, his older brother told him to shut up and go back to his sheep, but David wasn't fazed. He said, 'I'll go out there right now and fight him for you.'

"The king and Captain Abner tried to talk the lad out of this rash idea, for they knew that the giant would kill him with one stab of his sword, but David was persistent. He didn't boast that the big man would be dead meat when he finished with him. He just simply said, 'The Lord will give this heathen into my hand.'

"We put King Saul's armor on him and gave him a sword, a spear, and a pat on the back and sent him off to meet this giant, but he came back in a few minutes. We thought that he had lost his nerve, but it wasn't that way at all. He just didn't feel right in that heavy armor. So he took it off and started out to where the giant was with only his shepherd's staff and his slingshot. We watched him as he picked up a few stones from the brook that ran between the camps of the two armies; then he acted like he was ready to take on the whole Philistine army.

"When Goliath saw this young man coming out to do battle without armor, sword, or spear, he laughed so loud that everyone could hear him. 'Am I a dog that you come to me with sticks?' And the Philistine cursed David by his gods. But David didn't answer him at first and it made the big man real mad.

"He said to David, 'Come to me, and I will give your flesh to the birds of the air and the beasts of the fields.'

"The shepherd boy kept coming, and he answered the Philistine giant. 'You come to me with a sword, with a spear, and with a javelin. But I come to you in the name of the Lord of hosts, the God of the armies of Israel whom you have defied. This day the Lord will deliver you into my hand, and I will strike you and take your head from you. And this day I will give the carcasses of the camp of the Philistines to the birds of the air and the wild beasts of the earth that all the earth may know that there is a God in Israel. Then all of this assembly shall know that the Lord does not save with sword and spear, for the battle is the Lord's, and He will give you into our hands.'

"I must tell you, Prince Jonathan, there wasn't a sound from the ranks of either army. Everyone in both camps had gathered as close as possible to watch these two men, for everybody was wondering what was going to happen. Even the giant Goliath was quiet. He stopped his pacing and pushed his helmet back over his forehead so that he could see this young shepherd from Bethlehem better.

"Then, without another word, young David began to run toward the giant, and as he was running, he put one of the stones he had picked up from the brook in his sling. He swung it around his head a couple of times, and then he threw it at the Philistine with all his strength. The stone hit Goliath in his forehead. That was the only place that wasn't covered by armor, and it sunk in deep. The giant immediately fell to the ground like a log. Then David ran up to him, drew the Philistine's sword from out of its scabbard, and cut off the giant's head.

"When all of the Philistines saw that their champion was dead, they lost heart and were immediately in a panic. They began to scatter to the four winds. They left their tents, their horses, their extra weapons, their extra food, and everything else they had brought with them to the battle site. We followed them all the way to the gates of Ekron and killed thousands of them along the way. It was a great victory for Israel, and it reminded many of us of your faith assault at Michmash.

"Now everyone is singing the praises of David. As we were marching back from the Valley of Elah to Gibeah, the women came out on the road to meet us with tambourines, and they sang, 'Saul has slain his thousands, and David his ten thousands.' I don't think your father liked that demonstration very well. He shouted at some of the women to go home."

The courier looked at Jonathan with questions in his eyes. Jonathan didn't comment, so the man continued his report.

"Your father wants to question David at the court tomorrow at mid morning. Captain Abner will be bringing the shepherd to the court, and your father is requesting your presence at that time. He is certain that you would want to meet this new Israelite hero. That concludes my report."

The courier prepared to leave, and Jonathan ordered the man's horse to be brought to the war tent. Jonathan thanked the messenger profusely for such a complete report, and Zereth added her thanks. The prince was thrilled to the depths of his being by the report of the aide.

He and Zereth bowed in the war tent in a prayer of thanksgiving for the way God had used this humble shepherd boy to gain a great victory for Israel. As they finished, Zereth touched her mate's arm. "Jonathan, this triumph of David at the Valley of Elah resembles your victory at Michmash, doesn't it?"

"Yes, it does. And even though I haven't met this young man as yet, I already feel a special kinship with him."

She nodded, "I understand your feelings and also share them. I'm quite certain that you are planning to be at court tomorrow when Abner brings David in."

"Yes, I am. I hate to leave you, but I must meet this kindred spirit named David."

She hugged him. "I will miss you very much, but I want you to go."

Jonathan immediately informed Nebal of his plans and ordered horses to be prepared for him and a few aides for a speedy trip to Gibeah of Benjamin.

He was in the king's chamber standing directly behind the king when Abner ushered the new military hero into the presence of the king. The head of Goliath was still in David's hand, and Saul wasted no time on preliminaries.

"Whose son are you, young man?" the king asked.

"I am the son of your servant Jesse, the Bethlehemite," David answered.

As King Saul continued to question David about his home background and his work, Jonathan was greatly impressed with the candor and lack of braggadocio on the part of the young shepherd. David insisted on giving the God of Israel all the credit for the amazing feat of killing the giant Goliath. He said simply that he had become acquainted with the Lord while caring for his sheep.

He testified. "The Lord helped me to protect my sheep from the wild animals that would attack during the night seasons. When a lion or a bear came and took a lamb out of the flock, I went after it and struck it and delivered the lamb from its mouth, and when it arose against me, I caught it by the beard, and struck and killed it. Your servant has killed both lion and bear in the strength of the Lord. I knew that God, who has given me the strength to kill the lion and bear, would also give this uncircumcised Philistine into my hand."

As Jonathan listened to David's testimony before the king, he recognized the kindred spirit in this young Israelite that he had sensed in the messenger's report. For the two of them, the shepherd and himself, it was the sympathy of a common faith—a common devotion to a holy idea—the glory of Jehovah and the good of God's people, Israel. The prince considered this attitude a priceless virtue that the Lord had given to him as a child, and he could see that this young man from Bethlehem shared this virtue with him.

Jonathan felt the impulse of a special love for David begin to beat in his heart. And from the moment that the king finished his interrogation of the shepherd lad, the soul of Jonathan was knit to the soul of David, and Jonathan loved him as his own soul.

When the interview was over, the King and Abner soon left the court and only Jonathan and David and an aide remained. The two, the prince and shepherd, moved toward each other, and as they met in the center of the king's throne room, there was a moment of special bonding. They embraced each other as if they were friends of long standing, and they felt a kinship for each other that was stronger than that of brothers in the flesh. Jonathan made a quick heartfelt decision. Actually, it wasn't a decision of the moment, but rather the fulfillment of a promise made to the Lord years ago in the city of Amalek.

When Samuel rebuked King Saul for his sin of sparing Agag and the choice cattle at Amalek, he had announced that God would replace Saul as king with a neighbor who was better than he and who would do the Lord's will. The announcement by the prophet had paralyzed the king and made him a recluse in his own court for many months.

Of course, the declaration by Samuel had also greatly troubled Jonathan. For the moment his world was turned upside down. If his father lost his kingship, there would be no succession, and he would never be king.

At first he was a bit angry with Samuel, and a tinge of bitterness crept into his heart against the Lord Himself. As Samuel delivered his diatribe to Saul, Jonathan was standing with his troops just to the left of the prophet, but Samuel completely ignored him. He had acted the same way at Gilgal. When he had finished rebuking the king for offering the unlawful sacrifice, he had disregarded Jonathan and turned on his heels and went back to Ramah.

Jonathan was in anguish. Had the Lord considered him guilty as well as his father? He realized that he must spend much time in prayer to put his mind at ease and erase any bitterness between his heart and Samuel and the Lord. So he retired to his tent and spent time in earnest prayer to the God of heaven.

As he prayed, the thought came to him, and he knew that the Lord had spoken. "Jonathan, I know your heart has been hurt by the decision I have made. I cannot give you the details of My plans at this time, but if you will be patient and trust My judgment, it will work to your good and the good of My people, Israel. I will impress you with the person I have chosen and will put it into your heart to love him and to pass on to him the tokens of your position as prince, for he will be the next king of Israel."

Jonathan's heart was at peace, and there in the king's court, the Lord spoke to him again. "This is the man that I have chosen, so you must carry out My will for him."

"David, my friend," Jonathan spoke with a smile on his face and no reservation in his heart. "I have gifts for you, and you must accept them for my sake."

The prince took off his cloak and belt and untied his tunic, but David stopped him. "No, Jonathan, you are the prince, and I am a commoner. I should be the one giving the gifts. It has always been the custom that those of higher station receive gifts, but I have nothing to give." He spread his hands helplessly.

Jonathan smiled. "I know whereof you speak. It is customary for the lesser in rank to give gifts to the greater, but God has shown to me that I must reverse that custom. If you will indulge me for now and accept the tokens of my love, I will explain later the compelling reasons for my actions."

David nodded. "It will be my privilege to receive gifts from my new dear friend, Jonathan, the prince of Israel."

Jonathan took off his cloak, his armor, his tunic, and his belt, along with his sword, his spear, and his bow and gave them to David. And for the moment, Prince Jonathan stood naked in the king's court, except for his breechcloth.

It might have appeared to some that the gifts of Jonathan were rather tacky. They were all secondhand, even to the sword and spear and bow. Being a prince, he would be expected to give the very best of gifts to a friend, and this is what he did. The genius of the gifts was the fact that every item was from the person of the prince, not from an extra wardrobe.

For many centuries the eastern people had considered the simlah, the long-flowing outer garment termed the cloak or robe, to be symbolic of the person's deepest, most innermost feelings and desires. In an external sense, it was identification of one's person and of his attitude toward his god. It was worn continually day and night. By day it was protection from the elements, and at night it also served as a blanket and shield from the cold when the wearer was in the field. When combined with the tunic, the cloak (simlah) became, in a vital sense, an integral part of one's person. Thus Jonathan, in essence, gave a part of himself to his new friend David. This would not have been true if the prince had gone to the marketplace and bought a new set of garments for David.

The eastern peoples usually wore the simlah until it became frayed and a change became mandatory. Even with the prince, there was not a wardrobe full of robes hanging in his closet. After all, the rich, doting Jacob made only one coat of many colors for his favorite son, Joseph.

Since David was a shepherd by trade, his dress was that of the Israelite herdsmen. It was a short outer garment of fleece and there were no accessories such as shoes, boots, or a cap. While with his flock, he had no need for the long outer garment since he slept among his sheep at night. But now the young shepherd lad was court musician for the king and an officer in the king's army by order of the king.

During the interview of an hour ago, the king had instructed Jonathan to commission David as captain in the army. He would be serving under the tutelage of Abner for a time, so he needed the royal garments to grace his frame as an officer, and Jonathan's garments, which had been created by the king's tailor, would fit his needs. But, of course, Jonathan had an even more compelling reason for giving David his princely clothing and his implements of war. It was because of the voice that had spoken to him years ago in his tent at Amalek city.

"I will impress you with the person whom I have chosen to be the next king, and I will put it in your heart to love him and to pass on to him the tokens of your position as prince, for he will be the next king of Israel." And today that same voice had said, "This is the man."

Jonathan faced his new friend in the king's court. "David, I will now tell you the reason for my gifts. God has impressed me that you will be the next king of Israel. My sword, spear, and bow have been proven in battle. They were used in my hands, and by the power of the God of Israel, in the slaughter of the Philistines at Michmash. My garments are kingly garments, so they will be fit for the next king of Israel.

They embraced again, and there were tears in David's eyes. "Thank you again, my dear friend Jonathan," he said simply.

So David, the former shepherd from Bethlehem, but of late the hero of the battle of Ephes Dammim and a captain in the royal army, was clothed in the accouterments of a prince, while Jonathan was garbed in new clothing from the king's tailor.

Jonathan left David at the king's court and headed home to his beloved Zereth. The eyes of the princess widened as she saw the new apparel gracing the body of her husband, but she said nothing. She immediately began to search her memory for any suggestions he had made relative to a change of clothing, but her mental pursuit yielded nothing. So she smiled, kissed and hugged him, and waited for a report.

When they were seated, Jonathan spoke. "Zereth, do you remember our talks together about the Prophet Samuel's statements to my father that God had chosen someone to replace him as king over Israel?"

She nodded but knew that there was more to come, so she remained silent.

"We wondered just who it would be the Lord had in mind for Father's replacement," Jonathan continued.

"Yes," Zereth said eagerly. "Have you found out who the man is?"

"Yes, I have. Today I listened to the king question the young shepherd from Bethlehem who killed the giant, Goliath, at Ephes Dammim and who played his harp for my father when he was depressed. This young man gave such honest and humble answers to my father's questions that I was greatly impressed with him."

The prince leaned forward and his face lighted up. "As I listened to the exchange between my father and David, a voice spoke to my heart, 'This is the man who will be the next king of Israel.'"

Zereth drew in her breath, and her eyes were large. "Jonathan," she whispered, "are you absolutely convinced that it was the Lord's voice that spoke to you? This man is so young and inexperienced in the art of warfare and the administration of a kingdom, how could he possibly serve as the king of this great nation?"

Jonathan nodded. "At first I had the same thoughts as you have expressed. There was a battle in my heart. I thought this unsophisticated shepherd surely wasn't the one to replace me as the next king, and I wondered if the impression on my heart was divine. But Zereth, the conviction persisted and grew stronger until I bowed my head and offered a silent prayer—'Lord, I will accept your decision'—then my heart was at peace."

They sat in silence for a few moments, and then Zereth spoke. "Jonathan, I trust your convictions. You are a godly man, and I firmly believe that it was the Spirit of God that spoke to your heart. So we must accept the Lord's decision."

"Thank you, Zereth. I was quite sure that when you heard my account of my father's interview of David and of the impression that God laid on my heart, you would agree with me about David's appointment. My heart was impressed to make another decision there at court that I hope you will approve of. I gave David my robe, tunic, belt, armor, sword, spear, and bow. These were all tokens of my position as prince that I transferred to David. So, in truth, I am no longer prince and you are no longer a princess. But we will still keep the title. That is the reason for my new wardrobe."

Zereth's eyes lighted with understanding, and she arose and embraced her husband warmly. "Yes, as soon as you came in the house, I noticed your new clothing," she admitted. "And, of course, I wondered at the reason for your change. I heartily approve of your decision. I am so glad that you did what you believe the Lord wanted you to do.

"And, Jonathan, as I mentioned to you before, I am relieved that you will not be king of Israel. You have been acting as king now for a long time because of the inability of your father, and I'm afraid that the burdens are making you prematurely gray. Perhaps you can serve as advisor to David when he takes office. You have so much wisdom and commonsense; I am sure that he will want your assistance."

The two were quiet for a few moments, and then Jonathan spoke. "Zereth, I want you to meet this unusual young man, David. Next to you and Mother, he is the most important person in my life, and yet, I have known him for such a short time."

The princess smiled. "I'm so glad, my Jonathan, that you put me first and your mother next. And, yes, I certainly want to meet this man who has made such an impression on your heart. Because of your usual good judgment in choosing friends, I am quite certain that I will not be disappointed. Perhaps I should invite him to be the special guest at a dinner I will give at our home."

"I am sure that David would be pleased by an invitation from you," agreed Jonathan.

The date was set, and invitations were soon delivered to special guests for the banquet at the home of Prince Jonathan and Princess Zereth. The invitations specified that the feast was in honor of David, the hero of Ephes Dammim and now a captain in the king's army. All of the royal family accepted the invitation to this special occasion with grace, except the king.

He declined with the rude retort, "I have more important things to do than attend a special meal in honor of a commoner."

Jonathan was thrilled that Zereth and David became good friends so quickly. It was a bonding similar to his relationship with the young Bethlehemite.

A few days after the banquet, Jonathan received an order from the king to move his army back to Gibeah of Benjamin immediately. The message read that a home was already being prepared for him and Zereth. It would be ready for their arrival. Tents would be supplied for the troops.

Jonathan was glad that Zereth would now be closer to his mother and he would be closer to David. Jonathan and Zereth had barely settled in their new home when a teary-eyed visitor knocked on their door. It was Jonathan's older sister, Merab. Through her tears, the girl told Jonathan her troubles.

"Jonathan," she sobbed. "Father has promised me to David as a wife, and I am in love with Adriel. I am fond of David as a brother, but I could not love him. Adriel and I have been planning to ask Father for permission to marry but hadn't found the right opportunity. I tried to tell Father that I didn't want to marry David, but he wouldn't listen. Then he said something strange. He said, 'You will probably be a widow soon, then I will give you permission to marry whoever you wish.' Do you have any idea why he would say that?"

Jonathan was shocked at the implications of her statement but he gave no indication.

His sister continued. "Jonathan, you have more influence with Father than anyone else, so would you talk to him for me? Just so you know, Michal is in love with David and would like to marry him. Please ask Father to let me marry Adriel and let Michal marry David. I would appreciate it so much."

She looked at him with hopeful eyes, and he took her in his arms. "Merab, dear, I will intercede for you with Father. If you love Adriel you should be allowed to marry him, and if Michal is in love with David, she should have her choice. I'm quite certain that David would welcome her for a wife. I will also speak with David."

"Thank you, Jonathan," Merab breathed gratefully. I will be hoping and praying that Father will be favorable to your suggestions."

Jonathan was beginning to suspect what he didn't want to believe, that his father was plotting the death of David and would even use his own daughter to achieve his purpose.

Evidently, Saul was now suspecting that David was the one who would replace him as king. He had heard the women praising David with their tambourines, dancing, and singing on the way back from the battle of Ephes Dammim, and they had sung somewhat of a serenade, "Saul has slain his thousands and David his ten thousands."

Jonathan was certain that this disparity in credit had hurt the pride of the king quite deeply. Thus, his deranged mind had probably become suspicious that David would use his new fame to unseat him as the king and take over the kingdom. The prince shook his head in an attempt to dispel these unwelcome thoughts.

The next morning Jonathan went to visit the king about Merab's problem. The king admitted him with a wave of his hand and listened quietly as Jonathan pled the case of Merab and Adriel and also of Michal, who loved David and wished to marry him.

Saul pondered the situation for a few moments; then he shrugged his shoulders. "I will concede to the switch from Merab to Michal, but only if David will promise to be very aggressive in his wars against the Philistines and commit to a very substantial dowry for Michal. Since she is the baby of the family, she is very close to her mother and to me."

Jonathan was speechless for a few moments. The audacity of the king was beyond his comprehension.

"But father," he protested. "David doesn't have any money for a dowry. You haven't allowed him to go back to his home in Bethlehem since the battle of Ephes Dammim, and he hasn't received any army pay as yet. He probably has friends in Bethlehem, and I have heard that his parents are quite wealthy, but he is not the type to sponge off his parents."

The king had a wicked gleam in his eyes. "The dowry that I am asking for will not involve money. Please call David in now. I will give him my permission to marry Michal and will also acquaint both of you with the expected dowry." He laughed shortly. "Perhaps when he hears the choice of the dowry, he will not want to marry the princess."

Jonathan was puzzled about the king's statement. He wondered what the unbalanced mind of the king had dreamed up as a pre-wedding assignment for David that might possibly frighten the hero of Ephes Dammim.

He found David with the troops making plans for another raid on a Philistine garrison. The king was very pleasant and civil to David as Jonathan brought him into the king's court. David bowed respectfully, stepped back a few paces, and waited.

The king didn't speak for a few moments as he looked David over from head to toe. Then he looked at Jonathan with a questioning look in his eyes. Jonathan knew that his father had recognized Jonathan's garments gracing the body of David and his suspicious mind began forming an evil conclusion, but he held his tongue and smiled at David.

"Captain David," he said officiously. "I have noticed your zeal for the Lord and for our nation, Israel. You have already proven yourself to be an able warrior and commander, and I desire to reward you by making you a part of the royal family. I had promised you my older daughter, Merab, in marriage, but I was rather hasty in that decision. She is in love with Adriel the Meholathite, and thus was in a great deal of agony when she found that I had promised her to you. But my younger daughter, Michal, is in love with you, and therefore, I will give her to you instead of Merab. The crown will give the two of you a royal wedding here in the palace as soon as arrangements can be made."

David started to speak, but the king held up his hand, indicating that he had more to say.

"Usually a dowry is expected for the proposed bride. Since your parents have seven older sons, I am quite sure that they have paid some dowry?"

David nodded.

"Since my daughter, Michal, is a member of royalty, the dowry would be much higher than with a commoner. But since you are not a wealthy man, I am willing to make an exception for you. If you will bring me one hundred foreskins of my enemies, the Philistines, I will be satisfied."

Jonathan could hardly believe his ears. His former thoughts that the king was plotting the death of David were confirmed by this deadly request. Evidently the king was confident that asking for such a bloody dowry would surely send the Bethlehemite to his death.

The prince was about to protest, but David, after he had bowed humbly before the king spoke first, "My lord, the thought of marrying the king's daughter and thus becoming son-in-law to the king, overwhelms me. I am a poor, lightly esteemed man, and my family is one of the lesser families in the tribe of Judah. But since you know this, O king, and have still offered your daughter to be my wife, tomorrow I will most gladly bring to you the tokens of your proposed dowry."

He stepped back, bowed again, and left the court. Jonathan also left the court sick at heart.

Later in the day, David sought out Jonathan. "My dear friend, Jonathan," he said as he clasped Jonathan's hand. "I have made arrangements with a special company of my men to go down to the camp of the Philistines tonight. I would have asked you to go with me, but I prize your life highly and will not expose you to such a dangerous mission. I hope you understand."

"Yes, I understand your concern, but I am also greatly concerned for you. My father was not fair in requesting such an unusual dowry from you. I would like, with your permission, to go back to my father and plead for a change of settlement for Michal. I would be glad to provide a sensible financial dowry for you."

David patted his friend on the shoulder, "Jonathan, I am so grateful for your concern and offer, but I will not accept it. I know how much your father hates the Philistines, and I share his feelings. I am sure that I can help to satisfy his revenge against them, and at the same time win your lovely sister. I believe that God will protect me from these uncircumcised barbarians, and thus I go with His blessing."

Jonathan watched the young Bethlehemite walk away. He thought, *I hope and pray that David returns safely from this insane assignment and thus disappoints my father.*

That night Jonathan and Zereth spent much time in special prayer for David's safety and success in his raid on the Philistine garrison. Jonathan also knew the men that were accompanying David. Several of these men had families, so the men and their families were included in the special prayers of the prince and princess. As they finished their prayer, they embraced and the eyes of both were moist.

The next morning Jonathan hurried to the king's court. He knew that if David was successful in his crusade for the barbarian foreskins, he and his company would be in motion the entire night. There was the march to and from the battle area and then the battle itself. One hundred bloody tokens would take some time to acquire, so David would, no doubt, want to meet with the king early so that he could get to his rest.

Jonathan was in court when an aide announced the arrival of the honorable captain of the army, David. The young man came in before the king and Jonathan with a large bag in his hand. He bowed to them and presented the bag to the king.

"My lord," he addressed Saul. "God gave success to your servant and his helpers. We were able to kill two hundred of your enemies instead of the one hundred you requested, and the full tally is in the bag. I would be glad if you would have an aide certify the total."

"That won't be necessary," the king said rather gruffly. "I will accept your count."

David bowed. "Thank you. I would also like to report that not one man was lost in this incursion. We are very thankful to the Lord for His safe keeping."

Saul hesitated. "Captain David, you have fulfilled the requirements of the dowry for my daughter, so I will give my permission for you to marry her. You have the king's blessing."

The king turned to Jonathan. "Captain Jonathan, I charge you with the responsibility of notifying Michal and those who will be responsible for the arrangements for the royal wedding." He waved the two out of his presence.

David grasped Jonathan's arm as they stepped out of the palace. "My dear friend, Jonathan, I feel so greatly honored to be a son-in-law of the king and thus a brother-in-law to you."

Jonathan smiled. "Welcome to the family," he said with emotion.

"Now," Jonathan continued. "I will invite you to go with me to see Michal, and as soon as I tell her about the king's wishes, perhaps you will want to speak with her."

"I would like that," David responded.

Michal hid her emotions well when Jonathan and then David spoke with her, but Jonathan could tell that the pretty princess was excited to be betrothed to David. Jonathan invited her to go with him to visit with their mother and Zereth regarding preparations for the wedding.

The wedding was only a one-day affair, thus there was not any tent city. However, there was one feature that was sadly missing in Jonathan and Zereth's wedding that was very visible in Michal and David's marriage. The king was there in full regalia. Jonathan was pleased.

Jonathan and David wasted no time after the nuptials were over. They were men of purpose. Jonathan took his men on many incursions on the Philistine outposts, while David took the company of men assigned to him by Abner and went in another direction.

Jonathan always had good success in his incursions, but invariably, David inflicted greater losses on the enemy and captured the most spoil. His prowess as an army commander was remarkable, but Jonathan was not envious. He commended his friend.

There was one problem that Jonathan noticed with increasing concern, but he made no move to interfere. David would, in an excited manner, report to the king the results of every raid that his company made on the Philistine outposts. At first, the king acted pleased, but Jonathan noticed a gradual change in his mood.

He again reverted to sitting on his throne all day long with his spear in his hand. He was churlish to his aides and testy to all that approached him. He would allow David's entrance to the court and time for his report, but now the accounts were received with a scowl, rather than a smile. In his exuberance, David failed to notice the change of the king's attitude toward him, but Jonathan noticed, and he was deeply concerned. The prince could see that every report from the new army commander reminded Saul of Samuel's declaration at Gilgal and Amalek, and also the chant of the women on the road back from the slaying of Goliath. Jonathan could see in his father's actions that the king also now believed that David was the man who would supplant him on the throne.

It was the calm before the storm, but the prince was certain that the storm would soon come.

# JONATHAN'S HEART

## CHAPTER 5

The king was a man possessed of a demon. He paced back and forth in the court while Jonathan and the servants waited. Finally, with his eyes bloodshot and blazing and his body trembling with intense anger, he turned to face the waiting group. There were flecks of foam on his lips. He tried to speak but the words choked in his throat. When he was finally able to form the words, the tone was guttural.

"I demand that all of you join with me in hunting down David and killing him." He paused to let the words sink in before continuing. "He is a threat to our nation and to me personally, and therefore, he must be killed. Do you hear?" he shouted.

The servants bowed in acceptance, but Jonathan remained standing. His heart was churning. He had known for some time that the king was not as favorable toward David as he had been at the first, but he hadn't realized that the king's favor had turned to hate. The hate was so deep that he wanted his son-in-law put to death. Jonathan knew now that the king had come to realize that David was the man who would replace him on the throne of Israel, and this thought had pushed him over the edge. Jonathan knew that the servants were also deeply troubled by the king's order, since David was a very popular figure in the king's court.

Jonathan wanted to speak with his father about reconciliation with David, but he realized that now was not the time. The king's ire could be turned against him quite easily since he knew that Jonathan and David were now bosom friends. Saul's ire must cool first, and then perhaps he would listen to reason.

David was with his troops making plans for another raid on a Philistine outpost when the prince found him. David could tell by the look on Jonathan's face that his friend was not bringing good news.

"David," Jonathan said with emotion choking him. "I have bad news. My father is determined to kill you, so you must hide until mid morning. Only a short time ago, the king called the servants and me to a meeting, and there he ordered us to find you and kill you. Now, my friend, you are a favorite among the servants, but I am sorry to say that a few of them are not to be trusted. In order to curry favor with the king, they would stab you in the back. You must hide tonight, and when my father's anger has cooled, I will speak to him and then report to you. Hopefully he will be favorable."

The two friends embraced and wept together, and then David went into the forest and Jonathan went home to Zereth.

Jonathan and Zereth invited Michal to spend the night with them, and the three prayed together for David's safety in the forest and from the wrath of the king. Zereth cradled Michal in her arms and the two wept together.

The next morning, armed with a prayer in his heart, Jonathan approached his father. As usual, he was sitting on the throne with his spear in his hand. He didn't smile when Jonathan entered, but he did beckon the prince to approach by a wave of his hand. Jonathan was quite sure that the king knew what his mission was, so he made his case quickly.

"Father, I know that you are angry with David, but I hope that you and your servants will not cause him bodily harm. He is doing so well in his raids against the Philistines that I believe those barbarians will soon request peace. So far, in all of his many battles, he has not lost a man. That is so unusual. He esteems you highly and feels honored to battle your enemies and to have your daughter and my sister as his wife. He would gladly give his life for you and Michal.

"You must remember how he saved your army and our beloved nation at Ephes Dammim when he killed the giant, Goliath. Not one of your soldiers would do battle with him, but David took only his sling and some stones and risked his life to go out and fight with Goliath. It was a wonderful act of courage and faith. I remember that you and your troops rejoiced when the giant died and the Philistines were chased all the way to Gath and Ekron.

"Father, I hope that you will change your heart toward David and rescind your order to have him killed, because you would have innocent blood on your hands."

Jonathan paused and waited for the king to reply. He had seen a change of expression on Saul's face as he was making his plea for David, so he waited hopefully. The king shifted his position on the throne and his grip on his spear relaxed. But he was struggling.

"Perhaps I was too hasty in my order for David's execution," he admitted. "He did serve us well at Ephes Dammim. Had he not killed the giant when he did, the barbarians would probably have attacked us and we had little to withstand them. They would have overwhelmed us by their numbers. Also, from what I hear from him and many of his troops, he is doing a good job in raiding the Philistine garrisons. He brings back much spoil and thus far hasn't lost one of his men.

"So . . . ," the king waved his spear, "I am giving another order. As the Lord lives, David will not be killed. I command you, Jonathan, to send a message in the king's name to all of the servants and the troops to protect David from harm."

The king gestured for Jonathan to leave. The interview was over.

Jonathan bowed. "Thank you, Father. I will send the order out immediately."

He was elated as he left the king's presence, but there was a cloud on the horizon. He recognized that the king's edict was a reprieve rather than a total victory. His father was sick and, therefore, was unpredictable.

Jonathan sent two messengers out with the king's order to the servants and troops. Then he went to find David. He found an eager, hopeful David at the edge of the forest.

"David, my friend, I have good news for you. I have just come from an interview with the king. He was in a much better mood this morning than he was yesterday. He welcomed me and listened respectfully to my plea. His face is again favorable to you, my friend. He vowed by the Lord of hosts that you were not to be killed, but rather be protected by all of the servants and the soldiers." The two friends embraced at the edge of the forest and rejoiced together.

"Now," Jonathan continued. "I know that you are anxious to see Michal. Then you need to go in before the king so that he can verify the order that he gave me this morning."

There was peace again in the king's encampment, but it was a troubled peace. The king was neglecting the business of the realm, so Jonathan was involved more and more in managing the affairs of the kingdom.

As always there were both civil and military cases to decide as well as petty and grand penalties to assess. The judgment of the prince was tested to the limit many times. Even though by nature Jonathan was a very judicious man, he always felt a personal lack and a need to seek the wisdom of God. The priest, Ahijah, was a local resident, and the prince leaned heavily on his revelations obtained through the Urim and Thummim.

Jonathan was torn. He felt a need to spend more time in his crusades against the Philistines. The pesky barbarians were always threatening to push their boundaries into Israelite territory, and thus they were always taking advantage of the king's complacency. David was making inroads into their districts and was destroying many of their outposts and capturing much spoil. But lately, just as Jonathan was forced to spend more time in running the kingdom because of the king's inaction, David was ordered by royal order to spend more time in making music to combat the king's depression.

Often as Jonathan worked in the chamber, he heard sweet music coming from the king's court. David was at work soothing the king's spirit. When time permitted Jonathan would vacate the chamber and listen to David as he played. The music was a balm to the prince's heart as well.

One day as Jonathan watched, he noticed the king acting strangely. Usually he sat impassive on the throne with his spear in his hand and an unearthly gleam in his eyes, but now he was stirring as if he had just awakened. His hands were twitching and his face was contracting. Suddenly, he raised his spear and with all his might cast it at David. The king was an unusually strong man and had the spear struck David it would have gone completely through his body, but David dodged, and the weapon buried itself in the opposite wall. For a moment David looked at the king in surprise; then he walked out of the king's court.

Jonathan also left the king's court, sick at heart. He had hoped that his father had abandoned his vendetta against David, but evidently the hate had returned stronger than ever. The two friends met on the palace grounds and embraced but for a few moments; both were mute.

Jonathan broke the silence between them. "I don't know what went wrong," he said helplessly. "I knew that the bad spirit had been troubling him more than ever lately, but usually your music calms him and makes him less combative. It appears that the old man of hate has possessed him again, so my friend, you will not be safe anywhere that he can find you. I am quite sure that he will attempt to have you killed tonight, so you must flee for your life. Good-bye, dear friend, I will do my best to keep in touch."

The next day Michal confirmed Jonathan's prediction. Saul had sent messengers to capture David that night, but Michal let him down through a window, and he had escaped. Michal then told the messengers that David was sick and had put a simulated body in his bed so it would throw them off and give David more time. Later, Jonathan learned that David had escaped to Ramah and was staying with Samuel.

With David gone, the raids against the Philistines ceased. Jonathan called Abner into the official chamber and requested that he take over David's agenda against the Philistines, but the veteran army officer was almost insolent in his refusal.

"I take orders only from the king," he informed Jonathan, "and the king would prefer that I keep the men ready to meet any attack from outside of our borders."

Jonathan could have invoked royal authority and demoted the captain to a foot soldier, but he was quite sure that Abner would appeal to the king and the king would reinstate him immediately.

Jonathan was in a quandary. There were so many items of business demanding his attention at the palace, but he must also take time to harry the Philistines lest they get aggressive and double their forces like at Michmash.

It had been a bad day for the prince. He had taken time away from his duties at court to lead a raid against the Philistine garrison, and in the skirmish, he had lost two men by enemy arrows and two others were badly wounded. He was hurting. As the captain, he had become acquainted with and emotionally attached to each man in his regiment, and he felt personally responsible for their safety even in battle. Up to this point in time, not one man had been lost in the many incursions his army had waged against the enemy outposts. He felt so grateful to God for this safety record and had given special thanks to His heavenly commander after each battle. He would do the same today but with tears in his voice.

He was anxious to get home to Zereth, for he knew that she would drive the clouds away and comfort his wounded heart. She would also go with him to notify and comfort the loved ones of those who were lost in the battle. He left Nebal in charge of marching the troops back to camp and mounted his horse for a quick trip to his home.

As he made his way homeward, his thoughts centered on his army's change of fortunes. What was the reason for the loss of life? Had he possibly become too complacent because of the many trouble free incursions and thus let down his guard, or were the pagans becoming more bold and aggressive in their retaliation? He shrugged his shoulders in frustration and reasoned that in future raids he must make better preparations in both spiritual and military areas.

His thoughts diverted for a few moments to his friend David. He felt so badly that David was now a fugitive and was being hunted like an ordinary criminal by the king. The prince knew that Michal missed her husband greatly, and so many others were inquiring about him. Jonathan was quite sure that David would contact Michal and himself by courier as soon as he was situated.

The thoughts of the prince were again diverted to a very pleasant vision of Zereth running out to meet him with outstretched arms and ruby lips eager to meet him. He could always count on her love. She had never failed him.

He topped the hill overlooking the capital city. There was the palace standing almost in the center of the city, and off to the left he could see the red roof of his own home. Nearby were the tents and houses where the soldiers were billeted. It was a comfortable setting. As he neared the city gate, he looked closely. *Surely*, he thought,

*Zereth is looking out the window facing the front gate, and she will soon see me and come running to meet me.*

An aide took his horse, and the prince began to walk from the gate to the front door of his home. He was puzzled, for there was no Zereth. His hands trembled on the latch as his heart told him that something was wrong, but he had no idea what it might be.

As his eyes grew accustomed to the semi-darkness within, he made out the still form of his wife lying on the bed in the corner of the room. He rushed over and picked her up in his arms.

"Zereth, my dear, what's wrong?" he cried with fear in his voice. "Are you ill? Tell me what is wrong."

The living bundle in his arms stirred and a sob shook her slight frame. She shook her head. "No, Jonathan, I am not ill, but I am terribly troubled."

"Tell me what is wrong," he pleaded anxiously. "Is it something that I have done?"

She shook her head again. "No, Jonathan, you are always sweet and kind. The trouble is with me. You see, we have been married now for several years, and I have not yet conceived. As a prince, you must have an heir, but I have failed you. I am afraid that I am hopelessly barren. Up to this time, I have been living in hope and have suffered in silence over the matter, but today my heart broke. I can no longer ignore my deficiency. What shall I do?"

She raised her pretty tear-stained face, and Jonathan kissed the tears away.

"Oh Zereth, my dear, I was so afraid that you were ill, and my heart was crushed. Please, let your heart be at ease. I will love you with all my heart regardless of whether or not you give me an heir. Naturally, I would love to have a son, in fact several children, but you are worth more to me than a dozen children. So dry your eyes Princess Zereth and give me those open arms and pleasant lips that have strengthened me so much after every battle." She hastened to respond.

As they relaxed, a thought came to him. "By the way, did you know that Prophet Samuel's mother, Hannah, was unable to conceive for several years? She too was greatly concerned about her barren condition. Her husband Elkanah's second wife, Peninnah, was very fruitful and had several children. She would taunt Hannah mercilessly for her inability to have children. Then one day when Hannah was at the temple in Shiloh, she poured out her heart's desire to Eli the priest. He had special prayer for her, and God opened her womb. Soon Samuel was born, and later three other sons and two daughters were born to her."

As he finished speaking, Zereth clutched his arm, and her eyes were shinning. "Jonathan, that is the answer. I will give you permission to marry a second wife, and if she would have children, perhaps I could take one for you."

He looked into her dark questioning eyes and shook his head vigorously. "No, dear, that would never work. I do not wish to have a second wife. You are all I want. You probably are not aware that my father has a second wife and several concubines. Actually, the second wife is also a concubine, for he never formalized a marriage contract with her. She has a son named Ishbosheth, and although he is my half brother, I have never met him. I have wanted so much to get acquainted with him, since we are almost the same age, but his mother is very aloof and will not meet any of our family. When father first suggested that he was planning to take a second mate, Mother was greatly troubled and pleaded with him not to do so. But Father, stubborn as always, went ahead with the arrangement. Later, Mother graciously accepted the union and attempted to get acquainted with the other woman, but her efforts were rejected.

"I remember as a child Mother reading to me from the writings of Moses that God knew that multiple wives were never a good plan. He warned that men who, in the future, might serve as kings should be content with one wife. He knew that trouble would result from the ungodly practice of multiple marriages."

The two sat for a time, locked in each other's arms, their hearts beating as one. Jonathan broke the silence. "The prophet Samuel still lives at Ramah, and although he is very infirm, he is still powerful in mind and spirit. I am sure that he would count it a privilege to intercede for us."

Zereth was quick to rebut. "But Jonathan, you told me that in both instances when Samuel came to rebuke your father, he completely ignored you. Do you think now that he would waste time on our behalf?"

The prince answered with spirit. "Zereth, I have reflected much on the prophet's actions toward me when he chastised Father. I don't believe that it was an intentional snub to me. Rather, I believe that he trusted me to understand and accept the Lord's decision without serious question. That would be a compliment rather than a slur."

Zereth looked deep into her husband's eyes. She lovingly laid her hand on his arm. "Jonathan, I am so grateful to the Lord for you. You are one in a million. You are so willing to take a lesser role even though you have such outstanding leadership ability. If God sees fit to give us a son, I hope and pray that he will be like his father. Now tell me more about people whom we can enlist to petition the Lord to heal my barren condition."

"Well, I confess that I have lost some confidence in Priest Ahijah, but after all, he is a man of God, and therefore, we should enlist his intercession. Then, you must confide your fears to my mother and to your grandparents and request their special prayer. Their special prayers joined with ours, Samuel's, and Ahijah's will hopefully bring a positive answer from the Lord, and then you will rejoice with child."

She nodded. "This is our only hope." She looked at him again with questions in her eyes. "Jonathan, if God says 'no' to our petitions, will you still love me as much as before?"

He squeezed her waist. "Zereth, I promised at our wedding to love you until 'death do us part,' and my promises to you are never with reservations. My love for you grows stronger every day, and I will truly love you to the day of my death. If you bear me a son, I will love him with all my heart, but if you cannot give me a son, it will not lessen my love for you."

She relaxed and her heart was at peace.

Jonathan had an inspiration. "Zereth, since all of these prayers will be rising daily to the throne of God for your conception, we must act in faith. You should start making preparations for the child that the Lord will certainly give us. Start knitting garments and blankets for the baby as though God has already given you the signs of pregnancy."

Her face brightened. "That is a wonderful idea. I will begin immediately."

A few days after Zereth's announcement of her barren condition, Jonathan was making a routine review of the troops. He noticed that David's former company was not full strength, and he wondered why. He immediately summoned Captain Abner to give an account of the disappearance of David's former troops. Abner was curt but responsive.

"Those rebels ran off to join David in the wilderness. When Saul finds David, these men will be treated as deserters and will be put to death without a trial. That's all I have to report."

"Thank you, Captain Abner," Jonathan offered. He hesitated then continued, "Do you go with the king every time he goes out after David?"

"Yes, I do, I am as anxious to catch that renegade as the king is. He must be captured and killed."

"I have two more questions for you then. Will you please, tell me what David has done to deserve to be killed?"

Abner set his jaw. "I don't have to answer such a foolish question. And besides, you certainly should know that David is an enemy of the king."

"I have one more question. The last time I spoke to you, you informed me that the king needs you here in the capital to meet any enemy threat that might come across our borders. It might be of interest to you to know that while the two of you, with picked troops, are chasing one man the Philistines are plotting a major offensive on our southern border in the near future. We captured a Philistine soldier only yesterday who was willing to give us quite a few details about their plans. So perhaps while you and the king are chasing a mouse, a lion will come in the gate. You are dismissed."

During the next few weeks and months, Jonathan divided his time between administration at the court and incursions against the Philistines. He heard from David weekly through a nightly courier. The last message informed the prince that David had left Ramah for sanctuary in the wilderness.

Jonathan had just returned from another raid on a Philistine outpost when two visitors came to his home. The first one was an official courier bringing a summons from the king to appear at the New Moon Feast the next day at the palace. Jonathan was always bored at these functions and would prefer to skip them all, but to do so would constitute an open affront to the king. He would make the sacrifice by attending and act as though he were enjoying the affair.

The other visitor was David. The two hadn't visited together for some time, so they embraced warmly, but Jonathan could tell that his friend was greatly troubled.

"My friend, Jonathan," David said with desperation in his voice. "Tell me what sin I have done to incur the king's wrath? I had thought that the Lord was blessing my efforts against the Philistine enemies of the king so well that he would rejoice with me, but he is chasing me as the hounds chase the hart. I am certain that one day he will find me and kill me."

Jonathan's heart was pained for his friend. "David, I am quite certain that my father's hatred of you will soon cool and he will welcome you back to the court. He knows how close we are to each other, so I hope that will calm any evil intentions he has against you."

"Yes," David agreed, "your father certainly knows that I have found favor in your eyes, so he will probably reason, 'I don't want Jonathan to know that I am dedicated to kill David, for it would grieve him too much.' Jonathan, as the Lord lives and your soul lives, there is but a step between me and death."

Jonathan was greatly agitated at his friend's suggestion that he was near death at the king's hands. He spread his hands in frustration. "David, what can I do? I will do whatever you suggest."

The former shepherd did have a suggestion. "Jonathan, tomorrow is the New Moon Feast, and as a captain in the king's army, I should be present. I am quite sure that the king has attempted to reach me with a summons, but I have been hiding in the forest and could not be reached.

"Jonathan, I must not go to this festival, for I have reason to believe that the king would take advantage of this occasion to kill me. He will notice that my chair is empty, for I usually sit on his immediate left, as you do on his right. At first, he will notice my absence and say nothing. Later, he will question you about my empty seat. When he asks you why I am not at the feast, please tell him that I asked permission of you to go to Bethlehem to attend a yearly sacrifice for the family. If he says, 'it is well,' then it will be safe for me to return to the king's court, at least for the present. But if he becomes extremely angry, I will know that evil is determined against me, and I will remain in hiding.

"I loathe this life of the pursued, but I have no other option at this time, since I have no trusted friends except you, Zereth, Michal, my family, and a few soldiers and the forest.

"Jonathan, I trust that you will believe in me and be my friend regardless of your father's decision. If you see iniquity in me at any time, please kill me yourself, for I would deserve to die, and you would be blameless."

The two friends embraced warmly, and for a few moments both were mute. Then Jonathan spoke. "David, I will always believe you, and I will do all in my power to shield you from my father's wrath. I will tell you immediately if my father has planned evil against you. I will do as you say. If after I tell him that you have asked permission to go to your home in Bethlehem, he says 'it is well,' I will come running, for it will be good news. But if he becomes angry, I will know that all is not well, and I will come warn you.

"On the third day, if you will come down to this part of the forest and hide behind the stone Ezel, I will bring a lad out with me as if I am practicing with my bow and arrows. When the boy goes to find the arrows, I will either say, 'the arrows are on this side,' which will be a signal for you to come to join me since you will enjoy safety and not harm, or 'the arrows are beyond you,' which means that you must flee for your life since the king is more determined than ever to kill you."

The two friends embraced again, and Jonathan went home to Zereth, and David went back into the forest. The next day Jonathan joined the king's staff at the festival of the New Moon. The first day of the festival Jonathan sensed that his father was missing David, for he would often glance at the empty seat on his left. But as David had predicted, the king said nothing about his absence on the first day of the feast. By the second day, Saul could no long hold his peace. He turned to Jonathan with an angry scowl on his face.

"Why has the son of Jesse not come to eat either yesterday or today?" he demanded.

Jonathan was ready with an answer. "David earnestly asked my permission to go to Bethlehem. He told me that his family was having a sacrifice in the city and his older brother had commanded him to be present. That is the reason, my lord, that he has not come to the feast."

Saul was livid. He knew that his oldest son was protecting the king's mortal enemy, and his anger blazed against his firstborn. He groped for a moment for the words to describe his great rage.

"You son of a perverse, rebellious woman!" he shouted. "Do I not know that you have chosen the son of Jesse to your own shame and to the shame of your mother's nakedness? For as long as the son of Jesse lives on the earth you shall not be established, nor your kingdom. Therefore, send and bring him to me, for he shall surely die."

Jonathan's heart was churning, and he was mute as the king extended his tirade. The prince had anticipated that the king would speak a few choice invectives against David because of his missing the feast, but he had not expected that his father would so blatantly blaspheme the character of his mother. In a very real sense, the king had accused Jonathan's mother of being a wench.

For a moment the bitter phlegm of hate arose in the throat of the prince against his father. It almost choked him, but the Spirit of the Lord dissipated the foreign matter quickly. The king had profaned two of the dearest people in the life of the prince, and he was hurting deeply.

Jonathan was quite sure that he knew why his father had chosen to disparage his wife's character. Several times Ahinoam had lovingly and tactfully cautioned the king regarding presuming against the Lord's commands. She knew about the unlawful sacrifice at Gilgal and the sparing of Agag and had reminded him that the blessings of the Lord were vital to the success of his reign over Israel.

"My dear husband, you are destined to constantly fight against our pagan enemies today because our leaders of yesterday disobeyed God. Please, do not repeat their mistakes."

The king had resented his wife's suggestions and stubbornly gone ahead with his presumptive experiences at Gilgal and Amalek. Now he presumed to strike back at his wife through the stigmatizing of her name to her favorite son.

When the king paused in his harangue, Jonathan spoke to him from his wounded heart. "Why should David be killed? What has he done?"

He hoped his father's anger would cool quickly so that he could reason with him, but his wish was unfulfilled. The king was beyond the point of logic. He was insane. Without answering the prince, he lifted the spear, which always seemed to be in his hand of late, and cast it at Jonathan with all his might. Jonathan easily dodged the deadly missile, and without another word, he arose from the table and left the room. He knew now that David was right. Saul had planned to kill David at the festival, and his disappointment at being thwarted was so great that his mind again became unbalanced.

Jonathan hurried home to Zereth. He was confident that she would provide balm for his wounded heart and would also satisfy his hunger pains since he had left the New Moon table without eating.

His wife quickly noticed the troubled look on his face. "Jonathan, what is wrong?" she questioned. "Please come and tell me what the trouble is."

As they sat together, he told her about his father's tirade against David, the disparaging remarks against Ahinoam, and the demand that David be killed.

"When I spoke for David, he tried to kill me with his spear," Jonathan lamented.

She patted his arm. "Jonathan, I know how badly you are hurting for you love your mother so much, but I think that it would be best if we do not tell your mother about the king's remarks. She is so kind and would certainly understand, but I am afraid it would hurt her deeply."

Jonathan nodded. "I think you have spoken wisely. Mother does understand my father's moods very well, but despite his many failings, she still loves him and prays daily for a change of heart for him. So we will keep this abuse to ourselves."

"Tomorrow, I must share the gist of my father's remarks with David. I dread this assignment, since both David and I were hoping, but not really expecting, reconciliation between them, but it isn't going to happen, so David must stay in hiding."

They sat in silence for a few moments and then Zereth ventured. "Jonathan, do you think that you will be safe in your father's presence after that torrid meeting between you two? Since he actually attempted to kill you, should you trust yourself with him in the future?"

Jonathan thought for a few moments. When he answered, his voice was not completely convincing. "I would like to believe that when Father's anger cools, he will feel ashamed of his actions against me and will try to make amends. Now, I don't mean that he will apologize. That would strain his proud heart too much. Of course, I will be sure to always keep my guard up when I am in his presence, since his fits of intense anger seem to plague him more regularly of late."

Jonathan paused and shook his head. "I wish that we could invite David and Michal to spend the night with us before David leaves the neighborhood, but I'm afraid that would put him in greater jeopardy. I also wish that you could go with me when I bid him good-bye tomorrow, but that might be a red flag to my father's spies. They will be watching me rather closely from now on to see if I might give David's hiding place away."

The next morning, according to the plan, Jonathan took his bow and a quiver full of arrows as though he were going hunting. He took a little lad with him as a diversion and to fetch his arrows. He said to the boy, "Run, find the arrows that I shoot."

As the lad ran, Jonathan shot an arrow beyond him. When the boy came to the place where the arrows landed, Jonathan cried out "Is not the arrow beyond you?" Again, the prince shouted, "Make haste, hurry! Do not delay!"

Jonathan's helper gathered up the arrows and came back to his master. He was not aware of the role he was playing between the two friends. Then Jonathan gave his bow and arrows to the boy and said to him, "Go; carry them to the city."

As soon as he was gone, David came out of his hiding place, and the two friends met in the glade of the forest. They clasped each other firmly and wept together. It was a tender and sad moment for the two who were bound together by the cords of love. Neither knew if they would ever be able to meet again.

Jonathan said to David, "Go in peace, since we have both sworn in the name of the Lord, saying, 'May the Lord be between you and me, and between your descendants and my descendants forever.'"

With sorrowful hearts the friends parted. Jonathan went to his home, and David went deeper into the forest.

When Jonathan first met with his father after the debacle at the New Moon Festival, Saul was stiff and officious, but Jonathan's sweet attitude soon melted the king's icy front, and he became genial again with his son.

The king's chase of David with his cadre of picked men always provided the gist of the conversation around the army base, so Jonathan was able to keep up quite well with David's movements. Also, an aide of the king, who was friendly with Jonathan, was helpful in giving the prince details of Saul's chase. According to this aide, the king was now bragging that he was closing in on his mortal enemy.

One day news came through the aide that made the blood of the prince run cold. Apparently, the king had learned, through the chief of his herdsmen, Doeg the Edomite, that David had visited Priest Ahimelech at Nob and had received the sword of Goliath as a personal weapon and holy bread from the altar to feed the young men who were with him. In retaliation for the act on the part of the priest, Saul had murdered Ahimelech and his entire priestly order of eighty-five men. Only Abiathar, son of Ahitub, had escaped and had joined David in the wilderness.

Jonathan was deep in thought as he rode homeward after another attack on a Philistine outpost. His usual mild disposition was a bit heated on this day, and his heart was troubled. His mood had nothing to do with the raid, for that had gone well. None of the men had been hurt, and the army had collected much booty. Also, his soldiers had set the enemy garrison on fire, and the Philistines had been forced to retreat.

He reasoned that he should be feeling euphoric, but instead, his spirit was rather dejected. The day had not started out well. During the early morning hours, he had been called from his bed to squelch a riot in the army housing. The inaction of the king's soldiers was giving rise to more and more infighting while the king was off with his special group chasing David.

Later, Jonathan was called to hold two cases of court for city businessmen. The court recorder notified him that several other cases were demanding administrative attention, but he brushed them aside. He knew that it was very important for him to spend more time in the field with his regiment, for the Philistines were pressing closer and closer to Israel's boundaries.

The prince hadn't heard from David for several weeks, but he assumed that no news was good news. He was certain that the moment his father laid hands on David, the tidings would be carried to every part of the kingdom by order of the king.

On several different occasions of late, Jonathan had observed evidences of David's raids against the Philistines. David's signs of conquest would have been missed by most, but Jonathan could see his friend's pattern of complete destruction. No one was left in the outpost to identify the assailant to other garrisons.

Jonathan admired the work of his friend. Here was a young man who was being relentlessly pursued by a demented king, and yet he dared to lead his men in war against the king's enemies. The prince knew by experience that these forays were a great risk to David.

*Of course,* Jonathan reasoned, *David is forced to acquire provisions for his troops, which number about four hundred. Instead of burdening his countrymen with his needs, he is taking spoil from the enemy and thus weakening the pagans.*

Jonathan's thoughts switched from David to Zereth as he reached the gate of the city. His heart anticipated her welcome as he began the walk from the city gate to his home. She didn't disappoint him as she met him with open arms and welcome lips. But even though the reception was the usual, there was a different air about her and a merry gleam in her eyes.

She released herself from his embrace and stepped back. "Jonathan," she whispered, "rejoice with me, for I am with child."

For a moment he was so stunned by the exciting news that he was speechless. She stood still, eagerly waiting his response. Then he found himself, swept her up in his arms, and for several moments the usually dignified prince danced shamelessly in the street with his pregnant wife in his arms. Then he put her down and looked at her closely. "Zereth," he questioned. "Are you certain beyond a doubt?"

"Yes, I am. In fact I have known for several weeks now. I wanted so much to share the news with you, but I wanted to be certified by the midwife first. I didn't want to disappoint you."

He laughed a happy laugh. "It seems almost too good to be true, but yet, this is what we have prayed for, so I shouldn't have been surprised. Perhaps I'm too human.

"Zereth, we must share this good news with Mother and your grandparents right away. They will want to rejoice with us."

Jonathan saw a look of uncertainly in her eyes, and she hesitated a moment before she answered. "Jonathan, I hope you won't be angry with me, but your mother and my grandmother already know of my condition. I wanted them to assist the midwife in attesting to my pregnancy."

He understood immediately. "That's all right, dear. But can we visit Mother this evening and talk with her about our good news?"

"I would like that," she agreed.

"And," Jonathan continued, "I must find our friend David soon and share this good news with him. He has notified me by every courier that he is praying daily that you will bear me a son."

She grasped the arm of the prince as he spoke, and her eyes were wide. "Oh, Jonathan, I almost forgot. I heard some bad news in the village while you were gone. Your father sent a group of soldiers to kidnap Michal, and he sent her to be the wife of Palti, the son of Laish, who lives in Gallim. I also heard that Laish is a wealthy businessman who is close to the king. I am quite sure that by now David has heard of his loss and is in need of much encouragement from his best friend. You should find him as soon as possible, my dear."

The prince was stricken by the news, and for a few moments, he was mute. "Thank you for sharing my father's crime with me. I am sure that if anyone else, outside of our family and particularly my father, had practiced such a foul trick on David he would have paid them a deadly visit before the sun would set. But he is so conscientious that he will not lift his hand against the king regardless of the circumstances. He says that it is a crime against God Himself to harm the Lord's anointed. However, Palti should lay low for awhile, for David will be searching for him."

For the next several days, Jonathan was deluged with affairs of state while the king ignored the business of the kingdom in favor of searching the length and breadth of the land for David. It was the proverbial cat and mouse chase. Jonathan marveled at the ability of David to outfox his father. Even though spies were constantly notifying the king of the whereabouts of David, he was able to move to another location before Saul arrived.

In the dead of night, a courier from David brought a message for Jonathan. David was in the Wilderness of Ziph and was anxious to see his best friend. Would Jonathan please come?

Jonathan made arrangements to leave for the meeting the next night, since he was certain that spies for the king were watching his every move all day long. The two friends met in the middle of the forest. They embraced warmly, but both were quiet for a few moments.

"David," Jonathan spoke, "I was so sorry to hear about the kidnapping of Michal. For awhile I felt guilty that we hadn't moved her to our home, but the king was determined and would have taken her from our home and probably would have harmed Zereth."

David nodded. "Yes, it crushed my heart to lose Michal, but I will get her back. As soon as I can relax my raids against the Philistines, I will visit Palti in Gallim. He knows that Michal is my wife, and therefore, he has no excuse."

"Tell me, my friend, how is it going with you and Zereth?"

Jonathan laughed cheerily. "David, rejoice with us. Zereth is pregnant. Your prayers have been answered."

David clapped his hands and raised his eyes to heaven. "Praise be to Him who does all things well. I was sure that God, who loves to give us good things, would give you your wish for a child, and there is little doubt but that it will be the son and heir that you need. I only wish that I could be with you both when she delivers. But . . . ," he paused, and his voice quivered as he continued, "it seems that I am fated to constantly be on the run from the wrath of the king. Perhaps one day he will find us, and I'm sure he will deal with us quickly. I would die before I would raise my hand against the Lord's anointed."

Jonathan lifted his hand. "David, I do not believe that my father will catch you. God has His hand over you. My father knows, and I know, that you will be the next king of Israel, and I will serve next to you."

David clutched the shoulder of the prince. "My dear friend Jonathan, you are such a humble man. I am so glad to call you a friend. You have given me courage to go on. This could possibly be the last time we will be able to meet, so let us renew our covenant together.

"Jonathan, you must believe in me regardless of what you might hear, and I will do the same about you. I know that you will stay by your father because you are loyal and true. I would be disappointed if you would abandon him. He needs you. Let us be true to Jehovah. His ways are mysterious but are always best."

They clasped hands as they prayed together in the Wilderness of Ziph. Then Jonathan took his leave.

The raids by Jonathan's and David's forces on the Philistine outposts appeared to have weakened the resolve of the barbarians for an all out war, so for the time they pulled back the troops that had been massing on Israel's southern borders. This gave Jonathan more time to spend on the business of the kingdom.

Lately, military disputes had become almost as great in number as the civil cases. Since only about one hundred picked troops went with Saul and Abner on the crusades against David, most of Saul's army and David's former company were inactive for long periods of time. They were fighting men, and this passive situation bred infighting in the ranks of those who stayed behind. Many were hurt and some even died in the riots. Jonathan held military court often and punished the offenders with prison sentences, but as soon as King Saul and Abner returned from an expedition, the malefactors would be released.

Jonathan endured these indignities without umbrage or bitterness, but his tender heart was wounded. The time of Zereth's delivery was fast approaching. For Jonathan, the nearness of this blessed event brought a sense of foreboding, but for Zereth, it was a time of ecstasy, for at last she was giving Jonathan an heir.

Jonathan notified his mother and older sister Merab that the time was here. Both had done midwifery work before, but he also went for the community midwife. Then he began pacing in the yard in front of his home. Even though he prayed earnestly, he couldn't shake the thought that this would be a time of loss for him. He could hear the occasional screams of Zereth, and his heart ached with every scream. He knew that the pains of childbirth were a part of the curse that sin had brought upon women, but this knowledge didn't make the ordeal any easier for him.

Time dragged by. *Surely she should have had delivered before now,* he thought, but no one came to bring him word.

Finally his mother appeared in the doorway, and he could tell by the look on her face that the news was not good. He had heard the baby cry for a few moments, so he had assumed that it was a live delivery, but perhaps not.

"Son," Ahinoam put her hand tenderly on his arm, "you have a beautiful son waiting for you, but you must take care of him by yourself, for Zereth didn't live. It was a very difficult delivery, and her heart gave out."

Jonathan was in a daze. Zereth, the love of his life, was gone after only five years of life with him. His heart was crushed. He laid his head on his mother's shoulder and wept unashamed. Then he dried his tears and straightened his shoulders. He knew that he must be strong now for the child whom Zereth had left in his care. This little one was a part of Zereth, and he must love him and care for him as she would have done.

He turned to his mother. "Mother, tell me what I will need to do for my little son. I am quite sure that I must employ a wet nurse and also a nurse to take care of his daily needs."

"That is right," Ahinoam agreed, "and I have a suggestion for you. Last week one of my maids gave birth to a stillborn child, and she has plenty of milk. She is also an excellent maid and, therefore, could take care of all of the other needs for your son."

"Thank you, Mother. I knew you would help me."

"You will also need to choose a name for your son and my grandson. Zereth's grandmother is already calling him Meribbaal, but that sounds a bit too idolatrous to me. If you would like, I will help in selecting a name for him."

"I would like that, Mother."

"I am sure that you would like to see your son and heir and also have a last look at your dear wife before they take her away."

Before he took his son in his arms, Jonathan took a long loving look at Zereth. His already severely wounded heart was wrung afresh. She had desired so much to give him an heir, and the effort had taken her life. As he looked at her lying so white and still on the bed, he thought of the five short but wonderful years God had given them together. Then his mind reached forward to the resurrection—she would live again, and they would be together in the kingdom with the son she would never know on this earth. There they would love anew.

Jonathan turned to the little one who was sleeping peacefully. Zereth had satisfied his hunger pangs before her death, but this little one would never know on earth the mother who died to give him life.

With his Mother's help, Jonathan gave his son a permanent name, Mephibosheth—he who scatters shame. The love that the prince showered on his son helped to heal his own wounded heart.

# JONATHAN'S HEART

## CHAPTER 6

The official time of Jonathan's mourning for Zereth had ended, but the pain in his heart over his great loss had not abated. Jonathan's mother and older sister Merab had been wonderful comfort to him since the day of Zereth's death, and his friend David had sent condolences and assurance of his prayers several times, but the king had not bothered to attend the royal funeral. Jonathan was well aware that the king was furious because of the relationship he and Zereth had enjoyed with David, but disregarding the funeral of the princess was a royal affront.

Jonathan's heart was bleeding for his father's physical, mental, and spiritual health. He would meet the king from time to time in the king's court and would notice the permanent look of rejection on his father's face. The frustration of his eternal but unsuccessful pursuit of David was taking its toll.

The king had not yet met his new grandson, Mephibosheth. Ahinoam had confided to Jonathan that the few times the king had come in the palace from his pursuit of David he had slept in the throne room and left early in the morning without visiting her.

The queen was hurting. "Jonathan, I am so concerned about your father," she announced. "He is unconcerned about any other matter except the capture of David. I am afraid that he is mentally unbalanced. He has an unearthly look in his eyes now.

"I was caring for Mephibosheth one day when he came in the living room, and I asked him if he would like to see his new grandson. He ignored my question, picked up something, and left the house without answering. He acts like a man who is lost spiritually, so son, we must pray earnestly for him."

"I agree with you, Mother. He appears to hate me almost as much as he does David. He hasn't thrown his spear at me again, but he often watches me suspiciously as I work, as if I was his enemy. I am on guard at all times. He has lost all interest in the affairs of state. When I read legal matters to him, he will often leave the room while I am reading as though the material is totally unimportant to him. Of course, his consuming interest is the capture of David, so I am forced to tend to all of the business of state."

"But Mother, despite the troubles his fetish is causing, since he is my father and also the anointed king of Israel, I have promised my Lord and myself to stay by him regardless of his behavior. At the same time, I must be loyal to David since he is the Lord's anointed to succeed Father. You can see that my role is often frustrating."

Ahinoam looked at her firstborn son with fondness. "Jonathan, your father has no idea, and I doubt if David is fully aware, what a jewel they have in you. In your father's state of mind, he will probably never appreciate you. Most men in your place would have deserted him long before now, but I am so glad that you are determined to stand by him. I am proud of you."

Soon after Jonathan arrived back at the king's court from visiting his mother, the king and Jonathan's younger brothers, Abinadab and Malchishua, returned from another futile chase of David. The two brothers were always in the forefront of the company in the pursuit. They often boasted that soon they would catch this impostor who was a threat to their father's kingship and he would then pay the full price for daring to usurp the royal succession.

While Abinadab was civil to Jonathan, sometimes helping the prince with business matters, Malchishua was openly insolent to his older brother. He challenged Jonathan one day as the two met in the king's court.

"Why is it," he blustered, 'that you would aid a man who is plotting to destroy the rights of our family? Believe me, if I were next in line to the throne as you are, I would have every soldier in our armies looking for him."

Jonathan faced his younger brother with a prayer on his heart. He thought, *How can I possibly convince this angry young rebel to see that the king's crusade against David is contrary to God's will and that the Lord has directed my decision to assist David*?

"Malchishua," he said quietly but with conviction. "I have not abandoned our father. He is king and also my father. I will be loyal to him to the end of his life. But twice he disobeyed God openly, once in Gilgal when he offered an unlawful sacrifice and again at Amalek when he spared Agag and the best animals after God had told him, through the prophet Samuel, to destroy everyone and everything. On both occasions God sent Samuel to tell him that God no longer considered him as king, and therefore, there would be no succession. At the same time, he told father that a neighbor would take his place.

"I have found that, at God's direction, Samuel anointed David to be our next king, and the Lord impressed me that David would take my place in the succession to the throne. I will admit that I was looking forward to wearing the crown some day, and therefore, at first I was very disappointed, but Malchishua, I would rather obey the Lord's command than to be the king. I only hope that you and Abinadab will understand my position. Now lastly, we share the same mother and father. I wish that you would listen to your mother in this matter. She would have words of wisdom for you." As he finished, Jonathan's voice and eyes were pleading for his younger brother to understand, but the boy was resolute in his rejection. He turned on his heel and left the court.

Jonathan was sick at heart. He had failed miserably in his appeal to his younger brother, and Abinadab was also unbending in his rancor against David. Jonathan could see that his brothers had drunk too deeply from the cup of royalty, and now could not bear the thought of becoming commoners again. Their personal decisions had committed them against the will of the Lord. Jonathan was convinced that their crusade against David would eventually lead them into the same mental and spiritual condition as their father was experiencing.

Jonathan closed up his work at court and went to visit with Nebal and the troops. He found a very excited Nebal. "My lord Jonathan, Captain Abner came by only a few minutes ago to notify us that every man must be ready to march at a moment's notice. He said that David has collected almost six hundred men and he would be difficult to capture when he is found. So the king is taking every soldier with him on the next crusade, including our own one thousand men and also David's company. Has the king discussed this with you?"

"No, he hasn't, and he really doesn't need to since he is the commander-in-chief of all the armies. Of course, I wish he would have mentioned this arrangement when I saw him at court today, but he doesn't communicate with me very much of late."

That night a courier came with a message from David. "Dear Jonathan," the prince read, "I am in the Wilderness of Ziph and would like very much to see you and get the reassurance of your loyalty and love. I had a bad experience only a few days ago that has left me rather shaken and depressed. The Philistines were fighting against Keilah and robbing their threshing floors. The leaders of that city appealed to us to come and help them, and when I inquired of the Lord, He answered that we should help them. So we went to Keilah and, with the Lord's help, we were able to deliver the city and destroy the Philistines. The people were very grateful for our help and invited us to stay with them, but the king found out that we were in Keilah and came with a large company of soldiers to capture us. I inquired of the Lord if the people of Keilah would betray us to the king, and He answered that they would give us up, so we immediately moved to the Wilderness of Ziph. Will you please come?"

Jonathan was sure that the king had placed his spies at the gates of the city, so he had Nebal secure his horse in a small glen outside the walls of the city during the daylight hours, and under the cover of darkness, Jonathan scaled the walls, mounted his horse, and rode off to the Wilderness of Ziph.

He found David in the wilderness, and the two communed together for several hours. The fellowship of the friends strengthened the heart of David and renewed his courage. They repeated the covenant that bound them together and vowed everlasting loyalty to each other.

"Do not fear David," Jonathan assured him, "for my father shall not find you. I am confident that God has placed a shield around you, and you shall be king over Israel, and I shall be next to you. My father surely knows that this is God's will."

The two friends embraced, prayed together, and wept together. They were quite sure that this would be their last meeting together until Saul would end his search. David stayed on in the wilderness, and Jonathan went back to his home to little Mephibosheth.

The two kept in touch by courier, but the lines of communication were always fragile. The king's spies were more aggressive than ever, and it was only a matter of time before they would make an interception.

As Jonathan made his way to the court, he could hear the clamor of a crowd, and then he noticed the animated crowd on the front grounds of the palace. It was the spot where the public whipping post was located. He could hear the sound of the whip slapping and tearing human flesh. He quickened his pace and pushed through the excited observers. There in the center was one of his faithful couriers with his hands tied to the whipping post, and one of the king's aides was wielding the whip. The prince was furious. He strode over and tore the whip from the aide's hands.

"Who authorized you to whip this man, and what is the charge?" he demanded.

The king's aide was mute for a moment; then he pointed to Abner who was standing in the front of the circle of human flesh.

"He told me to do it. He said that it was an order from the king."

Jonathan turned to Abner. "Do you have a written order from the king authorizing the public scourging of this innocent person?"

Abner shifted his feet. "No, I don't have a written order, and furthermore, I don't need one. The king ordered me less than an hour ago to put the lash to this man since he was found carrying one of your letters to the traitor, David. Also," Abner continued with a defiant pose, "he ordered me to publicly whip every man who is caught carrying messages from you to David and the men who carry messages from David to you."

"Please untie Reuben and have his wounds treated."

Again, he addressed Abner. "This man was carrying out orders—my orders! He is a trusted and obedient servant. I am the one who is responsible for giving this message to him to deliver, so if the king must punish someone, I am the one to whom his wrath should be directed. Please give him that message for me."

He turned to the waiting crowd. "The show is over. You are all dismissed."

Jonathan could hear his father raving even from outside the palace doors. As he entered, he could see through an open door that the king was pacing with the ever present spear in his hand. The servants were grouped around the room, and their faces mirrored the terror they felt when the king was in a snit. Each man knew that if he so much as shifted his weight when the king was ranting, he might be the target of the spear.

Jonathan was quite sure of the reason for his father's rage. It was the content of the letter his courier was taking to David. In that message, he had renewed his covenant with his friend.

"All of you have conspired against me!" the king shouted. "My son has made a covenant with my enemy, and none of you told me about it. You have covered up for him."

Jonathan noticed that the servants were all shaking their heads in denial of the king's charge, but Saul raged on. "My enemy is planning to kill me and take over the kingdom, and when he becomes king, he will kill all of you and fill your places with his friends."

The king stopped his pacing and glared at each of the servants around the room as if daring any to deny his statement. No man moved a muscle.

The king had not seen Jonathan enter the corridor, so after the prince had watched the king display his venom to the servants in the throne room, he was able to make his way to the work chamber without detection. Jonathan half expected before the day would be over that soldiers would arrest him for insubordination. But even though the king came into the work chamber for a few minutes, he ignored Jonathan, who was sitting at his desk.

The next morning a courier brought news to the king that Samuel, the esteemed prophet and judge and spiritual leader of Israel for many years, was dead. It was an unsettling and unwelcome announcement to the nation of Israel, and especially to Jonathan who had been very fond of the pious priest. The prince was aware that Samuel had been declining in health for many months, but he seemed to be ageless in his work of spiritual reform for Israel.

Jonathan remembered with pain that Samuel had hoped for his sons to follow him as the spiritual leaders of Israel, but it was not to be. While the young men bore the name of their father, they were not endowed with his character. In fact, they tended to be copies of the indecorum of the sons of Eli who were called by their peers, "the sons of Belial."

Saul hated Samuel because of the prophet's censures, but he felt that he must declare a time of mourning for the popular leader, so he sent letters by courier to all of the provinces announcing Samuel's death and an official time of mourning. During this time, to the king's credit, he ceased all action against David although his heart still fumed against the supposed contender to his throne.

During the time of official mourning for Samuel, Saul also relaxed his spying so that a courier from David's camp was able to reach Jonathan without challenge. As the prince unrolled the message, he particularly noticed its length.

"Dear Jonathan. We have moved from the Wilderness of En Gedi to the Wilderness of Paran. While we were in En Gedi, I did a bad thing and my conscience smote me. We were being closely pursued by the king's men, but we outdistanced them and went into a large cave to hide. The king's troops didn't notice our tracks leading to the cave. When they came to the cave, your father entered the cave to relieve himself and to rest. As he rested, he fell asleep. Several of my men urged me to kill him, but I refused. I did, however, cut off a part of his robe. When he awakened and left the cave, we waited for a time, and then I came out of the cave and shouted to the king. I showed him the piece of his robe and reminded him that I could have killed him but would not harm the Lord's anointed. He was very remorseful and actually wept. He promised that he would never attempt to kill me again. I haven't seen him since that time, so I hope that he will keep his word.

"Also, while we were in En Gedi, we ran low on supplies. You see, I have almost six hundred men with me now, and some have their families, so they consume a lot of food. I sent a detachment to a rich man in Maon, by the name of Nabal, with a request for provisions for our army. Since we had helped guard Nabal's flocks and herds in the wilderness, I expressed the hope that he would want to help us. However, my men brought back word that Nabal not only refused to help but also treated the men very rudely. I vowed vengeance on this nasty fellow, and we were on our way to deal with him. But his very wise and charming wife came to meet us with liberal provisions and a plea that I would ignore the rudeness of her husband and not kill him. We honored her plea. A few days later, Nabal died of a heart attack. I sent for his widow, whose name is Abigail, and married her.

"Jonathan, I'm still in love with Michal and am hoping that I will soon be free to go to Gallim and take her back from Palti. I love you, my friend, and am praying that God will see fit to reunite us soon."

Jonathan became bored with his duties at the court, so he took time to lead his army against a Philistine outpost. It was a profitable venture. Not only were they able to take a good store of spoil from the enemy and send the barbarians running, they also captured a young Philistine soldier who gave Jonathan some very disturbing news. The Philistines were making plans to amass an army at Shunem that would be equal in size to the army at Michmash. Their goal was to destroy the armies of Israel and overrun the land.

The prince went to his chamber at the court to reflect on this unsettling news and to pray. He realized that the military power of Israel was at its lowest point in years. The king had exhausted the treasury of the realm by his eternal pursuit of David and had been lax in the collection of taxes to replenish the public fund. Many of the king's soldiers had deserted the army because of lack of pay. Jonathan had made certain that his men were paid, and not one had deserted, but their numbers would be so insignificant against such a large Philistine host. The prince wanted to share the news obtained from the Philistine soldier with his father, but as usual, he was out chasing David.

Saul came in from his pursuit of David with special news about his prime enemy. To the king's deranged mind, this news overshadowed the message that Jonathan shared with him

"Aha," he shouted, "one of my men has informed me that your friend, David, has joined with the Philistines. Achish, son of Maoch, who is a mortal enemy of Israel, has given David and his men the city of Ziklag for their own city. Of course, that means that David and his men will join our enemies in any future battle against us. Perhaps you will now believe that your supposed friend is a traitor since he has joined with our enemies. What further proof do you need?"

Jonathan had no answer for the king at the moment, but he was confident that David would soon clear up this seemingly traitorous move on his part. He didn't have long to wait, for that night a courier came with a lengthy message from David for the prince.

"My dear friend Jonathan, I wish with all my heart that I could visit with you personally, but since that is impossible I am sending you this account of my latest activities. Please do not think, for one moment, that I have become a traitor to you or your father or my beloved nation of Israel. You have probably heard that I am now living among our enemies, the Philistines. That is true, but we have not become a part of them.

"The reason for our move was to get beyond the reach of your father and also to accommodate our families. I now have six hundred men with me, and most of them have wives and some have children.

"I have recently married Ahinoam, the Jezreelite, and you will remember that I also have Abigail, the widow of

Nabal of Maon. We could no longer dwell in the wilderness with all of these dependents, so we have secured the city of Ziklag from Achish. It is much more comfortable for our families. I have developed a friendship with Achish, and he trusts me. He doesn't know that I have been raiding the camps of the Geshurites, the Girzites, and the Amalekites, since I leave no evidence behind that will implicate me.

"I do have a concern, Jonathan. I am hearing reports that the Philistines are preparing to do battle with the armies of Israel soon, and of course, my army would be expected to help them. I trust that you will join me in earnest prayer that God will not let that happen. Please know that my devotion to you and my love for you is stronger than ever. I pledge myself anew to you as your friend."

Jonathan finished reading the message and put it away. His heart was at ease now, for he knew that his father's contention regarding David was wrong. Even though David was in the camp of the enemy physically because of the king's pursuit and the care for the families, his heart was still with his beloved nation and his dear friend, Jonathan.

The plight of David bothered Jonathan. The enemy would consider David a great asset to their cause since his fame as a military leader was well known throughout the pagan world, and now since he was living among them, the Philistines would probably demand that he join with them in their war against Israel. The future looked bleak. Certainly, only the mighty God of miracles could bring about the conditions that would keep David and his six hundred men from fighting against God's anointed, King Saul, his friend, Jonathan, and his beloved nation, Israel.

Jonathan bowed his head in the king's court and placed the situation in God's hands.

The prince finished his work at court and went home to Mephibosheth. His little son was always a joy to his troubled heart. He was growing so fast. He was five years old now and very much attached to his father. Jonathan cherished the moments that he was privileged to spend with the little fellow.

It was just as the Philistine captive had reported and the Israelite spies had predicted. The Philistines soon gathered their armies together at Shunem with the obvious intention of doing battle with Israel, destroying their armies, and taking over the land. The barbarians had built up their armies since Michmash and Ephes Dammim, and the host now gathered at Shunem matched the force at Michmash.

Saul had no other option but to discontinue his pursuit of David and move his decimated army to Mount Gilboa where he faced the massive host of the Philistines. When Saul saw the army of the Philistines, he was terrified, and his heart trembled greatly. When he inquired of the Lord, the Lord did not answer him, either by dreams or by Urim or by the prophets.

Jonathan pleaded with his father to send out a call to arms to the ends of the kingdom with the hope that there would be a response like that of Jabesh Gilead and Amalek where hundreds of thousands volunteered to fight for Israel.

The king rejected Jonathan's request with the excuse that he had no arsenal of weapons to offer volunteers. They would be facing a well-equipped enemy with nothing in their hands, and thus, most would desert in the heat of the battle. The prince accepted the reasoning of his father and said nothing further.

King Saul was a spiritually lost man. The line between heaven and his own heart had been severed, not by the Lord, but rather by his own stubbornness of spirit. He had ignored the services of the priest and the prophet at Michmash and Amalek, and now he had nowhere to turn for divine counsel, so he turned to a spiritualist medium, a source that God had condemned centuries ago. Even the king had proscribed the practice when he first began his reign as king.

Jonathan's heart was in agony when he heard that his father had gone to seek advice from the Witch of Endor since divine communication had been denied him. The prince knew that by this act of desperation and denial that the king had forged his final and fatal separation from God, but the love and allegiance of the prince to his father never faltered. He determined anew that he would stand by him to the end.

In the meantime, Israelite spies had brought word to Jonathan that David and his troops were assembled with the Philistine leaders at Aphek where the pagans were finalizing their plans for the battle against Israel.

After bringing the prince this report, the Israelite spies were forced to withdraw from the areas around the Philistine camp because of increased enemy patrols. The night before the battle at Gilboa, Jonathan didn't know if he might meet his dear friend, David, face to face in the heat of the battle. The prince lifted his heart in prayer that somehow David would be exempted from the battle at Gilboa.

Jonathan went to his tent to spend time with the Lord. His heart remembered Michmash. This present situation here at Shunem was very much like the one at Michmash, but probably the forces of the barbarians at Michmash were larger than here and more heavily armed. There were no chariots here.

He remembered that as he sought the Lord in his tent at Michmash, God had answered his prayer in a very positive and wonderful way. It was as if the Lord had spoken to him face to face, "Jonathan, if you will go out by faith to meet the host of the enemy, I will give you my presence and the victory will be mine," but tonight was different than at Michmash. He felt the closeness of the Lord as though he could touch the divine form, but the voice was mute. There was no assurance of great success on the morrow.

The prince forgot himself in his prayers, and his heart was blessed. Then he sat back and let his thoughts dwell on his relationship with his Lord, his mother and father, and David. His relationship with God had been his first consideration since that day many years ago when he had pledged eternal fidelity to the One who had given him physical life and promised him eternal life. It had been a most pleasant relationship for him all these years.
There were some ways that God had led him that Jonathan didn't understand, but he had accepted these perplexities as God's best plan for his life. He had given God special thanks for a godly mother, a wonderful caring wife, and a beautiful son. He concluded that God and he were on good terms.

He thought for a time about his beautiful wife of only five years. Their love for each other had been so deep, and he had hurt so badly after her untimely death, but the little son she had left him had helped to mollify the deep wounds in his heart. He had pledged at her bedside that he would meet her one day in the kingdom, and by God's grace he would help their little son to meet with them.

He had been blessed with a wonderful mother. She was so patient and understanding. She had taught his heart to love the Lord and obey Him at all times. She had been such a balm to his heart since Zereth's death.

His thoughts lingered on his father for many minutes. While he had never enjoyed a close relationship with his father, he had always admired the man who became the first king of Israel. He was so tall and handsome, and in his early years as king, very decisive and successful, but as a boy, Jonathan had seen his father wander farther and farther away from the Lord. Then his unlawful sacrifice at Gilgal and his disobedient sparing of King Agag and the cattle at Amalek had been a watershed of sorts both on his kingship and his personal life. From that point on, he became a shell of a man and king in name only. And now, instead of receiving direction from the Lord through the Urim and Thummim, he was led by his twisted thinking to visit the proscribed Witch of Endor.

Samuel had told the king that the days of his kingship were numbered, and now, mused Jonathan, perhaps Gilboa would be the point of termination. Again, the prince vowed that he would be loyal to his father to the end.

His thoughts moved to David. Was he being forced to fight with the Philistines against Israel? Jonathan's heart went out to his dear friend who had been harassed so incessantly by a jealous king that he had no place to hide except in the camp of the enemy.

Even as Jonathan reflected on the plight of David, he heard a stirring in the camp and someone shouting his name. He stepped out of his tent and saw a rider headed his way. He had never seen the man before, but he knew instinctively that he was a courier from David's camp.

The rider saluted Jonathan and spoke in an excited voice, "I have a message for you, Master Jonathan, from Captain David."

"Come into my tent," the prince invited.

The courier stepped into Jonathan's tent but refused the proffered seat. It was obvious that he was in a hurry.

"My lord, David wishes to inform you that he, with his company, is back at Ziklag. He was ordered by King Achish to meet with the Philistine lords at Aphek where they were planning their war strategy against you and your father. David was concerned that he would be forced to fight with the Philistines against Israel, but the Lord intervened. He put into the hearts of the Philistine commanders to order his army back to Ziklag. David knew that you would be pleased to hear this news. He also wanted me to tell you that he would like to bring his army to Gilboa to help in the battle against the Philistines, but he doesn't think that your father would accept his services."

The messenger finished and prepared to leave. Jonathan thanked him and asked that the courier also take his thanks and prayers back to David.

As the messenger departed, Jonathan thought again of his pleasant relationship with David. He remembered that it was not without some agony that he had accepted the decision of the Lord that David would be king in his stead, but God implanted love for this young man from Bethlehem, and Jonathan was at peace. He then hoped that he could have the privilege of being David's right-hand man, but with the dire situation here at Gilboa, it didn't appear that God had this relationship in mind. In the shadows of this impending disaster, Jonathan would need to be patient and wait for God's direction. He thought that possibly his presence in David's body of officers might be too disruptive.

Jonathan knew and appreciated the fact that he was greatly loved in Israel. Many people had confided to him that they would be glad when he became king. While the words were tempting to his human heart, he prayed more earnestly that God would erase any desire from his heart to be king of Israel. God had said, "No," and God always knows what is best.

The night before what he was sure would be a battle was a time of struggle and decision for the prince. His experience as a warrior in the field gave him certainty that if the Lord did not work for Israel as he did at Michmash the course of the nation would be a lost one. The physical numbers pitted against them were much too great to overcome by human methods. He thought of his little boy of only five at home with his nurse. If he became involved in this battle, he would leave Mephibosheth without father and mother so early in life. His stomach wrenched at the thought. His thoughts extended along this line. If the battle went against Israel, the Philistines would surely follow up their advantage and raid the land. Their first objective would certainly be Gibeah where his little son, the son's nurse, Jonathan's mother, and Merab were stationed.

A voice spoke to his heart, and he was quite sure that it was not the voice of God. *You must escape before it's too late. Your father is responsible for this impossible situation, and he should be the one to pay. There isn't any reason why you should be a martyr with him. Take your son and go to David at Ziklag. He will welcome you with open arms.*

The thought was tempting but unacceptable to the loyal heart of the prince. He had pledged before God to stay by his father to the end, and he was a man of his word. He shook his head to rid himself of these venal thoughts, got up from his knees, and went outside to view again the enemy across at Shunem. Many torches lit up the countryside around the pagan army, and it appeared to be a large number of watchmen stationed along the borders. There was abnormal activity among the main body of troops. It appeared that the Philistines were planning on an early morning attack.

Jonathan went back inside his tent and fell into a brief troubled sleep. He awakened early in the morning, and for a few moments, he was disoriented. He thought that he was back in Gibeah, and he should see Mephibosheth. Then his mind cleared and the thought struck him, he might never see Mephibosheth again. He knelt down for his morning prayers, and when he had finished, he stepped outside his tent. His father was also standing in front of his tent, as were Abner and Jonathan's brothers, Abinadab and Malchishua. All were watching the activity of the Philistine army across at Shunem.

Jonathan moved toward his father with trepidation, for he had no idea how the king would receive him. He knew that his father heard his steps as he approached, but the king ignored him until the prince stopped close beside him. Then the king turned slowly to face his oldest son. There was fear in his eyes, and the look on his face was grave, but it was not unkind or condemning.

Neither spoke for a few moments; then the king broke the silence.

"It looks as if they will attack in a few hours, so we should get the troops ready. We will let them meet us here, which could give us a bit of an advantage. We will need all of the advantage that time and terrain will give us," he added wearily.

By this time the two brothers and Abner had joined the two at the entrance of Saul's tent. The king looked at each of his sons in turn. "Jonathan, Abinadab, and Malchishua, I will give you three the privilege of leaving before the battle begins. I wouldn't count your leaving as desertion, since unless we have a miracle, we will all be lost."

He hesitated for a few moments as if questioning the wisdom of what he was going to say next; then he shrugged his shoulders and turned to Jonathan. "I'm sorry, son, that I spoiled the succession for you. You would have made a great king, and all Israel would have been proud of you. But it will never happen now." There were tears in the king's eyes, and his voice quavered.

He turned to Abner. "Captain Abner, I have heard that you have talked of leaving before the battle begins, but since you are the commissioned leader of these troops, you must stay by with me. Now, you are dismissed to get your troops ready. They should have a quick meal right away; then you must line them up for battle." As the king finished speaking, his shoulders slumped and he turned away.

Jonathan stepped forward and grasped his father's arm. "Father, I have pledged to stay by you to the end, so I have no plans of deserting you. You can count on me." The two brothers also pledged to stand by their father.

The king nodded. "I appreciate your loyalty. You are good sons, and you deserved a better father. I wish that you would have chosen to leave, but since you won't leave, let us go and eat what could be our last meal together."

It was midday before the pagan troops began moving toward the Israelite position on Mount Gilboa. It was a massive host, so they moved rather awkwardly. Also they were densely packed in their ranks, which gave the Israelites some advantage, but the strength of the enemy was in their superior numbers. Their lines stretched for a long distance in every direction over the field.

The king and his three sons fought valiantly. The king, rather than being isolated by his troops at the rear of the lines, instead led the charge against the enemy. He was out in front. Jonathan admired the courage of his father. Bodies were soon scattered widely over the battlefield and riderless horses numbered in the hundreds. They were neighing in terror and dashing about wildly. One beautiful black stallion attempted to attach himself to Jonathan. It was tempting to the prince, for he could have easily ridden out of the battle area. However, Jonathan slapped the horse on his rump, and the temptation immediately disappeared.

Suddenly, Jonathan saw Abner grab the reins of one of the horses, mount up, and quickly ride out of the battle area. He was deserting as the king had mentioned. Jonathan didn't have time to reflect on Abner's desertion, since the battle was raging around him. He fought the enemy with sword and spear, and many died at his hand, but others pressed into the gap made by their fallen comrades. The prince saw his father and his armor bearer fall on their swords and only a few seconds later his brothers fell by the swords of the enemy. Then an arrow pierced the heart of the prince of Israel, and he fell mortally wounded on the field of battle.

The heart of Jonathan was still at only forty years of age. But the influence of his heart has transformed and inspired many for good down through the ages and will continue to bless through eternity.

A very famous religious author of the past century penned a beautiful elegy for Jonathan that is somewhat of a summation of the life of this prince of Israel.

"Jonathan, by birth heir to the throne, yet knowing himself set aside by the divine decree; to his rival the most tender and faithful of friends, shielding David's life at the peril of his own; steadfast at his father's side through the dark days of his declining power, and at his side falling at last—the name of Jonathan is treasured in heaven, and it stands on earth a witness to the existence and the power of unselfish love" (Ellen G. White, *Education*, p. 157).

# DAVID'S HEART

## Introduction

Probably more than any other man in Bible chronology, the life record of David declares that, while sin can bring only shame and woe, God's love and mercy can reach to the deepest depths and, through faith, lift up the repenting soul to share the adoption of the sons of God.

His Psalms picture dwelling on the mountaintop with God; offering praise, thanksgiving and adoration to his Creator and Helper; and, later, sitting in the ash pit of bitter repentance and sorrow for sins that impacted not only himself but also his precious people.

David was declared to be a man after God's own heart even before his secret anointing as king and his introduction to the history of Israel.

He was greatly blessed by having the sagacious Samuel as his mentor and the loyal and unselfish Jonathan as his best friend. From a human standpoint, he could not have attained the prominence as the greatest king of Israel without the potent influence of these two men in his life. He mourned deeply for both men at their death. He even wrote a song to honor his friend, Jonathan. It was called the "Song of the Bow."

As with Moses, David learned to know God as a personal friend and Savior through his tenure as a shepherd. As he lay among his sheep at night and looked up into the starry sky, his heart was convinced beyond the shadow of any doubt that a personal and loving God was in charge of the heavens and the earth and that man existed only by God's plan and design. Several of his Psalms reflect this thinking in the night seasons about God and his care for man.

David's installation as king over all Israel was a slow and painful process, but it did develop in him a strong sense of patience and trust, which served him well during the turbulent years of his reign.

One author of over a century ago observed that, "Through years of waiting and perils, David learned to find in God his comfort, his support, his life. He learned that only by God's power could he come to the throne, only in his wisdom could he rule wisely."

He was a strong king but a poor parent, and his sons' evil habits reflected the weakness of his parental discipline.

David's last days of life were spent in comparative isolation. He did have the virgin Abishag as his constant companion, but their relationship to the very end was strictly platonic.

He died of old age and was buried with his fathers, but his name has endured through the ages. It should be noted that his dying charge to Solomon was, "He that ruleth over men must be just, ruling in the fear of God."

## DAVID'S HEART

# CHAPTER 1

"I will rejoice in the Lord and in His holy law . . ." the boy, David, sang. His voice broke on the high notes, and he coughed in embarrassment.

Two of his older brothers, Eliab and Abinadab, were nearby, and both men looked up and groaned. Eliab shook his head. "I wish you would practice that babbling out with those miserable sheep of yours, 'sister boy,' instead of irritating your family. And besides, if you must sing, why don't you sing regular songs instead of that made-up stuff of yours."

David was repentant. "I'm sorry that I annoyed you, but something is happening to my voice. I can't reach those high notes in my songs like I used to do."

The brothers laughed loudly. "Haven't Mother and Father told you about your voice changing at your age?" Abinadab asked as he laughed. "Besides," he added with a wink at Eliab, "you were supposed to be a girl. We already had too many boys before you showed up, so you should be singing real high like a girl."

David had known for several years that most of his six brothers resented him. They had informed him many times that they had collectively prayed for a sister. Thus when he was born their disappointment was so great that they nicknamed him "sister boy." He hated the nickname but accepted the slur with grace.

"What in the world are you making?" Eliab wanted to know.

"I'm making a harp to provide music for my songs when I'm out with the sheep," David explained patiently.

"I will sing to the sheep every night, and this instrument will help me to make better music for them."

Abinadab laughed. "So that's the reason that old ram Luna is getting so mean. I've noticed that he wants to fight everything that comes around him. It's probably because you've stirred him up with all of that singing you do to entertain your sheep."

David smiled. "Old Luna is always friendly with me, but he doesn't like strangers, so perhaps, if you two would trade work with me for a week or so, Luna might learn to like you too."

"Bah," Abinadab growled. "I wouldn't be caught dead with those smelly animals. I'll stick with the good old farm work."

"Who showed you how to make a harp? I can't believe that you can make anything that makes any kind of music, even music the sheep will tolerate."

David ignored the slur. "I saw a harp of eight strings in a shop in Bethlehem a few weeks ago. I felt sure that I could make one just like it, so I got all the materials together, and I'm almost finished with it." He held the partially finished instrument up for the brothers to see.

Eliab and Abinadab looked at the object skeptically. "Where did you get all of those strings?" Eliab wondered.

"Do you remember the old ewe that died a few weeks ago?"

The brothers nodded.

"I took gut strings and muscle strings out of her and scraped and dried them. I will use them for strings on this harp."

Eliab was unconvinced. "Do you mean that you plan to make music with those meat strings?"

"That's right. When I attach them to this sounding board, I expect that I will be able to make beautiful sounds that my sheep will love. You might like to hear me play sometime."

The two men looked at their youngest brother for several moments. He was really an enigma to them. They had resented him and teased and tormented him since he was first able to follow them around, but he had loved them and treated them sweetly in return. At times they were frustrated with his response and ashamed of their actions toward him. They wouldn't admit to one another the feelings they often experienced as they watched him at work and play. There was a certain quality in his demeanor that spoke of a sense of destiny. They had no power of prognostication, but he seemed to always be bound for a prominence. Thus, the torment he received from his own flesh and blood was simply a step on the ladder he must climb or the road he must travel.

As the brothers watched him, they were often reminded of Joseph and his brothers. They feared that in the family of Jesse the Bethlehemite there might be a repeat of the experience of Joseph and his twelve brothers.

Eliab and Abinadab walked away from David with their thoughts in turmoil, and David continued his work on the harp.

"Mother, would you like to hear part of a song I am writing? I will play it on the new harp I have made."

David's mother paused in the work she was doing, and her eyes widened in wonder at her youngest son. "Do you mean, my son, that you have made an instrument all by yourself that makes music?" she asked in amazement.

"That's right, Mother. I just finished it, and I wanted you to hear it before I go back to my sheep."

Zeresh wiped her hands dry and sat down on a stool. "Come, David, and play and sing for me."

David sat down on a stool near his mother and began to play his new harp and sing in a clear tenor voice

"The Lord is my shepherd; I shall not want. He maketh me to lie down in green pastures; He leadeth me beside the still waters. He restoreth my soul; He leadeth me in the paths of righteousness for His name's sake."

David stopped and looked at his mother with questioning eyes. "That's all I have written on that song so far," he said apologetically. "But I hope that the Lord will help me finish it in few days." He paused. "Did you like it Mother?"

Zeresh had been listening and watching her youngest son with misty eyes and a prayer of thankfulness in her heart. She arose and grasped her son to her breast. "David, that was beautiful. It stirred my heart so deeply. But tell me, son, where you learned to make such beautiful music? You haven't had any teachers."

"I was in Bethlehem a few weeks ago with Father, and I saw an eight-stringed harp in one of the shops. The shopkeeper was so nice. He let me play on it for several minutes, and he showed me which strings to pick in order to make music. God helped me to remember every word he spoke, so I made this harp just exactly like the one in the shop."

Zeresh was amazed. She looked at her youngest son for several moments with love and adoration in her eyes. "Yes, David, I truly believe that God did help you to remember the instructions of the shopkeeper, for your music was beautiful. You must play for your father and your brothers soon."

The boy shook his head vigorously. "Oh no, Mother! Eliab, Abinadab, and Shammah wouldn't like to hear my music, and Father is always too busy to listen to me." His face brightened, "But I'm glad you like it. And since my sheep always like to hear me sing, I'm sure that they will like my music too. I'll play for them, and when Ezri can watch my sheep again, I'll come in and play for you."

Zeresh's heart was hurting for her precious little boy. She had been aware for several years of her older sons' feelings toward David, and her mother's heart sensed what the root of the problem was. They were envious of the natural serenity and wisdom of their youngest brother and were frustrated at the total absence of resentment on his part of their constant maltreatment.

David interrupted his mother's thoughts. "Mother, I need to get back to my sheep. Ezri was so kind to watch them for me while I finished this harp, but he needs to bring the cattle in soon. And," he added with a big smile, "I'm anxious for my sheep to hear my music."

Zeresh nodded. "You are so faithful to care for your sheep. Your father has mentioned several times that he wishes he had more faithful workers like you for his farm. But son, I am always concerned that you are out with the sheep every night all by yourself. I am worried that some large wild animal will attack your flock and you. What would you do?"

"Oh Mother," the boy answered quickly, "I'm not by myself. God is with me all the time, and He is much stronger than bears or lions. He keeps me safe."

His face brightened. "Only last week, a bear came to take one of my lambs. Just as he caught it, I ran up to him and thrust my shepherd's staff into his side. He dropped the little lamb and turned to attack me, but I thrust my staff into his open mouth, and while he was struggling with the staff, I killed him with my rod. I skinned him and am curing the hide for you, Mother. It will be ready soon."

Zeresh's eyes were wide. "David, you mean that you killed a big bear with only your staff and your rod?"

"That's right, Mother, and the Lord has just now given me several more lines for the song I just sang for you."

"Yea, though I walk through the valley of the shadow of death, I will fear no evil; for Thou art with me; Thy rod and Thy staff they comfort me."

David looked to his mother with shining eyes, and Zeresh hugged him to her breast again. "Son, that was so beautiful. You must sing the entire song for me when you have finished."

"I will, Mother; I promise."

David could tell that old Luna liked his singing and the music from his new harp. As the boy played, the old ram lay quietly among the flock, but as soon as the music stopped, the animal became restless. He roamed among the ewes and lambs and even nudged David, which the boy interpreted as sheep language for "play me more music." So David played more music, and again the ram lay quietly. Finally, the fire died down and the flock slept.

As he played for the flock, David could hear the barking of jackals fairly close. Jackals were the greatest pests to the shepherd boy. Often they attempted to steal a lamb or ewe from the flock, and David had killed several with his sling as they came within range, but it seemed to him that two more always took the place of the one he killed.

David had practiced with his sling until he could now cut a single leaf from the twig of a tree at twenty to thirty paces, so any of the smaller varmints that ventured too close to his precious flock were usually food for the vultures the next day.

While the jackals were barking, a lion suddenly roared. The jackals immediately were silent and David's sheep stirred uneasily. The shepherd boy had seen a few lions of late near his flock, but as soon as he moved out to the edge of the sheep, the big cats disappeared.

David lit a torch from the coals of his fire and with his weapons in hand walked out in the direction from which he had heard the roar of the lion. He saw the intruder not far away, but as he raised the torch, the lion didn't slink away as the others had done. In the moonlight David could see that it was an old male lion probably starving to death. A lamb would be a tender morsel to his broken teeth and empty stomach. A stone from David's sling hit the big cat in his protruding ribs, and he roared in pain, but he didn't turn tail and run. He was ravenously hungry, and hunger made him bold.

As David readied his spear and club, the lion suddenly ran up to the flock and grabbed a lamb from its mother's side. The little animal bleated in terror. Before the would-be killer could turn around, David was upon him. He thrust the spear into the beast's side and made a huge gash. The cat dropped his prey and turned to face his tormenter. David dropped his spear, took his club in his right hand, and grabbed the lion by the hair under its jaws. The beast tried vainly to grab David's body, but the boy kept hitting him on the head with his club. The weakened animal was soon subdued and lay at David's feet. David dragged the carcass of the lion out into the thicket and left it as a dubious feast for the jackals. Then he went back to check on the little lamb. He discovered that no physical harm had been done to the lamb because of its heavy coat of wool and the old lion's broken teeth. The lamb's mother was comforting her little charge, and the lamb was bleating softly.

The flock was restless now because of the lion's attack, so David took his harp and played and sang for them until they settled again and went to sleep. David also slept among his sheep.

David never led his flock close to the main routes of travel, but quite often vagrants, roaming Philistines and bandits, shunned the well traveled roads and would come too close to David's charges. Most of these travelers were on a mission and thus passed by without trouble, but some were looking for plunder. When David would see these unwelcome visitors, he would pray earnestly for divine help and get his weapons ready.

One day two men, who David suspected were bandits, left the course they were taking, which should have bypassed his flock, and came directly toward him. When they were about one hundred paces away, David held up his hand for them to stop, but they ignored his sign.

David hailed them. "Don't come any closer to my sheep as they are afraid of strangers. Please keep on your way."

The men halted momentarily and looked around to see if there were any other shepherds. Evidently they concluded that the boy was alone with the flock, so they separated a bit and came on with quickened pace.

David armed his sling and took aim at the nearest man's legs, and the bandit fell heavily with a badly injured leg. David quickly re-armed his sling and called out to the unharmed bandit. "If you come any closer, I will aim a bit higher on you, so take your crippled friend and be on your way."

The man hesitated for a few moments while his wounded companion groaned with pain. Then he reached down, drew the injured man to his feet, and slowly left the area. David watched them until they limped out of sight.

With thankfulness in his heart, he reached down and picked up his harp and sang the beginning of a new song.

"In Thee, O Lord, do I put my trust; let me never be ashamed: deliver me in Thy righteousness. Bow down Thine ear to me; deliver me speedily: be Thou my strong rock, for an house of defense to save me. For Thou are my rock and my fortress; therefore for Thy name's sake lead me, and guide me."

In the past few days, David had seen several small bands of Philistines in full battle dress heading north past the flock's grazing ground. The soldiers seemed preoccupied and ignored the boy and his sheep. They were on a mission, but David had no idea where the troops were heading. These pagans had grown bolder in the passing months and had infiltrated many of the cities of Israel. David had seen many Philistine soldiers lounging in the marketplace of Bethlehem and had seen several pagan altars in the groves and on the tops of the highest hills. He had heard from passing Israelites that the soldiers were boasting that they would soon launch an all out war against Israel and would take their land back from the intruders.

David's heart was stirred. He wished, with great desire, that he was old enough for army service. Several of his brothers were presently serving in the royal army, but David had heard their remarks that King Saul was not aggressive enough in fighting the pagans.

David had never met the king, but he prayed for him every day. He was the Lord's anointed, and therefore, he deserved the loyalty and respect of every person in the kingdom. Thus, his heart was hurt when he heard his brothers criticize the king.

David was mystified. The Philistine troops that had passed a few days ago had not returned, but now there were hundreds of Philistine civilians traveling hastily south and west toward their own land. Many were on foot with burdens on their backs, while others had ox carts full of clothing and furniture and were leading cattle and donkeys. No one bothered to stop and inform the shepherd boy as to the cause of their exodus. In fact, none of the travelers were conversing with one another. They were all in a hurry.

For David, the mystery continued till the next day when his brother Raddai came out to replenish the shepherd's food supply. As soon as they embraced, Raddai exclaimed, "David, something wonderful has happened. About a week ago, hundreds of thousands of Philistine soldiers had gathered at Michmash to fight our small army of three thousand men. But Eliab told us that when it came time for the armies to fight, only six hundred of King Saul's troops and eight hundred of Prince Jonathan's troops were still around. The rest had fled to the pits and woods, and some had even deserted to the enemy.

"Eliab said that King Saul was so afraid that he didn't wait for Ahijah or Samuel to offer a sacrifice to the Lord, but instead, he offered an unlawful sacrifice of his own. When Samuel came, he chided the king, and it made Saul mad. So instead of taking the troops that were left in his army and fighting the Philistines, he went out and sat under a pomegranate tree and pouted. But Prince Jonathan didn't quit. He and his armor bearer decided that God would be with them, so they climbed up the cliff that separated the two armies and began to fight those pagans. They were killing hundreds of the Philistines when the king and the Israelites saw what was happening. So the army and the king joined in and pursued the Philistines all the way back to Beth Aven. They killed thousands of the enemy on the way.

"Even though Jonathan had been the one who had gained this great victory, the king wanted to kill him because he had violated an order that Saul had given forbidding any of the men to eat anything until the battle was over. Jonathan hadn't heard his father's order, so he ate a little honey as he was going through the forest. The men thought that it was a silly order, so Abinadab said that when the king declared that he was going to kill his own son, Jonathan, the troops voted against the king and saved Jonathan."

Raddai was not finished. "Two days ago King Saul made a pronouncement in every city that any Philistine found in the kingdom at the end of seven days would be treated as traitors, so the pagans have been leaving the cities by the scores."

"Yes," David offered. "I've seen hundreds go by, but I had no idea what was happening." He paused for a moment. "Raddai, I would surely like to meet Prince Jonathan. Wouldn't you like to meet him too?"

"Yes, I would," agreed Raddai.

"I have heard," David said, "that he is only twenty-five years old, but he must be a man of great faith."

The two were silent for a few moments.

"David," Raddai hesitated. "Mother told me a few weeks ago that you have made a musical instrument called a harp that you play when you sing to the sheep. She said that you played so beautifully for her and sang a few verses of one of the songs you are writing. Would you play and sing one of your songs for me?"

David's eyes lit up. "I will be glad to sing and play for you. And I will play a part of a new song that I just started writing today."

Raddai sat and listened, and the sheep gathered around David as he played and sang.

"The Lord is my light and my salvation; whom shall I fear? The Lord is the strength of my life; of whom shall I be afraid? When the wicked, even mine enemies and my foes, came upon me to eat up my flesh, they stumbled and fell. Though a host should encamp against me, my heart shall not fear; though war should rise against me, in this will I be confident. One thing have I desired of the Lord, that I will seek after; that I may dwell in the house of the Lord all the days of my life, to behold the beauty of the Lord, and to enquire in His temple."

As David finished his song, Raddai grasped his arm. "David, that was beautiful. Thank you so much for playing for me."

Then he turned to David with a troubled look on his face. "David, I know that our older brothers torment you endlessly. But you also know that I do not join them. I am sure that the main reason they trouble you so much is because they are jealous of you. I'll admit that I am also guilty to a point. All of us have a kindred feeling that one day you will be a great man, and we will look up to you, but because of your loving and forgiving nature, you won't try to get revenge. To your mind, we will always be your loving brothers."

David looked at his older brother for a long moment. "Raddai, if I am ever a great man, it will be because God makes me so. I would never be anything without Him."

After Raddai left, David thought for many long moments about his brother's prediction. *Does God have something great and special in mind for me?*

# CHAPTER 2

It was obvious to David that his brother Raddai had been weeping, for his eyes were red and they mirrored his inward pain. David was alarmed at his brother's apparent distress. For several moments the older brother was mute with his grief. Then between sobs, he told David the reason for his sorrow.

"David, Mother is dead. She died last night in her sleep. Father is in a state of shock, so the brothers will have to take care of the burial. Ezri is on his way out to tend your sheep so you will need to come as soon as he arrives."

David nodded. Then he bowed his head and wept for several minutes. His heart was crushed. His dearest earthly friend, the mentor and comforter of his entire eighteen years of life, the one who had agonized to bring him into this world was gone.

He turned to Raddai. "Raddai, I will miss Mother so much. She was such an encouragement to me. When I could get away from my sheep for a time, I would go to visit her and would sing and play for her, and she would always tell me how my songs would bless her. Sometimes she would sing my songs with me, and we would have such a pleasant time together." He got teary eyed again. "But those times are only precious memories now."

As he reminisced with Raddai about his mother, David remembered a promise he had made to her that he had not fulfilled. "Raddai, many months ago I sang and played on my new harp part of a new song I had just written about the Lord being my shepherd. Mother liked it very much and made me promise her that when I finished the song I would sing the entire song to her. I finished that song only a few days ago, but I didn't have the opportunity to sing the rest of the song to her. Raddai, could I sing the last part of the song to you? It would help my heart feel as though Mother listened to it."

Raddai nodded. "Yes, David, please play the last part of the song to me."

David sang with deep feeling and Raddai was blessed.

"Thou preparest a table before me in the presence of mine enemies: Thou anointest my head with oil; my cup runneth over. Surely goodness and mercy shall follow me all the days of my life: and I will dwell in the house of the Lord forever."

Raddai smiled his pleasure. "Thank you, David. I know that Mother would have been greatly blessed by those words. Now I must go back and help my brothers with the burial service. Ezri should be here at any moment, and then you must come and join us."

The two brothers embraced again, and Raddai left for home.

David began to reminisce about his mother again as soon as Raddai left, and the opening words of a new song came to him. He picked up the harp and began to sing.

"Rejoice in the Lord, O ye righteous: for praise is comely for the upright. Praise the Lord with harp; sing unto Him with the psaltery and an instrument of ten strings. Sing unto Him a new song; play skillfully with a loud noise, for the word of the Lord is right and all his works are done in truth."

David had been so intent on his singing that he hadn't noticed Ezri coming into the camp. The young servant listened quietly as David sang and played. Ezri was like a brother to David, and whatever was hurting David was also hurting the servant boy. So when David finished his song, without a word spoken between them, the two embraced for several long moments there in the midst of the flock, and they wept together.

Ezri stayed with the sheep while David went to his home and to the burial service for his mother. The service was so quiet that the beating of the eight individual hearts could almost be heard during the ceremony. Their father, Jesse, was still in a state of shock and the seven sons were non-communicative as they bore their mother to her final resting place. After the funeral service, David immediately went back to Ezri and to his sheep.

After a brief period of mourning, David's father married a widow from the community. Leah had been married to Nahash, an Ammonite, and had given him two daughters, Abigail and Zeruiah, and a son, Shobi. Nahash had been a soldier in King Saul's army and was killed in a raid on a Philistine outpost.

Now the sons of Jesse had the sisters they had wished for when David was born.

Ozem, David's brother, appeared to be in a hurry and not in the best of moods as he came running out to where David was watching his sheep. The man was out of breath.

"David!" he gasped. "Prophet Samuel is making a surprise visit to our city and to our home, and he wants to see you immediately."

For a few moments David remained in his place, not grasping the report and summons he had received from Ozem.

"Samuel is at our house and wants to see me?" David asked in disbelief. "How could he possibly know about me?"

"He asked Father if he had any other sons, and father told him about you." Ozem's brow furrowed with anger. "Now stop asking silly questions and get on your way to the house. And remember, as soon as you find out what Samuel wants with you, hurry back to your miserable sheep. I don't want to watch them one minute longer than I have to."

David picked up his harp and sling and prepared to leave, and then he hesitated. "Ozem, sheep sense whether you like them or not, and since it is obvious that you hate them, they might give you some trouble. But if you will speak to them kindly, they should obey your commands."

Ozem grimaced. "It will be difficult for me to be civil to these smelly animals, but I'll do my best. Please hurry to the house and back."

David was almost to his home when he remembered the old ram, Luna. The animal didn't like strangers, and Ozem would certainly qualify as a stranger. The beast was always obedient to David. He liked the servant boy Ezri, and he tolerated David's brother Raddai, but any others who came close to him would provoke a chase. David was sorry for his lapse of memory, but it was too late now to retrace his steps and warn Ozem.

His heart was beating fast with anticipation as he neared the place of meeting. He had never met the revered man, Samuel, but he had been anxious for several years to make his acquaintance. He had heard so many good things about the chief priest and only one bad report. Samuel had sons who had been judges at Beersheba, and it was rumored that they accepted bribes and cheated some of the lay people. David had dismissed the report as a baseless rumor, and it had not affected his exalted view of the prophet, priest, and judge.

When David came into the house, he saw Samuel act as if he were listening to a voice, and then the aged priest turned his piercing eyes on David and came forward with a smile to embrace the shy son of Jesse.

Without explaining his actions, Samuel took a vial from a pouch at his side and poured the contents on the head of David. Then Samuel motioned for every member of the family to kneel while he placed his hands on David's head. He offered a beautiful prayer of dedication over the young shepherd and then lifted David to his feet, embraced him, and without further remarks left the house.

When David first came into the room, he noticed that the city elders of Bethlehem were with his family, and he wondered why they had been invited but decided against inquiring about their presence. However, as soon as Samuel left the room, these elders began to question David's father as to the reason for Samuel's visit. Several of these honorable men began speaking at once.

"What was the meaning of Samuel's visit? Did you invite him to your home without our knowledge?"

Jesse spread his hands in frustration. "Brethren, I do not know the answers to your questions. I did not invite him, but when the chief priest and supreme jurist of our land requested a meeting in my home, who was I to refuse the man of God?"

The elders nodded their heads in accord. "Yes, yes. You could not deny him the right to meet in your home."

The men turned searching eyes on David, and one of them spoke. "Son, the most honored man in all of Israel surely must have anointed you for some special purpose. So you must pray that God will reveal to you the special purpose for your life."

David nodded. "I will do that, my lord."

True to his promise, as soon as the interview with Samuel was over, David hurried back to the sheep and Ozem. As he traveled, he was in deep thought. Questions that he couldn't answer at the present were troubling his mind. *What is the meaning of the anointing service Samuel just performed? Did the priest anoint any of my brothers before I arrived?*

His mind was so occupied with the peculiar actions of Samuel that he almost bypassed his flock. Ozem's cries for help brought his mind back to the present, and he almost laughed out loud when he saw the predicament of his brother, but he restrained himself.

Ozem was sitting on the limb of a tree just out of reach of Luna. The beast was stamping its front feet in a very threatening manner and was snorting sheep curses at the intruder in the tree.

"Come and get this killer away from this tree so that I can get down and go home!" Ozem yelled.

David decided to pay him back a bit for the teasing he had endured. "Would you like to hear what Samuel said to me when I met him?" he asked.

Actually, he just now realized that Samuel hadn't said one word to him. Aside from the prayer of dedication, it was all action—the embrace before the prayer and the anointing, then a second embrace after the prayer.

"I don't want to hear anything right now but the sound of the steps of this demon of a ram leaving this tree!" Ozem stated with conviction.

"Very well," David said. "As soon as I take him away, you can climb down and make a run for it. He won't follow you."

As David prepared to take Luna away, the thought occurred to him. "Ozem, I left my rod and staff with you. Why didn't you use these on this contrary animal? After a few lashes with the rod, he would have left you alone."

"Hah," Ozem grunted. "I didn't have a chance to use anything, since he struck me from behind when I wasn't looking. He struck me three more times before I could get to this tree and once when I was climbing. If I could have broken one of these limbs off, I would have used it on him, but I picked the wrong tree. Now, are you going to take that varmint away so I can get down?"

David grabbed the aggressive animal by the horns and led him away while Ozem wasted no time in descending the tree and heading for home on the run. David sat down and gave in to his laughter.

David was watering his flock at a favorite watering hole when a company bearing the royal insignia of Israel crested the horizon and came directly toward his flock. The shepherd felt that he had nothing to fear from representatives of the king, so he waited for the caravan.

A kindly looking man, who appeared to be the leader, greeted David with an embrace and a kiss. "Greetings from the king, my son. I have been to Hebron on business for our beloved king and am returning to Gibeah. Could we have permission to drink from these waters and water our animals?"

David laughed. "God made these springs, so they belong to Him and are, therefore, free to everyone. Please drink your fill and water your animals."

As the helpers were busy watering the animals and filling their water skins they were carrying, the leader visited with David. He saw the harp in David's hand and was interested.

"Do you play that instrument?" he wanted to know.

"Yes, I do," David answered quickly. "The music calms my sheep when they are restless at night, and," he laughed, "it puts them to sleep most of the time." He added modestly. "I sing songs to them that I make up myself. Of course, I believe the Lord inspires me to write these songs."

The man's face brightened. "That is wonderful news. Would you consent to play for our company?" he asked.

"Yes, I will," David offered. "And I will sing for you a part of a new song that I wrote only last night."

By this time the men had filled the water bottles and watered the animals. Everyone sat down in a circle and waited for David. David readied his harp and began to sing in his clear tenor voice.

"The heavens declare the glory of God; and the firmament showeth His handywork. Day unto day uttereth speech, and night unto night showeth knowledge. There is no speech nor language, where their voice is not heard. Their line is gone out through all the earth, and their words to the end of the world. In them hath He set a tabernacle for the sun, which is as a bridegroom coming out of his chambers, and rejoiceth as a strong man to run a race. His going forth is from the end of the heaven, and his circuit unto the ends of it; and there is nothing hid from the heat thereof."

As David finished his song and laid aside his harp, the leader arose and came forward and embraced the shepherd lad again. "My son, your music spoke to my heart."

He smiled. "No wonder your sheep love your music so much. I envy them. I wish that I could come to your camp every night and be lulled to sleep among your sheep. You certainly must come and play for the king sometime. I am sure that he would love your music as much as we have." All of the men around the circle nodded their heads in agreement.

The leader changed the subject. "Do you lose many of your sheep to bandits and wild animals?"

David smiled and shook his head. "I have never lost any of my sheep to bandits or wild animals. I know all of my sheep and lambs by name, and I check on each one every night. I have had jackals, lions, bears, and bandits attempt to steal lambs, but God has helped me to kill them or turn them away."

"You have killed bandits, bears, lions, and jackals?" the man asked in amazement.

"I have never killed a bandit," David said, "but I have crippled several. I broke the leg of one, and I felt sorry for him and made a splint for his leg so that he was able to walk. I have killed jackals, bears, and lions."

The man looked at David for several moments. "My son, you are a very unique person. You have many sheep here and you care for them all by yourself, yet you have not lost one to thieves? The king's court must hear of your exploits.

"We must be going now, but I hope that we will meet again. My name is Elah, and I am the chief servant for the king. If you ever come to the palace in Gibeah, you must ask for me."

David laughed. "I'm sure that I will never have any business at the king's palace, but if I do have occasion to visit there, I will certainly ask for you. My name is David, and I am the youngest son of Jesse, the Bethlehemite."

Among the few regular visitors to David's camp was his brother Raddai. David always looked forward to his older brother's visits since he would always bring him news of home and the kingdom. This particular day Raddai appeared to be bursting with news.

"David, Abinadab came home on leave from the king's army yesterday and brought a very interesting report about the king that I felt would be of interest to you."

David was excited. "Yes, please sit down and share it with me."

"Abinadab reported that over a month ago Samuel came to Saul at Gibeah with a message from the Lord that the king was to make war against the Amalekites and destroy every man, woman, and child, besides all of their property, including stock, personal goods, gold, and silver. The reason for this order was because the Amalekites had attacked our forefathers when they were on their way from Egypt to Canaan, and now the entire race had filled up their cup of iniquity, so they were to be wiped out.

"Abinadab said that the king organized his troops so well that the Amalekites were on the run in just a short time and almost all of them were destroyed. But Saul spared King Agag and the best of the cattle. The king's son Jonathan pleaded with his father to kill Agag and destroy the cattle, but Saul insisted that he wanted to spare Agag for a time and the cattle would be used for a sacrifice to the Lord.

"The prophet Samuel came to the camp soon after Saul had marched his army back to Gilgal, and he said that the Lord was highly displeased because Saul had disobeyed Him by not destroying all of the Amalekites and their property. Then, according to Abinadab, Samuel made a very strong statement. He said, 'Saul, you have been rejected by the Lord as king over Israel. The Lord has chosen another man who is better than you to be king in your place. This man will be obedient to the Lord's commands.'

"Abinadab said that the men of the army began to speculate among themselves as to whom Samuel was referring. They all liked Prince Jonathan very much and were looking forward to the time when he would be king in his father's place. But Samuel's announcement sounded as if a stranger would take Saul's place."

Raddai stopped talking abruptly, and for several long moments he stared at his brother. A strange thought struck him with force as he was speaking. *Could it be possible that my younger brother, the favorite object of teasing and torment by my brothers, the only one who was anointed by the prophet and priest Samuel in the presence of our family and the elders of Bethlehem several months before, could be the next king of Israel?*

He wanted to banish the thought immediately, but it was so pervasive and intractable that it refused to go away. He shook his head to clear his jumbled thoughts, and David noticed.

"Raddai, is something wrong?"

"No, nothing is wrong," Raddai assured him. "I just had a thought of what I must do tomorrow.

"Now, back to Abinadab's report. He said that Samuel demanded that Saul bring King Agag out to him, and he then said to Agag that he must die in the same way that he ordered others to be killed. Then Samuel hacked him to pieces with a sword in front of the entire army. After worshiping with the king, he left for Ramah.

"The king then ordered that all the Amalekite cattle be destroyed, which he should have done in the first place. Abinadab said that Saul appeared to be very angry and agitated, and he left immediately for his palace in Gibeah. The reports that are now coming back to the army are saying that the king sits all day long on his throne with his spear in his hand as if he is looking for someone to show up and demand his place on the throne. It is also rumored that Jonathan is compelled to act in the king's place."

David was sad. "Raddai, I am so sorry for King Saul. He is the Lord's anointed king of Israel, but now he is fearful that the Lord might cause him to be forced out of office at any time so that the prophecy of the new king could be fulfilled. He must be a very miserable man."

David paused for a few moments. "But Raddai, God is so longsuffering and forgiving, thus He surely must have determined, in His infinite wisdom, that He could no longer trust Saul to rule His people fairly."

When David mentioned the word "anointed," Raddai winced, and the thought of David's possible kingship returned even stronger than before. He knew that Samuel didn't make a practice of going to the cities and picking someone at random to anoint. There had to be something very significant about the service that day in his father's house. He remembered later that his father and brothers had discussed the reason for Samuel choosing David out of the seven sons to be anointed, but they had never reached an agreement.

Raddai felt certain now that he could tell his father and brothers the reason why Samuel chose David for the anointing service that day. But he also resolved that he must keep his suspicions to himself because his brothers would certainly laugh him to scorn if he would suggest such an insane idea.

David was speaking again. "But Raddai, what about Prince Jonathan? Samuel's statement to King Saul would surely imply that Jonathan would not succeed his father as king. Instead, a stranger will be the next king. That doesn't seem fair to Jonathan. He is such a good man and a man of great faith. It seems that he has earned the right to be king. I hope that Israel will never forget what he did by faith at Michmash."

Raddai agreed. "I understand your feelings. Both Eliab and Abinadab feel the same way. They say that every man in the army loves Jonathan and would obey him to the death, but God has spoken and He always knows what is best."

David nodded. "You have spoken well, Raddai."

"I must be getting back to the farm," Raddai announced, "but I will visit you again as soon as I have further information."

David embraced his favorite brother warmly. "Thank you, Raddai. I appreciate your visit and report very much, and I will look forward to your next visit."

The palace servants were frustrated. For weeks now the king had refused to communicate with them. He would sit on his throne for hours at a time with a spear in his hand, and they were often afraid to approach him with food and water.

Jonathan was now managing the affairs of the kingdom, and the servants appealed to him for help in serving the king, but Jonathan couldn't help them. In fact, he was having troubles of his own with his father. Often there were certain letters and documents that needed the approval of the king, but Saul ignored them. The king could neither read nor write. Thus, a scribe always wrote his letters, and the king would affix a certain mark that passed for his signature, but often he refused to add his official mark.

Tension mounted by the day in the palace. One day the chief servant, Elah, had a bright idea, and he called the other servants quickly about him.

"Many months ago," he recalled, "I was returning to the palace from Hebron when I met a young shepherd lad from Bethlehem at an oasis. He was so kind to us. He helped us fill our water skins and water our animals. As I was talking with him, I noticed that he held a musical instrument in his hand. He told me that he had made the harp all by himself and that he sang and played to his sheep every night. I asked him if he would play for us, and he consented. He played and sang a beautiful song that he had written only a few days before. I believe that this young man's music would be a great blessing to our king."

The servants nodded in unison. "We agree, Elah. You should go right now and get the king's consent to send for this young man so that he can play for the king and drive that distressing spirit away."

With an anxious heart, Elah went in before the king. He had no idea what kind of reception he would receive, but Saul smiled at his chief servant and raised his hand in recognition. Elah relaxed.

"Honorable king, your servants are concerned for your welfare since we believe that it is a distressing spirit from God that is troubling you. Will you now command your servant to seek out a man who is a skillful player on a harp? When he plays his beautiful music for you, I believe that the distressing spirit from the Lord will go away and you will be well."

Saul considered the suggestion for a few moments; then his face brightened. "That is a wonderful thought, Elah. I will command you this moment to find such a man and bring him to me."

Elah was elated. "Honorable king, I know of such a man as I speak. When I was returning to the palace from Hebron one day, I met a young man from Bethlehem at an oasis. At my request he played and sang beautifully for our company, and I am sure that you will also enjoy his music. His father's name is Jesse."

"Very well," Saul decided. "Send messengers to Jesse at Bethlehem immediately and request him to send his son David to the king's court."

It was mid morning and David was watering his sheep when Ezri came again. He was a young man of few words, so he immediately got to the reason for his visit.

"David, messengers from the king are at the house, and they have asked for you to come immediately. I know that they are expecting you to go with them to visit the king in his palace at Gibeah, so I will keep your sheep until you return."

David's eyes widened. "Ezri, I hope that you are not joking with me. What would the king want with a shepherd boy?"

Ezri spread his hands. "My friend, David, I would not think of playing such a serious joke on you. The two men are at the house and are waiting for you. Your father said that you must not keep them waiting."

Ezri had his own rod and staff and sling, so David gathered his equipment and hastened to the house.

The two men arose and bowed before David as he entered the room, and the older man spoke. "Master David, we have been sent by the king to request your presence at the king's court. The king has heard that you play beautiful music on a harp you have made, and he believes that you might be able to help him."

The man hesitated for a moment; then proceeded. "Our king has been plagued with a distressing spirit from the Lord, and we believe that your music can drive this spirit away and restore him to sanity."

David was astounded at this request from the king, but he wasted no time with questions. "If you will kindly grant me a few minutes to gather some personal belongings, I will be glad to go with you to visit the king."

The men nodded in agreement.

The men were almost non-communicative on the way from Bethlehem to Gibeah, and David was glad. He had so many thoughts of his own to sort out before he was to meet the king. Thus, the silence of the trek was a blessing to him.

He wondered greatly why he would be chosen for the special task of playing for the king's depression. *Surely,* he thought, *there must be many musicians in the kingdom more proficient than I am.*

The first person he met when he entered the palace was Elah, the chief servant of Saul, and the mystery of his choice to serve the king was solved. Elah had recommended him.

Elah embraced David warmly, and then explained to him the condition of the king. "He is terribly depressed, and I believe that there is a quality about your music that will relax him and give him peace. He is expecting you, so are you ready to meet the king?"

David nodded. "Yes, I am ready."

As Elah led David into the king's chamber, Saul turned his piercing eyes upon the shepherd, and before Elah could speak, the king asked. "Who are you, my son?"

"I am David, the son of Jesse the Bethlehemite," David offered, "and I am the shepherd of my father's sheep."

"How old are you?" the king asked.

"I am twenty-one years old, my lord," David responded.

"Very good." The king sounded satisfied. "My servant Elah tells me that you play the harp beautifully, and he believes that your music will help my depression. Will you play for me?"

"Yes, my lord," David agreed. "I will gladly play for my lord, the king."

The king motioned David to a stool nearby and then assumed a listening position.

David prayed a silent prayer and began to pick the strings of his harp and sing in his rich tenor voice.

"God is our refuge and strength, a very present help in trouble. Therefore we will not fear, though the earth be removed, and though the mountains be carried into the midst of the sea; though the waters thereof roar and be troubled, though the mountains shake with the swelling thereof. There is a river, the streams whereof shall make glad the city of God, the holy place of the tabernacles of the most High. God is in the midst of her; she shall not be moved: God shall help her, and that right early. The heathen raged, the kingdoms were moved; He uttered His voice, the earth melted. The Lord of hosts is with us; the God of Jacob is our refuge."

As David played, the king nodded his head in approval, and a smile touched and transformed his face. His form began to relax as he listened. Finally, he laid his spear down on the floor by his throne and placed his hands in his lap. It was obvious that, for the time, the music was driving the king's depression away.

Soon Queen Ahinoam, accompanied by two beautiful girls who David assumed were the king's daughters, came into the room and smiled and nodded their pleasure.

When David finished his offering, the king motioned for him to come near and the queen and daughters surrounded him.

"My son," the king said gratefully. "I was greatly blessed by your music. I want you to become my court musician. I am sending a royal edict to your father, Jesse, informing him that you will stay here at the palace and play for me whenever the depression comes upon me. Are you willing?"

David bowed in consent. "My lord, your servant is always willing to serve the king, the Lord's anointed."

"Very well," the king determined. "It shall be so."

# CHAPTER 3

"Thank you very much for what you are doing for my father," the princess said gratefully. "I don't know what would have become of him if you wouldn't have come, since the physicians all gave up on him. But he is responding so well to your music that I am hoping for complete healing for him soon." She paused and looked at David hopefully. "Do you believe that he is getting better?"

"Yes, I do see signs of improvement in your father's behavior. It appears that the seizures are decreasing both in number and intensity. Perhaps God will see fit to heal your father soon."

The princess looked at David for several moments. "It sounds as if you have a lot of faith in God," she ventured.

David nodded. "I do trust Him every day for wisdom and protection, and He has never failed me, but I always pray for more faith." He turned to her. "What about you?"

Her gaze wavered, and she answered uncertainly. "I believe in God, but I often wonder if He is too busy to pay attention to us."

Her face brightened. "You must talk to my brother Jonathan. He is a great believer in God. In fact, he has told me often that God will do anything for us that we ask if we obey Him and ask that His will be done." Her eyes became starry. "He is such a wonderful brother, and I know that you would like him too."

"I have been anxious to meet your brother. I have heard so many good things about him."

"He is at Gilgal now with his army, but he comes here quite often to judge court cases and take care of other business of the kingdom. You see, father hasn't handled any kingdom business for months." She said the last statement rather apologetically.

David nodded. "It would be impossible for him to do business in his condition."

"Jonathan's wife, Zereth, is here in the city," Michal informed him. "You must meet her also. She is almost as nice as my brother," she added with a twinkle in her eyes. "Now, you probably have already guessed; I am Michal, the king's youngest daughter."

"It is certainly my privilege to meet and visit with you, Michal. I see Elah motioning to me, so I assume that I am to play again for the king."

David's ministry to the king with his fits of depression was exhausting, even to the hardy shepherd. Often in the middle of the night, the king would suffer an attack, and David would be summoned. The posture of the king during these seizures was always predictable. He would sit on his throne like a figure cut from stone with his spear in his hand, his eyes glazed, and only the music and singing of David would relax him and give him rest.

David suspected that the king's depression was really a spiritual malady, probably caused by guilty feelings from his disobedient actions at Gilgal and Carmel. There was also the fear of the loss of his kingship that constantly preyed on his mind. Thus, the only complete healing of his disease would depend on a renewed relationship with his Lord, so David chose to sing songs that spoke of God's mercy and forgiveness.

The king seemed very agitated today, and instead of his usual stance, as that of a statue, he was in motion. The muscles in his face and arms twitched convulsively, and he changed position often as David played. He didn't lay down his spear but clutched it even tighter.

David wondered about the drastic difference in his demeanor from former sessions, but he had no clue as to the change in his actions.

Finally, the king arose from his throne and dismissed David with a wave of his hand. As David turned to leave the room, Michal stopped him. Her eyes were wide and dark with fear. "I'm sure that you noticed the difference in father's behavior this morning. Late last night Captain Abner brought news to him that the Philistines are gathering in large numbers at Ephes Dammim and are threatening to make war on our army. Uncle Abner insisted that Father must come to the battle site immediately to encourage our troops so that they will not desert as they did at Michmash. Mother pleaded with Father not to go to the battle site because of his mental and physical condition, but Father is stubborn and feels that he must go for the sake of the men. Now, because of his mental agitation, he will, no doubt, forget about you, so I assume that you are free to go back to your home. When he gets back from Ephes Dammim, I am sure that he will call for you again." She touched David's arm. "I will certainly miss you and your beautiful music."

David looked into her beautiful eyes and the manhood in him was deeply touched. "I will surely miss you also Princess Michal. Perhaps fate will bring us together again."

He left then to gather up his belongings and go back to his home in Bethlehem and to his sheep.

Ezri seemed troubled as he greeted David, and the reason for his unease was soon revealed. "David, I am a poor shepherd," he confessed. "I lost a lamb and a ewe to a jackal and a lion, and both were taken in the daytime. The jackal took the lamb when I was treating another sheep that had fallen into some brambles. When I finally saw the thief, he was too far away for me to give chase. I did fight the lion that took the ewe, but I was no match for him." Ezri spread his hands in frustration. "As I get my earnings from your father, I will pay for the sheep."

David embraced Ezri. "I would not accept any payment from you, my friend. I know that you are a very dependable person, and therefore, the loss of the sheep could not be helped. So forget about any thought of payment. I am very glad that you were not hurt by the lion."

"Thank you, David," Ezri breathed. "You are a wonderful friend."

David had to get acquainted with his sheep all over again. He had been gone from them for almost a year now, and a number of new lambs had been born during that time. He named the new lambs, and after looking over his flock, he surprised himself by remembering the names of the ewe and lamb that had been taken by the lion and the jackal.

The lions and the jackals continued to threaten his flock often. He killed several jackals with stones from his trusty sling and drove off many lions, but they came back again and again. It was a labor of love but also of eternal vigilance.

David had been back with his sheep only a short time when Ezri again came out to replace him. "David, your father has a task for you, and he has asked me to care for your sheep again until you return." The servant hesitated for a moment. "David, will you trust me with your sheep again?"

David embraced him warmly. "Yes, Ezri, I will gladly trust you with my sheep. You are a very dependable person, and my sheep love you. Now, about the ewe and the lamb that were lost, it is very possible that they would have been taken even if I was with them, so don't feel guilty any longer over their loss.

"I have no idea what kind of a chore Father has in mind for me, Ezri, but I promise that I will be back as soon as possible." David had no idea at that moment that he would never return to his sheep.

"David, I need for you to take some foodstuff down to your brothers, Eliab, Abinadab, and Shammah, who are with the king's army in the Valley of Elah. I understand they are getting ready to fight a large Philistine army, and I am sure that they would enjoy some food from home. They have been there for many days now, so take an ephah of dried grain and these ten loaves to them and take these ten cheeses to the captain of their company. Bring back news of their welfare as soon as you can," Jesse instructed him.

David took his shepherd's staff and his sling and the provisions for his brothers and their captain and went down to the Valley of Elah.

David hadn't seen his three oldest brothers since the day Samuel had visited their home in Bethlehem, so he was anxious to see them and find out how they were faring at the battle site.

When he thought of Samuel and the actions of the chief priest toward him that day at his home in Bethlehem, he almost forgot his present mission. He wondered again what the anointing service meant. The thought had possessed him often while he was watching his sheep, but so far any solution had eluded him.

He heard the shouting before he reached the headquarters, but he noticed that the army didn't appear to be in motion, so he wondered about the loud noise. The armies of Israel were drawn up in battle order, and as he looked across the Valley, he saw that the enemy was also poised for battle. David left the cheeses with the supply keeper with instructions to give them to the captain of his brothers' company, and then he went to find his brothers with the food and gifts in hand.

David expected that the brothers would be glad to see him since he brought them greetings and gifts from their father, including foodstuffs to supplement their army rations, but he was disappointed. All three of his brothers were in a foul mood. They ignored the provisions and the gifts and didn't even acknowledge him with an embrace or a handshake. They appeared to be mesmerized by something or someone out in the valley between the armies.

David ventured a question to Eliab, "My brother, please tell me what is of such great interest to all of you in the valley?"

Eliab continued to ignore him, but a soldier standing next to the three brothers answered David's question. "Young man, if you will look out in the valley now, you will see the cause of our troubles. Do you see that giant man? Every day this giant Philistine, Goliath, comes out into the valley to defy the God of heaven and every man in the army of Israel. He claims that his god, Dagon, is stronger than our God, and therefore, none of our soldiers can fight him and kill him.

"Every day he challenges our men to come out and fight him. He says that if one of us will fight him and kill him that the entire Philistine nation will be our servants forever. On the other hand, if he kills our warrior, we must be servants of the Philistines forever." The soldier hesitated for a moment, and he shuddered. "None of our men have dared to fight him, not even our king, who is also a giant."

Another man spoke up. "I know that Prince Jonathan would fight and kill him if he was here, but the king has refused to call him and his army from Gibeah."

David was amazed. "How long has this Philistine been making this challenge to the army of the Lord?"

"Every day for forty days this man has been taunting us," the soldier answered.

Eliab had been listening to David's questions and the soldier's answers, and he now spoke up. "Why did you come down here to the battle site in the first place, sister boy? And with whom did you leave those few miserable sheep? I know your pride and the naughtiness of your heart. But your nosey questions are distracting the men, so why don't you go back to your sheep where you belong?"

David looked for a long moment at his oldest brother, but there was no rancor in his look. He was wondering why one of his three brothers hadn't accepted the giant's challenge. They were big men and experienced in battle.

"Brother, I'm sorry if I offended you, but I am amazed that every man in the king's army has allowed this uncircumcised pagan to defy the God of heaven and the king's men for forty days without answering him back."

He turned to the soldier again with whom he had spoken. "What does the king say about this heathen?"

"The king has promised that any man who fights this giant and kills him will receive his daughter in marriage and his father's house will get an exemption."

David made a decision. "I will go out and fight this pagan in the name of the Lord of hosts."

"My foolish brother, you haven't even seen this giant of a man yet, but you are already boasting that you will go out and fight him," Abinadab said in an accusing tone. "There he is ranting again out there in the valley, so why don't you listen to him for a few minutes and look at his size before you decide to go out and let him chop you in pieces?"

David looked out into the valley and saw the man of whom they were speaking. As he looked at the man, he remembered his mother's stories of the giant sons of Anak who had fought against the Israelites as they traveled from Egypt to Canaan. This man was truly a giant, and perhaps he was a descendent of Anak.

The giant was shouting and David listened. "Why have all of you Israelites come out to fight against us?" he ranted. "You are the servants of Saul, but you are all afraid of me. I am a Philistine, and I defy the armies of Israel to give me a man who will fight against me. If any of you men dare to fight me and kill me, I swear by the great god Dagon that all of our people will consent to be your servants. But if I kill the man you will choose, you must agree to be our servants."

The giant shook his spear in the air in his anger. "Is there not a single man among you who will accept my challenge?"

At that moment there was a stir among the soldiers as a man stepped up and grasped David by the arm. "The king wishes to see you," he said curtly.

The king was standing in front of his tent watching the actions of the giant in the valley as David came up.

"This is the man who has said that he will go out to fight the giant, Goliath," the servant explained to the king.

Saul looked at David searchingly. "Haven't I seen you somewhere before, my son?" he asked.

"Yes, my lord, you have seen me at your palace. I am, David, the son of Jesse the Bethlehemite, the one who played and sang for you at the palace in Gibeah."

The king's eyes lit up. "Yes, yes, I remember that you were the lad. You were a great blessing to me. But my son, how can you go out and fight this giant of a man? You are only a bit above average in size, and you are not battle tested. This man would probably kill you with one stab of his sword or spear."

"Yes, my lord," David answered. "As you say, I am not battle tested, but I will not go in my own strength. This man is armed only with his great size and his sword and spear. I will go in the name of the Lord of hosts who made heaven and earth. He helped me to kill lions and bears and jackals that threatened my sheep, and I have faith to believe that He will give this uncircumcised Philistine into my hands. You see, my lord, someone must surely fight this pagan, for he has defied the God of heaven and the armies of Israel, and he must be answered."

Saul looked long at David. He liked this young man who had driven his depression away on many occasions. *Perhaps*, he mused, *God might use this daring young man here at Ephes Dammim like he used Jonathan, at Michmash.*

Suddenly the king turned to David. "Do you realize, young man, that if I let you go out to fight this man and he should kill you that the Philistines will expect us to be their servants forever?"

David nodded. "Yes, I heard him make that statement," he admitted. "But are we not already their servants if we don't have the courage to go out and fight the giant?"

"Yes, you are right. Very well, you will go with my blessing and hopefully with the blessing of the Lord.

"Abner, bring my armor for David. He must not go out to fight this giant without armor."

David had never been suited in armor before, and the attire was cumbersome to him. He lifted his sling in his right hand as if to throw a stone, but the action was not natural. He knew that this weight could possibly deflect his aim.

*However*, he reasoned, *I am covered from head to toe with the metal greaves which could divert the thrust of the giant's sword or spear.*

So he picked up his staff and started out toward the valley, but the hand of the Lord stopped him, and he turned back. He knew that he must not wear that which he had not tested.

When he returned the armor, he made only a brief apology. "I have not tested this armor. Therefore, I must not wear it to fight this man. I will go instead in the armor of the Lord."

The king's heart was immediately assailed with serious doubts. Should he allow this vulnerable youth to go out to fight this giant who was in full armor? He was certain that the outcome would be a disaster. David would die by the hand of Goliath, and the Philistines would be emboldened to demand that the terms of the fight by kept.

He started to give the order for Abner to stop the youth, but the words stuck in his throat. He watched helplessly as David walked toward the valley with his sling and staff in hand.

The army of Israel watched David start out toward the valley, and David's brothers also watched him go. For perhaps the first time in their entire twenty-two year relationship with him, their hearts were anxious for him. Each of the three thought, for a moment, about going out to join him, but selfish fear kept their feet in place.

David was not in a hurry as he walked out to meet the giant. His faith assured him that God was with him, and thus his movements were unhurried. He tested his arm with the sling to make sure that the weight of the heavy armor had not caused any muscle spasms.

There was a small brook before him, and he stopped to replenish the stones in his shepherd's bag. He chose five smooth stones, and then he turned his full attention on the giant standing immobile in the valley.

Goliath was puzzled. When he first saw David leave the ranks of the Israelite army and come across the valley toward him, he thought that the man was playing a joke on him. The man had no armor, no sword or spear, yet he was on his way across the valley as if he were planning to do battle with him—a giant in full armor. The Philistine noticed that the man was much smaller than himself. He was certain that he could do this rash, pestilent fellow in with one slash of his sword. This victory would really be too easy—no contest. He pushed the visor of his helmet up over his hairline so he could see his opponent better. He had no idea that David had prayed for the Lord to expose the forehead of the giant.

David was walking faster now and the two foes were approaching each other rapidly. The Philistine laughed harshly. "Am I a dog," he cried out, "that you come to me with sticks and stones? By the name of my god Dagon, I swear that I will cut you in pieces and give your flesh to the birds of the air and the beasts of the field, and this day your people will be delivered into our hands."

David responded quickly. "You come to me with a sword, a spear, and a javelin, but I come to you in the name of the Lord of hosts, the God of the armies of Israel whom you have defied these forty days. This day the Lord will deliver you into my hands, and I will strike you and take off your head. And this day I will give your carcass and the carcasses of these Philistines who are with you to the birds of the air and the wild beasts of the field. Then all this assembly shall know that the Lord does not save with sword and spear, for the battle is the Lord's, and He will give you into our hands."

Then David ran to meet the giant. As he ran he put his hand into his shepherd's pouch, took out a stone, armed his sling, and slung the stone with all his might at Goliath. The stone went true to its mark. It struck the giant in his forehead and sunk in deep. Goliath fell heavily to the earth. David immediately ran and took the giant's sword out of its scabbard and cut off his head. For a few moments the men of both armies were frozen in place; then the Philistines broke and ran in terror.

Suddenly, there were shouts from the army of Israel, and the soldiers leaped into action. They rushed across the valley and began to pursue the fleeing Philistines, who were totally disorganized. They chased the pagans as far as the gates of Ekron, and thousands of the Philistines were killed or wounded along the way.

When David returned from chasing the Philistines, he picked up the severed head of Goliath, along with his sword and armor, and prepared to take them back to Bethlehem. He wondered, briefly, why he would bother to save the Philistine's head. Was it a sign of pride on his part—a token of a personal victory—or was the object a symbol of God's victory over the enemy? He chose to believe the latter.

Soldiers crowded around David to congratulate him and thank him for fighting a battle that each man knew they should have fought forty days ago. David's brothers were among those who were congratulating him, but their attention bothered him. They had been very rude to him before his battle with Goliath, but now that he was famous, they seemed proud to call him brother rather than "sister boy." David felt sorry for their pettiness.

As David prepared to leave with the heavy armor, the sword, and the head of the giant in hand, Captain Abner pushed through the crowd and grabbed him by the arm. "The king wishes you to ride with him in his chariot back to Gibeah," the officer announced.

David had never ridden in a chariot before. His former method of transportation was by foot. But here he was, not only riding in a chariot, but riding in the personal chariot of the king of Israel.

"You are to stay at the palace tonight," the king informed him. "And tomorrow you will be presented to the king's court and to my son Jonathan."

In every village and hamlet where the king and David passed through on their way back to Gibeah of Benjamin, people were waiting to welcome the victorious pair, "Long live the king and David the giant killer," they shouted.

The king appeared pleased with the multitude, but there were a few groups of women playing tambourines who sang, "Saul hath slain his thousands, and David his ten thousand." David noticed that the visage of the king darkened when he heard this unfavorable reference to himself, but he made no mention of these pestilent groups. He welcomed David to the palace and ordered Elah to make the shepherd comfortable.

# CHAPTER 4

David awoke with a start and felt around him, but there was no feel of wool. Then he remembered; he was not with his sheep; he was in the king's palace at Gibeah and was soon to be presented to the king as the hero of Ephes Dammim.

"What is your name, young man, and whose son are you?" the king asked.

David thought the question a strange one since he had played before the king for an extended period, had met with the King and Abner before going out to fight Goliath, and had ridden with the king in his chariot from the Valley of Elah to Gibeah only yesterday. However, he answered the ruler respectfully. "My name is David, my lord. I am the son of Jesse the Bethlehemite, and I am the keeper of my father's sheep."

Saul looked at David for a long moment. "And you are the man who killed the Philistine giant Goliath and made possible a great victory for Israel, are you not?"

"That is right, my lord. I killed him in the name of the Lord of hosts, and God gave us a great victory."

The king nodded. "Because of your great service to the Lord and to Israel, I decree that you shall no longer go back to your home in Bethlehem. Instead, you must stay at the palace in Gibeah and give yourself completely to the service of the kingdom. I am assigning you a position of leadership in the royal army, and you will be answerable only to Captain Abner and me."

David bowed. "Yes, my lord, I will accept the charge and will serve you and the kingdom with my whole heart."

The king raised his hand and waved to signify that the interview was over; then he left the throne room with Captain Abner. David stayed in place, not knowing where he should go or what his next assignment would be.

David had noticed a tall young man standing behind the king's throne during the royal interview, and he assumed the man was the king's son, Jonathan. As the King and Abner left the room, Jonathan came forward to where David was standing, and the two men looked at each other for a long moment. It was as if an electric current passed between them and welded their hearts together. They embraced warmly as if they had been bosom friends for years. In a moment of time, a bond was forged between the two that would last to the death. They loved each other as their own soul.

"David, I have gifts for you and you must accept them, and then I will explain the reason for my giving them," Jonathan said with deep feeling.

David shook his head. "No, no, my lord Jonathan, I am the one who should be giving the gifts, since you are the prince and I am the commoner. But," David spread his hands helplessly, "I have nothing to give."

Jonathan smiled. "David, my friend, I understand your feelings. But if you will allow me the honor of giving my gifts to you, I am sure that when I explain the reason for my giving them, you will be satisfied."

David nodded. "I will accept them."

"Thank you," Jonathan responded. There in the throne room, Jonathan took off his robe, his armor, sword, bow, and belt and gave them to David.

David bowed in acceptance and humility as Jonathan gave him the treasured items; then he straightened up. "Jonathan, please explain the reason for giving me these special gifts."

"David, in the first place, these gifts are tokens of a covenant that I am proposing between us this day. From this time and place, we are brothers and will therefore love and trust and protect each other to the death."

David clasped the right hand of his new friend, and they locked arms to signify the ratification of the covenant.

Jonathan continued. "The second reason for my giving these gifts is even more compelling. Please, be patient with me as I explain." His face twisted in pain. "Two different times now my father has disobeyed a direct command of God. The first time was when he offered an illegal sacrifice on his own at Gilgal. An unusually large Philistine army was threatening war against our very small Israelite army, and Father claimed that he needed a word of counsel from the Lord. A resident priest, Ahijah, was at hand who could have offered the sacrifice and the Prophet Samuel was scheduled to visit the camp soon, but Father wouldn't wait. He was proud and stubborn and thus made his own rules.

"The second incident happened when God, through the Prophet Samuel, commanded him to destroy the entire Amalekite nation. Their sins had mounted up to heaven, so the king was commanded to destroy every man, woman, child, stock, and all goods. Not a particle was to be left."

Jonathan shuddered. "But Father saved King Agag as a trophy of war and the best of the stock as spoil. He claimed that the stock was saved for a sacrifice to the Lord and that he would soon kill Agag. I pleaded for him to obey the Lord fully, but he was firm in his disobedience. On both occasions that I have mentioned, Samuel came into camp soon afterward and brought a stern message of rebuke from the Lord. Twice he made the statement that since Father had disobeyed the Lord so shamelessly, God was rejecting him as king of Israel. He said that God had chosen another to be king in his place who would do His will and follow His orders.

"Now, of course, Samuel's statements that someone from outside of our family would be the next king also affected my future. I had naturally assumed that one day I would succeed father as king, but Samuel's statements dashed my hopes.

"At first, I was disappointed and somewhat bitter at the thought of not being king. But I prayed earnestly that God would help me to accept the fact that I would never be king, and the Lord answered my prayer. I have accepted my lot and am at peace."

David had been listening attentively to Jonathan, but now he spoke up. He was agitated. "But Jonathan, that wouldn't be fair. Surely God didn't reject you because of your father's sin. You are the prince. You are a man of great faith and our beloved nation needs you as its next king. Perhaps you misinterpreted the message that God gave to your father through Samuel."

Jonathan shook his head. "No, David, I did not misinterpret God's message, and the reason I am so certain is part of my story."

David relaxed again and listened.

"My wife, Zereth, is very happy that I will never be king. You see, David, for many months I have acted in Father's stead since he has been unable to carry on the king's business. The task has been very tiring and frustrating because of the great press of business to attend to when I come to the court. Also, there are some documents that require the king's mark. He can neither read nor write but he does have a royal mark that he must affix to special records. Sometimes he will refuse to make that mark and the documents pile up. The hours have been long and the results very meager. I will be glad when Father can again assume his royal responsibilities or the new king will be installed.

"Back to my story. Zereth and I have prayed earnestly for God to reveal to us the person who will succeed my father as king, and God has answered our prayers. David, you are the man whom God has chosen to be the next king of Israel."

David was stunned. The thought of being king had never entered his mind. But then he remembered the anointing by Samuel, and he realized that Jonathan was right. However, the thought of God choosing him to be king over Israel overwhelmed him. He bowed his head and was silent for several minutes as he wrestled with thoughts that he had no answers for at the moment.

*Why is God choosing me out of all of the people to be king over Israel? I am only an insignificant shepherd. Why is God bypassing Jonathan?* That thought hurt his heart. *What plan does God have for removing King Saul and installing me as king? Surely there must be some mistake; Jonathan is wrong and Samuel is wrong. They have misread God's signs, and the mistake will soon become evident.*

Then the Spirit of God touched him and settled his thoughts. *If God has chosen him, as it appears He has, He will provide the answers to these questions in His time and His way. I must be patient and wait for the providence of God.*

Jonathan noticed David's agitation but remained quiet. David raised his head, and there were tears in his eyes. "Jonathan," he said softly, "let me share with you. Several years ago Samuel came to the town of Bethlehem for the purpose of offering a sacrifice. Afterwards, he invited the elders of the town to meet in our home with our family. Strangely, he interviewed my brothers one by one, and then asked Father if he had any more sons. I was out in the field with my sheep at the time, so Father sent for me. As soon as I came into the house, Samuel embraced me and then anointed me. He appeared to be in a hurry, for immediately after the anointing, he placed his hands on my head, gave a short prayer of dedication, and then left for Ramah. He offered no explanation to anyone for his actions, and naturally, everyone present was mystified."

David paused and reflected. "It has been almost four years since Samuel's visit. He has never returned to Bethlehem, so I have not had an opportunity to question him about the reason for the anointing, but I am quite sure that the chief priest doesn't conduct anointing services without a divine mandate. However, since so much time has elapsed since my anointing, perhaps the purpose of the service is no longer in force." David looked at Jonathan. "So, my friend, it is possible that you will be king after all."

Jonathan shook his head vigorously. "No, David, time doesn't change God's mind. As I have already told you, God gave me an unmistakable impression that you will be the next king of Israel, so let's not discuss the matter any further."

They embraced again and renewed their covenant.

The invitation to the royal banquet came to David by special courier. The message was beautifully engraved on expensive papyrus and was scented with perfume of the most pleasing fragrance.

David was to be the guest of honor, but the shepherd boy from Bethlehem had never attended a banquet. He was used to the simple fare of the herdsman and the occasional bliss of a meal at his mother's table, so he feared that he would feel out of place at a royal banquet.

In the many months of his music ministry to the king, he had never eaten at the king's table. He had supped with the servants, so he was greatly concerned about this present invitation, since the formal repast was to be a royal affair.

The royal family awarded David the honors of a hero. A royal carriage came for him and carried him to the banquet hall. Prince Jonathan met him at the door with the beautiful Princess Zereth on his arm. In only the few moments that David was privileged to visit with Zereth, he loved her as he loved his friend Jonathan.

A royal servant escorted David to the banquet table and seated him between the king's two daughters, Merab and Michal. The queen was seated opposite of David at the table, and she smiled her welcome. The king was missing.

Except for his mother, David had rarely mingled with members of the opposite sex. His stepsisters were older by several years, and he hardly knew them. Thus, he was rather shy in the presence of women. Merab was quiet and pensive, but Michal was talkative and interesting.

"Father said that you went out against the Philistine giant without a sword or a spear, only with your sling and your staff. Weren't you afraid that he would quickly stab you with his oversized spear?" Michal asked.

David smiled. "I didn't plan to let him get that close."

Michal laughed sweetly, and Merab listened intently.

"But," Michal insisted, "according to Father's account, Goliath was suited in full armor, so how did you know where to aim the stone?"

David responded quickly and firmly. "As I went out to meet him, I prayed that God would impress him to push up his visor over his forehead, and that's what he did. So I knew exactly where to aim the stone."

Both Michal and Merab looked at David for a long moment. "Do you actually believe that God impressed him to push his visor up so that his forehead was exposed?" Michal asked in amazement.

"Yes, I do," David said quickly. "I was going out to fight him in the name of the Lord God of hosts, and I knew that I had the advantage."

Jonathan, the host of the banquet, proposed a toast to David, the hero of the battle of the Valley of Elah, at that point, thus interrupting his conversation with the two princesses.

As the food was served and the guests began to eat, Michal again became inquisitive. "So you are a shepherd by trade?" she asked.

Before David could answer, Merab chided her younger sister. "Michal, let the man eat his meal. He will surely think that you are a nosy churl."

David laughed. "I assure you, Princess Merab, that the idea of your sister being a nosy churl had not entered my mind."

He turned to Michal. "Yes, I have been a shepherd for as long as I can remember. You see, Princess Michal, the work of a shepherd is not the most coveted task on a farm. You must stay out with your sheep day and night through storm and sun, and you must protect the sheep from wild animals and bandits. Since I was the youngest of seven sons, I was assigned the job that none of my other brothers wanted. But strangely, I have loved being a shepherd."

Michal's eyes sparkled. "Elah told me that you have killed many jackals and even lions and bears and crippled bandits who were trying to raid your sheep."

"That's right," David concurred modestly. "Up to the time I left to go to the Valley of Elah, I had not lost a single sheep to wild animals or bandits."

Michal was impressed, and even Merab viewed him with new interest.

David was loath to see the pleasant evening end, but a servant notified him that his carriage was ready. Michal touched him on the arm as he prepared to leave. "Will you play and sing for me sometime soon? I enjoyed your music so much when you played for my father."

"I would be happy to sing for you at your convenience, Princess Michal," David said with a bow.

"Thank you very much, and thank you for such a pleasant evening," she said sweetly.

"Captain Abner requests your presence in the war tent at the eighth hour," the aide informed David.

"Please tell Captain Abner that I will be there at the eighth hour as he has requested," David responded.

The captain was crisp and officious as he welcomed David into the war tent. "The king has ordered me to assign a company of soldiers to you, and you are to raid the Philistine garrisons that are close to our border. I will identify the garrisons week by week that you are to attack. You will be expected to destroy these outposts so that the enemy will be compelled to move farther back into their own territory. For the present time, you will report the results of your raids to me, but it is possible that the king will have you report to him personally at a later date."

David bowed. "I am at your service, Captain Abner. Please introduce me to the men that will make up my company."

As Abner brought the soldiers out one by one, it was quite evident to David that they were an undisciplined lot. *Perhaps,* he mused, *Abner is giving me the most hopeless of his two thousand.*

The men were slow in their movements, and many of them slouched in line. David welcomed them enthusiastically and asked them to speak their names. He wanted to get acquainted with them personally, for they were now his sheep, and he was their shepherd. He must teach them obedience and purpose.

"Men," he said firmly, "we must learn how to work together, so for the next five days, we will march for three hours on the parade ground. Then, after an hour of rest, we will practice jousting for two hours. Next week Captain Abner will give us an assignment, and we must be prepared to attack the target and return to home base without losing a man. Do you have any questions?"

Several of the men began to grumble. David ignored the disorder for a few minutes; then he raised his hand for silence. "I will not tolerate talking in line without official permission. Even the first offense will be treated harshly. It will warrant a night in the guardhouse."

David paused for a minute to let his statement sink in. The men had grown strangely quiet.

For several weeks David led his company on successful forays against the Philistine garrisons. Not a man was lost, and much spoil was brought back to put in the Lord's treasury and parcel among the troops. The men of David's company praised his leadership, and the entire census of Abner's troops was energized. In fact, other soldiers of Abner's army were requesting to join David's regulars.

Abner was waiting for David when he came in from his latest raid. "The king wishes to see you in the throne room immediately," the army commander notified him.

Jonathan was in the throne room with his father. David relaxed when he saw the smile on his friend's face. The king greeted him without preamble. "I have heard such good reports of the raids you are leading against the pagan garrisons, and Abner tells me that many of his soldiers are requesting to join your company, so I am assigning you as captain over one thousand troops of Abner's army. That will give us three armies of one thousand troops in each. You will no longer be answerable to Abner, but you will report directly to me."

The king continued, "I will plan to go with your company on your next raid. Your men are reporting that your leadership gives them a great sense of confidence and none of your men has been lost so far."

David protested. "Oh king, it is true that the Lord has given us protection to this point, but I would not want to risk the Lord's anointed in any of the raids."

The king held up his hand. "I am anxious to see your method of leadership, so I will go with you. We will not discuss the matter further. When is your next incursion scheduled?"

David bowed in acquiescence. "I will need a few days to train the new men, so the time for our next foray is one week from today. Now, my lord, we have taken many horses in our raids, so all of my men are now mounted. You will need to come by chariot."

In the early morning hours, David took his company to the vicinity of the Philistine outpost, and at dawn he struck from three sides with every man screaming the Israelite's war song. It was a complete and total victory. Not one pagan escaped, and every man was put to the sword. Then David set the men to work destroying the garrison and gathering the spoil.

King Saul was pleased with the efficiency of the attack. He considered himself very proficient in the art of warfare, but he recognized that David was his superior.

On the return trip to Gibeah, David was dismayed, and Saul was greatly angered. Women came out of all the cities along the way with tabrets and instruments of music, and they danced and sang in response, "Saul hath slain his thousands, and David his ten thousands." It was a repetition of demonstrations in two cities when the king and David were returning from Ephes Dammim.

David made no move to acknowledge the women's adulation but instead looked straight ahead as he rode by. He was sick at heart. He had no idea who had arranged such a passionate demonstration since it was obvious that it was not spontaneous. And he wondered if perhaps, the king thought that he had encouraged the display.

Out of the corner of his eye, he watched the king as the women sang. The face of Saul darkened and the muscles of his jaw began to twitch with displeasure. The knuckles of his hands were white as he gripped the poles of the chariot, and his tone of voice was unusually harsh as he ordered his driver to greater speed. When the procession reached the palace at Gibeah, the king dismissed his chariot driver with a wave of his hand and without a word to David walked into the palace.

David dismissed the men and went to his room. He spent much time in prayer that night, asking the Lord for special wisdom in handling this threat to his relationship with the king.

The next morning he sought out Jonathan. Jonathan was busy at his work in the administration room, but when David entered he pushed aside his work and embraced his dear friend.

"David," he asked eagerly. "How did the raid work out yesterday? Was Father pleased?"

David's face twisted in pain. Jonathan noticed and became anxious. "Jonathan, the raid itself worked out perfectly. We destroyed the garrison, put every man to the sword, and gathered much spoil. Your father was pleased."

He hesitated, and then continued. "But on the return trip there were demonstrations in every town and city along the route that I'm quite sure hurt your father deeply. Women came out with musical instruments and sang a song, 'Saul has slain his thousands, and David his ten thousands.' It was like our return trip from Ephes Dammim but on a much larger scale.

"I know that the women meant well, but it was very unfortunate. My own heart was hurting for your father, and as I watched him, I could tell that he was raging inside. He was gruff to his driver, and when we reached the palace, he ignored me."

David spread his hands helplessly. "I am at a loss. Someone must have organized those demonstrations, but I have no idea who it could have been. They were certainly not spontaneous."

Jonathan smiled and nodded. "David, you will probably find that the army men were behind those demonstrations. They love you and simply wanted to let you know how they feel about you. They had no idea that the king would be with you on this latest raid."

Jonathan touched David's arm. "Father likes you very much, David, and perhaps after a time he will forget this slight on the part of the women." Jonathan shuddered. "His moods are so unpredictable. I only hope that he doesn't slip back into those fits of depression again."

Their conversation was interrupted by the appearance of the head servant, Elah. The servant was apologetic in his attitude, and David suspected the worst. "Captain David, the king is experiencing one of his moods of depression again, and the servants have requested that you come and play for him as you used to do."

David looked at Jonathan, and the prince nodded. "I hope that you will do this for my father, David."

"Yes, Elah, I will play. Give me a few minutes to get my harp and my music."

"Thank you, Master David," Elah whispered.

It was a familiar sight that greeted David as he stepped into the throne room. The king sat immobile. He was staring straight ahead and the spear was held so tight in his right hand that his knuckles were white. As David started to play, there was a change in Saul's attitude. He turned toward David, and his eyes were fierce. He had heard this music before, and it had calmed his fears, but today was different. It was the same musician, but Saul had changed.

His deranged mind saw in David now as the man who would attempt to take his place on the throne. Hadn't

Samuel told him the usurper would be a neighbor of his? This man fit that description. Hadn't the women attributed to this man a place above him, the king? What more could he have but the kingdom itself? *This music,* he reasoned, *is just a screen to cover up his evil plans to overtake the throne.*

Over and over again these thoughts coursed through the twisted grooves of his mind. *I must get rid of this man,* his mind screamed. He raised his arm and threw his spear with all his might at David, but his aim was not true, and the missile lodged harmlessly in the opposite wall.

Despite the danger he had already faced in the throne room, David continued to play until Saul relaxed and began to rest. Then David took his harp and left the room.

The next morning Elah again came looking for David. The servant found David on the parade ground with his men. "Master David, the king requests for you to meet him in the throne room immediately. He is in a much better mood this morning," the servant assured him. "He doesn't have his spear in his hand, and he is smiling at the servants."

David nodded. "Please tell the king that I will be with him in a few moments." He gave tasks to several of the men, dismissed the servants, and headed for the palace.

Elah was right. The king was in a much better mood. He dismissed the servants he was visiting with and welcomed David with an uplifted hand and a smile.

"Captain David, you will remember that I promised to give my daughter in marriage to the man who would kill the giant Goliath."

David nodded. "Yes, I remember."

"I have not forgotten that promise, and I plan to follow through. You may have my older daughter, Merab, for your wife."

David's eyes widened, and his heart was racing. "My lord, I am not worthy to be a son-in-law to the king. So I would not hold you to your promise to give your daughter to the man who killed Goliath."

The king laughed. "I was quite sure that would be your reaction, but I insist. You fulfilled your part of the contract, and I must fulfill my part."

David bowed in acquiescence. "My wishes are subject to the king's wishes," he said humbly. Then a thought struck him forcefully. "Is your daughter Merab willing to marry a commoner in Israel?"

The king smiled. "My daughters are also subject to my wishes. I will speak to Merab tonight, and I will meet with both of you here in the throne room at the ninth hour tomorrow." He waved his hand to signify that the session was over.

David left the king's presence with mixed emotions. He had not been impressed with Merab, but Michal had pleased him greatly. He would much prefer Michal, but the choice was not his to make. The king's wish was law.

As David relaxed in his room that evening, he couldn't know that at that very moment a teary-eyed Merab was visiting with her brother Jonathan. She had been in session with her father, and she rebelled against marrying David. She was in love with Adriel, the Meholathite, and wanted Jonathan to intercede with her father to allow her to marry Adriel. She assured Jonathan that Michal was in love with David and wished to marry him.

David also couldn't know that the king's desire for him to marry one of his daughters was a selfish one. His twisted mind had reasoned that possibly his daughter could unwittingly lead David into a death trap with the Philistines.

The next morning David met with the king and Jonathan in the throne room, but Merab was not present. The king welcomed David with a smile, and Jonathan welcomed his friend with an embrace.

The king cleared his throat. "Captain David, it appears that I misspoke when I promised you my daughter Merab. She is in love with Adriel, the Meholathite, and I have given them permission to marry. However, my daughter Michal is in love with you, and therefore, I am giving Michal to you instead of Merab. Perhaps I have disappointed you, but I have done what I thought was best.

"The crown will give an order for a royal wedding for you and Michal. The date will be set by the two of you with the advice of the queen." There was an evil glint in the king's eyes now, and David wondered.

The king continued. "Usually the groom is required to give a dowry for the bride, and since Michal is the youngest of our children, the dowry her mother and I would ask for could be quite large. However, we recognize that you are a shepherd and a poor man, so I am proposing a non-financial dowry. I am asking for a dowry of one hundred Philistine foreskins to be delivered to me personally within ten days."

David saw Jonathan open his mouth to protest such a deadly bequest, but the king ignored him and waved David from the room.

David went immediately to the soldier's quarters to seek volunteers to go with him to glean the one hundred Philistine foreskins. It was a dangerous mission, and he could only risk volunteers. David was pleased that more of the men were willing to go than he could use, so he used a version of Gideon's method to select the men he needed.

As he was choosing his company, Jonathan came into the quarters. He had a concerned look on his face. He looked at David for a long moment. "David, I'm sure you are aware that Father believes that he is sending you on a death trip."

David nodded. "Yes, I read his intentions quickly. But Jonathan, I am in love with your sister, and I want her for my wife. I am also impressed that God wants me to go for the king's sake. If God will keep the men and me safe and give us a successful mission, perhaps the king will be helped spiritually.

"I have explained to the men the extreme danger of this venture, so they are not going blindly. Thank you, Jonathan, for your concern. I am confident that you and Zereth will be praying for our safety."

David and his men made careful preparations and left for the chosen Philistine city in the middle of the night. They chose a moonless night. The raid was quick and decisive, and the pagans were surprised in their sleep so that not a spear was raised nor a sword unsheathed by the enemy. The surviving Philistines were in a panic.

David and his chosen few rode back to Gibeah with their grisly trophies in two bags instead of one. They had doubled the number of foreskins requested by the king.

# CHAPTER 5

Elah ushered David into the king's presence. David held the dowry for Michal in two bags. The king seemed surprised to see his new army captain, but he did his best to hide his surprise and the shadow of disappointment that passed over his face. He welcomed David with a weak smile and a lukewarm greeting. David was pleased to see Prince Jonathan with the king, and the two men embraced each other warmly in the king's presence.

The king motioned for David to speak.

"My lord, the king," David said respectfully. "I wish to report that last night I led a company of men into the Philistine city of Ekron. We engaged the Philistines in the fourth watch of the night and gathered twice the tally of foreskins that my lord required. We returned without one of our men being harmed."

David offered the two bags of foreskins to the king. "Perhaps, my lord, you would like for one of your servants to check the total."

The king waved the receptacles aside. "There is no need for an examination," he said curtly. "I will accept your count."

He turned to Elah who was standing near. "Elah, have one of the servants bury these two bags immediately."

Then he turned to Jonathan. "Prince Jonathan, it appears that Captain David has fulfilled the requirements of the dowry for Michal, so I am ordering you to arrange for the wedding between my daughter Michal and Captain David as quickly as possible."

Jonathan bowed. "Yes, my lord, your orders will be carried out speedily."

As Jonathan and David left the throne room, Jonathan clapped David on the shoulder. "Just think, my friend, we will not only be brothers but also brothers-in-law."

David nodded. "Yes, Jonathan, but I am not worthy to be a son-in-law to the king. So perhaps I should decline this royal privilege."

"Nonsense, my friend," Jonathan responded. "You did a great favor to the kingdom when you killed Goliath. You deserve all of the honors the crown can bestow upon you. "Besides," he added, "you would certainly disappoint my little sister and me if you refused to marry her."

David laughed. "Jonathan, you are a good persuader. It would pain my heart to disappoint either you or your sister."

The royal wedding was only a one-day affair, but people came from all points of the kingdom to share in the festivities. Most people came to meet the hero of Ephes Dammim; David's name was on every tongue.

King Saul was present to pronounce his royal blessing on the union of his younger daughter and Captain David, but the praise that was openly bestowed on David by the multitude greatly vexed the troubled king, and he left the ceremony in a pout.

Jonathan observed the dark frown on his father's face and his sudden departure from the wedding festivities. The heart of the prince told him that there would be dark days ahead for David and Michal, but Jonathan couldn't have known at that moment just how dark those days would be.

The raid on the Philistine outpost was the bloodiest attack that David and his men had experienced thus far. He had planned the foray well and had gained the Lord's approval through the intercession of the resident priest, but it appeared as though the Philistines were expecting an attack, and they fought back fiercely.

All of the enemy soldiers were slain but David also lost one of his men and several were wounded. An enemy arrow had even pierced David's left arm. It was a solemn and silent company that wended its way back to camp at Gibeah.

Even though he was weak from loss of blood, David took time to order the burial of the dead soldier and care of the wounded. All of the men were a precious trust to him, and he mourned openly for the slain hero. David was consoled somewhat by the fact that the dead soldier left no dependents. He was an orphan.

When he had finished with his special duties, David walked with effort to his home and to his new bride, Michal. Michal's eyes were wide as she saw the blood on her husband's tunic.

"David, you're hurt," she whispered. "Come, lie down on the bed and let me examine your wound." David was proud of his wife as she worked efficiently to stop the flow of blood and bind up the injured arm.

When she had finished, David grabbed her with his good arm and kissed her passionately. She returned the embrace with ardor, then leaned back, and with mock severity chided him. "My dear, Captain David, you must control yourself or you will open that wound again. You cannot afford to lose anymore of your precious blood."

David laughed. "That kiss was worth several drops."

She pulled a chair close to the bedside. "David, please lie back down and tell me about what happened today."

David relayed to her the bloody details of the raid, and she listened quietly. Her face was grave. She nodded.

"David, if the trajectory of that arrow would have been only a few inches to the right, I would have been an army widow at this moment." She shuddered, and her eyes were bright with fear. "This is what my father is hoping will happen. When he told Merab that he had promised her to be your wife, he assured her that if she would agree to marry you she would soon be a widow and could then marry Adriel with father's blessing.

"But Merab was madly in love with Adriel, so she went to Jonathan to get him to intercede with Father. When she told Jonathan what Father had said about her soon being a widow if she married you, Jonathan was horrified. He visited Father early the next morning and persuaded him to let Merab marry Adriel. Then Jonathan told Father that I was in love with you and wanted to marry you, so Father consented and said that I would be just as good as Merab."

She shuddered again and grimaced. "Then he asked you to pay him that deadly dowry for the privilege of marrying me."

She hesitated. "Jonathan told me that you actually doubled the size of the dowry. Is that true?"

"Yes, it is," David replied. "And I found it to be a very reasonable dowry for my beautiful wife." He drew her to him again.

Michal was puzzled. "David, why does Father want you destroyed? If it hadn't been for you, the battle at Ephes Dammim would, no doubt, have turned out much different than it did. Now you are the only one who is keeping the Philistines at bay. Abner is sitting on his hands, and Jonathan is busy acting as king in Father's stead. Father should be so grateful for you, but . . . ," she faced him with question marks in her eyes. "Tell me, David, what does Father have against you?"

David looked at his wife for a long moment. Conflicting thoughts troubled him. *Should I tell her of God's rejection of her father as king and of my anointing by Samuel at*

*Bethlehem? Does Jonathan want her to know of his divine impression that I will be king instead of Saul or himself? Perhaps her love for me might turn to hate if I reveal these things to her.* He shook his head to clear his thoughts, and Michal noticed.

"David, what's wrong?" she asked in alarm. "Is it something really bad that Father has against you?"

"No, Michal! It isn't really a bad thing, but perhaps I am not the one who should tell you what the trouble is. You probably should ask your brother Jonathan about your father's rancor."

Michal shook her head vigorously. "No, David, I will not ask Jonathan. You are my husband now, and you must share with me what you know about Father's bitterness. I will not rest until I know what is bothering him."

David bowed his head in submission. Michal was right. She deserved to hear the truth from him rather than Jonathan, and if she turned against him because of knowing the truth, God would give him strength to bear the blame.

"Michal, since your father became king, on two different occasions he has deliberately sinned against the Lord's commands. At Gilgal he offered an illegal sacrifice, and at Amalek he saved the king and much spoil after God had specifically ordered him to destroy everything. Each time, Samuel came later with a divine rebuke for your father, and on each occasion he said that God had now rejected him as king over Israel and had chosen another to be king in his place."

David paused and pain showed on his face. "One day, soon after these transgressions of your father, the Prophet Samuel made a surprise visit to Bethlehem and specifically to my home. He called the city elders together and announced that he had come to offer a sacrifice. I was out with my sheep and, therefore, missed the sacrifice. After the sacrifice, Samuel asked my father to bring all of his sons to him. He met my brothers one by one, but none appeared to satisfy him. He then asked Father if he had any more sons, and Father told him about me, so he asked Father to send for me immediately. As soon as I came into the house, Samuel nodded as though I was the one he was looking for, and then he anointed me in the midst of the elders and my family. He didn't explain his actions to anyone, and he left for Ramah immediately. Since I had no idea what the anointing meant, I went back to caring for my sheep.

"Soon after the anointing service, I was called to the palace to play for your father who was depressed over the statements that he was no longer the legitimate king.

"Then came Ephes Dammim and the slaying of Goliath. Afterward, your father ordered me to stay with him at Gibeah, and he made me captain over one third of his army with the understanding that I was to lead continuous raids against the Philistine outposts. God gave my company good success, and one day your father asked to accompany us on a raid. I attempted to dissuade him, but he insisted. The raid was successful, and as we were marching back to Gibeah, many women came out from the towns and cities along the way dancing and singing, 'Saul has slain his thousands, and David his ten thousands.' He has acted strangely toward me since that day. He was agreeable to our marriage, but it appeared that his reasons had nothing to do with our happiness.

"Now, Jonathan revealed to me that he had an impression from the Lord that I will be the next king of Israel, and he believes that your father also has this belief. This is the reason for his hatred of me."

As David finished, Michal embraced him warmly. "Thank you, David, for sharing with me. I know that it was difficult for you to relate these matters because of your loyalty to Father and also your natural inclination to humility, but I am so glad that you had the courage to share."

David relaxed. "Michal, I was so afraid when you fouud out that I am possibly a threat to both your father and brother to the throne of Israel that you might hate me."

Michal was shocked. "Why, David, I love you. I have loved you for several years. I know that what you have related to me is not a plan of yours to replace Father and deny Jonathan. It is God's plan and we must accept it."

"Michal, I am so grateful for your understanding. I am planning to continue our raids against the Philistines with the hope that your father will see that the Lord is blessing, and perhaps I can regain his favor."

There was fear in her eyes as she nodded her agreement. "Yes, I understand that as an army officer you must carry on these raids, but please be careful. I have no desire to become a widow."

David was puzzled. For several weeks now he had led his men on raids against the Philistine garrisons, and the Lord had given him success over his enemies. The company had destroyed each of the outposts without the loss of one man and a large amount of spoil was brought back each time. It was stored in the army storehouse.

David reported to the king in person after every raid, but it appeared that Saul was bored by the accounts. He would shrug his shoulders and dismiss David quickly with the wave of his hand. *Perhaps*, David mused, *the only news that would interest Saul from these raids would be the news of my death.*

David hadn't played for the king for several months, but he knew that the time clock was ticking. One morning as he was preparing the troops for another raid, Elah came to him. The servant's face was grave. "Master David, the king is in a very depressed mood this morning, and the servants all agree that the only remedy for his condition is your music. Will you please come and play for him?"

"Yes, I will come, Elah," David assured him.

He dismissed the troops, took his harp, and went to the king's chamber. It was a familiar sight that greeted him. The king was sitting, as though chiseled from stone, with his spear gripped tightly in his right hand. His eyes were staring vacantly. As David began to play, the king's body began to move, but not to the beat of the music. Rather, his movements were by tenuous jerks. He turned his head and fixed his fierce gaze on David. His right arm began to twitch uncontrollably and the knuckles on his right hand were ashen white. David watched the king carefully. Soon the right arm of the king began to lift with effort; then, with a sudden thrust and a demonic laugh, he threw his spear with all his strength at David. The aim was erratic and the spear pierced only air until it embedded itself in the opposite wall. Without a word, David left the king's presence and went home to Michal.

Michal was surprised at David's presence and concerned about the pained expression on his face. "David, what's wrong?" she asked anxiously. "And why did you decide against going on the raid today?"

He motioned for her to come and sit beside him. "I had made all preparations with the troops for the raid today, but at the last moment, Elah came to the field with an urgent request for me to play for the king. He indicated that your father was having one of his very worst days yet and the servants were in turmoil. They all agreed that the only remedy for your father's depression was for me to play and sing for him. Since I am a servant of the king, I decided immediately that it was my duty to minister to him. I dismissed the troops, took my harp, and went to the king's chamber. I could see immediately that Elah was right. The king was in a deep depression."

David shivered as he spoke. "Usually I play for an extended time, but this time it was different. As soon as I started playing, your father began to react to the music. He turned and glared at me with a look of hate I had never seen before. His body began to twitch, and suddenly, without warning, he threw his spear at me with all his strength. His aim was bad, so I wasn't in great danger, but I decided that I should leave him immediately."

David looked at Michal and spread his hands helplessly. "I'm certain that I will not be safe in his presence from now on, so I will spend my time with the troops."

Michal had listened silently. Her face was ashen, and a tremor passed over her body. Her voice was only a whisper. "David, my father is insane, isn't he?"

David pondered for a moment before answering. "It is possible that he has brooded so long over the statements of Samuel about losing his kingship that he has become mentally unbalanced. Perhaps later he will come to his senses and be sorry for his actions of this morning, but I feel that it would be better for him and me if I were not in his presence."

Michal nodded in agreement. She clutched his arm. "David, would you please stay home with me today and comfort my heart, for I am so anxious for your safety?"

He pulled her to his chest. "I will be most happy to spend the day with my new bride."

Jonathan came to visit that same evening, and David could tell by the grave look on his friend's face that he was a bearer of bad news. David and Michal listened quietly as he shared with them.

"Today, my father called a meeting of all of the servants and me and demanded that each of us watch for an opportunity to kill you. He claimed that you are a threat to his kingship, my succession, and the position of all the servants."

Michal clutched David's arm as Jonathan told of the deadly plot.

"But there is more," Jonathan added. "Later today I saw Abner and several soldiers go into the throne room, so I am quite sure that he has given orders to arrest you. Abner probably welcomed the order, but the soldiers like you, and this command would be distasteful to them. David, I think it would be best for you to hide in a secret place, because the soldiers might come tonight."

He looked to Michal. "Michal, you will need to act the widow tonight. Perhaps nothing will happen, but we can't take chances since Father is very unpredictable."

Michal nodded. "I understand Jonathan. David told me that Father tried to spear him this morning as he played on the harp."

Jonathan's eyes were wide. "I wasn't aware of that incident, but that is more reason why we must be very careful."

"David, in the morning I will talk to the king about you. I will attempt to convince him of the blessings you have already given to him through your slaying of Goliath at Ephes Dammim and the successful raids you are conducting against the Philistine outposts. Also, he needs to know that you are the only one who is raiding the Philistines at present. I don't have the time, and Abner will not take the time. So perhaps father can be convinced that you are an ally, rather than an enemy. After I talk to the king, I will find you and give a report of his reaction. We will know at that time what course God would have us to take."

David and Michal nodded in agreement. "You have spoken wisely, Jonathan," David consented.

He turned to Michal. "Dear, if you will prepare some food and a night cover for me, I will spend the night in the woods."

Jonathan left then. After an embrace and a kiss from his wife, David took his provisions and cover and slipped out into the night.

The next morning Jonathan sought out David in the forest. The face of the prince was wreathed in a smile. "David," the emotion in his voice choked him for a moment, "Father has remanded his order to kill you and has sworn that you will not be harmed. He asks for you to return to your place at the court and to the head of your army."

The two friends embraced warmly in the sanctuary of the forest. David took courage at the news that he was again in the good graces of the king, and he continued to raid the Philistines as a man possessed. He led his men in forays against the outposts of Ekron, Timnah, Gath, and other cities, and the pagans fled before him. Not a man in his army was lost, and the name of David became a household name throughout the nation of Israel and the land of the Philistines.

David no longer reported his exploits to the king. He realized that his successes were an irritation to Saul rather than a time for rejoicing. But the soldier's wives, who were servants in the palace, told Elah of David's mastery of the Philistines, and Elah relayed the news to the king. Once again, the king lapsed into depression.

Elah met David as the captain and his men returned from another raid, and David feared what the chief servant had in mind. He reasoned that he would rather face a score of Philistines than to go in before the king.

"My lord, David, the king is deeply depressed today, and he has requested that you play for him," Elah lied.

David suspected, and rightly so, that the request had come from the palace servants instead of the king, but he consented to play. He prayed that the Lord would use him to be a blessing to the king, while at the same time, protecting him from the wrath of the king.

He found the king in his usual form during his fits of depression; yet he seemed a bit different today. David played for several minutes before the king moved, but this time it was evident that the move had been planned.

The king arose from the throne, walked quickly over to David, and attempted to pin him to the wall with his spear. Only David's quickness saved him. The king drove the head of his spear deep into the wall, and while he was attempting to extract it, David fled from the room. He went immediately to his home and to Michal.

Michal met him at the door with quivering lips. It was evident that she had been crying. She was getting ready to tell David the reason for her tears when she saw his own ashen face and shaking body.

"David, what's wrong?" she asked quickly. "Did you have a bad raid today?"

David shook his head as he embraced her. "No, Michal, we had a very successful raid today, and all of the men were in good spirits. But as soon as we arrived back at camp, Elah met me and asked if I would play for the king. He claimed that the king requested me, but I suspected that the culprit was Elah. As soon as I saw the king, the thought struck me that he was acting, but I ignored my suspicion and began to play. I had only been playing a few minutes when suddenly your father got up from his throne, came quickly over to where I was playing, and attempted to pin me to the wall with his spear. Only the hand of the Lord prevented me from being killed."

Michal's red eyes were wide with fear. "David, I am convinced that Father will not rest until you are dead."

"Yes, I agree with you," David said quickly. "But Michal, you have been weeping. Tell me dear, what is wrong?"

Pain twisted her features. "One of the palace servants came today to tell me that Father is planning to kill you tonight. They are going to wait until you are in bed; then several of Abner's soldiers are coming to take you to the king. He is bragging that he will cut off your head even quicker than you cut off the head of Goliath." She lowered her voice. "Two soldiers are secretly guarding the front door of our home right now. They have been there most of the day. But none are guarding the rear window, so if you will change your garments, I will let you down through the back window so that you will be able to escape. I have packed food and covers for you in case you need to spend several days in the forest. Perhaps, in a few days, Father will tire of his deadly game and you can come back to me again. When they come to take you tonight I will tell them that you are sick. I have already put a fake body in your bed so they will believe me."

The two young lovers embraced warmly, and Michal sobbed on his breast. Then she let David down through the back window, and he disappeared into the darkness. David longed to go back to Michal the next day, but he was sure that the king would have the soldiers posted at his home in case he would tire of the forest and come home to his wife.

He wondered what he should do next, and he made a quick decision. He would go to Samuel at Ramah. He hoped that Samuel would welcome him and give him direction from the Lord.

David had seen Samuel very briefly once before, but he was certain that he would recognize the aged priest. *Will Samuel recognize me and remember the anointing at Bethlehem?*

When David was ushered into the prophet's presence, he thought to introduce himself, but Samuel brushed the introduction aside. He threw his arms around David and embraced him warmly. "David, my son," he said with emotion, "you are a welcome sight to these aging eyes. I have thought about you and prayed for you every day since I met you at your home in Bethlehem."

His eyes were sad. "I know why you are here, David. You are now a fugitive from the king. Saul believes that you are a threat to his kingship, and thus, he is determined to kill you."

David nodded. "The rumors you heard were right. The king has twice tried to kill me with his spear, and only a few nights ago, he sent soldiers to my home to take me. My wife heard of the plot and got me away safely. The king's soldiers are now watching my home to take me to the king if I return."

David looked at the prophet helplessly. "Master Samuel, what should I do? Do you have counsel for me? Am I fated to run from the king until he finds me and kills me? Please tell me what I should do."

Samuel looked at the troubled young Bethlehemite for a long moment, and his eyes were misty. "David, my son, I am confident that God will keep you from the clutches of Saul."

He paused, "I thought when I anointed you that day among your family and the elders that God would soon place you on the throne of Israel, but it hasn't happened as I expected. However, it will happen in His time. David, God works in mysterious ways, and we must learn to accept His plan and wait on Him for its fulfillment.

"You have asked me what you should do. Since you are God's anointed, I am confident that He will give me an answer for you, so you must stay with me here at Ramah until God directs you to go elsewhere."

David stayed with the students of the school of the prophets in Ramah while Samuel inquired of the Lord about David's future decisions.

David was hurting. He longed to go back to Michal and Jonathan at Gibeah, but he knew that such a move would be unwise. Surely the king's soldiers were watching his home day and night, and if they captured him,

Saul would show no mercy. He would charge David as a traitor to the crown and quickly execute him.

The days passed without the Lord giving Samuel a direct vision of what David should do next, so the two tarried at Ramah. They knew that with Saul's network of spies the king would soon find out that David was with Samuel at Ramah and would then send soldiers to capture him.

And so it happened. A spy notified Saul that David was at Ramah, and the king sent soldiers to take him, but the Holy Spirit frustrated the would-be captors. When the soldiers arrived, Samuel was leading the sons of the prophets in the act of prophesying, and the Spirit of God fell also on the troops, and they began to prophesy. The usually irreverent soldiers didn't remain long under the spell of the Spirit, and when they recovered their poise, they forgot their deadly mission and immediately left shamefacedly for Gibeah.

Saul was livid as the troops reported their experience with the prophets. He immediately sent for Captain Abner. "Lock these stupid swine up for the night," he ordered, "and tomorrow I will decide their fate. Tomorrow you will send another company to Ramah, and they must bring David back to me or they will die."

"Yes, my lord," Abner answered quickly. "I will carry out your orders."

The next morning Abner sent another company of soldiers to Ramah to capture David, but they returned in the evening empty-handed with the same report of prophesying with the prophets of Ramah as the former company. A third company was sent out with the same results.

King Saul was puzzled, but resolute. The enemy was within his grasp, and he must not let him escape. So he decided to go to Ramah in person. He was determined not to fall under the same spell as the soldiers had, but when he saw Samuel leading the young prophets in the act of prophesying, the callous heart of the king was overcome. He took off his regal robe and fell down before Samuel in the position of prophesying. He remained in this prone position all of that day and the next night as the words of the Lord flowed from his compromised lips. The next morning he arose, abandoned, for the moment, his deadly plan, and returned to Gibeah.

David was elated. Could it be that the king would now permanently forsake his plot to kill him? But the Lord's word that came to him through the prophet Samuel dashed his hopes.

"David, you must not stay here in Ramah, because Saul has not changed his mind. The reprieve is only a pause with the king. He will soon pursue you with vengeance, so you must plan to spend time in the wilderness in the future."

David decided on a bold move. Under the cover of darkness, he returned to Gibeah, spent time with Michal, and then sought out his friend Jonathan. The two embraced warmly, and David told Jonathan of his stay with Samuel and of the experience of the soldiers and Saul at Ramah. Jonathan praised the Lord.

David faced his friend with tears in his eyes. "Jonathan," he asked plaintively, "what sin have I committed against your father that he is so determined to kill me? Surely one of these days I will die at his hand."

The face of Jonathan had a stricken look. "David, surely you are wrong. I am aware that Father went to Ramah to take you and was frustrated in his attempt by prophesying with Samuel and the prophets. The report of his experience with the prophets has gone to the uttermost parts of the kingdom, and he hasn't been out of the palace since that time. So I am hoping that he has given up his rancor against you and will now accept you back into his graces."

David shook his head. "I was hoping the same thing, Jonathan, but the Lord gave me a different message through Samuel. He told me that your father's vengeance against me will soon be renewed and that I must resign myself to living as a fugitive in the wilderness for months and possibly years."

Jonathan was silent for a few moments as he digested this information; then his face brightened. "Tomorrow is the beginning of the New Moon Feast, and Father will surely expect you to be present. Perhaps then we can test his feelings toward you."

David looked for a long moment at his friend. "Jonathan, since the Lord has warned me against your father's rancor, I cannot attend the New Moon Feast since I believe that he would attempt to kill me. But we can still test your father's intentions. If he asks why I am not at the feast, you will say, 'David asked my permission to go the Bethlehem to attend a family sacrifice, for his brothers demanded that he be present.'

"If he accepts my excuse graciously, I will take that as a good sign and will come back to my home and to Michal, but if he gets angry, I will know that he has planned evil against me and will remain in the forest."

Jonathan concurred. "Yes, David, you have spoken well. You will remain in the forest until I return with Father's reaction."

The two friends embraced again and renewed their covenant there at the edge of the forest.

It was the second day of the New Moon Feast, and David had come down to the stone Ezel, which was the prearranged place where he was to meet with Jonathan. David's heart was anxious. He saw Jonathan coming toward him across the field with a boy to fetch his arrows. David waited in silence. As Jonathan shot his arrows, he shouted to the lad. "Are not the arrows beyond you? Make haste, hurry; do not delay."

David's heart fell, for he knew by Jonathan's charge to the boy that he was fated to spend his future days in the wilderness. When the boy gathered up the arrows,

Jonathan gave him the bow and arrows and said to him, "Go, and carry them into the city."

As soon as the lad was gone, David arose from his place at the stone and fell on his face at Jonathan's feet. Then he arose and the two friends embraced and kissed each other.

"David," Jonathan spoke with a halting voice, "it happened just as you suspected. Father made no mention of your absence on the first day, but on the second day, he asked me, 'Why is not the son of Jesse at the feast?'

"I answered him as we had agreed. I said, 'David asked my permission to go to Bethlehem to attend a family sacrifice. His brothers had demanded his presence.'

"Father then became very angry and threw his spear at me. He cursed my mother and raved that I would never come to the throne as long as you were alive. So David, my friend, you will not be safe in his presence any longer. Go in peace, my friend, and may the Lord be between you and me and between your descendants and my descendants forever."

David's heart was breaking, but the Spirit of the Lord gave him grace and courage. "Jonathan," he said in a firm voice, "do not think harshly of your father because of his hate for me. Stand by him in this time of great trouble. And, my friend, please take care of my wife, Michal. I have no one else but you and Zereth to commend her to."

Jonathan pressed his hand, "That I will do."

So David went into the wilderness and to his loneliness, and Jonathan went back to the city and to Zereth.

# DAVID'S HEART

## CHAPTER 6

David lay on the mossy floor of the forest and reflected on his precarious situation. He was now a fugitive from the king of Israel, the most powerful man in the nation. The fact that he was son-in-law to the king and anointed by the chief priest of the nation to succeed the present king appeared to make no difference at all. He was a proscribed outlaw and subject to arrest and execution as a traitor to the crown. He knew that he was innocent of all the charges against him, but he had no court in which to plead his case.

He yearned for the warmth of his wife, the loyalty of his friend, Jonathan, and the comfort of his sheep. But for the moment, these were only memories.

As he mused, he heard the sound of many horses coming through the forest and the sound of men conversing together, and he hid himself. Then he heard his name being called, and he recognized the voice of one of his trusted lieutenants, so he threw caution to the winds and stepped out from his hiding place.

David was somewhat overcome with emotion, for there before him in the forest was his first lieutenant Joram and twenty men from his army. They were leading a horse for him. All of the men embraced David warmly and expressed their pleasure at seeing him again.

Then Joram spoke. "Jonathan told us where we would find you, and we have come to join you in your exile. Many of the other men are coming to join you within a few days and some of Abner's men are coming with them."

David tried to speak, but the words choked in his throat and his eyes were moist. He looked at each of the men with love in his eyes and called them by name.

"I can't let you do this," he said with emotion. "It is such a great risk to be hunted by the king's army. If he should capture any one of us, he will show no mercy. You would be executed as a traitor without a trial. Also," he continued, "you will no longer eat at the king's table. You will have to forage, and that will mean dangerous raids on the Philistine and Ammonite outposts."

The men nodded in unison, and Joram spoke again. "Captain David, we have discussed the dangers and the physical needs we would face by joining with you, and yet we decided unanimously that we would come. You are a very fair and loyal man, Captain David, and all of the men love you. We would die for you, so please do not think of sending us back."

David could tell by the looks on the men's faces that all shared the plea, so he yielded. "You will stay," he determined quickly. "And may the God of heaven bless you and keep you safe from the clutches of the king and give unto you the necessities of life."

"Thank you, Captain David," the men exclaimed in chorus.

"Now," Joram said with a smile on his face, "we saved half of our rations from the last two days, so we will have a feast with you here in the forest tonight, and perhaps, tomorrow the Lord will send us manna or quails."

David laughed, and suddenly it seemed to the fugitive that there was light in the forest. "You are a clever man, Joram."

David realized that the men were both a blessing and a curse to him. They were fully armed, mounted, and well trained, and thus would be a formidable foe to any comparable number of the king's troops. But since the king now knew that the men had deserted to David, he would surely use a much larger company in pursuit of his hated foe, and since the men would make it more difficult for him to hide in the forest, he would need to keep on the move.

As he pondered these things, he decided to go to Nob to visit the high priest, Ahimelech. Perhaps the priest would have a word for him from the Lord and would also provide some food for him and his men. He must be cautious, since he had no idea whether Ahimelech had heard that he was now a fugitive of the king, so he left the men in a secret place outside the city and went in by himself.

The priest appeared nervous when David came in by himself, and he asked in a fearful voice. "Why are you alone? Why is no one with you?"

David decided that he must use subterfuge on the fearful priest, so he answered. "I am on a secret mission for the king, and I have sent the young men who are with me on ahead. I will join them tonight, but we are in need of provisions. Do you have five loaves of bread that you could give us?"

"I don't have any common bread here today, but I do have plenty of shewbread. If your young men have kept themselves from women, you may have it."

"Yes," David answered. "It has been three days now since the men have touched women, so they are holy and would be able to partake of the shewbread."

As Ahimelech prepared the bread for David, the fugitive remembered that the sword of Goliath was on loan here at the temple. David already had a sword and a spear that the men had brought him, but he wanted this treasured weapon.

"Do you have any weapon here that I could have?" he asked. "The business of the king was so urgent that I left without sword or spear."

Ahimelech hesitated for a moment. "All I have here is the sword of Goliath the Philistine whom you killed in the Valley of Elah. You may take it with you."

The priest took the sword from behind the ephod and gave it to David. David cradled it to his breast. There was none like this crafted sword of the giant Philistine.

As David was returning to his men in the secret cave, he met two merchants from Bethlehem who knew him and were friends of his. They brought bad news from Gibeah. King Saul had sent out couriers to every city and town in the kingdom announcing a liberal reward to anyone who would take David dead or alive, and early tomorrow morning the king and Captain Abner, with one thousand soldiers, were starting out in search of David. They were boasting that soon David would be as dead as Goliath.

David's heart was racing as he joined the men and shared the news with them. The men were disappointed and angry. Two of the men had visited a local market and bought several fish and some cheese. They were fairly certain that David would bring the bread, so they were anticipating a feast for the midday meal.

David calmed them. "Look, I have bread from the temple, and you have supplied the fish and cheese. The King and Abner are not on their way yet, and we have a secluded place here, so let's have a feast. Then we will decide where we should go from here." The men were soon in good spirits again as they ate a tasty meal in the hidden cave near Nob.

David had seen King Saul's chief herdsman, Doeg, at the temple, so he was fairly certain that by morning light the King and Abner and their troops would be on the road to Nob.

The men had dined well and were in a good mood, so they listened closely as David outlined plans for their move from Nob.

"I think that the king will expect us to go farther north to keep out of his reach," David confided. "So I propose that we go south into his face. We will skirt the main roads and the cities and head for Judah." He shivered. "We might even choose to stay in a friendly Philistine city."

The men nodded in agreement, and Joram spoke for the group. "That sounds good to us. You lead and we will follow."

It was much slower traveling since they were using only trails, but they bypassed the cities and steadily made their way south toward Judah. Soon David saw familiar landmarks of his sheep's grazing grounds, and his heart longed to go visit Ezri and his sheep and also drop in to see his father and stepmother, but he knew that it would be too dangerous. Also, the king would proscribe his family if they helped him in any way.

They camped near the Philistine city of Gath, and the next morning David made a decision that almost cost him his life.

He decided, without seeking the Lord's counsel, to visit King Achish, the Philistine. He found an ally in Achish, but the servants and military leaders who were at court warned the king. "Be careful. This man is a powerful person in Israel. Don't you remember that they sang of him after the battle of Ephes Dammim, 'Saul has slain his thousands, and David his ten thousands'?"

David knew the language of the Philistines, and he was alarmed when he heard the warning of the servants and military officers. He knew that he was in danger of losing his life, so, once again, he resorted to subterfuge. He fell down before the king as if he were suffering a seizure and feigned madness. He rolled on the floor and foamed at the mouth and jabbered unintelligently.

Achish was alarmed at the actions of David and chided his servants for allowing David to come into his presence. "Remove this man immediately," he cried. So the servants took David out of the court and deposited him outside the city gate. David wasted no time getting back to the men and leaving the area.

After much discussion and prayer for divine guidance, the group decided to go down to the cave of Adullam. As they made camp that night, David wrote a psalm in memory of his deliverance from the Philistines at Gath. He sang part of it for the men and played on his harp.

"I will bless the Lord at all times: His praise shall continually be in my mouth. My soul shall make her boast in the Lord; the humble shall hear thereof, and be glad. O magnify the Lord with me, and let us exalt His name together. I sought the Lord, and He heard me, and delivered me from all my fears. They looked unto Him, and were lightened: and their faces were not ashamed. The poor man cried, and the Lord heard him, and saved him out of all his troubles. The angel of the Lord encampeth round about them that fear Him, and delivereth them. O taste and see that the Lord is good; blessed is the man that trusteth in Him. O fear the Lord, ye His saints; for there is no want to them that fear Him."

The men nodded and smiled their approval.

The cave of Adullam was a haven for David and his men for several weeks, and it was here that his family increased many fold. His father and stepmother and his brothers and sisters heard that the king was planning retaliation on them because of David, so they came to join him at Adullam.

Eliab spoke for his brothers. "David, we have treated you shamelessly since the day you were born because we had prayed for a sister, so you have every right to hand us over to the wrath of the king. We are very sorry for our actions and hope that you will forgive us and let us be a part of your army." David embraced them warmly and welcomed them into his band.

Many others joined with David at Adullam. Everyone who was in distress, those who were in debt, those who were discontented, and many of his former troops came to him, and David became captain over them. There were now about four hundred men with him.

David's father and stepmother were aged, and life in the forest was very tiring for them, so David took them to Mizpah of Moab and presented them to the king of Moab.

The king was honored to have David, the famous hero of Ephes Dammim, ask a favor of him. So David's parents stayed with the king of Moab while David was a fugitive from the king of Israel.

The day came that David had dreaded. He knew that life had become too comfortable at Adullam, which was confirmed when the Prophet Gad came to the camp one day with a message for David.

"Captain David, the Lord says that you are no longer safe here at Adullam. You must go farther south into the land of Judah and specifically into the forest of Hereth."

So David and his army broke camp at Adullam and journeyed south to the forest of Hereth in Judah. Travel was much slower now with the increased number of people, and many of the men had their families with them. But David's army was capable of fighting at least twice the number of the king's troops. They were all fully armed and mounted, and they trained several hours each day there in the forest.

The third day in the forest brought a visitor to David's camp with news that broke his heart. The visitor was Abiathar, the son of Ahimelech, the high priest at Nob.

"Master David, you remember that King Saul's chief herdsman was at the tabernacle the day that my father gave you the shewbread and the sword of Goliath. Evidently, he told the king about the incident, and the king assumed that my father was helping you in a revolt against his kingship. So the king summoned every one of the priests to Gibeah, and as soon as we arrived, Saul accused us of treason to the crown. He ordered the soldiers to kill us, but they refused. So Doeg began the bloody work. I was the only one that escaped out of the eighty-six priests. Then the king sent a company of soldiers to Nob to kill our families." When Abiathar had finished, he and David wept together for an extended time.

"I feel that I caused the death of all the people in your father's house, Abiathar," David said, "but we cannot bring them back. You must stay with me now, for you will be safe here. He who seeks my life also seeks yours, but our men will keep us safe."

A few days later two armed men passed the guard and came to David in the forest. They introduced themselves as representatives of Keilah, a Canaanite city not far from David's camp. David motioned for the men to dismount and state the reason for their visit.

"Captain David, we need your help," the spokesmen said. "The Philistines are constantly attacking our city with the intent to take it for their own. They are robbing our threshing floors and threatening us with starvation unless we surrender to them. We have a very small army and thus are no match for them, but we have heard of your fame as a man of war. We are hoping that you will come and fight these Philistines and deliver our city. The elders have promised to give your company provisions if you will come." The men looked at David with a look of desperation on their faces.

David nodded. "I will consider your request and will speak with the men. If we decide to help you, we will strike the Philistines at our time and without any further communication with you, but it would be soon."

The men nodded their agreement. Again the man spoke. "We hope you will decide to come, otherwise we will soon be servants of the Philistines."

David pondered the request of the men from Keilah for an extended period. He knew that it would be a dangerous mission, but if he should lead his men against the Philistines and deliver Keilah, perhaps the city of Keilah would give him and his company sanctuary from the pursuit of Saul. If that happened it would be the end of a torturous journey for him. So he called Abiathar.

When the priest fled from the murderer Doeg, he brought his ephod with him. So David asked the priest to inquire of the Lord for him if he should attack the Philistines.

And the Lord responded, "Yes, go and attack the Philistines and save Keilah!"

When David placed the matter before the men, they were very positive. "Look, we are afraid of the king here in Judah. So how much more dangerous would it be for us to go to Keilah to fight the Philistines."

David petitioned the Lord through Priest Abiathar a second time. "Shall I go to Keilah?"

The Lord gave him the same assurance as before. "Go and save Keilah, and I will be with you."

David led his men to Keilah, and they smote the Philistines a mighty blow. The Philistines fled before them, and the besieged city was saved.

The liberated inhabitants of Keilah danced in the streets and thanked David and his company again and again. They gave David's army the spoil of the defeated Philistines and then heaped upon them much booty from their own stores. The elders of the city called a public meeting and invited David and his company to make their home in the city of Keilah, but David was uneasy.

Keilah was a well-fortified city with walls, gates, and bars, but it could become a prison for his company if Saul should come to take them with a large army and threaten to destroy the city unless they would hand over David and his men.

Once again, David called Abiathar and asked him to inquire of the Lord for him. "O Lord God of Israel, your servant knows that Saul will soon come to destroy the city for my sake. Will the men of Keilah deliver me into his hand?"

And the Lord said, "Saul will come down to Keilah to destroy the city for your sake, and the men of Keilah will deliver you into his hand."

David was in agony, so he called his men together, and they departed the city and went to the strongholds of the Wilderness of Ziph, which was a part of the forest of Hereth. Saul sought him every day, but the Lord kept David and his men hidden there in the forest.

It was morning in the forest, and most of David's men were still asleep when David heard the challenge of the guard and the pleasant response of the visitor. David sat up quickly, for the voice sounded like that of his friend Jonathan. In a few moments, Jonathan rode into the camp.

The prince dismounted quickly, and the two friends embraced warmly. Then Jonathan stepped back and looked into David's eyes. "David, my friend, I am so sorry to be a bearer of bad news, but two weeks ago Father sent soldiers to your home, kidnapped Michal, and gave her to Palti, the son of Laish."

Jonathan hesitated and tears formed in his eyes as he continued. "David, I feel so guilty about this happening because I had a premonition that Father might do this very thing because of his hate for you and his frustration at not being able to catch you. Zereth and I urged Michal to come and live with us, but she was hopeful that you might come back to her at any moment, and she wanted to be there for you. Later, I felt that I should have used my powers of administration to demand that she come with us, but I hesitated, and we lost her." He spread his hands helplessly. The two friends wept together there in the forest.

Jonathan continued. "I sent an official letter to Palti, warning him that Michal was not his and that he was not to touch her. He would pay the price later if he violated her. I haven't received an answer from him as yet."

David grasped his friend's arm. "Thank you, Jonathan, for your concern. Tell me again why your father hates me so much? Surely some day he will find me and kill me."

Jonathan shook his head vigorously. "No, no, David. Do not fear. The hand of Saul, my father, shall not find you. You shall be king over Israel, and I shall be next to you. My father knows this to be true."

The two men confirmed their covenant there in the Wilderness of Ziph, and Jonathan prepared to leave.

"David, my father has soldiers watching your house and mine twenty four hours a day," Jonathan said with emotion. "So it was very difficult for me to leave without being discovered. The night before last my aide, Nebal, hid my horse in the woods behind my home, and as soon as it was dark, Zereth helped me out of our back window. I found my horse without being discovered. It will be more difficult to return to my home again so I would request that you pray for me."

The two friends knelt together on the floor of the forest and prayed for each other and for Michal and Zereth and for their loved ones. David prayed for his enemy, King Saul.

Before mounting to leave, Jonathan had a final word. "David, I will send you news by courier if you will keep me informed as to your location. When you send news to me, direct it to Nebal, and he will give it to me." The two friends clasped hands, and Jonathan went back to Gibeah while David stayed in the wilderness.

The king had sent out word to all of the cities of Israel that anyone, or any city, that would harbor David or give him assistance in any way would be destroyed. He used the murders of the priests of Nob and their city as an illustration of his threat. Thus, David and his men were forced to shun the cities and dwell in the wilderness areas at all times. They had been hiding in the Wilderness of

Ziph for several months now, and the area seemed fairly secure to them.

It was a long distance from the king's base at Gibeah, and the area was abundant with game and wild berries. But Saul's deadly threat made the Ziphites, the descendants of Caleb, son of Hezron, fearful that the presence of David near their city might rouse the ire of the king, so they sent representatives to the king at Gibeah with the message that David was in the wilderness near their city. They told the kind that they would lead him to the hideout of the outlaw.

The king took personal charge of a large company of soldiers to go down to the Wilderness of Ziph to capture David. But some friendly Ziphites came to David's camp and informed him of the intention of their leaders, and David moved his company to the Wilderness of Maon.

Again, local residents betrayed David's location, and Saul came to the Wilderness of Maon seeking him. It was a precarious time for David and his men, for it appeared from a human perspective that he could not escape the clutches of Saul. David and his men were on one side of the mountain, and Saul and his men were on the other side. The king and his men were encircling David and his men, but at the critical moment, a messenger came with news for the king that the Philistines were invading the land. So Saul broke off his pursuit of David to go fight the Philistines, and David and his entire group knelt and thanked the Lord for His marvelous deliverance. Then they arose and sang praises to the God of their salvation.

David wrote a song to commemorate the divine deliverance, and he sang part of the song to the company around the fire that night.

"Unto thee, O Lord, do I lift up my soul. O my God, I trust in Thee; let me not be ashamed, let not mine enemies triumph over me. Yea, let none that wait on Thee be ashamed; let them be ashamed which transgress without cause. Show me Thy ways, O Lord; teach me Thy paths.

Lead me in Thy truth, and teach me: for Thou art the God of my salvation; on Thee do I wait all the day. Remember, O Lord, Thy tender mercies and Thy lovingkindnesses; for they have been ever of old."

David was certain that when Saul took care of the Philistine threat he would again be in pursuit of his fabricated enemy since it was a passion for him. For the moment he was trading the hours of depression, when he would sit on his throne with his spear in his hand, for the hours of the chase. Apparently, he was stimulated by the thought that if he could destroy the man whom he thought to be the one God had designated to supplant him, his kingship would survive. His twisted mind wouldn't allow him to realize that he was fighting against God, and therefore, he had no hope of success.

David moved his company, which now numbered more than six hundred, to the Wilderness of En Gedi. Again, spies betrayed his position to the king, and Saul came down to En Gedi with three thousand men to capture David.

There were several large caves in the forest with rooms extending out from the main corridor, and David and his company took refuge in one of these caves. David posted sentries throughout the forest to alert him of the approach of Saul and his men.

Soon, just as David had expected, Saul and his three thousand men entered the forest in search of David, but one of David's sentries saw them and immediately warned David.

David and his people were staying in the inner recesses of the largest cave, but they had entered the cave by a hidden back entrance, so there were no telltale signs at the front entrance of the cave to betray their location.

Saul's men stopped to rest at the entrance of the cave, and Saul came in to relieve himself and take a brief rest.

He soon fell asleep, and thus presented a tempting target for the harassed people within the cave.

"God has put your enemy within your grasp this day," several of the men reminded David. "So just say the word, and we will run him through with a spear; then our exile will be over."

David considered the situation for several minutes. It appeared that Saul's defenseless position in the cave was an answer to prayer, but an inner voice reminded David that the king was still God's anointed, and until God took him away, he must be spared and protected. So David arose and cut off a corner of Saul's robe. Even that gesture bothered David's conscience, but he felt that his action was justified.

Soon Saul awoke and went out to join his men. The king's army started off into the wilderness in search of David.

David waited for a few minutes, and then he went out to the entrance of the cave and called after the king. "My lord, the king," he shouted.

Saul was startled by the voice, and as he looked behind him, he saw David standing at the mouth of the cave with a piece of cloth in his hand. David stooped with his face to the earth and bowed down. "My lord, why do you constantly pursue your servant David? Today the Lord delivered you into my hand and some urged me to kill you, but I have determined in my heart that I will not stretch out my hand against the Lord's anointed.

"Now, my father, you can see that the corner of your robe is in my hand. I cut off the corner of your robe, but I did not kill you, so you can surely see that there is neither evil nor rebellion in my heart. Let the Lord judge between us, and let the Lord avenge me on you, but my hand shall not be against you."

When David had finished speaking to Saul, the king was smitten in his heart, and he lifted up his voice and wept. Then he acknowledged, "David, you are more righteous than I, for you have rewarded me good whereas I have rewarded you evil. The Lord delivered me into your hand, but you did not kill me. Therefore, David, may the Lord reward you good for what you have done for me this day. And now I know that you will be king, and the kingdom of Israel will be established in your hand. Therefore, David, swear to me this day that you will not cut off my descendants after me or destroy my father's house."

So David swore to Saul. Saul then returned home to Gibeah, and David went up to his stronghold.

A courier from Jonathan informed David that Samuel had died and the king had proclaimed an official time of mourning to honor the revered priest, jurist, and prophet.

David had been privileged to be with the man who anointed him as the future king of Israel only a short time, but during that brief period, the great man had taught him much.

It was during the early days of Saul's pursuit of David that he had fled to the protection of Samuel. David had shared with Samuel that he feared Saul would soon find him and kill him, but the priest had said that it wouldn't happen. Samuel assured him that God would protect His anointed and would, in His time, bring David to the throne of Israel. Now, his mentor was dead, and David felt lonely as he had when his mother died.

David was having difficulty providing food for his six hundred men and their families. The men were good hunters and the women gathered berries and nuts, but at times their diet was scant.

For some time the company had camped in the southern part of the Wilderness of Judah near the town of Carmel. Since the death of Samuel, the king hadn't pursued them, so the only challenges they had faced were the ever present need of food and protecting the flocks of a rich man by the name of Nabal who lived in the area. David's company had protected the flocks from bandits and wild animals on several occasions, and the shepherds were very grateful. David had not asked for one animal as payment for the security they had afforded the shepherds.

But it was now shearing time, and David was sure that it would be a festal occasion at the home of Nabal. So David decided to press for partial payment for the protection they had provided for Nabal's flocks.

David sent ten of his young men to Nabal. "Greet him in my name," David instructed them. "And say, peace to you and your house. We heard that you are shearing now, and we want to let you know that we protected your flocks from bandits and wild animals while we were with your shepherds in the wilderness and thus helped to enlarge the abundance of your harvest. Ask your young men, and they will tell you how we helped them in protecting your flocks. Therefore, let my young men find favor in your eyes on this feast day. And please, give whatever comes to your hand to your servants and to your son, David."

But Nabal was churlish, and he answered the young men roughly. "Who is David, and who is the son of Jesse? He is probably just another servant who has deserted from his master and now wants a handout. Am I supposed to take my bread and meat from my shearers and give them to a stranger? Tell this man, David, that I have nothing for him." Nabal turned his back and walked away.

The ten young men went back to David empty-handed and reported to him all the words of Nabal. David was livid with anger by the time the young men had finished their report, and he made a quick decision. "Gird on your swords," he ordered the men. "We will go to Maon and deal with this pestilent fellow. As I live and breathe, before the sun rises tomorrow, there will not be a live male in the entire household of Nabal."

So David and four hundred of his men started for Maon, and two hundred stayed with the supplies. But the Lord was at work to keep David from shedding innocent blood.

One of the shepherds, who had been a beneficiary of David's kindness in the wilderness, heard the harsh response of Nabal to the ten men from David's company, and he was sure that his employer had not heard the last from David. So he immediately went to inform his mistress, Abigail, of the danger that awaited Nabal from the wrath of David.

"Mistress Abigail, David sent messengers from the wilderness to greet our master, and he cursed them. David's company was very good to us when we were in the wilderness. They were like angels to us, but I fear for our master. He is such a scoundrel. I am very certain by morning light, David and his men will be here to avenge the unjust treatment of the men of their company. I know you are a very wise and discerning woman, so consider what you should do, for I know that harm will be planned against our master and against his household."

Abigail considered the appeal of the servant for a few moments; then the sagacious lady made a decision. She ordered her servants to prepare two hundred loaves of bread, two skins of wine, five sheep, five ephahs of roasted grain, one hundred clusters of raisins, and two hundred cakes of figs. These were loaded on donkeys and, with servants preceding her, she rode out to meet David without her husband's knowledge.

When she met David and his men, she dismounted from her donkey and fell at the feet of David in an act of utter contrition and humility. "My lord, let the guilt rest on me for the evil actions against your young men. I did not see the men myself, but a servant informed me and it hurt me greatly. Please disregard the rudeness of the scoundrel Nabal, for as his name means fool, so he is. Now, my lord, since the Lord has held you back from bloodshed and from avenging yourself with your own hand, let your enemies and those who seek harm for my lord be as Nabal. When the Lord has appointed you ruler over Israel, as I am sure He will, you will not have shed blood without cause. And now, please accept this present, which your maidservant has brought to you, and let it be given to the young men who follow you."

David's conscience was smitten as he considered the wisdom of the godly woman. He realized immediately that the Lord had used her to keep him from an act of folly, which would have stained his record for years.

He blessed the God of heaven who had sent her, and he blessed her from the bottom of his heart and thanked her for her wise counsel. "You have been an angel to me," he said.

Then David received from her hand what she had brought, and he said to her. "Go in peace to your house. See, I have heeded your voice and respected your person."

About two weeks later, one of Nabal's herdsmen found David in the wilderness and informed him that Nabal had died. "Blessed be the Lord, who has pleaded the cause of my reproach from the hand of Nabal and has kept his servant from evil! For the Lord has returned the wickedness of Nabal on his own head," David responded.

David was lonely. He missed Michal, his first love, very much, but as long as he was a fugitive from the king, he had no hope of taking her back from Palti. Quite a few of the troops had their wives with them, and whenever David would see these men sporting with their wives, he would long for female companionship.

Because of the prevailing polygamy in the land, he had no qualms about taking a second wife or more, but he was fearful that, should he choose a second wife, he might hurt his dear friend Jonathan. Perhaps he would think that he was putting someone else in Michal's place.

David knew that Jonathan was monogamous and had no desire to take a second wife. Zereth had proposed a second wife for him when she believed that she was permanently barren, but Jonathan would not discuss the proposal.

These thoughts raced around in David's mind as he lay under the stars the night after he had heard of Nabal's death. He thought of Abigail, Nabal's widow. She was young, wise, and beautiful, and now she was a widow and would soon be lonely. As he lay there on the floor of the forest, he decided to propose marriage to her. At morning light he would send ten of his young men to her home with the proposal, and if she accepted, the men would assist her in moving her personal possessions to the forest.

His decision prompted him to rise from the forest floor, and by the light of the embers of the dying campfire, he wrote his proposal to Abigail. His heart still pained him about Jonathan's possible reaction to his decision, so he also wrote a letter to Jonathan. He finished the letter and placed it in the pocket of his tunic. He would wait to send it until he heard from Abigail.

Abigail welcomed David's proposal, since she had determined not to observe a period of mourning for her dead husband. She herself was lonely, as was David, because she had despised the man to whom she had been married for several years. She had married Nabal, a much older man, to save her parents from financial ruin, but her exercise of love and loyalty had gone for naught. Before her parents could use the money borrowed from Nabal, bandits had broken into their home, stolen the money and killed them both. Abigail suspected that Nabal was behind the bloody raid on her parent's home, but she couldn't prove her suspicions, so she lived with her frustrations during her years with Nabal.

Abigail quickly put her chief herdsman in charge of her estate, gathered up her personal belongings and, with five of her maidens accompanying her, followed the young men to the forest and became the wife of David.

But David had another matrimonial problem to care for before he moved his company back to the Wilderness of Ziph. A young man and his sister from Jezreel, a city in the northern section of Israel, had recently joined his company, and several of the young men were vying for the affections of the maiden, Ahinoam. She was beautiful in face and form and very discreet in her actions toward the men. Thus the men were frustrated by her lack of interest in their advances. Two of the men had fought over her, and David had disciplined the men. It soon became evident that the maiden was in love with David, so David married her. He now had two wives plus his lingering relationship with Michal. He reluctantly sent the letter to Jonathan that he had written that night by the light of the dying campfire.

David moved his company back to the Wilderness of Ziph, and again, representatives from Ziph hastened to Saul with the news of his location. So Saul, with three thousand chosen men, came down to the wilderness to capture the king's mortal enemy.

One of David's sentries informed him of Saul's presence and his men, and David moved his company farther into the interior of the forest. David thought it strange that the king didn't use all of the prevailing sunlight to pursue him but rather chose an early camp. David waited until the camp was quiet, then he decided on a bold move.

"Who will go with me to the king's camp?" he asked.

Abishai, the brother of Joab, answered quickly, "I will go with you."

So David and Abishai went to the king's camp and found everyone asleep. Even Captain Abner and the sentries were in a deep sleep from the Lord. Abishai was anxious. "God has delivered your enemy into your hand this day," he said. "So please let me strike him now with his own spear. I will not have to strike him a second time."

"No, Abishai," David responded. "The Lord forbids me to stretch out my hand against the Lord's anointed. As the Lord lives, the Lord shall strike him. His day shall come to perish, perhaps in battle, but my hands must be clean from his blood. But Abishai, take the water jug there by the king's head and his spear and let us go."

David and Abishai went to the top of the hill and looked down on the king's encampment. Then, David shouted down to the king and the people with him and especially to Captain Abner. "Captain Abner, answer me!"

Abner awoke, and in a fearful voice answered back, "Is that you, David?"

"Yes, Abner, this is David. Now tell me Abner, aren't you supposed to be the guardian of the king? Then why did you go to sleep and leave your lord the king unguarded? Surely, Abner, as the Lord lives, you are worthy of death for leaving the Lord's anointed as you did. Now, if you will notice, the king's spear and his jug of water are missing. I have them here in my hands."

Then the king called out. "Is that you, David, my son?"

"Yes, it is," David replied. "Why are you constantly pursuing me, my lord? If I am guilty of treason or some other sin against you, may the Lord deal with me harshly? But if my sin is only in the mind of man, may they be cursed before the Lord. Behold, you were in my hand today, and again I was urged to smite you, but I will not lift my hand against the Lord's anointed. So, my lord, the king, since I value your life so much, let my life be valued in your sight. Send one of your young men here, and I will give him your spear and your jug of water."

Then Saul called out. "May you be blessed, my son David, and may you do great things and prevail." Then

Saul went back to Gibeah, and David remained in the forest.

Several of the older men and the men with families were tiring of the constant moving from place to place, so a delegation came to meet with David.

"Captain David, we are so glad to be a part of your company, but we feel that we need a more permanent camp for our families," the spokesman said. "You have always been fair with us and have always been concerned for our welfare, so we have nothing but praise for your leadership. But we were wondering if we could raid a Philistine city and take it over for our company, then we could settle down for a longer period of time. We will abide by your decision."

David nodded. "I knew when you joined with me that the constant moving from place to place in order to escape the clutches of the king would become tedious for most of you. It has also been very wearing on me. I had no idea at first that we would have families, but I am glad for them. It has made our exile much more pleasant. Let me consider your proposal tonight and tomorrow, and I will give you an answer," David promised.

The men agreed unanimously with David's proposal and returned to their tents.

David prayed earnestly to the Lord that night for wisdom. "What shall I do, Lord?" he pleaded "It isn't fair to the families of these men to always be on the move, but it doesn't appear that Saul is going to declare a halt to his pursuit anytime soon. Because of the king's hatred of me, any member of my company that would fall into the hands of the king would be dealt with like the priests of Nob."

The thought came to him. *Go to King Achish again. He will give you sanctuary*. The thought was repulsive to him at first when he remembered his previous experience with the king of Gath, but the thought of sanctuary with Achish persisted. He wished that Abiathar would have been present with the ephod, but the priest had gone back to Nob for a few days.

Many of the men were skeptical at the idea of refuge with Achish, but they trusted David's judgment.

The next day David met with Achish, and he found a friend in the Philistine king. He knew that Saul was relentlessly pursuing David, and he felt a kindred spirit with the fugitive from Israel, so he offered David and his company the city of Ziklag as a permanent home.

When Saul heard that David and his company were with the Philistines, he chided Jonathan for the unfaithfulness of his friend, but he no longer pursued David.

Later, David found himself in a very tough situation because of his relationship with the Philistines.

# CHAPTER 7

David realized too late that he had gotten his men and himself into a very perilous situation because of his lies. His conscience was stricken.

In his desperation to secure a more permanent camp for his company and a safe place against Saul's pursuit, he had told Achish, king of the federation of Gath, that he and his men were outcasts from Israel and were seeking permanent residency among the Philistines. So Achish welcomed them with open arms and gave them the city of Ziklag for their own.

When they had settled in Ziklag, David and his men began to raid the cities of the Geshurites, the Girzites, and the Amalekites, but David told Achish that they were raiding Israelite cities in retaliation for their banishment from their homeland. Achish was greatly pleased with this demonstration on the part of David to permanently sever his relationship with Israel, and David increased in favor with the king.

In order to keep his lies from being found out, David destroyed every living thing in the cities of their raids, but they usually brought back much spoil, which they shared with Achish, thus cementing the union between David and his benefactor.

But the day of reckoning was sure to come. Achish now innocently expected a payback for his goodness to David. The Philistines were gathering at Shunem to fight against the Israelites who were gathering at Mount Gilboa, and Achish said to David, "Surely you and your men will go out with me to fight against our mutual enemies."

David's heart began to race, and his thoughts began to collide, but he didn't allow his face to betray his feelings as he answered Achish. "Surely you know what your servant can do."

David felt for the moment that his feet were in a steel trap and Achish was holding the chain. The implications of the statement, "Surely you and your men will go out with me to fight against our mutual enemies," were overwhelming to the young fugitive. If he would go out with the Philistines to fight against his beloved nation and his dear friend Jonathan, he would be a traitor, both in the eyes of Israel and also in his own eyes. On the other hand, he had obligated himself to the Philistines, and he couldn't think of turning against his benefactors in the heat of the battle. If he would be so traitorous, his name would be forever odious to both the Philistines and the Israelites.

Waves of guilt swept over him as he realized that he was largely responsible for his present difficulty because of his deceptions. He cried silently to the Lord for deliverance from his crisis, and the Lord heard him and delivered him. While Achish loved and trusted David like his own son, many of the Philistine leaders still remembered that David slew their local hero, Goliath of Gath, at Ephes Dammim. Thus they mistrusted his loyalty in battle, and when Achish suggested that he go with them to battle against Israel, they rebelled.

"Look, this is the man that Israel reveres. Don't you remember how they sang about him at Ephes Dammim, 'Saul has slain his thousands, and David his ten thousands'? Make him go back to Ziklag, for he will surely become our adversary in battle and reconcile himself with his master and all Israel with the heads of our men."

So Achish called David and informed him, with tears in his voice, that he could not go with them to battle after all. He must return to Ziklag.

Relief flooded over David's heart, and he breathed a silent prayer of thanksgiving to the Lord God of Israel.

But to Achish he said, "But what have I done? And to this day what have you found in your servant as long as I have been with you that I might not go and fight against the enemies of my lord and king?"

The heart of Achish was in pain as he answered. "David, I know that you are as good in my sight as an angel, but the princes of the Philistines have spoken and there is no recourse. So early tomorrow morning you and your men must go back to Ziklag."

David and his men's spirits were high as they rode back to Ziklag. God had greatly blessed them, and they were singing His praises. He had given them a city for their families, relief from the pursuit of Saul, and had delivered them from the threat of fighting against their friends and relatives in Israel.

They were nearing the end of their three-day journey from Shunem to Ziklag. Most of the men were dreaming of the joyous reunion they would receive from their loved ones, but when they crested the hill and looked down on their dream city, Ziklag, they lifted up their voices and wept. The city was in ruins. Smoke was still rising from smoldering logs, and not a person was stirring in the plundered city.

They galloped down to the site of their ruined city and sat for a while in muted grief. Then several of the men turned to David, and the spokesman was severe. "We ought to stone you, Captain David, for taking us on that silly trip to Shunem and leaving our families completely unprotected," his voice broke. "We have lost everything." Several of the men nodded in agreement with the spokesman.

David bowed his head in submission, and then he spoke. "If it will make you feel better and help to atone for your families, gather up your stones, for I am to blame. However, since there are no bodies in the ruins, we have reason to hope. Before you throw the first stone could we have Abiathar consult the Lord through the ephod and see what He would have us to do?"

The men nodded in unison.

David inquired of the Lord. "Shall I pursue this troop, and will I overtake them?"

The Lord answered. "Pursue them, for you shall surely overtake them and without fail, recover all."

The men's spirits were revived at the Lord's answer, and they again promised to follow David.

One of the men in David's company was an excellent tracker, and he soon determined that from the signs around the camp the attackers were Amalekites from south of Simeon. He also proposed that since the rebels had gathered so much loot from Ziklag and the surrounding areas, they would be traveling very slowly and could possibly be overtaken within two days time.

They started on the trail of the raiders at a fast pace, but since they had been traveling hard now for several days with limited rest, many of the men were faint, and when they reached the Brook Besor, west of Beersheba, two hundred of the men could go no farther. So they stayed at the brook while the other four hundred continued the chase.

Providentially, they found an Egyptian servant on the trail that had been left behind, and he led them to the Amalekites.

It was nighttime and the raiders were celebrating their great success with feasting, drinking, and dancing. David and his men attacked the raiders with a fury born of desperation. The Amalekites were spread over the face of the earth, but David's men surrounded them and penned them in. They fought them for the balance of the night and all the next day. Only four hundred young men mounted on camels escaped the wrath of the four hundred avengers. All of the captives were rescued, and

David's company recovered a large amount of spoil. It was a satisfying victory.

When the men returned to Ziklag with their families and the massive amount of booty, they pitched their tents and began to make plans to rebuild their ruined city. Then David played the politician. He sent portions of the spoil to the elders of Judah, Bethel, Ramoth of the South, Jattir, Aroer, Siphmoth, Eshtemoa, Rachal, the cities of the Jerahmeelites, the Kenites, Hormah, Chorashan, Athach, and Hebron, and all other places where their company had found friendly refuge during their years of exile.

David was anxious for word from the battle between Israel and the Philistines at Mount Gilboa. He was sure that the army of the Philistines was much greater in the number of troops than that of Israel, somewhat like at Michmash; thus, the only advantage Israel could hope for would be the faith of Jonathan.

But David couldn't have known that God had other plans for the faith of Jonathan at Mount Gilboa. The prince was not to be the savior of the nation as he had been at Michmash; rather, he was to be a sacrifice for David.

It was the third day after David and his men returned to Ziklag from the slaughter of the Amalekites that word came from the battlefield of Mount Gilboa. A young Amalekite brought the news, but it was framed in a lie and it doomed the messenger. The man's clothes were torn as if from hand-to-hand combat and dust was on his head to portray a sense of mourning, and David feared the worst.

"Where have you come from?" David asked.

"I escaped from the camp of Israel at Mount Gilboa," the young man offered.

David leaned forward, but there was fear in his heart. "How did the battle go?" he asked anxiously.

The young man feigned sorrow of heart. "The battle went against Israel and many of the troops were slain. King Saul and Jonathan, his son, are also dead."

"How do you know that Saul and Jonathan are dead?" David pressed him.

"I saw Jonathan die by the sword," the Amalekite professed. "And then, by chance, I came upon Saul. He was leaning on his spear, and the chariots and horsemen were all around him and pressing him hard. I knew that he was doomed. When he saw me, he called to me and asked me to kill him before the heathen Philistines got to him. He said that he was in anguish of spirit and wanted to die. So I stood over him and killed him as he requested, and I took the crown from his head and the bracelet from his arm and have brought them to you, my lord."

David was certain that the Amalekite was fabricating much of his story in his desire to impress David, but the crown of the king and his bracelet in the man's hand was proof that Saul was dead, and there was no doubt in David's mind that Jonathan was also dead.

The heart of David was in agony at the thought that his dear friend Jonathan was dead. Their friendship had been so warm and precious but also so short. David tore his clothes as an act of great sorrow, and all of the men followed his example. Then the entire company mourned, wept, and fasted for the rest of the day.

After David had gained his composure, he looked at the young Amalekite for a long moment. He was sure that he detected a touch of smugness on the man's face as though he had attained some sort of triumph. David's ire was raised.

"How was it that you were not afraid to put forth your hand to destroy the Lord's anointed?" David asked him.

The man's face showed fear for a moment, and he spread his hands helplessly but remained mute.

David called for one of his men and the man came quickly. "Execute this man," he ordered. "He raised his hand against the Lord's anointed, and therefore, he deserves to die."

The man died in front of David's tent in Ziklag because he had claimed to kill the king, but he had lied, for Saul died by his own hand.

David mourned for both Saul and Jonathan, but his sorrow was deepest for his dear friend Jonathan. In his grief, he wrote a song to memorialize their friendship, and he called the song "The Song of the Bow." He reserved the last part for Jonathan.

"How the mighty have fallen in the midst of the battle! Jonathan was slain in the midst of your high places. I am distressed for you, my friend, Jonathan. You have been very pleasant to me; your love for me was wonderful, surpassing the love of women . . . ."

David was hurting. Israel was now without a king, and he feared that the Philistines would soon take advantage of the absence of leadership and overrun the land.

He was convinced that God had anointed him to take Saul's place. But he was fearful that any immediate move he made to assume the kingship would seem disrespectful to the names of Saul and Jonathan, thus resulting in the resentment of the people of Israel toward him.

So he sought out Abiathar and the ephod. "Shall I go up to any of the cities of Judah?" he asked the Lord.

And the Lord answered quickly. "Yes, go up."

"Where shall I go?" David asked further.

"Go up to Hebron," the Lord directed.

So David took all of his men with him and their households, his two wives, Ahinoam, the Jezereelitess, and Abigail, the widow of Nabal, and went to Hebron. And when the people of Judah heard that David had moved to Hebron, they came up quickly and installed him king over all of Judah.

As David considered his present position, he was tempted to question his divine anointing by Priest Samuel to be king over all of Israel. Judah had welcomed him with open arms, but Judah was only one tribe in twelve. None of the other eleven tribes had made a move to accept him.

He reasoned that since Judah was the strongest tribe in the nation, it would be possible to bring the other tribes into a national union by force, but he rejected the thought immediately. He knew that the Lord didn't have force in mind for uniting His people. A united Israel must be a willing Israel. Thus, he would wait for further instructions from the Lord through Abiathar and his ephod.

David was directing the building of a palace when a courier came with a message from King Ishbosheth of Israel, who was residing at Mahanaim. David could hardly believe his senses. In only a short time a man had established himself at Mahanaim and was proclaiming himself king over Israel. The letter in his hand was sealed with the royal seal.

He shook his head as if to clear his thoughts. He had certainly not anticipated an impediment of this nature. He remembered that he had heard Ishbosheth's name several times through his friend Jonathan, but he had never considered this son of Saul, whose mother was a concubine, as a serious contender to the throne of Israel. But the letter in his hand was sealed with the name Ishbosheth, king of Israel. The letter informed David that he and his court would now need official permission from the king to travel in any province in the nation outside of Judah.

David sat for a time in deep thought with the royal letter in his hand. Questions surfaced in his mind about this pretender, Ishbosheth. Certainly this man, with no name or influence outside the precincts of his home city, would not be so rash as to presume that he could proclaim himself king of Israel and expect to be accepted without question. Someone with a national reputation would have to sponsor him, but who could it be?

As he mused, the name Abner suddenly came to mind. "Yes, the culprit must be Abner."

He had heard that Abner survived the carnage at Mount Gilboa, and he wondered how that could have happened. Several of David's men had openly expressed the thought that Abner had deserted his troops in the midst of the battle and fled the area.

The men were right in their assumption. Abner was a deserter, which was a crime punishable by death. His decision to leave during the heat of battle had saved his life but filled him with guilt, and his installation of Ishbosheth as king over Israel was an effort to mitigate a part of his guilt. His intention was to honor Saul by putting a member of his house on the throne of Israel and thus perpetuating the king's succession.

He hated David, and as a relative of the king, he had shared Saul's belief that David was a threat to the kingship of Saul and the succession of Jonathan. Also, he was still smarting from the chiding David had given him in the Wilderness of Ziph for falling asleep while guarding the king. Thus, the installation of Ishbosheth as king of Israel was a double-edged sword in the hand of Abner. He was honoring Saul to mitigate some of his guilt, while at the same time, opposing David.

David now had six wives, and each of his wives had given him a son. It appeared that in regards to family his plate was full, but he still yearned deeply for his first love, Michal, daughter of Saul and sister of his dear friend Jonathan.

Many times in the night sessions he would dream of going to Gallim and taking Michal by force from her imposter husband, Palti. But for years the constant harassment by Saul had made the dream impossible of fulfillment. Now he was free from the threat of Saul's pursuit, but there was a new impediment. He was banned by an official edict of the king of Israel to travel outside the boundaries of Judah. The edict did give him the right to ask for official permission to travel in the other provinces, but he was fairly certain that when he would explain the reason for the excursion to either Ishbosheth or Abner, they would deny his request.

Another reason for his deep desire to have Michal back with him was because of her relationship to Jonathan. If she were here, he reasoned, a part of his dear friend would also be with him.

He grieved the loss of Jonathan and often would ask his associates for suggestions as to how he could further honor the memory of the loyal prince of Israel.

During his days of exile in the wilderness, David had appointed Joab, the oldest son of his stepsister, Zeruiah, as commander of his army. Joab was a headstrong man, very daring and confident, and thus, he was difficult to control. But he was loyal to David and was loved by the troops. He knew that David was fretting with the confines of Judah, so without David's knowledge, he decided to challenge the strength of Abner. He sent a messenger to Abner requesting a meeting with him, so with his two brothers, Abishai and Asahel, and a chosen company of his young men, he breached the boundaries of Israel and met with Abner and a company of his men at the pool of Gibeon.

It was not a friendly meeting at Gibeon. Joab and his company sat on one side of the pool while Abner and his men sat on the other side. For a time there was no communication between the two groups. Then Abner spoke.

"Shall we have several of our young men from each side fight before us?"

Joab agreed. "Yes, that would be good. If you will choose twelve men from your company, I will choose twelve from mine, and we will see who prevails."

It was a bloody contest there at the pool of Gibeon. As soon as the twenty-four young men came together, each grabbed his opponent by the hair of his head and thrust his sword into the side of his enemy. All twenty-four men fell down on the field and died together.

This was the beginning of a fierce battle between the two armies, and Joab and his men routed Abner and his men.

During the hasty retreat of Abner and his army, Abner killed Asahel, the younger brother of Joab. This incurred the hate of Joab and Abishai and later was the cause of Abner's death.

There was a long drawn out war between the house of Saul and that of David, and Saul's forces grew weaker while David's grew stronger.

Abner was frustrated. Things weren't working out as he had planned. While he was gaining strength over Ishbosheth in the kingdom of Israel, he was losing ground against the growing influence of David. It was becoming more evident to the devious opportunist that his future was dependent on an affiliation with David. He hated the thought, but he saw no other way of protecting his leadership and dignity. As he thought on the change he must make, the irresolute king himself gave Abner the opportunity to split with Ishbosheth.

Abner's wife had died, and the lonely army captain had begun consorting with one of Saul's former concubines, Rizpah. However, this relationship bothered Ishbosheth. He considered this to be a violation of his father's legacy, so he complained to Abner. "Why have you slept with my father's concubine?" he demanded.

Abner was irate. He hadn't thought for one moment that his relationship with Rizpah was improper in any way. He was a widower and lonely, and she was a liberated concubine and also lonely. Both individuals had entered into the relationship with pleasure.

Bile rose up in Abner's throat. "What are you saying to me?" he wanted to know. "I have been loyal to you as I was with your father. I put my life on the line to install you as king over Israel and have fought against David and his army to keep you on the throne. Now you accuse me of an improper relationship with your dead father's concubine. I haven't raped that woman. She was just as eager for the relationship as I was." Abner glared at the king for several moments, and Ishbosheth quailed before his gaze.

Abner made a decision. "May the Lord do so to me and even more also," he said through clenched teeth, "if I do not transfer the kingdom of Israel to David and leave you with nothing, you ungrateful wretch. I will set up the throne of David from Dan to Beersheba." With those words still echoing in the throne room, Abner walked out and left Ishbosheth to his fears.

Abner considered his steps very carefully. He knew that David still felt strong lingering loyalties to the family of Saul because of his relationship with Michal and the memory of Jonathan. So the transfer of the kingdom from Ishbosheth to David would need to be a bloodless one.

Abner met with the elders of many of the cities of Israel to determine their attitude toward David becoming king of the entire nation. He found a very favorable impression of the king of Judah. They would welcome David with open arms, as had the elders of Judah.

Abner was ready to make his move. He sent messengers to David at Hebron, and a servant ushered the messengers from Abner into David's presence. The king wondered what the crafty Benjamite had in mind now. He knew that Abner was the power behind the throne of Israel; Ishbosheth was only a figurehead. So whatever the message from Abner might be, it would have the weight of Israel behind it.

David motioned for the men to speak.

"Master David," the leader spoke respectfully. "Our commander, Abner, has commissioned us to bring a message of friendship to you. He is proposing a covenant between you and himself, and if you are willing, he promises that he will bring all Israel under your leadership. He will convince Ishbosheth to abdicate in your favor. Our commander, Abner, is convinced that all Israel should be united, and he believes that you are the only man whom all Israel will accept. The transfer would be a bloodless one."

It was a moment of weakness for David. He chose to ignore the fact that Abner had installed Ishbosheth as king over Israel partly because of his hate for David. Also his spiritual sense should have warned him to test the sincerity of the Benjamite before he agreed to any type of covenant. He should have asked the ambitious warrior what he was expecting in return for such a liberal offer. But the thought of being established as king over all Israel without bloodshed stilled his agitated conscience for the moment and made him naively receptive.

Without consulting the Lord through the ephod, he answered the messengers. "Good. You may tell commander Abner that I will make a covenant with him and will await his invitation for me to accept the rulership of all Israel. But," David added, "before I see Abner face to face, he must bring my wife Michal, Saul's daughter, back to me. He took her from me when I was a fugitive from the king, and therefore, I am ordering him to bring her back."

The men bowed. "Very well, we will carry your answer and also your request to Abner. We are certain that he will have an answer for you soon."

The men returned the next day with an answer from Abner. "My lord, David, if you will send a formal request to King Ishbosheth that Michal be returned to you immediately, I will personally see that your wishes are carried out. The reason I am suggesting that the request be sent to the king is because of the royal authority that will accompany the order to Palti."

So David sent messengers to King Ishbosheth asking that his wife Michal be returned to him. "I betrothed her to myself for one hundred foreskins of the Philistines, and she was taken from me by force. I want her back."

When Ishbosheth received the request from David, he was reluctant to remand the order of his father, but Abner spoke in a tone of authority. "Go ahead and order it to be done. I will see that the order is carried out."

So Ishbosheth sent and took Michal from Palti and brought her to David's home in Hebron. David was away when she arrived, but he could hardly wait to welcome her home. He was alarmed when he returned to his home, for instead of a warm and anxious Michal, he found a teary-eyed and rebellious woman. He attempted to take her in his arms but she repulsed him.

"Michal," he exclaimed with disappointment in his voice. "Aren't you glad to see me? I have been so anxious to have you back."

She turned on him with her eyes blazing. "You are so anxious to have me back, are you? What are those six wives doing in my place? Because of Jonathan's letter, Palti never touched me all the time I was with him, and I was anxious to get back to you. But in these few years that you were supposed to be longing for me to come back, you have married six other wives and every one of them has children by you.

"My father had multiple wives, and it was very difficult for Mother and the family. But my brother Jonathan, who was supposed to be your best friend, would not take a second wife, although Zereth assured him that she would allow it."

Michal was out of breath. She threw herself on the bed and wept aloud. David longed to take her in his arms and comfort her, but he knew that she would reject him. So he left her to her tears.

Abner felt that he had everything in place to establish David as king of Israel, so he made a personal visit to David at Hebron. "Master David, all things are ready," he said confidently. "I will go and gather all Israel to my lord the king that you may rule over the nation."

David was pleased, so he made a feast for Abner and the men who were with him. Afterward, he sent them away in peace.

But David hadn't reckoned with his army commander Joab, which was a very serious omission on the part of the king. Joab and his brother Abishai were very bitter toward Abner because of the murder of their brother Asahel, and both were planning vengeance on Abner at their earliest opportunity.

The two brothers and their troops came in from a raid with much spoil soon after David had sent Abner away, and Joab was incensed when he heard that David had made a covenant with Abner and sent him away in peace. He went to David with hate in his heart and fire in his eyes.

"What have you done?" he said between clenched teeth. "Abner came to you and you sent him away in peace. Don't you know that he was actually spying on you to find out how he can best attack you at his convenience?"

David didn't answer him, so he stomped out. As soon as he left the presence of David, he sent several of his young men to bring Abner back on the pretext that David wanted to have further word with him. When Abner returned, Joab took him aside as though he would converse with him, but instead, he stabbed him in the stomach, and Abner died there in Hebron for the death of Asahel.

David and all Israel mourned for Abner, and David wrote a song of lamentation for him.

"Should Abner die as a fool dies? Your hands were not bound nor your feet put in fetters. As a man falls before wicked men, so you fell."

David publicly charged Joab with the murder of Abner, and for a time there was a stricture between David and his nephew.

The death of Abner brought profound changes in Israel. Ishbosheth lost heart because his mainstay was gone. He had only been a front for the power and influence of Abner, and now his impotence as a ruler would be visible to all.

The army of Israel was especially troubled by the loss of their commander since there was no one with the strength of leadership to take his place.

Many of the soldiers remembered David's military leadership and talked about going as a company to Hebron with an invitation for David to be the commander of their army and king of their land.

While they hesitated to put their plan into practice, two low-life fellows decided to be the innovators. Baanah and Rechab, sons of Rimmon the Beerothite, went to the palace of the king at Mahanaim and murdered Ishbosheth as he lay asleep. They cut off his head and brought the grisly trophy to David at Hebron. They hoped that David would reward and honor them for their evil deed. But they found a different David than they had expected. He ordered them to be executed as he had the young Amalekite who brought the story of the killing of Saul at Mount Gilboa.

With the death of Ishbosheth, it appeared that there was no longer any impediment in David's way to the rulership of all Israel. The people of Israel were ready, and every tribe sent their leading elders to David at Hebron and made a covenant with him there to rule over all Israel. So, at age thirty-seven, David began to rule over all the land of Israel from Dan to Beersheba.

David's present capital was at Hebron, and Ishbosheth had ruled Israel from Mahanaim, but David felt that he needed a more central city from which to rule and to call his own, so he chose Jerusalem. But the Jebusites were there, and they were strongly entrenched.

David consulted the Lord about attacking the city, and the word came back. "Go up, for I will surely give you the city."

So David and his men went to attack the city, and the Jebusites prepared to resist him. David challenged his men. "Whoever climbs up the way of the water shaft and opens the city to us will be our chief."

Immediately the intrepid and temporarily ostracized Joab stepped forward, climbed the water shaft, and against imposing odds opened the city gates for David's army to march in and claim the city. True to his word, David reinstated his nephew Joab as the commander of his army.

David dwelt in Jerusalem and called it the city of David. He built his palace and seat of government there, and Jerusalem became a great city under David's leadership.

As David surveyed the length and breadth of his kingdom, he thought of his dear friend Jonathan. How good it would be to have him here with him as second in command as they had planned in the forest that day. Except for the sins of Saul, Jonathan should be ruling this vast empire instead of himself.

Then he reconsidered. Perhaps it was never the intent of the Lord for Jonathan to be king over Israel. God always knew what was best. As he pondered, he wondered what he could do further to honor the name of Jonathan in the kingdom. He faintly remembered that Jonathan had told him that a son had survived the birthing death of Zereth, and he wondered if that son might still be alive. He also remembered the name of a servant of Saul, Ziba. So he called for Ziba, and the servant informed him that the son of Jonathan, Mephibosheth, was still alive and living in Lo Debar.

Ziba was specific. "My lord, King David, when the nurse who was tending the infant son of Jonathan heard of the death of Saul and Jonathan, she picked the boy up to flee from the Philistines, but she dropped him, and he became crippled in both feet."

David listened intently. Then he ordered Ziba to bring Mephibosheth to the palace, restore to him all of Saul and Jonathan's property, and give him a permanent place at the king's table.

Michal was overjoyed when David told her about his plans for Mephibosheth, and the relationship between David and Michal was greatly improved.

# CHAPTER 8

While David was with Samuel at Ramah, the aged priest shared with him the story of the tragic journey of the Ark of God.

Hophni and Phinehas had taken it with their carnal hands from its berth in the temple at Shiloh to the battle of Ebenezer, where the Philistines killed Hophni and Phinehas, captured the Ark of God, and carried it to Ashdod as a trophy of war.

The pagans believed that they had captured the god of Israel and had displayed it in several of the cities. But wherever it was shown, plagues had descended on the people of those cities, and the Philistine lords became alarmed. So they sent it back to Israel on a new cart pulled by two recently freshened heifers that had never worn a yoke. There was no visible driver for the cart.

The first place in Israel to receive the Ark was Beth Shemesh, and the people were overjoyed. But some people violated the sacred vessel, and as a result, several people died quickly of a plague, so the people of Beth Shemesh sent it on to Kirjath Jearim, where it had resided now for more than twenty years.

During the many years the sacred vessel had been at Kirjath Jearim, Samuel had longed to bring it to Ramah and house it in a special room his father, Elkanah, had built for it in the tabernacle. But for these long years, the room had remained vacant.

David was puzzled. "But Master Samuel, why haven't you sent for the Ark and brought it to Ramah? You are the most influential man in all of Israel, and people are at your beck and call. I'm sure that you could have found more than enough of your fellow Levites to carry the Ark from Kirjath Jearim to this place."

Samuel's face twisted in pain. "You are right, David. I found many Levites who were anxious to transport the Ark from Kirjath Jearim to Ramah, but the elders of the city would not allow the sacred chest to be brought to this place. They feared that some of the people in Ramah might dare to violate the Ark, as did the people of Beth Shemesh, and the entire city would suffer a serious plague. I assured them that the room would remain locked at all times except when the Ark would be in use for a special service. But the elders have been inflexible."

David broke in. "Master Samuel, have they considered how many blessings they are missing by not having this sacred vessel here in their midst?"

Samuel nodded. "Yes, I have reported to them the great blessings the house of Abinadab is enjoying, but they were unimpressed."

Samuel's face brightened. "David, will you promise me that when God installs you as king over Israel, you will prepare a room for the Ark in your capital city and move the Ark from Kirjath Jearim?"

David nodded. "Yes, Master Samuel, I will promise."

David sat on his throne in the capital city of Jerusalem and thought of his promise to Samuel regarding moving the Ark of God from Kirjath Jearim. He was now king over all of Israel, so it was time to fulfill the promise, but there were major impediments.

The sacred vessel should be housed in a temple where the holy and most holy places could be divided, but it would take several years to build a temple, and he would need to get the Lord's permission. A tabernacle, with a special room dedicated to the holy chest such as Samuel had prepared at Ramah, could take the place of a temple for a time but that too seemed remote.

Then he remembered. For hundreds of years the Ark had been housed in a tent. Yes, that was the answer. He would have workman prepare an elaborate tent in which to put the Ark of God.

There was another very serious obstruction that would delay the move of the Ark. The Philistines were now threatening the very gates of Israel. They had decided to test the strength of David and had gathered in large numbers in the Valley of Rephaim planning for an all out war.

After the death of Saul and Jonathan at Mount Gilboa, the Israelites had fled the cities on both sides of the Jordan, and the Philistines had immediately moved into them. This gave them a base inside the precincts of Israel, and through the intervening years, they had used their strength in these cities to take over other peripheral cities.

Knowing that David was a mighty man of war, they feared that as soon as he had established himself on the throne of Israel, he would challenge their right to these cities, so they decided to strike first. David realized that his strength was in the Lord God of Israel. So he petitioned the Lord for wisdom through Abiathar and the ephod, and under the direction of God, he defeated the pagans twice and drove them back to the gates of Gezer. He spared his old friend and former benefactor, Achish, king of Gath, but he reduced the extent of his territory.

With the Philistines now in subjection and the tent prepared to receive the Ark of God, David was ready to bring the sacred chest from its present berth in the house of Abinadab at Kirjath Jearim to Jerusalem.

He gathered thirty thousand of the choice men of Israel to assist in transporting the Ark. But David erred in the method of moving the sacred chest. He had ordered a new cart to be built on which to carry the Ark, and the two sons of Abinadab, Uzzah and Ahio, were to drive the oxen. The 30,000 men were to make music, dance, and celebrate as the Ark moved along.

But God had originally ordered that poles be made and covered with gold. These poles were to fit into loops on the sides of the Ark and were to be borne on the shoulders of four picked Levite men.

This error on the part of David didn't become critical until the procession came to Nachon's threshing floor. The road leading into the threshing floor was deeply rutted due to many carts loaded with grain coming into the mill. One of the oxen stepped into a deep rut and stumbled. The cart leaned dangerously, and it appeared that the Ark could fall, so Uzzah put his hand on the Ark to steady it. God immediately struck him dead. In a moment of time, the oxen stopped their forward motion, the musicians were suddenly mute, and the dancers ceased their dancing. The entire procession halted as one man.

David was overcome with emotion. A man had died before his eyes, partly because of his omission regarding the proper transportation of the Ark. He was reminded, however, that Uzzah knew better than to touch the sacred vessel. He was the eldest son of a chief priest, and the Ark of God had lodged in their home for many years. He had witnessed firsthand the rich blessings the sacred Ark had brought to their home. He had often assisted his father in sacrifices involving the Ark, but he had grown somewhat careless in his attitude toward the vessel that symbolized the presence of God. Thus, when the cart leaned to one side and threatened to dislodge the Ark, he treated the sacred chest as a common object, and as a result, he suffered the displeasure of God.

The joy of the thousands accompanying the Ark on its journey to Jerusalem turned to sorrow at the death of Uzzah, and many in the procession questioned the fairness of this violent act of God.

David was angry. The thought of the divine judgment on the people of Beth Shemesh where a few people had violated the Ark came to his mind, and he wondered if perhaps the people of Jerusalem would violate the Ark and call down these same judgments. So he decided that he must seek further counsel from the Lord before moving the sacred chest to Jerusalem.

He sought out a Levite friend Obed Edom, who lived in the area of Gath Rimmon and was a musician in the procession accompanying the Ark.

"My friend, Obed Edom, I am fearful that if we move the Ark to Jerusalem at this time plagues might accompany its arrival. Would you be willing to house the Ark at your home until the Lord gives further directions regarding its future?"

Obed Edom nodded eagerly. "Yes, my lord, my house will welcome the Ark of the Lord."

David was in the throne room when the messenger from Beth Shemesh was ushered into his presence. He motioned for the man to speak.

"My lord and king, I am from the city of Beth Shemesh but have been visiting recently in the village of Gath Rimmon. I found that the talk of the town is the way the Lord is richly blessing Obed Edom and his household by the presence of the Ark of God. Several of the people of the city asked me to report to you about the many divine favors enjoyed by Obed Edom, and they believe that you might want to move the Ark from Gath Rimmon to Jerusalem immediately."

David thought on the messenger's words for several moments, and then he nodded. "Yes, the people are right. It seems that now is the time for the Ark to be moved to the tent in Jerusalem." He paused. "I must reward you for bringing this message to me. Ask what you would desire from the royal storehouse."

"No, my lord, I desire nothing for myself. I am among those who greatly desire to have God's sacred Ark in a permanent place in the capital city. The vessel has been in exile much too long."

David eyed the man with new appreciation. "Thank you very much for taking the time and trouble to bring this message to me. I will make immediate plans to carry out the wishes of the people."

David didn't make the mistake of putting the Ark on a cart this time as he had at Kirjath Jearim. Instead, he chose many quartets of Levite men to carry the Ark on their shoulders. They would serve in succession. After every six steps, the bearers of the Ark would stop while the priests sacrificed oxen and sheep. Thousands of people came out of the cities and joined the procession accompanying the ark on its journey to Jerusalem. The multitude clapped and sang and danced as the Ark moved along, and the sound of the trumpet was heard all along the way. David sang and danced before the Ark with inspired passion. He reveled in the thought that the sacred Ark of God would finally have a permanent home in the city – the city of David.

As the procession came into the city with David at its head, Michal, Saul's daughter and David's wife, looked out of a window and saw the king in his exuberance, and she despised him in her heart.

After the Ark had been put in its place in the midst of the tent David had prepared for it, he had the priests offer burnt offerings and peace offerings before the Lord. Then, after giving gifts to all the people, he hastened home to bless his own household.

A tempestuous Michal met him at the door.

"How glorious was the king of Israel today," she chided him, "exposing himself in the sight of his servant girls like any empty-headed fool."

David was both shocked and angry, and he answered her in a pique. "I sang and danced before the Lord today, for he has chosen me before your father and his entire house to be ruler over Israel. I will play more music before the Lord and act more undignified in praise and honor to Him, and by the servant girls to whom you refer, I will be honored in their eyes."

David and Michal did not live together as husband and wife from that day forward, and Michal had no children to the day of her death.

David wasn't satisfied. He had promised Samuel that when he was installed as king over Israel he would move the Ark from Kirjath Jearim to his capital city. That part of the promise he had fulfilled, for the Ark was now berthed in Jerusalem. A larger part of the promise he had made to Samuel was that he would build a temple to house the holy chest; instead, he had built a tent.

The main reason for choosing a tent over the temple was the extreme length of time to build a temple. But there was a larger reason: he needed divine permission to build a temple. He remembered that God had commanded Moses in the wilderness, "Let them make me a tabernacle (temple) that I may dwell among them." The presence of the Lord would dwell among them in the most holy place and that would require a temple, so David called the Prophet Nathan to him in the throne room.

Nathan came quickly, and David faced the man of God. "My lord, here I am dwelling in a house of cedar while the Ark of God is dwelling in a tent. That doesn't seem fair to me. Would you petition the Lord for me to see if He will allow me the privilege of building a temple to house the holy vessel?"

"Yes, my lord, I am sure that I can give you an answer from the Lord on the morrow."

The next day the prophet came back to David, but his countenance was troubled. David motioned for him to speak.

"My lord, the king, I placed your request before the Lord yesterday, and the Lord has given me an answer.

"The Lord said to me. 'Tell my servant, David, that in all the years I have dwelt among the children of Israel, My home has been in a tent or tabernacle, never a temple. Thus, I appreciate the desire of my servant, whom I took from the sheepfold and made him to be king over my people, Israel, to build Me a temple where I may dwell. Tell my servant, David, that because his heart is inclined to exalt me among the people, I will greatly bless him and will give him rest from all of his enemies. But he is not to build a house for Me. He is a man of war, a man of blood, and therefore, he is not to build this sacred house. A son of his, who will succeed him on the throne when he rests with his fathers, will build Me a house, and I will be his father and he will be My son.'"

David bowed in submission. "The Lord has spoken. Blessed be the name of the Lord."

Since building a temple would not be occupying his time and energy, the king made plans to make war on the enemies of Israel. He made war against the Philistines, the Moabites, the Syrians, and lastly the Ammonites. Everywhere he turned the Lord blessed David, and these pagan people were soon chattels of Israel and were paying tribute money. So the nations were at peace with Israel.

David was bored. He was a man of war, and all of the nations round about Israel trembled at the mention of his name. Most of these nations were now paying tribute to the nation of Israel. There were still a few pockets of resistance in the nation of Ammon that needed to be subdued, including the capital city, Rabbah, but these spots were not a big challenge to the king. There were pressing business matters of the kingdom that needed his attention, so he called his army commander Joab into the war room.

Joab came quickly and waited patiently for the king to speak. David dismissed the servant who had brought Joab in and turned to the commander of his armies. He looked at Joab as if he were seeing him for the first time. He deeply disliked this proud, cruel nephew of his, but he needed him.

Joab had no peer in the nation of Israel in the art of warfare except David himself. Thus, David tolerated him and kept him as the commander of his armies despite his distasteful feelings toward him.

David spoke. "Commander Joab, it's time for us to destroy the pestilent cities of Ammon that are constantly harassing our border cities and at times threatening our capital city, Jerusalem. Perhaps we should put them all, including their capital city, Rabbah, to tribute." He paused and waited for Joab to respond.

"Yes, my lord, I agree with you," Joab answered. "I will make arrangements immediately for a large company of soldiers to move against Ammon. It will take a few days to make full preparations, but we should be ready within a week."

He paused. "Is my lord the king planning to go with us?"

David shook his head. "No, I will plan to stay by at Jerusalem. The business matters of the kingdom have greatly increased during the past few months, and I must make some very important judicial decisions. I have confidence, Commander Joab, that you can take care of the Ammonites with dispatch. However, when you begin the siege of Rabbah, please send a messenger to me, since I feel a need to be there to accept their surrender."

Joab bowed. "Yes, my lord, I will carry out your instructions carefully."

David counted sheep time and again with the hope that sleep would come, but he remained wide-awake. Sleep was elusive. He knew the reason for his wakefulness; he wanted to be out in the field with his men of war. The business of the kingdom was tedious to him while battle excited him and quickened his heartbeat. His wives and children were asleep and thus offered him no company. So he arose from his bed, walked outside, and made his way to the roof of the palace. The devil met him there.

The light of a torch burning on a housetop several doors away caught his attention. By that light he could see clearly the facial features of a very beautiful lady bathing herself. Evidently the lateness of the hour made her secure in the thought that no one would spy on her. But David watched her cleanse her comely body parts for several minutes from his dark nook on the palace roof.

Thoughts, as dark as the night that hid him, began to battle against the voice of reason in his mind as his animal nature desired passionately to have this woman for the night. But reason argued that he could wake up one of his wives or concubines, even at this time of the night, and they would gladly share their bed with him. As David continued to watch the beautiful bather, passion and reason wrestled together in the confines of his heart. Finally, he determined that he would send a messenger to find out who the lady was. This decision gave passion the edge in the battle.

The messenger met him in the throne room and bowed respectfully. "My lord the king, the woman about whom you have inquired is Bathsheba, the daughter of Eliam and the wife of Uriah the Hittite, who is presently with the king's army in Ammon."

David's heart pained him at the announcement that she was another man's wife, but passion had already won the battle. He immediately ordered his servants to inform the woman that the king requested her presence at the palace.

At first, Bathsheba was alarmed at the request of the king. She was a very pious woman, and as a fairly recent bride, she was deeply in love with her soldier husband. However, even though she suspected that the king might desire her for one of his concubines, she had been taught from childhood that one must not deny the wishes of a priest or the king. So she immediately went with the messenger.

David paced the floor nervously as he waited for Bathsheba. Reason hadn't given up easily and even now he considered sending other servants to abort the visit of Uriah's wife. But he hesitated and the proper moment passed. The servants soon brought the lovely Bathsheba into his presence.

The woman bowed before the king, and he noticed that she was even lovelier than he had thought at first. David dismissed all of the servants and the two strangers. The king and Uriah's wife visited for a time in the throne room. Then David invited her into his bedroom, and she went with him.

The next morning the two went their separate ways. She went back to her home and David to his place in the administration room. Both left the king's bedroom with a load of guilt on their hearts.

For several weeks David's religious devotions were strained, and the Lord seemed remote. No new songs came to his mind. But as the weeks passed in succession, his guilt began to decrease, and the thought even possessed him that as king it was fitting and proper for him to take whatever his heart desired. The thought brought a balm to his troubled heart.

As he surveyed the length and breadth of his kingdom, it was evident that God was blessing him. The only trouble spots were those of Ammon where Joab had not yet reached, but reports from the battle sites indicated that things were going well. Joab sent word that soon he would begin the siege of Rabbah. Then like a thief in the night, trouble came in and imposed itself on David's pleasant life. The servant delivered a note to the king written by Bathsheba, Uriah's wife. The message was terse.

"My lord the king, I am with child."

David's heart twisted in pain as he reread the contents of the letter. He hadn't given a thought to the possibility of such a revelation resulting from the night with Bathsheba. Uriah hadn't been with his wife for several months now, so the child couldn't possibly be his. It had to be the product of his night with Bathsheba, and the thought brought a new dimension to the problem. Either he would have to admit to his adulterous affair with Bathsheba, or she could be in danger of being stoned as a harlot when her pregnancy became obvious to her neighbors.

He needed help to untie the knots of his duplicity. He thought of calling for Abiathar and the ephod. Perhaps God would ignore his sin and give him an answer to his dilemma. But God seemed so far away now. For a moment the thought struck him that God might even laugh in his face, so he decided on another plan; he would send for Uriah.

Uriah came in before the king in a rather hesitant manner. He was a career soldier, and therefore, wasn't accustomed to visiting in the king's palace. He felt much more comfortable in a tent on the battlefield. His face revealed that his heart was questioning what the king wanted with him.

David attempted to relax him and put him at ease. "How is the battle going against Ammon?"

The soldier relaxed as he answered. "The war is going very well. We have crushed many of the Ammonite cities, and Commander Joab reported only last night that we would probably be at the gates of Rabbah in a few weeks."

David smiled. "I would like to have been in the field myself, but business at Jerusalem has been very pressing, and I was forced to leave it all in the hands of Commander Joab. He is a very capable leader, isn't he?"

The soldier's face lit up. "Oh yes, Commander Joab is a great leader. He doesn't expect anything of anyone that he is not willing to do personally. The men love him very much."

David now resorted to subterfuge. "Your neighbors tell me that you are a newly married man and that you have been away at war now for several months while your bride is yearning to see you and spend some time with you. So I brought you home for a few days that you might fulfill the desire of your wife. Go down to you house tonight and spend the night with your bride."

David dismissed Uriah, but he didn't go down to his home as David expected. Instead Uriah spent the night with David's servants.

David was frustrated and also irritated when he learned the next morning where Uriah had spent the night. He called the soldier again into the throne room. "Uriah, I asked Joab to send you home so that you could spend time with your wife, but instead of going home to your wife, you spent the night with my servants. Why didn't you spend the night with your wife?"

Uriah spread his hands in a helpless gesture. "My lord, the Ark of God is residing in a tent and Joab and my fellow soldiers are encamped in an open field. So how could I go down to my house and eat and drink and lie with my wife? As your soul lives I would not think of doing my own pleasure."

David looked at Uriah for a long moment and shame came up in his throat and threatened to choke him. He thought of his own actions that night when lust drove him to commit adultery with this man's wife. But Uriah would not do his own pleasure with his wife because it would be a sin against his fellow soldiers.

For a few moments David was speechless; then he found his voice. "You must stay by here for a few days and perhaps you will then desire to visit your wife."

Uriah stayed by at the palace for several days, but he did not go to visit his wife. He continued to spend the night with the palace servants.

David recognized that his original plan for covering up his sin with Bathsheba would not work because of the pious stubbornness of Uriah, so he formed a second plan: a deadly one.

He sat down and wrote a message to Joab telling him to put Uriah in the very front of the battle line and make sure that he would be unprotected and thus be killed. He sealed the letter with his royal seal and sent it to Joab by the hand of Uriah. A few days later a messenger came from Joab with the news that Uriah the Hittite was dead. David commended his commander discreetly for carrying out his orders.

After Bathsheba observed a period of mourning for her husband, David sent for her, and she became his wife. David was now confident that his sins would be forever hidden from the sight of men.

Shortly thereafter, Prophet Nathan visited the palace. He seemed a bit tense, and when David offered him a seat, he indicated that he would prefer to stand. David motioned for him to speak.

"My lord the king, there is a certain rich man who has many flocks of sheep and herds of cattle. In the same city there is a poor man who had only one little ewe lamb. The lamb grew up in the poor man's home and became a member of the family. It lay in his bosom and ate at his table.

"One day a traveler came to visit the rich man and be his guest. The rich man made preparations to entertain his guest, but instead of looking to his own flock, he took the one ewe lamb from the poor man and prepared her for his guest."

Nathan paused. "I await the judgment of the king on this man."

David's face became livid, and anger boiled up in his throat. "This man deserves to die," he said with passion, "and he must pay the man fourfold for the ewe lamb. If you will tell me who this vile wretch is, I will personally see that the sentence is carried out."

Nathan nodded, and his eyes were misty. He pointed his finger. "Thou art the man, oh, king! God has given you houses and lands and many wives and children, but you took the one ewe lamb from Uriah as your own. Then to make matters worse, you plotted to have him killed in battle and have acted as if it were nothing in the sight of the Lord."

David felt as if a dart had been driven by the hand of the Lord through the tender flesh of his heart, and he bowed his head and wept bitterly. When he raised his head, he sobbed through his tears. "I am guilty, and I deserve to die. May the Lord have mercy on my poor sinful soul."

Nathan shook his head. "No! God has determined that you will not die. However, since you have despised the commandment of the Lord by killing Uriah and taking his wife to be your wife, the sword shall never depart from your house. I will raise up an adversary against you from your own house that will take your wives and lie with them in the sight of all the people. You sinned secretly, but I will do this thing before the sun. Moreover, because of this deed, you have given occasion to the enemies of the Lord to blaspheme. The child also who is born to you shall die."

The first of the afflictions predicted to fall on the house of David came quickly as the child born to David and Bathsheba died. The child's death was a painful reminder to David that even this innocent child was impacted by his sin. And, according to the judgment of the Lord, many other innocent people would be hurt before the plague would run its course.

In his mental and spiritual anguish, a song of appeal for forgiveness and reinstatement to the favor of the Lord came to the king. He wrote it down and sang it before the Lord.

"Have mercy upon me, O God, according to Thy loving kindness; according unto the multitude of Thy tender mercies blot out my transgression. Wash me thoroughly from mine iniquity, and cleanse me from my sin. For I acknowledge my transgression; and my sin is ever before me. Against Thee, Thee only, have I sinned, and done this evil in Thy sight; that Thou mightest be justified when Thou speakest, and be clear when Thou judgest . . . . Purge me with hyssop and I shall be clean . . . . Create in me a clean heart, O God; and renew a right spirit within me. Cast me not away from Thy presence; and take not Thy Holy Spirit from me. Restore unto me the joy of Thy salvation; and uphold me with Thy free spirit. Then will I teach transgressors Thy ways; and sinners shall be converted unto Thee."

David comforted Bathsheba in her bereavement, and he lay with her. She conceived and gave birth to Solomon, beloved of the Lord.

# CHAPTER 9

When David determined that the fictitious rich man of Nathan's parable should pay fourfold for his injustice to the poor man, he was pronouncing his own sentence for his sin against Bathsheba. Four of his own sons would fall, and the loss of each would be a result of his sin.

God made the world and so ordered human life that every seed brings forth fruit of its kind and every action issues in a corresponding result. This is a constant invariable law. Thus, David's sin brought affliction to him and to his family in later life commensurate with the depth of his sin and the eminence of his position.

While David was an outstanding king and a bloody and inflexible warrior in battle, he was a weak and indecisive parent. He never disciplined or chided his sons, and consequently, most of them were extremely selfish.

Amnon, his firstborn by Ahinoam the Jezreelitess, was a handsome lad with the bearing of a prince, but his father or mother never seriously disciplined him.

He came to David one day with quivering lips and tears in his eyes. David was alarmed at the pain of his little son. He took the boy in his arms and stroked his beautiful hair. "Son, tell me what is wrong? Perhaps Father can fix it."

Amnon looked up with his large expressive eyes and nodded. "Mother told me that you would help me."

"Yes, son, I'm sure that I can help you."

Amnon's face brightened at his Father's assurance. "Aziz has a sling that he made himself, and it will kill birds and animals and . . ." The boy got teary eyed again. "I want it, but he won't give it to me. He told me to make my own sling, and I don't want to make my own sling. I want Aziz's sling." He looked to his father in appeal. "You will get it for me, won't you?"

David was in a dilemma. He remembered that the boy, Aziz, was the son of a very influential banker in the city of Jerusalem. David couldn't afford to stir up the boy's father by demanding his son give Amnon his sling, so he made a very painful decision.

"Amnon, you have heard of the giant Goliath that I killed with a sling and a stone at the battle of Ephes Dammim, haven't you?"

The boy nodded. "Yes, Father, I have heard."

"I still have that sling here at the palace. I will give you that sling and you won't need Aziz's sling."

Amnon shook his head vigorously. "No, no, Father! You don't understand. That is an old sling, but Aziz's sling is a new sling. It's better than your old sling."

For a few moments, David was at a loss for words. He thought surely that giving up his treasured trophy would satisfy his son, but he had been rebuffed. He was back to his original dilemma. Perhaps he could deal with Aziz.

"Amnon, would you find your friend Aziz and tell him that the king would like to visit with him here at the palace? Ask him to bring his sling with him."

The boy nodded eagerly. "Yes, Father, I will find him right away."

Aziz followed Amnon into the king's presence with obvious reluctance. There was fear in his dark eyes, but his jaw was set in a posture of defiance, and he clutched his precious sling so firmly in his hand that his knuckles were white.

David greeted the lad with a smile and a pat on his shoulder. The boy relaxed a bit.

"Aziz, thank you for coming to see me," David said softly. "Have you ever been in the palace before?"

Aziz nodded and swallowed and Amnon answered for him.

"Oh yes, Father, Aziz comes into my playroom often. He is one of my best friends."

"That's good Amnon. I'm glad to hear that you share your playroom with your friends."

The king turned to Aziz. "Amnon tells me that you have made a sling with which you kill small animals and birds."

The boy nodded.

"You must have made a very strong sling. May I see it?"

Aziz offered the sling, but he held on to one of the strings. David looked it over carefully and with obvious approval. "That is a very nice sling, Aziz. I can certainly understand why your friends would like to own it."

Aziz smiled his appreciation.

David continued. "When I was your age, I was a keeper of sheep, and I had to protect my sheep from jackals, bears, lions, and bandits. So I made a sling like yours Aziz, and with it I killed many jackals and drove away lions and bears and bandits that tried to steal my sheep. With that sling I also killed the giant Goliath at Ephes Dammim. Would you like to see that sling?"

The boy nodded eagerly. "Yes, my lord, I would like to see your sling."

David spoke to a servant who quickly brought the treasured sling. He held it up before the two boys. "Aziz, would you like to have this sling?"

There were stars in the boy's eyes, and he nodded quickly. "Yes, my lord, I would love to have your sling."

Amnon broke in. "Father, I have changed my mind; I would like to have your sling."

David hesitated for a moment. He hadn't expected this change of heart by Amnon. But the moment passed, and he determined quickly that he had passed the point of no return in his dealings with both boys.

"No, Amnon, you had your chance, and now Aziz will have his. Aziz, will you trade your sling for mine?"

The boy pushed his sling forward. "Yes, my lord, I will trade my sling for yours."

David passed his sling to Aziz and accepted Aziz's sling in return, which he handed to Amnon. Amnon's face twisted in a pout as he looked covetously at the sling in Aziz's hand.

David's heart was in pain as the boys left the throne room. His family had grown large in only a few years, while at the same time, his regal responsibilities had multiplied. Time with his family was minimal, and as a result, his sons were growing up without paternal training. Most were selfish and grasping as was Amnon.

As David considered the problems of his family, the thought possessed him for a moment that he was reaping the results of ignoring God's counsel to the king: "neither shall he multiply wives for himself, lest his heart turn away."

There were several bright spots, however, in the census of his sons as a result of good maternal training that gave him hope. There was Chileah, son of Abigail, widow of Nabal; Shephatiah, son of Abital; and Ithream, son of Eglah. These boys were always polite and well behaved at court and had no part in the interminable pranks of several others.

Absalom, son of Maacah, daughter of Talmai, king of Geshur, had very little maternal training. The mother's unusual beauty had attracted David to her, and he had married this pagan princess against the dictates of his own conscience.

Absalom was the most handsome of the king's sons and also the most aggressive. He was a born leader, and while very young, he established himself as the indisputable captain of the king's sons other than the oldest son, Amnon. Amnon was a leader in his own right, but his followers were fewer in number than those of Absalom.

Absalom would remind his followers that he was not only the son of a king, but also the grandson of a king, and therefore, he would be king someday. There was good reason for his boasting. His mother, Maacah, would often take her son to visit his grandfather, Talmai, king of Geshur. The aging king would impress his young grandson with the thought that he was born to be a king and, therefore, must always act in a regal manner.

Talmai taught the boy the strategy of winning the support of the people, and Absalom was a fast learner. He would come back to his home with his mind full of ideas about recruiting more followers. Soon his disciples were filling the streets. The followers of Absalom and the followers of Amnon often clashed in the streets. Absalom always declared his group the winner. Then his followers would put a crudely made crown on Absalom's head and a scepter in his hand and would proclaim him king. His imaginary throne was under the sword of Goliath that David had hung in the trophy room.

Absalom boasted many times that when he became king the sword of Goliath would be his and he would use it to kill all his enemies.

David sat in the throne room and his soul was in reflection. There was peace over all the land of Israel, and the national treasury was full to overflowing. The natives were paying a modest tax, but the bulk of the income was from the nations paying tribute. Everywhere the king looked in the land, the picture was of prosperity.

David began to hope that God had canceled the afflictions that were promised as a result of his sin with Bathsheba and his murder of Uriah. But it wasn't to be. The blight had not been canceled but rather was delayed. In time it was sure to come.

Amnon was in a bad mood. He was in a love with Tamar, the beautiful sister of Absalom. His desire for her was so strong that he could neither eat nor sleep. She was always on his mind, but Absalom had forbidden him to touch her. In fact, he had warned his older half brother not to go near his sister. So Amnon pouted.

His friend Jonadab, the son of David's brother Shammah, noticed Amnon's strange behavior and was concerned. "Amnon, my friend, what is wrong with you?" he asked in alarm. "There must be something really troubling you. Could you share with me?"

Amnon nodded and turned his troubled face to Jonadab. "Jonadab, I am madly in love with Absalom's sister Tamar, and I cannot live without her. I am sure that my father wouldn't give her to me in marriage, and Absalom has threatened to have his company of ruffians beat me up if I touch her. So I don't know what to do. Jonadab what should I do?"

The impious Jonadab was ready with a solution to Amnon's dilemma, and there was an evil glint in his eyes as he whispered the plan to his questionable friend. At first, even the dissolute Amnon was shocked by Jonadab's suggestion, but his passion for the girl was so strong that conscience was muted, and even the threat of Absalom was forgotten. He decided immediately to follow Jonadab's suggestion.

"Now remember," Jonadab reminded him. "You are to lie down on your bed and act as if you are very ill. Your father will, no doubt, come visit you soon and will be concerned for you. He will ask you what can be done to relieve your pain. You are not to answer him immediately, for it must appear that you haven't given the easing of your pain any thought. Then you will answer the king, 'Please let Tamar come and bake me several cakes in my sight that I may eat from her hand and get well again.'"

The evil plan of Jonadab worked perfectly for the incestuous Amnon. Tamar came quickly to her brother's bedside at the request of her father and baked the cakes as Amnon desired. But when she took the cakes to Amnon's beside, he refused to eat. Instead, he took her by the arm and asked her to commit fornication with him.

Tamar was horrified at her brother's suggestion. "Oh no, my brother," she protested, "do not force me. This would be the most grievous sin in Israel, and I would have nowhere to go from here. I would be an outcast among the daughters of Jerusalem, and you would be regarded as one of the fools of Israel. Please, speak to the king, for he will not withhold me from you."

But he would not listen to her appeal, and with his strength, he forced her and raped her. The anticipated satisfaction eluded him, however, as waves of shame and guilt washed over him, and in his bitterness of spirit, he ordered his servants to throw her out of his house. In her anguish of spirit, the girl tore her beautiful gown of many colors and left the rapist's house weeping bitterly.

All in the royal household soon knew about the sin of Amnon against Tamar, and lines of personal judgment were quickly drawn.

The wives and concubines of the king who had daughters despised the rapist prince and feared for the moral safety of their own daughters. They looked to the king to punish Amnon severely for his sin, but it was not to be.

David was angry at his oldest son's transgression and felt a need to administer some kind of judgment for this flagrant sin. Several months ago he had severely disciplined several of his soldiers who were found guilty of raping a captive maiden. But in the meantime, his administration of justice had suffered serious regression because of the memory of his own sins of adultery and murder. So he said nothing good or bad to Amnon.

Absalom was outraged at his brother's sin and heartbroken at his sister's condition. He comforted her gently in her sorrow, and she made her home with him.

Absalom vowed in his heart that one day Amnon would pay with his life for this grievous sin against Tamar. Several months before this occasion, he had threatened Amnon with a severe beating by his company of ruffians if he even touched his sister, but he quickly abandoned that plan in favor of one that now included murder.

The wily prince bided his time. He must not hurry. So whenever he met Amnon at the court or on the palace grounds he was always civil. Amnon was puzzled and disarmed by the attitude of Absalom. He had expected that Absalom would attempt to carry out his threat of mauling him, so he kept a few of his own rascals always by his side in case of a surprise. But there were no altercations. As time passed it appeared that all who were involved forgot the shaming of Tamar, but appearances were deceiving. Two years had passed since Amnon's sin against Tamar, and Absalom was now ready to administer his promised judgment against Amnon. Amnon's time was soon to end.

It was shearing time for Absalom's flocks at Baal Hazor, and according to his usual custom, he prepared a feast for his shearers and certain members of his family. For the past several years, Amnon hadn't been invited to the celebration, but this year the guest list included the older brother. It appeared to Amnon somewhat like an olive branch after the storm. He was pleased with this show of acceptance on the part of his formerly estranged brother and accepted the invitation gratefully. He would go as an ox to the slaughter.

The king declined Absalom's invitation to the feast, but all the king's sons were present and most imbibed freely of the wine from Absalom's vineyards. Absalom made certain that the wine jars were always full, and poor unsuspecting Amnon drank cup after cup of the intoxicating beverage. Soon he was addled and argumentative, and he picked a fight with the servant who was filling the wine cups. Actually, the servant provoked the brawl by deliberately spilling wine on Amnon's coat, but the wily aide of Absalom made the incident look like an accident. Amnon rose unsteadily to his feet and threatened the man with his short sword, but the servant drew his own weapon and thrust it into Amnon's side. So Amnon died in his drunken condition.

The death of Amnon brought a sudden end to the festivities at Baal Hazor. David's sons quickly mounted their mules and hurried back to Jerusalem. In the meantime a messenger brought the false news to David that all his sons had been slain by Absalom, and the king was greatly distraught. He arose and tore his robe and laid full length on the floor in the throne room. The servants joined him in his sorrow by tearing their garments and standing around his prone form. But Jonadab, the son of Shammah, David's brother, the one who encouraged Amnon to rape Absalom's sister, knew what had happened at Baal Hazor.

He came in before the king and spoke to him. "My lord the king, the report that all of your sons are dead is untrue. Only Amnon is dead. Absalom has been plotting the death of his sister's rapist for the two years since the deed was committed." As Jonadab was speaking, the sons of David came into the palace grounds.

Absalom felt vindicated. For two long years, he had hated Amnon with passion because of the rape of his sister, but he had forced himself to be civil toward his despised older brother. The object of his loathing was now dead, and the slate was clean, but he feared the wrath of his father, so he fled to his grandfather, Talmai, king of Geshur.

The exiled prince was with his grandfather in Geshur for three years, but he wasn't idle.

Every day he would sit for a time with his grandfather in the throne room and the hall of justice where he studied the art of administration. Then he would go out to the city gate and listen to the elders discuss the politics of the country. While at the city gate, he honed his skills of winning the hearts of the people by welcoming the visitors into the city and giving his blessing to those who were leaving. He dreamed of the day when he would replace his father as king over the great kingdom of Israel. The time of his ascension must be soon, he reasoned, since his father was aging and no longer had the strength or the wisdom to rule the nation of Israel. He further concluded, in his fantasy, that his father and all of his brothers would be an impediment to his kingship and, thus, would need to be destroyed.

The prince rejected all thought of a spiritual kingship, for in his mind, that was the greatest weakness of his father. So he determined that his reign would be patterned after the model of his grandfather who was a pagan.

David was concerned about Absalom. The errant son had been gone from Israel for three years now, and during the entire three years, there had not been any direct communication between the father and the son. David's wife Maacah visited her son and parents at Geshur twice each year, and she brought back news about her son's activities to David, but no greetings were ever exchanged and no appeal was ever sent by Absalom for permission to return to Jerusalem.

David had been consoled over the death of Amnon. He realized that, possibly, it was in mercy that the dissolute life of his eldest son was cut short. However, he also realized that the fact did not in any way mitigate the sin of Absalom.

David longed to go to Geshur and bring his son back to Israel, but he remained indecisive and, therefore, made no move to carry out his desire. Instead, he sat on his throne and brooded over his boy.

In Geshur, Absalom was anxious to return to his homeland, but he feared that his father would still administer justice for his sin against Amnon, so he sent no request to the king.

Finally, the wily Joab felt a need to intercede. He sent for a wise woman from Tekoa and instructed her with an appeal before the king, and he put the words in her mouth. The woman came in before the king and bowed her face to the floor. When she arose, David motioned for her to speak. "My lord, oh king, help me. I am a widow. My husband is dead.

"Your maidservant had two sons, and they fought in the field, and since there was no one there to part them, the one struck the other and killed him. Now I am in great trouble, for the family has risen up against your maidservant, and they are demanding that my only living son be delivered to them for execution. This would leave me with no son and my dead husband would be without an heir and a name."

She paused and waited for the king to speak. David detected a familiar thread running through the woman's story, but he held his tongue. Perhaps his impression was wrong. He looked at the woman for a long moment, and then he spoke. "Go to your house, and I will give orders regarding your case."

He dismissed her with a wave of his hand, but the woman made no move to leave. She spoke again. "My lord, please bear with your maidservant a few moments longer."

David nodded. "Please stay on."

The woman raised a bony finger and pointed at the king. He drew back in alarm. For a moment he relived the specter of Nathan pointing his finger at him and speaking those awful words of condemnation: "Thou art the man."

The woman noticed the king's reaction and hesitated for a moment. Then she continued. "Oh king, you have contrived to do this same wrong, as I have mentioned, against the people of God, for out of your own mouth you have condemned yourself. You have refused to bring back from exile the one you have banished."

David realized immediately why he had recognized a familiar thread running through the woman's story. The woman was still speaking, but David was not listening. He held up his hand and the woman paused. "Please, answer me truthfully," he said to her and the woman answered.

"Yes, my lord, I will be truthful to the king."

David looked her in the eyes. "Is Commander Joab the one who recruited you to speak to me about my son, Absalom?"

The woman answered without hesitation. "My lord, you are a wise and discerning king. Yes, your servant Joab commanded me to speak to you, and he is the one who put all of these words in my mouth. Now that I have delivered the message, I will leave it with the king to decide what he should do with his son who is longing for forgiveness and for permission to return to Israel." The woman bowed and left the king's presence.

David sat for several minutes with his head in his hands. He was struggling with a decision that he had delayed much too long. He then arose, called a servant, and sent for Joab.

Joab came quickly at the king's orders and bowed before him. His usual arrogant manner seemed to be tempered today with a trace of hope and humility, and for the moment, David found himself liking his hot-tempered nephew.

"Joab, I will accede to your wishes. Your clever ploy worked, so I am giving you orders to go and bring back Absalom from Geshur to Jerusalem. He has been in exile too long. But," he added, "I do not want to see his face until I am ready to send for him."

Joab fell on his face before the king. "Thank you, my lord, for showing favor to the wishes of your servant. I will certainly acquaint Absalom with your decision."

David waved the commander of his armies out of his presence.

The banning of Absalom from the king's court proved to be a very costly mistake on the part of David. In essence, the prince was confined to his home, so day after day his resentment against his father mounted as he sat in his house. He drew his plans carefully for treason against the king, but he recognized that he must have exposure to the people in order for his plans to succeed. Absalom was praised as the most handsome man in all of Israel. From the sole of his foot to the crown of his head, there was no blemish on him. But instead of his good fortune making him thankful to the Lord for His favors, he became very self-centered. Thus, while he sat in his house in his banishment, he dreamed of how he could use his good looks and charming personality to win the hearts of the people to himself.

For two full years, Absalom sat and dreamed and planned until he was ready to put his plan of treason into action. But he must first see his father and get released from his prison.

He sent for Joab so that he could request an appointment with the king, but Joab ignored the summons. He sent a second time for the army commander, but Joab continued to ignore his petition. So he resorted to a desperate strategy. He had his servant set Joab's barley field on fire, and Joab came to him quickly.

"I must see the king!" he informed the captain. "And I will not take no for an answer, so get me an appointment to see my father now."

Joab bowed in submission. "I will go to the king immediately with your request."

It was a tense meeting between the king and the rebellious prince in the throne room. Greetings were exchanged, and the king asked about his son's welfare, but there was no move toward reconciliation until Absalom broke the stalemate.

The prince stated his case. "Hear me out, oh king. I was banished to Geshur for three whole years, and then you sent for me to return to Jerusalem. But what good has it been for me to be in Jerusalem? I have been under house arrest in my own home now for two years when I could have remained free in Geshur." He spread his hands helplessly and looked to the king.

David looked at his handsome son for a long moment; then he put his head in his hands and wept. When he spoke, his voice broke. "Oh Absalom, my son, I have missed you so much. Why did you do it? Why did you murder your brother?"

Absalom's chin came up, and his eyes glistened fiercely. "My lord the king has spoken wrongly," he said between clenched teeth. "I did not murder Amnon—I administered justice. Surely the king should know that Moses commanded that if a man finds a virgin and he forces her and rapes her he is supposed to be put to death. I have the command delivered to Moses by the Lord with me, and I will read it to the King. 'But if a man find a betrothed damsel in the field, and the man force her and lie with her; then the man only that lay with her shall die.'

"Oh king, you placed my sister in harm's way. You requested for her to go and bake cakes for Amnon who was feigning illness just so he could have her alone with him and force her and rape her. My little sister and your daughter, oh king, has suffered much misery over the affair, yet no one made any move whatsoever to punish this vile offender, not even you, my lord, who is the supreme jurist of Israel."

David sat mute and unmoving on his throne for several moments before he answered. "You are right, Absalom. I am at fault and you are vindicated. I should have administered justice to Amnon immediately, but I listened to his mother and my own emotions instead of the counsel of the Lord. From this moment I absolve you from all blame in the death of Amnon, and you are free to go about all Israel at will."

David arose then and clasped his son to his breast, kissed him, and wept, and Absalom went out from the presence of the king.

Absalom bided his time. For four years he courted the favor of the people as his grandfather, Talmai, had taught him. He bought himself many chariots and hired fifty men to run before him as if he were already a king. He spent many hours each day at the city gate giving counsel to those who were in need and sympathizing with those who were sorrowing. Many times he would say, "Oh that I were appointed a judge in the land, I would hear every case and would administer fair justice to everyone." The people would nod in agreement with him and were drawn to him.

He was now ready to take over the kingship, but it must not happen in Jerusalem, for his father was too strongly entrenched in the capital city. He decided that he would go to Hebron, the city of his birth and the place where his father, David, had been proclaimed king. So he went in before the king with a strange but seemingly innocent request.

"My lord, please let me go to Hebron to pay a vow to the Lord that I made while I was in Geshur. I vowed that if the Lord would bring me back to Jerusalem and I would again find favor in your eyes, I would serve the Lord with all my heart. Since Hebron is the city of my birth, I would like to begin the fulfillment of my vow there." David was pleased with this pious request by his son, and he quickly gave his consent.

"Yes, my son, go with my blessings and may the peace of God rest upon you for the rest of your life."

Absalom had a twinge of conscience at his father's statement, but he quickly stifled it, bowed to the king, and left the throne room. He quickly summoned his charioteers and the fifty young men whom he had hired to run before him, and with two hundred young men accompanying him who knew nothing of his plans, he went down to Hebron.

He trembled a bit as he thought of the magnitude of the task before him, but he was resolute. He had laid his plans too well to abandon them now. When he arrived in Hebron, he made two more very critical decisions. As the king, he knew that he would need an experienced counselor to advise him on matters of strategy for the kingdom. His father had two very wise counselors whom he desired for his own advisers, but he wasn't sure if either of the men would desert the king in his hour of need.

He considered the two men. There was Hushai the Archite, but he knew that the aging sage was deeply loyal to the king. It was doubtful if he could be persuaded to turn against his old friend.

The second counselor was Ahithophel the Gilonite. He was a wise man, but to Absalom, he was the least desirable of David's two advisors. Absalom remembered that Ahithophel was the grandfather of Bathsheba and had criticized the king publicly for his adultery with Bathsheba and the murder of Uriah. However, the king and Ahithophel had seemingly settled their differences since then, and Ahithophel was in good grace at the king's court.

Absalom decided to test both men's loyalty to the king, so he sent a request to both of the men to meet with him at Hebron. Hushai ignored the invitation, but Ahithophel came quickly, and Absalom found a willing spirit in the veteran counselor.

Absalom's second decision was to send out spies throughout the tribes of Israel to recruit men in every city to join his rebellion. To these men were given the order, "As soon as you hear the sound of the trumpet in the marketplace of every city, you will rise up and proclaim, 'Absalom reigns in Hebron.'"

David was alarmed. A messenger had just come from Hebron with the news that Absalom had proclaimed himself king at Hebron. The messenger added, "The hearts of many of the men of Israel have turned to Absalom, oh king."

David chided himself for being so ignorant about the real reason for Absalom's request to go to Hebron. The realization washed over him that Absalom had been planning for years to take over the kingship of Israel, but he, the king, had missed the signs, and many of the signs were very obvious.

He pondered for a few moments about his lack of insight. Was it possibly the result of a guilt complex because of his sins against Bathsheba and Uriah, or was it a tendency of his to always think well of his sons? He couldn't sort it all out at the moment, but he realized that he was losing precious time.

If his impious son marched against Jerusalem with a large force, there would be much bloodshed. The entire royal family would be wiped out, and he would not be spared. He must leave Jerusalem immediately.

There was a great exodus from Jerusalem as David and all of the royal family and the servants fled before the threat of Absalom, but the king left ten women, concubines to keep the palace. The multitude passed sadly out of the gates of Jerusalem and over the brook Kidron toward the way of the wilderness, and everyone wondered when, if ever, they would return to their beloved city. The king encouraged them along the way.

The years of David's life in the wilderness, fleeing from the wrath of King Saul, served him well in his current situation. In fact, his faith in the Lord was strengthened as he led his people from their secure homes in Jerusalem to an uncertain dwelling in the woods of Ephraim.

The loyalty of many people was tested at this time, and some, including David's former counselor Ahithophel, proved false. To many, the belief that the young Absalom would win against his aged father was so strong that they cast their lot with Absalom.

David and his company were long gone from Jerusalem when Absalom and his followers entered the capital city. The rebel son was disappointed that his father had escaped him, but he was confident that he would find him and all of the royal family and would dispose of them. It was told to David that Ahithophel had deserted to Absalom. Knowing the wily and unprincipled counselor well, the king was sure that Ahithophel would counsel the prince evilly, but well. So he sent his loyal friend Hushai the Archile back into the city supposedly to join with Absalom and to frustrate the counsel of Ahithophel.

Absalom felt that God was certainly favoring him, for he now had both of his father's trusted counselors with him. He was certain that they would advise him well.

Since Ahithophel was the first to join with him, he turned to him now, "Ahithophel, tell me what I should do?"

Ahithophel assumed his most erudite position as he answered. "Since your father has left ten concubines to keep the house, if you will have intercourse with these women in the sight of all Israel, the people will hear that you are greatly despised by your father and your followers will be strong in your favor."

Absalom liked Ahithophel's counsel, so they pitched a tent on the roof of the palace and Absalom violated the concubines of his father. Ahithophel's plan of revenge against David was working well, so he continued his counsel.

"Now," he said to Absalom, "let me choose twelve thousand men, and I will pursue your father immediately. We will come upon him when he is weary and weak, and he will be easy prey for us."

Absalom and the elders nodded in agreement. "That sounds like a very wise idea," the rebel prince said. "But first let us ask Hushai what his counsel would be."

Hushai breathed a silent prayer before he answered. "The counsel of Ahithophel is not good at this time. You know that your father is a man of war, and the men with him are seasoned warriors. They are angry that they were made to flee like a hare before the hunter. So they will not camp with the people tonight but will hide in some pit or grove, and you will not be able to find them. My counsel is that you continue to gather all Israel unto you, and then you will be able to meet the king wherever he is camped, and you will overpower him and destroy him and those who are with him."

The Lord gave weight to the counsel of Hushai, and Absalom and all the men with him said, "Yes, the counsel of Hushai is better than the counsel of Ahithophel."

Then Hushai sent a message to David by the hands of Jonathan and Ahimaaz. "Do not spend the night on the plains or the wilderness, but speedily cross over the Jordan, so that you will not be found by the troops of Absalom."

And David and all the people with him crossed over the Jordan and came to the woods of Ephraim.

Soon Absalom and his host pursued the king, and the two bodies met in battle in the Wilderness of Ephraim.

Absalom chose Amasa, a cousin of Joab, as the commander of his army, while Joab, his brother Abishi, and Ittai the Hittite, shared the leadership of David's army.

It was a bloody battle there in the wilderness, but the raw undisciplined troops of Absalom were no match for David's seasoned veterans. Absalom's army was crushed, and the prince was killed by the hand of Joab as he hung from the limb of a tree by his head.

David was greatly agitated over the death of Absalom, and he wept long and loudly. In his grief, he cried out, "Oh my son, Absalom—my son Absalom!"

Joab was told of David's great distress over the death of Absalom. The irreverent warrior was both puzzled and extremely angry at David's attitude. He remembered that David had allowed his son to remain three years in exile in a foreign country without so much as a note. Then when Joab had persuaded the king to bring Absalom back to Jerusalem, David had kept his son under house arrest for two more years without seeing his face.

Thus, David's extreme display of sorrow over his son's death seemed a bit hypocritical to Joab. But there was another component of David's agony that bothered Joab even more than the hypocritical nature of his mourning. It was the sinister aspect of Absalom's treason against the crown. It was obvious that if the prince would have succeeded in his plan to take over the kingship of Israel, he would have destroyed the king, all of the royal seed, and all who were working for the king. But David was acting as if he would have preferred to expend all these people in order to save Absalom. So Joab went in before the king without a royal invitation. He even addressed David as he would a peer.

"Do you realize that today you have shamed all of your servants and their families who have saved your life? You are acting as though you love your enemies and regard as nothing those who have supported you at the risk of their lives. If all of us would have died and Absalom would have lived, would you be satisfied? Now stop your tears and go out and comfort your people and thank them lest you lose the loyalty of all those who have favored you. David obeyed, arose meekly, dried his eyes, and went out and sat at the gate and embraced and thanked all the people who came to him.

As David and his troops journeyed back to Jerusalem, the chastened king pondered on the treason of Absalom and his death. As he reflected, the wounds made by his sins of adultery and murder began to bleed anew. He remembered the words of Nathan: "The sword shall never depart from your house. Besides, I will raise up adversity against you from your own house." The sword had now taken three of his sons from him, and he wondered when it would strike again. He bowed his head on the way to Jerusalem and asked the God of heaven to help him to accept His judgments with grace and a willing heart. The rebellion of Absalom weakened David's rule in Israel for a time. Judah remained loyally behind him, but in other areas of the kingdom, there were hints of mutiny.

A Benjamite by the name of Sheba decided to declare himself king. So he blew a trumpet and shouted to the people, "We have no part in David or inheritance in the son of Jesse, every man to his tent, oh Israel." And the multitudes in the kingdom of Israel followed him. Thus, he became a greater threat to David's kingship than had Absalom.

David was angry with Joab because he had killed Absalom and had also chided him harshly because of his mourning for Absalom. So the king decided to set aside Joab as commander of his armies and appoint Amasa, son of his stepsister Abigail and a cousin of Joab, as the commander.

He commanded Amasa, "Assemble the men of Judah and present yourself here within three days, and we will pursue Sheba."

But Amasa was not able to assemble the men of Judah as quickly as David had requested, and David became impatient, so he chose Abishai to lead a company in pursuit of Sheba.

However, Joab was not so easily set aside. He commandeered a company of Cherethites, Pelethites, and a group of mighty men of Israel and joined with his brother Abishai in pursuit of the rebel Sheba. When they came to Gibeon, Amasa caught up with them, and Joab killed him there.

Joab and Abishai and their troop went on from Gibeon and besieged Sheba in Abel of Beth Maacheh. They would have broken down the wall of the city and destroyed all of the inhabitants, but a wise woman persuaded the people to kill Sheba and throw this head over the wall. Then Joab and Abishai blew a trumpet and withdrew from the siege. The rebellion of Sheba was ended.

Afflictions continued to fall on David as God had promised, but through it all he wrote a song of praise to God for his miraculous deliverances.

"The Lord is my rock, and my fortress, and my deliverer; my God, my strength, in whom I will trust; my buckler, and the horn of my salvation, and my high tower. I will call upon the Lord, who is worthy to be praised: so shall I be saved from mine enemies? The sorrows of death compassed me, and the floods of ungodly men made me afraid. The sorrows of hell compassed me about: the snares of death prevented me. In my distress I called upon the Lord, and cried unto my God: He heard my voice out of His temple, and my cry came before Him, even into His ears."

David stained the last days of his life by ordering a census of the children of Israel. Joab wisely tried to dissuade him, but David persisted and the Lord was angered by the prideful decision. So the Lord ordered an extra affliction to fall on the troubled king. He gave David three choices: seven years of famine on the land, three months of fleeing before his enemies, or three days of plagues on the land. David chose three days of plagues, and seventy thousand men died throughout the land.

Now David was old and could no longer rule the land with justice and equity as he had for the past forty years. So Adonijah, the son of Haggith and the oldest living son of David, decided to proclaim himself king in his father's stead. But David had chosen Solomon, the son of Bathsheba, to succeed him on the throne, so there was a problem for the aged king. He decided to abdicate in favor of Solomon, and Adonijah's dreams of kingship were dashed.

Later, Solomon had his half-brother, Adonijah, slain because he requested to marry Abishag, the virgin that lay in David's bosom during the last days of his life. Thus, the fourth son of David died in fulfillment of David's condemnation on himself in response to Nathan's parable.

David died and was buried with his fathers. As men have studied the life of David through the centuries, he has been both praised and cursed. As Nathan predicted, the weak points in his life have given occasion for the enemies of the Lord to blaspheme. But the strong points in his life, which demonstrated a God-given potential to humble himself in the dust under God's censure and to praise God for his afflictions, have buoyed the hearts of millions of God's people through the dark years.

Despite his dark and seemingly deliberate transgressions, he was truly a man after God's own heart.

We invite you to view the complete
selection of titles we publish at:

**www.TEACHServices.com**

scan with your mobile
device to go directly
to our website

Please write or email us your praises, reactions, or
thoughts about this or any other book we publish at:

P.O. Box 954
Ringgold, GA 30736

**Info@TEACHServices.com**

TEACH Services, Inc., titles may be purchased in bulk for
educational, business, fund-raising, or sales promotional use.
For information, please e-mail:

**BulkSales@TEACHServices.com**

Finally if you are interested in seeing
your own book in print, please contact us at

**publishing@TEACHServices.com**

We would be happy to review your manuscript for free.